COVER OF SNOW

COVER OF SNOW

A NOVEL

Jenny Milchman

DOUBLEDAY LARGE PRINT HOME LIBRARY EDITION

BALLANTINE BOOKS • NEW YORK

Published in the United States by Ballantine Books, an imprint of The Random House Publishing Group, a division of Random House, Inc., New York.

BALLANTINE and colophon are registered trademarks of Random House, Inc.

ISBN 978-1-62090-996-6

Printed in the United States of America

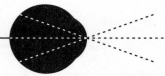

This Large Print Book carries the Seal of Approval of N.A.V.H.

This one is for my mother and father,
who in their different ways
gave me the gift of story.
And for Josh, who gave me everything.

COVER OF SNOW

CHAPTER ONE

My husband wasn't in bed with me when I woke up that January morning. The mid-winter sky was bruised purple and yellow outside the window. I shut bleary eyes against light that glared and pounded.

A second later I realized my toes weren't burrowing into the hollows behind Brendan's knees, that when I flung out my arm it didn't meet his wiry chest, the stony muscles gone slack with sleep. I slid my hand toward the night table, fingers scrabbling around for our alarm clock.

Seven-thirty.

It was late. As if drugged, my brain was making sense of things only after a dull delay. But it was a full hour past the time I always woke up. *We* always woke up. Brendan slept a cop's sleep, perpetually ready to take action, and I had been an early riser all my thirty-five years.

Bits of things began to take shape in my mind.

The morning light, which entered so stridently through the window.

Brendan not in bed with me. He must've gotten up already. I hadn't even felt him move.

But Brendan had been working late all week; I hadn't yet found out why. My husband had good reason to sleep in. And if he had risen on time, why didn't he wake me?

I felt a squeezing in my belly. Brendan knew I had an eight o'clock meeting with a new client this morning, the owner of a lovely but ramshackle old saltbox in need of repair. My husband took my burgeoning business as seriously as I did. He would never let me miss a meeting.

On the other hand, Brendan would know that if I slept late, then I must be worn out. Maybe getting Phoenix off the ground had taken more out of me than I realized. Brendan probably figured he'd give me a few extra minutes, and the morning just got away from him.

He must be somewhere in his normal routine now, toweling off, or fixing coffee.

Except I didn't hear the shower dripping. Or smell the telltale, welcome scent of my morning fix.

I pushed myself out of bed with hands that felt stiff and clumsy, as if I were wearing mittens. What was wrong with me? I caught a glimpse of my face in the mirror and noticed puddles of lavender under my eyes. It was like I hadn't slept a wink, instead of an extra hour.

"Brendan? Honey? You up?"

My words shattered the air, and I realized how very still our old farmhouse was this morning.

Padding toward the bathroom, one explanation for the weight in my muscles, not to mention my stuporous sleep, occurred to me.

Brendan and I had made love last night.

It had been one of the good times; me lying back afterward, hollow, cored out, the way I got when Brendan was able to focus completely on me, on us, instead of moving so fiercely that he seemed to be riding off to some distant place in the past. We'd even lain awake for a while in the waning moments before sleep, fingers intertwined, Brendan studying me in a way that I felt more than saw in the dark.

"Honey? Last night tired me out, I guess. Not that it wasn't worth it."

I felt a smile tease the corners of my mouth, and pushed open the bathroom door, expecting a billow of steam. When only brittle air emerged, I felt that grabbing in my gut again. Cold tile bit my bare feet.

"Brendan?"

My husband never started the day without a shower; he claimed that a night's sleep made him ache. But there was no residue of moisture filming the mirror, nor fragrance of soap in the air. I grabbed a towel, wrapped it around my shoulders for warmth, and trotted toward the stairs, calling out his name.

No answer.

Could he have gone to the station early? Left me sleeping while my new client waited at his dilapidated house?

"Honey! Are you home?" My voice sounded uncertain.

No answer. And then I heard the chug of our coffeepot.

Relief flowed through me, thick and creamy as soup. Until that moment, I hadn't let myself acknowledge that I was scared. I wasn't an overreactor by nature usually.

I headed downstairs, feet more sure now, but with that wobbly, airless feeling in the knees that comes as fear departs.

The kitchen was empty when I entered, the coffee a dark, widening stain in the pot. It continued to sputter and spit while I stood there.

There was no mug out, waiting for its cold jolt of milk. No light was turned on against the weak morning sunshine. No-body had been in the icy kitchen yet to-day. This machine had been pro-grammed last night, one of the chores accomplished as Brendan and I passed back and forth in the tight space, step-ping around each other to clean up af-ter dinner.

That thing in my belly took hold, and this time it didn't let go. I didn't call out again.

The sedated feeling was disappear-ing now, cobwebs tearing apart, and my thinking suddenly cleared. I brushed past the deep farm sink, a tall, painted cabinet.

With icy hands, I opened the door to the back stairs, whose walls I was pres-ently laboring over to make perfect for Brendan. Maybe, just maybe, he'd skipped his shower and called in late to work in order to spend time in his hide-away upstairs.

The servants' stairs were steep and narrow, with a sudden turn and wells worn deep in each step. I climbed the first two slowly, bypassing a few tools and a can of stripper, then twisted my body around the corner. I took in the faded wallpaper I'd only just reached after months of careful scraping.

Perhaps I didn't have enough momentum, but I slipped, solidly whacking both knees as I went down. Crouching there, gritting my teeth against the smarting pain, I looked up toward the top of the flight.

Brendan was above me, suspended from a thick hank of rope.

The rope was knotted around a stained glass globe, which hung in the cracked ceiling plaster.

Brendan's neck tilted slightly, the angle odd. His handsome face looked like it was bathed entirely in red wine.

Suddenly a small cyclone of powder spilled down, and I heard a splitting sound. There was a rip, a tear, the noise of two worlds cracking apart, and then a deafening series of thuds.

The light fixture completed its plummet, and broke with a tinkling sprinkle of glass. A tangle of ice-cold limbs and body parts slugged me, heavy as lead blankets.

And I screamed, and screamed, and screamed, until the warble my voice had been before became no more than a gasping strain for air.

CHAPTER TWO

Club Mitchell arrived, gun at the ready; I don't know when, or how he knew to come. He was Brendan's partner, and his best friend before that. Maybe Club and Brendan had developed some karmic connection. Maybe I called him. He might've heard me keening—there was no other word for it—on that back stair.

Club scooped me up in his well-muscled arms and carried me to our couch. Then he must've gone back to where he found me, because the next thing I heard was cursing.

"No. Oh no. What the fuck did you do?"

I screwed my fingers into my ears, but I couldn't block out the sound of Club Mitchell starting to cry.

My parents and sister arrived next.

Again, I had no idea how they'd been summoned. I let them in, trembling in clothes I didn't remember putting on, awash with outdoor chill. The wreath I'd made was still hanging on the front door, its gay ribbons motionless in the still air.

"Oh, Nora, darling." My mother stuck out both her arms, like tongs.

I stared over her shoulder as she enfolded me. My unblinking eyes settled on my sister, Teggie. She was shivering, her grass-blade arms wrapped around her narrow torso.

"Time," said my dad, his voice throaty, but brisk. "Time is what you need."

Unbelievably, fatigue was smothering me, and I yawned mightily.

"Heals all wounds," Teggie murmured, her tone so affable that only I would've heard the bite.

"That's right," my dad said, giving her a surprised, grateful look.

Teggie walked over to me. "Sit down," she said. "I'll make you some coffee."

"I can do it," my mother offered.

My father crossed the room and embraced me, his arm a weight around my shoulders. I fought not to shrug it off, and my sister rescued me, leading me over to a chair.

"Nora," my mother called from the kitchen, an apologetic note in her tone. "I'm just having a little trouble finding the—"

"It's all right," I barked. Then I dropped my voice. "Right now all I want is to sleep."

My father and sister glanced at each other, a rare private exchange between them.

My mom came back in. "All right," she said softly. "That sounds like a good idea. Need any help getting upstairs?"

I squinted at her, my mother's face suddenly unknown to me, a stranger's. "No," I replied in a tone odd to my own ears. "I don't need any help."

I mounted the front stairs and sank

into the yawning sea of our bed. After a minute or two, I got back out. My throat was filling up, my nose too; I couldn't breathe. I curled up on the wood floor, where it didn't seem to matter if I suffocated, down low, a place nobody would ever think to look. After a while, I reached one hand up and pulled a blanket down over me.

The sole, lone thing I cared about, in the entire shimmering universe, was *why*.

CHAPTER THREE

On the day of the funeral my family members appeared before me in a dark blur. I couldn't remember what I had put on, whether it was black, green, or nothing at all.

"Mom?" I asked. "Am I—okay?"

She didn't seem to understand what I meant. Her gaze didn't drop to my outfit; it offered no reassurance. In that moment my mother's face told me only one thing.

And all I could think about for the rest of the day—while snow splattered the cemetery and the Wedeskyull police strode over the rock-hard soil, doing their stately, mechanical dance; when they lowered my husband's casket into a frozen rift in the ground, before gathering stiff as tin soldiers at our tiny farmhouse—was my mother's expression. How she had once loved Brendan like a son, but now she'd come to hate him.

Club was the last cop to arrive at our house afterward. Once he came, there didn't seem to be enough space for everyone else. He was a solid man, filling a good chunk of the living room, and he sloshed coffee into a cup for me. I accepted the drink without question, knowing I wouldn't take a sip. Club had brought his huge black Lab, as he always did. I was allergic to dogs, but today I craved the lighter, easier side Weekend brought out in his master.

I felt as if I had an invisible force field around me. Our small house was packed with family, friends, the gray-uniformed bodies of Brendan's fellow police officers, people who had known my husband all his life. But I managed to roam between them, cutting wide swaths of

space, before settling, alone, in a corner.

Weekend trotted over. He butted my
hip, liquid eyes downcast. Force field
cracked by one brave soul, I thought.

Club was standing next to Police Chief
Vern Weathers, who oversaw the room
as if it belonged to him, and he had to
bear the hurt for everyone in it. I tried to
gather together a greeting for Vern while
Club cradled his holster in his palm,
eyeing me. These were Brendan's people, not mine, and while I felt comfortable enough with everyone, I'd never
really become a part of them.

Weekend's rough sheet of tongue
lathered my fingers.

When my nose began to run, I sniffed,
but didn't take my hand away from the
dog.

Not until Brendan's mother arrived.

I was still staring at the tight knot of
gray-clad men, their expressions frozen
in a way that couldn't be explained by
the temperature, and that I didn't quite
believe was caused by the circum-
stances, either. These weren't emotional

men. I didn't think grief would immobilize their features, make them move as if their joints were rusty, and cement themselves as far away from me as our small farmhouse would allow.

Icy air sheeted in, and I looked up to see my mother standing at the front door. It was dark out already. Two women came inside, their arms linked.

"Hello, Eileen," my mother murmured, the name tolling like a bell.

Eileen had arrived with her sister-in-law, Jean, a retiring presence despite her bulk.

I'd always thought that my mother-in-law and I would have a lot in common. She had a love of archeology; I had majored in art history and restored old houses for a living. But Eileen Hamilton despised me from the moment Brendan brought me home with him from college.

Her black dress was stiff, and its style somehow wrong: oversized flaps at the collar, the hemline long. Funeral garb might be understandably outdated, but all of Eileen's clothes tended toward this, like a wardrobe from a different age.

"I'm sorry," I told my mother-in-law, feeling as if I'd just admitted to something. Then I sneezed. Weekend rubbed against me.

My mother-in-law's mouth was the size and shape of a frozen pea. "Thank you."

"I am, too, Mrs. Hamilton," Teggie said. "Brendan was the only brother I ever had."

Eileen's mouth whittled further. "What do you intend to do now, Nora?"

I was trying to muster some compassion for my mother-in-law. She'd had one son die before Brendan. She was childless now, and a widow, too. "I'm sorry?" I said again.

Weekend twitched beside me.

A cough rattled in Eileen's throat. "Well, this isn't really your place, is it? Brendan's perhaps, although frankly, I was always surprised that he came back here."

She was voicing the same thoughts I'd had earlier, but her words, their tone, made my skin grow chill all over. I patted Weekend, thinking hard, at the same time trying not to think.

"It's not even your house," Eileen went on. "Jean must own nearly all of it still—"

Jean was standing in front of a table laden with serving plates and bowls, her wide back turned, and she offered neither protest nor affirmation. I watched out of the corner of my eye as she walked off.

"Mrs. Hamilton," Teggie began. "I think you'd better—"

"This isn't the time," I interrupted.

"No," Eileen said after a pause. "Perhaps not. Give yourself a few days then. I suppose final decisions can wait."

My sister's mouth opened again, but for once I spoke before she did. "It won't be the right time for me to decide anything for a while. Not until I find out what happened."

"What happened?" Eileen echoed.

"To Brendan," I replied unnecessarily.

Eileen frowned. Then suddenly she leaned forward, taking my hand in both her bony ones. It wasn't a touch; it was a way to keep me still. I could feel each slender digit, the points of her knuckles.

"Why do you think a man kills himself, Nora?" she asked, each word unflinchingly delivered, a jab in my ribs. "What reason do you imagine people will come up with?"

"I don't—" I had to work to swallow. Weekend's whine was a vibration in his throat. When I brushed my hand along his flank, he stilled. "I don't know what you mean."

"Everyone else will, though," Eileen said shrewdly. "The police have been giving you a break in deference to Brendan, I imagine. But I'm sure they have questions about his last days."

I stared at her, ruing the expression of incomprehension I knew must be on my face.

"Unhappy men commit suicide, Nora. And what makes a man unhappy—especially one who is widely known to love his job?" She spoke quickly now, words gathering momentum, like a train. "Why, trouble at home, of course. With his marriage. His wife."

"You heartless bitch," Teggie burst out. "They buried your son today—"

For just a second, I started to turn away. Teggie could take care of this. She would finish Eileen off, with her razor-sharp tongue, her fearless stare, better than I ever could. As a child, Teggie had her mouth honest-to-God washed out with soap more times than I could count. My father used to joke that the devil himself would turn away when Teggie got on a roll.

I swiveled back around.

"That's not why Brendan did this," I said, ignoring the shaking in my voice. "We were happy, and everybody knew that, as surely as they knew he liked his job." I paused to take in breath. "Did you think I wouldn't look further, Eileen? Because *it's not really my place*?"

On trembling legs, I turned and left the room, Weekend at my heels.

CHAPTER FOUR

My bedroom was the only place in the house I could think of to go. When I got there, the door had been pushed open. Weekend gave a lone bark as we entered.

"Jean?" I said, coming upon Brendan's aunt by the dresser.

She turned with uncharacteristic swiftness. "Oh, Nora," she said softly. "I'm sorry. I just—needed a little space."

"Yes," I murmured. "Me, too."

Jean's soft face folded and tears seeped from beneath her eyelids. I looked away momentarily. The dog began to snuffle around the spare pieces of furniture in the room—bed, trunk, dresser. I felt a brief pat on my back, and when I looked up again, Weekend and I were alone.

I woke the next morning alone in bed, and I knew it must be true.

For a moment I couldn't think how to put one foot onto the floor, then the other; how I'd ever do something as simple as get up again.

True, then.

Someone had come in the night and sealed up my whole body in clay. If I moved, I'd crack apart. What did I do now? My face splintered, broke, as I wailed aloud. At least, I thought it'd been out loud. I lay there, waiting for the patter of my family's feet.

But no one came. That one thought— *What do I do?*—kept flapping and cawing in my head like a bird, until I remembered the Wedeskyull P.D. I clutched at the memory like a buoy. Brendan's fellow officers had stayed so silent yesterday, retreating as if they'd never known me at all. And not in a stammering, well-meaning way, either. In a way that was wary.

I could start with them.

I sat up, my feet slapping against icy floorboards. Had this old wood ever felt warm?

I smoothed the rumpled side of the bed, patting both pillows—one that was damp, one that was arid—into place.

True.

"I'll do it, honey," I whispered. "I'll find out why."

My father and Teggie were in the kitchen cleaning up funeral detritus, a hundred half-laden paper plates, and cups sloshing with unfinished drinks. The house hadn't cleared out till late last night, though I'd missed much of it. They worked in silence, my dancer sister up-ending the cups over the sink with a careless kind of grace, my dad more ar-duously tipping plates into the trash.

I stared at the scene of uncommon peace, then walked to the fridge to take a look at the leftovers. I would divide up the food and distribute it to the bachelor

cops. Maybe that would get them talking to me again.

I noticed my mother as I began rum-
maging for supplies—Tupperware, tinfoil—in a cabinet. She was busy at the
stove. "Mom? What are you doing?"

My father looked up. "Tell Nora about
her call."

"What call?"

"Oh, yes!" my mother said, while stirring a pot. "Looks like you might have a
customer, darling."

"Says his name is Ned Kramer," added
my dad.

It took a moment, but a memory began to build. Ned Kramer was a reporter,
fairly new in town. We'd met when he
did a human interest piece on the
start-up of Phoenix Home Corp. *Local
resident opens business* kind of thing.
I'd just completed my first big job, the
restoration of a church that was being
transformed into a residence. Ned had
mentioned then that he was in the process of buying one of the historic homes
on the outskirts of town.

"His number's by the phone," my father said. "You could call right now."

"I don't know," I replied. "My head's a little far from work at the moment."

The statement came out with a hitching breath. Only a few days ago a call like this would've been cause for jubilation. Phoenix was still in the process of becoming established; I needed every referral I could get. I would've told Brendan the news and he would've insisted on taking me to Wedeskyull's one nice, candle and tablecloth restaurant to celebrate. The idea that my business might take off had seemed like a dream back when I was an admin assistant, stuck trying to dig a local psychologist out from under reams of insurance documents. But now Phoenix Home Corp. felt a little like a favorite doll from childhood, something you knew you'd once loved but couldn't quite remember why.

My mother's hand was slowing down. She pulled the spoon around in her pot. I imagined something meaty and thick, a sludgy brew.

"I understand," my father said, in a tone that said he didn't at all. "Unfortunately, life doesn't slow down for us."

I began to slice a pie into triangles,

wrapping each one in tinfoil. A small, tempting parcel to trade for information, and I never once wondered what I would be asking, nor why I should have to barter for it.

The phone rang.

I snatched it up. "Hello?"

My whole family was facing me.

"Hello?" I said again. Then I clicked off the phone and returned it to its console, shrugging. "Nobody there."

"I'm making soup," my mother said. "And there's also lasagna, chili, all labeled in the freezer."

Understanding dawned. "You're leaving."

"We know you must want things back to normal," said my father.

Suddenly I stashed my bag of leftovers on the ice-cold cellar steps. My mother's recitation of dishes, not to mention the thought of all those wedges of pie, bleeding fruit, had turned my stomach. I wasn't up for a confrontation with the cops today.

"The store." My mom was still speaking. "Your dad will have customers complaining. But I'll come back whenever you need me. Right, Jack?"

"I'll stay," Teggie added. "I have an audition but not until the third."

Later that evening, my sister served one of my mother's meals, and we sat over it for a while, neither of us eating. Teggie had never eaten in a way that could be called hearty, certainly not since she had started dancing professionally. But I had once enjoyed food.

She glanced over her shoulder toward a little porch. "What's out there?"

I pushed aside my full plate. "That's our balcony."

Teggie stood up. "I know that, but what's *out* there?"

The smell of the food was too strong. I got up to clear the plates. "What do you mean, what's out there?"

"Looks like glasses."

"Oh," I began.

"Nor?"

"Brendan and I had a drink out there the night he—the other night. It was really too cold but . . ." I turned, refusing to look. Nor did I add—it would've been unnecessary, a detail that would only make Teggie feel the sting of her solitary life—that as we went outside into the frigid air, wineglasses held aloft in our hands, I had known I would be warm soon enough, with my husband in our bed.

Brendan had touched me on the small of my back; he'd called me Chestnut. He joked that instead of cocktail hour, we were having a cocktail minute. Brendan was always the one to suggest a dive into the lake, or a sudden look at the stars. Without him, I saw myself turning into a person I didn't like, wretched and worn, someone who didn't take delight in anything.

Teggie unlatched the door, and white pellets instantly blew inside, stinging and small. We kept a small table and chairs out there, but they'd been unusable for months. The chairs wore extra seats of snow, twelve inches high, and the table was similarly capped.

"What the hell were you two drinking?" Teggie asked as she came back inside.

"Close the door!" I begged, hugging myself. "What do you mean? Wine."

"One of you at least," she added.

"What are you talking about?" I asked again.

"Weird, isn't it?" Teggie said, holding up a glass. "It's not just frost—that's what I thought at first."

I reached for the cold glass and stared at it. It was coated with a cloudy white film. The other glass was clear except for a scum of crimson at the base.

I brought the filmed glass to my nose, and sniffed, the act accompanied by an icicle of panic. That awful morning. How late I'd slept, my thick-headed stupor.

"There's something in this glass. In my drink. It knocked me out."

"Who would've drugged your drink?" Teggie asked, uncharacteristically naïve. But then my sister had always reserved unique faith for Brendan. "Oh, no. You think that Brendan—"

"He must've known what he was going to do," I whispered, cutting her off. The way he'd stroked my fingers after, instead of just dropping like a stone into sleep. How I'd felt him studying me in the dark. "And that he'd need privacy for it."

I didn't realize that my grip had loosened until Teggie snatched the glass out of the air, just before it would have splintered on the floor.

CHAPTER FIVE

The next day my sister was at it again.

"Look, I know you don't exactly like to deal with the tough parts."

I frowned, but not at her. Not at anything. At everything.

"Come on, Nor," Teggie went on, all but scoffing. "Unicorns and sunrises. Light stuff, happy stuff. That's the world you inhabit. Why do you think you couldn't hack it in the city?"

A strange memory appeared in my head. I'd been young—six or so—and I'd fallen down in my father's store. The floor was rough—I could still remember the scuffed wood that generations of workmen and contractors had trod upon—and my knee had bled for a long time. My mother had floated the possibility of stitches, but my dad had cast that idea aside in a tone not unlike Teggie's right now. "Scrapes," my mom had said a little while later, pressing a gauze pad very tightly to my knee. "Your father does better with scrapes than cuts."

I still had a jagged white line on my knee.

Teggie began talking again. "Why do you think Brendan did it the way he did?"

When I looked at her blankly, she went on. "Brendan was a cop. He knew his way around weapons, had access to them. So why a rope? Why hanging?"

I fiddled with a cup of tea.

"Wait a minute—you know something," Teggie said. She must've sensed that I wasn't going to answer, because she stood up. "Where's the rope? It must still be around here somewhere." The gruesomeness of the suggestion didn't seem to strike her.

"No, Teggie," I said, fidgeting hard

enough that the amber contents of my cup threatened to overturn. "Please." She was younger, but she'd always been the bossy sister, the one who assigned us fake names in our games, and choreographed the shows we put on.

Teggie turned, a dancer's spin, and left the kitchen for the pen of garbage bins outside.

When she came back inside, I averted my head from the unraveling mess of rope she held against her shivering frame. But I'd already caught a glimpse of rough, splintering fibers.

"No one's gone to the dump," my sister said. Tears filmed her eyes, and I was struck by two things. How seldom Teggie cried, and also by how much she'd loved Brendan.

I stood up and went over to the phone. There was only one person I could imagine seeing right now. Someone else who had known this rope in its deadliest incarnation.

"Nor?" My sister spoke as I dialed.

"Not now," I said. "Don't say anything else right now. Okay? Can you just for once in your life—"

The ringing ceased and I said, "Club?" into the phone before he'd even answered.

"Yeah?"

Teggie raised her voice. It was steady again. "Take a look at this."

"Can you come over?" I went on, loudly, to drown out my sister.

"Now? I guess so. Shift starts at four." Club paused. "You got any news?"

Why was Club the only person who seemed to believe there might be news?

"I'll be there in a few," he told me.

My sister stepped forward, still clutching her burden.

"I already looked at that rope." My voice held a dreadful calm. "I wonder if you even know what's strangest about it. Me, I couldn't really help but know, what I do for a living and all." I began to chuckle, a low, lilting laugh that scared me.

"What are you talking about?" Teggie demanded. Wisps of dry hemp drifted from her fingers like flyaway hair.

"Look at that thing," I burst out, blindly thrusting my hand toward one frayed end of the rope. My sister was right: I couldn't face it. But I would never forget the way it had disintegrated on the back stairs. "It's a goddamned antique."

My sister frowned. I probably cursed as rarely as she cried.

"That particular piece of rope," I went on, "has to be over twenty years old."

UNDERGROUND

The urge came upon Eileen as it always did, when the winter sun began to fade after its brief appearance in the sky, and another long night stretched ahead. Did she spend more time in the basement below during the frigid months that dominated the calendar, seven of them at least? Eileen Hamilton wasn't sure, and she'd never been a woman given to examination of her habits.

She got up stiffly from the chair in the parlor, a basket of mending forgotten beside her. Her knees creaked as she rose, a tight, brittle sound, which if she had been more inclined to study herself might have unnerved her.

She paused to locate her key ring.

Eileen had stopped locking the upstairs door sometime in the years after Bill died and Brendan had left home. There was no reason to secure it anymore, no one to keep out. But some habits died harder than others, and she couldn't bring herself to leave the final door unguarded.

Her knees sounded again, taking the narrow column of stairs, but her stride evened out as she crossed the vast space, keeping pace with the setting sun. By the time it was full dark, she intended to be hidden away.

It was warmer down here than in the rest of the house. Eileen kept the furnace set low, but a stone foundation provided good insulation, and buffered the house from winds. She unlocked the door and went in.

As always, a feeling of deep peace descended as she took in her precious collection, only to be stolen away by a wild, rocking fury. Her gaze grew muddy, then she couldn't see at all. The hands that had dropped to her sides balled into fists. Her shoulders rose as high as her head and she looked like a bull, ready to charge.

If she made noise down here, no one would know, even if someone came around; the stone walls were too thick. So perhaps she did, probably she did, for sometimes her own ears rang after she'd been in here for a while, as if they'd been subjected to a high, shrieking wind. There was other evidence of upset. Eileen sometimes had to spend hours cleaning up afterward, restoring her perfect displays, slicking things down with fingers wetted by tears. Her nails were often bent back, their beds dark with blood, as if she'd been tearing at concrete.

She began to quiet, her thin chest heaving. Once that chest had been lofty, lush enough to nourish children. It settled to its normal flat plane, motionless, no sign of her beating heart. The only remaining movement in Eileen lived in her hands, which continued to twitch and tremor, and would, she knew, for hours, long after she escaped upstairs.

Eileen watched her fingers as if they belonged to somebody else, moving as they were of their own accord, twisting and turning the remaining section of rope.

CHAPTER SIX

Weekend bounded in with an energy that belied what a large dog he was. Like his master, I thought, almost smiling as my hands got their watery massage.

"Here." Club's voice drew my attention and I looked up to see the bouquet of carnations he was thrusting in my direction. "From Dave."

"Dave?" I asked, beginning to peel off the cellophane wrapper.

"Yeah." Club shrugged. Only then did I recall that at the funeral, the Chief's brother was the only cop to approach me.

Teggie took the flowers before heading into the kitchen. "I'll just make some lunch or something," she said on her way out.

"Your sister's name is Terry?" Club said, still standing in the same spot. Not long ago, this house had been like Club's own. The sofa cushions took on his shape when he sat down; he even had his own special glass. But with Brendan gone, it was as if he didn't fit here anymore. Or maybe it was I who didn't fit, and everybody was just waiting around awkwardly, wondering when I would figure that out.

"Come on in," I said, flinching at Club's formal thanks. "It's Teggie," I went on, trailing him. "A family name," I added vaguely. Well, that was true enough, in a manner of speaking.

We sat down on the edges of our chairs, Club's a chintz that didn't suit him. Club blew into his hands, and I jumped up. "I can turn up the heat—"

"No, don't—"

Our wretched leanings toward politeness subsided when Weekend trotted into the room. I beckoned him over.

"Since when are you my dog's biggest fan?"

I rubbed my suddenly itchy nose and Weekend's flank simultaneously. The dog turned a few times, before lying down on my feet.

"I guess sneezing and sniffling used to bother me more."

Club eyed me. His hand made a habitual gesture, a sort of unconscious reaching for the gun he always carried, off duty or on.

He'd been a linebacker and a right wing at Wedeskyull High. Fifteen years from now he might be slightly soft, with that padded look muscular men get as they age. But for now Club was in top shape, face always reddened by the wind or sun, with big balls of muscle along his arms, a wide wall of a chest, and a tight, square jaw.

Brendan had described the way Club snapped handcuffs on as soon as they began questioning someone, the hours he spent at the shooting range.

I'd always been glad he and Brendan

were partners. I saw it simply, in black-and-white terms. If you were a cop it was better to have someone by your side who might occasionally jump the gun than a man who would hesitate. In exchange for that sense of security, I was willing to ignore the sense I got from Brendan that there was a darker side to Club—not just a readiness or willingness, but an eagerness.

Of course, in the end, even Club wasn't able to protect Brendan. Not from himself.

My eyes burned as if suddenly exposed to smoke. I wanted to see my husband then, with a pull so intense I didn't think I would survive it. Weekend jumped up on the sofa, draping his body over my form, which had begun to slump.

"Thinks he's a lapdog," Club said.

Why did Brendan do it, I thought to ask. *Do you know? Would you tell me if you did?* But before I could speak, two solid thumps sounded on the front door. Chief Weathers pushed it open as I struggled to get the dog off of me.

"What's up, Chief?" Club asked, already on his feet.

The Chief scowled, and I realized something must be wrong. Club had known instantly, but my instincts were off, dull now that I no longer heard Brendan taking the stairs at a run, slipping into his uniform jacket as he called out for me not to wait up. Already I was losing the rhythms of a cop's life, Brendan's readiness for action, the notion that off-duty spells—few and far between with such a small-town force—had to be borne until real time could begin again. I had the sudden, mad impulse to reach out and stop both men from going to whatever it was.

I settled for taking a step forward, and the police chief's face finally unfurled.

"Nothing at the moment," he said, and Club's broad shoulders relaxed.

"Will you stay for a sandwich?" I asked, remembering belatedly how distant the Chief had been the day of Brendan's funeral.

But that earlier distance had vanished—maybe it hadn't been coldness at all, only sorrow and grief—and the

Chief scuffed his boots before stepping forward into the house and placing a pale-fleshed hand underneath my chin.

"I haven't told you yet how sorry I am," he said, voice a low rumble. "This is more sadness than most folks have to bear in a lifetime."

I felt tears crowd my throat. "Thank you, Vern."

He looked across the room to Club. "She calls me Vern," he said, and I quickly realized my mistake. The truth was, before this, I hadn't had cause to address Brendan's boss very often.

"My mama called me Vern," the Chief went on. "My kindeygarten teacher maybe. Everyone else calls me Chief. It was my name long before I ever came to be one. Isn't that right, Mitchell?"

Club nodded.

"'Course, that was crazy."

"What was, Chief?" Club asked.

My lips raised in a smile, for I could tell where this was going, the two men launching into some oft-repeated routine. Maybe it was paranoid of me, but I also heard another note below the humorous one, in Club's voice a sort of dutiful drone.

"Mama and my teacher calling me by my Christian name." The Chief let out a laugh, genuine and broad. Rather than sounding ugly in this grief-stripped room, it brought back a little of its life. "They should've known I was gonna be Chief." He raised my chin with his hand then, gaze probing. "You call me Chief. Okay?"

My throat was still thick. "Yes," I said, low. "Okay." The Chief's presence was like a soft, enveloping blanket. I felt myself begin to unfreeze, just a little. I leaned into his pat, the way a cat will do as it sidles past your leg.

"Next time," he said, "I'll stay for a meal."

The Chief turned and ambled out before either of us could say goodbye.

Late that afternoon, the phone rang. "Hello?" I said into it, but received no reply. I uttered the next inquiry more impatiently before tossing the cordless aside on the bed. Both Club and Teggie had urged me to rest. And for some reason, I had agreed, even though I didn't want to rest, had the feeling I'd already spent too much of my life resting.

My sister entered the room. "I found it."

I was still focused on the phone. "Found what?"

"What Brendan used. In his desk drawer. Club was getting a book out of the study," she added quickly.

I patted the bed, indicating that my sister should sit down, but she ignored me.

"Don't you want to see?"

A pause. "Yes, of course."

She laughed, brief and bitter. "Really? Of course?"

Before I could answer, she held out her hand, palm up.

I lifted an amber plastic bottle. "Prescription pills?"

"Read the label."

I glanced at the white sticker. The type was dark and clear, but for a moment I couldn't make out what it said at all.

"They're for Brendan," I said at last. "You already said that."

"Name isn't all that's on a prescription label," Teggie said.

"Why do you sound that way?" I cried.
"Why are you being so harsh?"

"Harsh?" Teggie echoed strangely.
"You don't know what harsh is. You
don't know what harshness you're letting yourself in for. I may not, either, but
I have some sense of what happens
when you try and face up to the truth."
She hesitated. "I have a short lifetime's
worth of cred on that subject."

I glanced down at the label again.
"The physician is Doctor Bradley. He
works with the police when they need
medical help."

Teggie paused, then said, "Okay."

"He must've been on duty when these
were prescribed."

"Keep reading."

"The date . . ."

"Right," said Teggie, her voice an
ache, hardly confirmation at all.

". . . was January sixteenth." I tried to
swallow past a sudden blooming in my
throat. "January sixteenth?"

"Yes."

"No," I said stupidly.

Even Teggie had stopped speaking for the moment.

"If he got these on January sixteenth," I said, letting the words come slowly so they didn't choke me all at once, "then it means that Brendan planned this— that he knew what he was going to do—a week before he did it."

CHAPTER SEVEN

By six the next morning, I was no longer able to keep my eyes shut. My mind and guts were one roiling mass.

For five terrible days now, a belief had gripped me, unquestioned. That belief was in jeopardy, and I had to restore it. Period.

Except the questions were coming at me, like a river overflowing its banks, unstoppable.

To do what he did, my husband must have been clamped by a spasm of un-anticipated pain. Whatever caused him to be in such agony, I was sure that it had caught him completely and totally unaware.

Otherwise I would have known. Brendan would've shared with me, or if not that—for even I had understood that there were things my husband didn't say, dark reaches of himself he kept concealed beneath the surface fun and humor—then I would've intuited it. Something huge and catastrophic enough to end Brendan's life could not have gone unnoticed, unremarked.

If my husband had been wounded on January sixteenth, severely enough to hang himself on the twenty-third, I would have heard something about it. Seen it. *Smelled* it on him.

Except I hadn't.

Not if he'd decided on his course of action, gone so far as to procure some drug to grant him isolation, a full week before.

Was Teggie right? Did I turn away from the hard things, or had there simply been no real hard things in our life? We'd had enough money—Jean was generous about the rent, and the cost of living wasn't high up here—to enjoy

an occasional vacation, plus the everyday recreation and sport of the region.
Even in this small house, there sometimes seemed too much space, but I'd
held out hope that might change one
day. It was easy not to think about, because time spent just the two of us went
down so easily, filled with laughter and
distracting details from our days. Details
that now threatened to seem cata-
strophically superficial, compared to
whatever had been really going on.

I sat up in bed, pushing the covers
down from my waist. I was cold every
time I slept now, no longer able to bear
a blanket being drawn all the way up to
my neck. Even shirt collars brought back
intolerable visions of rope drawn tight
around someone else's throat, but I was
paying for this new phobia, my upper
body stiff as I walked to the bathroom.
In the shower, though, I didn't allow myself the luxury of a soak.

Because if Brendan got that prescription on January sixteenth, that meant
we went about our light, normal daily
lives for seven whole days beforehand.

Lived together. Slept together. Ate together. Showered together, at least once. Talked, made love, shared drinks. All while he was preparing to drug me and leave me alone forever? Planning to kill himself? It was impossible.

But the date on the prescription said otherwise.

I grabbed a sliver of soap, swiping opaque streaks across my goose-bumped skin.

Unless Brendan got the medication for another purpose, then used it in my drink on the spur of the moment.

That could be it, I went on, piecing together hopeful thoughts.

Amazing, the things you began to hope for.

Brendan could've had the prescription here in the house, filled on the sixteenth for some minor ailment I was guilty of overlooking, then been struck down on January twenty-third by an unbearable shock, some piece of news I had yet to uncover.

I kept going, trying to unravel my dead husband's last hours.

He decided to use the medicine to knock me out. Maybe he wasn't even sure it would do the trick, but once it did, as soon as I slipped into a weirdly solid sleep, there was nothing to keep Brendan from that hideous hank of rope and the light fixture on our back stairs.

What kind of medication was it? Why had the doctor prescribed it?

Shivering, I stepped beneath the blast of water, taking only a second or two under the stream before fumbling for a towel. Then I padded down the icy floorboards toward Brendan's study, taking care not to wake my sister.

I didn't bother sitting down. The chair in here was Brendan's, and I couldn't stand to be in that right now. In fact, almost everything here belonged to Brendan. Until recently, when I'd created a few files, I'd seldom had any need for a computer. And I wasn't one for lounging about reading, preferring instead to be out working with my hands.

I stared at the laptop on the desk, then identified a button that seemed to take a great deal of effort to depress. The machine came sluggishly to life, a series of bleeps and grindings that sounded very loud in the still morning. I glanced around, but my sister slept on securely, two rooms away.

Sonodrine, it said on the bottle she had found.

My right hand shook as I typed the word. I clutched at the towel with my left, clenched into a quaking fist. My shoulders were pebbly with gooseflesh and if I didn't get into some clothes quickly, I was going to start to cry with sheer discomfort and cold. I clicked on the first page that came up, then the next, and another, going back to read them all in quick succession, as fast as I could mouse between tabs. My gaze flicked left to right, but I took in hardly any words.

It didn't matter what the Internet came up with. The vast, infinitely tangled Web didn't know Brendan, and it certainly didn't know me. I hated technology, so cold and heartless compared to the warm, beating pulse I felt when I laid my hands upon plaster or wood. I needed a real, breathing human being who wouldn't offer me manufacturer warnings, chemical composites, or frequencies of use, but would instead tell me why Brendan might've taken this particular drug on that fateful night.

"Nora?"

Teggie, huddled in a robe, was standing in the doorway, blinking, her curls stuck up at odd angles.

"It's early, go back to sleep," I said, pushing past her to my room.

Teggie followed, yawning.

I yanked out clothes from a drawer, then dressed, leaving my top buttons undone. It was an insane way to dress in Wedeskyull in winter. From the time I'd arrived in this new, strange climate, a compressed fall succumbing to six or seven months of winter's biting cold, I had adapted to extra layers and multiple kinds of outerwear. But I could no longer bear the feeling of being bundled up to my neck.

My sister trailed me into the hall.

"Where are we going?" She sounded awake.

I hesitated. "I think I have to do this myself, Teg."

She eyed me, a look of understanding passing over her face.

I used to disbelieve the way people

got used to devastating events. Circum-
stances they once thought they could
never bear: a terminal diagnosis, or
losses so grievous that just the mention
of them before they occurred required
tapping on wood and begging God to
forbid.

Now I knew how they did it.

Your definition of what was bad
changed. The unthinkable turned into
the familiar, and other, more dire things
became what you needed at all costs to
prevent.

Brendan had hanged himself from the
top of the odd, crooked back staircase
I had been laboring to restore. He did it
after making sure I would sleep through
his monstrous machinations, after muffling my ears and brain against the dry,
reedy jolt of rope giving up its final slack.

Nothing could change that. The worst
had happened.

Unless he planned it in advance. That
would be even worse.

The prescription must have been purchased for some other purpose. But
what? Brendan never took medicine,
never had a single complaint beyond

the muscle aches that he called the tenor of a cop's existence. The holster was weighty when worn continually, and hours at the shooting range always tended to stiffen up his arms.

Sonodrine was a sleep aid primarily. That's what the first Web page had told me. But it could be used to dull pain as well. Had Brendan suffered some injury too mild to tell me about?

My sister stepped close, trying to hold me in her thin, reedy grasp. I pulled free.

Teggie frowned. "Let me fix breakfast," she said. "First."

How tempted I was, how much I wanted to give in, go back to how things once had been.

Although this wasn't really how things had been, was it, me setting off on a search for answers, Teggie suggesting we stick to the mundanities of routine?

I grabbed my bag, kept stocked for small, impromptu jobs or on-site meetings, turning around for one last look before leaving.

"Not hungry," I said. "You eat."

"I never eat before an audition," she replied. Her narrow shoulders seemed to settle. "Forget it then. Just come back quickly."

My response sounded bleak as I took the stairs at a reckless pace. "I don't know if this will be quick."

CHAPTER EIGHT

When I got out to the driveway, my car, unused now for the better part of a week, was frozen solid, its cherry color bled pink by layers and layers of ice. Every surface—windshield, windows, both side mirrors, and all four metal flanks—had turned into opaque, mottled sheets. The tires were stiff and glassy. My key wouldn't slide into the lock.

Once it became clear just how impenetrable the car was, I began to stamp around, boots slipping and catching on ice-coated lumps of gravel.

How did I not anticipate this? It was

January in Wedeskyull, New York. I'd lived in the upper Adirondack Mountains for nearly eight years now; I knew what it was like to have to keep a snow shovel inside so you could start carving out your path from the front door. If you didn't dig things out every day—porch, driveway, car—you'd find them entombed the next.

Entombed. My mind revolted against the word, and I paused in my frantic sliding and tripping, breath emerging in furious white huffs.

I couldn't keep avoiding all the words that clanged like a church bell, all the things that threatened to suffocate me. So long as I was doing that, I'd never discover why Brendan had done what he did.

Hanged himself.

Don't just think it, say it aloud.

No more lying, blinking, turning away.

"Hanged himself," I whispered into the frozen air. "My husband hanged himself."

I glanced up at the bedroom window—my window now, just mine—looking to see if Teggie would be occupying the room, her figure etched against the glass.

"He's dead!" I cried out. "Brendan killed himself!"

I hurled my oversized bag onto a solid hump of snow. It could've broken my camera, but I didn't care. Then I stomped over to the garage and ripped the door open, fighting a low drift that broke into solid pieces at my assault. Once I had succeeded, I plunged my fist into a bucket and yanked out a scraper.

I flung myself against the brittle car, tearing at its armor so that first hard chunks, then a fine spray, flew off the glass.

Words as splintery as the ice emerged from me.

"You used to do this for me, Brendan, but you'll never do it again!"

Only the grinding scrape of serrated plastic against lifeless things—metal, glass, and ice—answered back.

"I'll never wait for you to come inside, breath clouding your face. You'll never say, 'All done, Chestnut.' Never! Never! Never!"

I tore at the ice with the scraper until the green plastic began to whiten with wear. I realized that for the first time in days I wasn't chilled to the bone. My body was heated through, back clammy with sweat underneath my thick coat.

"I'll do it myself, like I'll be doing everything myself!"

Bangs and rips to the ice-choked car.

"But it's not about what I'll be doing, Brendan—"

The scraper snapped in half in my fist and I started to use my hands, snatching up broken slices of ice, and swiping at the leftover film until the car was finally clear enough to see.

"It's about what I'll miss," I said hoarsely. My throat was raw.

But not thick, threatening to cut off breath.

My chest heaved in my down jacket. I had torn the tips off six fingers on my gloves.

I tossed the broken pieces of scraper onto the lawn and dashed back to the garage for a canister of de-icer. Then I swept my bag up from the ground. As a glow of yellow lights began to light the houses of my neighbors, I threw myself onto the front seat, ground the clutch into reverse, and fishtailed out toward the highway.

I didn't see the whipping red lights, carnival-bright against all the whiteness around me, or hear a wail until the police car was beside me. Then I jerked the steering wheel to the right, and skidded onto the shoulder of the Northway.

I'd been married to a policeman; I knew that if a police car drove up next to you, the cop had been trying to pull you over for a while. I put my head down on the steering wheel, letting the window down blindly. A flurry blew across my bare face. It had started to snow without my realizing it.

"Want to look up at me, ma'am?"

I tilted my head to one side.

"Oh, Nora. Honey, I didn't see it was you. Your license plates are covered with snow."

"Sorry about that, Vern," I said. "Chief."

A big, meaty arm penetrated the window and the police chief lifted my face. His own was covered by a gray ski mask, which produced a particularly alien effect. "Fact is, you were driving mighty fast. Sliding a bit, too."

"Was I?"

"Didn't you hear me behind you?"

"No. I'm sorry. My head was . . . somewhere else."

The Chief peeled off his mask and peered in at me. "That wasn't why I pulled you over."

I was staring at Vern's gray-swathed chest, the familiar row of silver buttons, a sheen on his badge that I knew took work to maintain.

The Chief rested both hammy fists on my window bed, where a lip of snow had already gathered. "One of your taillights is out. Can't afford that in this weather."

"Oh, right," I replied. "I'll have to replace the bulb."

"Where you headed now? Away from Jean's house, I can see."

The desolate thought that it would never be my house washed over me. It wasn't even Brendan's. "To the pharmacy," I said.

"You having some kind of medical problem?"

"No," I said, a small smile creeping up on me. I could refer to something goopy, female, and the Chief would surely back off. Then I wondered why I wanted him to. Vern stood there, his breath emerging in steady, white plumes.

"I found some medication," I went on after a moment. "It's—it was—Brendan's, but I don't recognize the prescription."

I left out the fact that Brendan had drugged me with this particular pill.

"You're looking for 'how comes' and there aren't any here," the police chief told me gruffly. "Brendan died and I'm mad as hell, like you, but no good comes from wondering why."

I squinted through the snow-strewn air at the Chief's fleshy face. Died. Not killed himself. Was the Chief trying to tell me something? Or did he just want to spare me?

"I need to know as much as I can about how Brendan was doing. This medication is something he didn't tell me about. And I can't stand that right now."

Vern's face became even softer. "Okay. All right. But I'm gonna have to insist you take care of that taillight first."

A sudden swirl of snow momentarily blocked out sight of the Chief.

I glanced at the clock on my dashboard. "My taillight? Now?"

Vern Weathers was smiling, jowls lifted so they wrinkled his eyes. "Now, honey, there's already been one tragedy for the Hamilton family this year, and it's just a baby year yet. No more, all right?"

I nodded in resignation.

"In this weather it's not safe for you to be driving around one backlight down. You go on over to Al's, and he'll fix you up. When he's done you can play yourself a little detective. Heck, if you do a good job, maybe we'll hire you on." The Chief went silent for a second. "Don't mean to make jokes. The wife would have my head."

I had trouble picturing tiny Mrs. Weathers even reaching the top of her tree trunk husband, let alone doing anything to his head. Vern must've seen it on my face, for he chuckled in agreement.

I raised my window, pushed down to trigger the blinker, and reentered the Northway, scattering snow in front of my tires. Behind me, Vern pulled out, too, red lights twirling in an onslaught of flakes.

CHAPTER NINE

I made my way through empty streets, still but for the snow, toward the outskirts of town. They had turned slushy with salt and as I glanced in my rearview mirror, half expecting to see the police chief still behind me, I saw caramel-colored splashes instead.

Stopping at a red light, I peered through the foggy windshield.

A bait and ammo store sat directly in front of me, and just beyond it, my destination. Al's Gas & Service occupied one corner of Water Street, across from a new Mobil. I favored the latter, where

I could grab a cup of coffee after pumping my gas, but Al Meter serviced the cop cars and so I obeyed Vern's order. For all I knew, he might check.

Things like the two stations could make Wedeskyull a tough place sometimes. The town—whose ominous-sounding name, spoken as if someone were killing weeds, stood in stark contrast to its physical beauty—was not an entirely peaceful place. It was divided between newcomers and natives, the Mobil half and the Al's half. As the émigré bride of a man whose family had lived here for a hundred years, and elsewhere in the Adirondacks for a hundred before that, I didn't fit into either group.

But I loved Wedeskyull—and not only because of Brendan. There was a wealth of antique houses for me to pore over, all in differing degrees of dilapidation. Even if I'd never made many friends of my own here—*any,* came Teggie's voice, any *friends of your own*—the architecture made a surprisingly rich substitute.

It was Brendan who'd pointed out how many city expats poured fortunes into those places, and soon after that observation was made, my business was born. *You can do it, Chestnut. Ask for twenty percent commission.*

Memories. Reams of memories assailed me.

Like *Chestnut.*

I'd once asked Brendan why he called me that, and he answered dreamily, "Because you're my Christmas treat." But his face held something more.

It was true that we met during finals back in school in the city, just before winter break. Brendan had bought me a bag of nuts off a cart to celebrate the end of exams.

"One step closer to lawyerdom," he announced.

Brendan had settled on the profession because he wanted to deal with all the people who played games with the law. At least that's what he'd told me when we started dating, and he'd been filling out applications, and taking the LSATs. But when the time came to choose between law schools, something had radically changed. Brendan proposed. And then he suggested we return to his hometown, where he had gotten an offer to join the force. Being a cop gave Brendan good benefits, long-term security, and something else. A call to his heritage.

I stared up at the traffic light. It was the only one in town. Chance Carson, the owner of the bait and ammo store, had paid for that light. Made access to his parking lot easier.

Wedeskyull was a big small town, if that made sense. It had its own schools, jail, police force, and there were enough residents—especially with the newcomers coursing in—that no one could really claim to know or even recognize everybody. You could drive twenty miles and still be contained by the borders of Wedeskyull, but within its spread-out confines stood one central stalk, a deeply rooted tree, the branches of which went back to the town's inception and had witnessed its growth.

The now green light blurred before my eyes.

An engine gunned behind me.

I jolted forward, putting my hand up in apology, and turned into Al's lot.

Grimacing at the salt chunks that

broke beneath my boots as I got out, I tugged open a smeared glass door. The temperature inside and out differed by about sixty degrees, which led to condensation. Across the empty street, the Mobil lot was clear beneath a brightly lit overhang.

Now that I was inside, I could see that this place was more modern than its age and position in town would suggest. I'd been expecting something out of *Andy Griffith.* Instead there was a high bank of gleaming machines with buttons that lit up, tools that more closely resembled thermostats or telephones than wrenches, and some blue thing on wheels that looked like a friendly robot.

But no one to use all of this equipment. I was alone except for a crackling radio, set to the police channel. I backed away from its buzz of familiar voices.

"Can I help you, Missus?"

I had no idea where the voice had come from.

"Um, yes," I began.

The sole occupant of the dim interior showed himself. He was dressed in camouflage, the white kind for winter, and as I studied him, I realized he couldn't possibly help me. He was just a kid.

He moved out from behind a grimy desk, blue eyes squinting.

I tried a smile.

"What can I do you for?"

The boy had a dazzling smile to go along with those bright eyes. He was on the small side—not much taller than I was—and his light hair was tangled. The smile faltered when I didn't say anything. *"What can I do you for.* That's what my boss always says."

Now that he was standing in the open, I thought he looked vaguely familiar, like someone I might've seen around but never really met.

"Well," I began, "my car's outside and it's got a light out?"

The boy's smile broadened. "Let's have a look."

I found myself smiling back as we walked across the slushy lot.

"Messy out here," he said. And then to my amazement, the boy drew his camouflage-patterned sweatshirt over his head, and laid it on the asphalt. He hadn't bothered with a jacket back in the shop; now he stood unflinching in the air, which was cold enough to shatter, wearing only shirtsleeves.

I glanced down at the cloth.

"Stand on that, why don't you? Then your feet won't get as wet."

"Um," I mumbled. "No, that's all right . . ."

The boy turned an injured gaze on me, and I saw in that moment that I'd been wrong. He wasn't a child, he might be as old as twenty, twenty-five even. A faint scruff of beard on his jaw showed in the light, and his eyes also held more than anyone very young could've seen.

I stepped onto the white cloth, rapidly liquefying in the slush, and the boy's chunks of teeth showed again. "Think I got this one in stock. You stay right here."

I was trying to tease out the branches of his mind. Kindness paired with a lack of understanding about basic physical realities, such as what happens when cotton gets wet, or the fact that my boots would've protected me much better than his flimsy shirt.

The temperature was starting to wear on me by the time he returned with a small box. He crouched by my car, fiddling while I wrapped my arms around myself, wondering at his lack of response to the burning cold.

Why was I standing out here? It wasn't as if my help was needed. I started to turn and go inside—deliberating over whether to provide any explanation or excuse—when he spoke up.

"I'm awful sad about Brendan."

The cold took hold of me then, and didn't let go. "Did you know Brendan?" Then I paused. "Do you know me?"

"Know," he echoed, and I was about to pose another question when he went on, his tone making the words freeze on my lips. "Go, slow, row to hoe."

"Rhymes," I said senselessly, wanting to get out of there. Why hadn't I gone to the Mobil? I didn't know if this person was brain-injured or mentally retarded or some other variation of differently-abled—all deserving of equal rights and fair treatment and anything else they might want, only not by me, not right

now anyway. I had to get to the pharmacy.

"Want to turn 'em on?"

"What?" It came out more of a cry. I
didn't understand anything anymore.

"Your lights." He gestured to where
he'd been working.

"Oh." My face grew hot despite the
chill. "Sure." I stepped off the sodden
sweatshirt, drowned now in the lot, and
went to sit down on the front seat.

"Works real well!" the boy-man said
with delight. "Visible even in broad daylight." A pause. "*Risible* is the only one."

"What?"

"*Miserable*—no, that's cheating . . ."

Another rhyme, I realized belatedly. I
leaned forward, but didn't close my
door. "Thanks for taking care of this."

"Ms. Hamilton . . ." he said, and I
frowned again.

"Yes?"

"That'll be sixteen dollars. Just the
cost of the light. Labor's on the house."

"Oh," I said, starting to reach for my
bag. "Right. Thank you."

"That was his. Long time ago," he
said, and I followed his gaze to the sack

I used as both briefcase and purse, a castoff of Brendan's when he decided against law school.

So this person had indeed known my husband, in which case my uppermost guess about his age was probably closest to the truth. As I trailed him back to the garage to pay, I wondered if he knew anything else.

"I used to watch him skate," he said, opening the cash register.

Relief, which I didn't entirely understand, sank into me, weighing me down. Brendan couldn't have known this person, then, nor vice versa. In the eight long winters we'd lived up here, Brendan had never once set foot on a lake. He wouldn't join the hockey team the cops all played on. Brendan felt clumsy on ice, a standing he couldn't abide. He liked to be good at things—taking double-black-diamond trails easily, expert with a pickax and ropes—and consequently had always seemed to display an aversion to skating.

"Boy, did they have fun."

"Who?" I burst out. "Who are you?" I

added, hoping my rudeness might pass unnoticed amongst all the other things this person didn't seem to understand.

He trudged over to the dirty desk, pulling open a drawer that protested with a metallic shriek. He handed me a business card, the kind torn from a perforated sheet.

Dugger Mackenzie. Al's Gas & Service. Tender, loving care for your automobile.

"Dugger?" I said, and he grinned.

"Not like that." The grin washed away. His face looked almost unrecognizable without it. "Rhymes with *cougar.*"

I almost missed it when his hands started to curl into fists, and had to hurry to scare up a response as he started to pummel his own hips.

"Gotcha," I said in a deliberately easy tone. "You say your name with two 'o's."

The tension in his posture began to loosen.

I dropped the flimsy card into my sack. "Well, Dugger, it was nice to—"

"They kept us little guys off the lake. Not all the time then, not yet, but me they did almost always," Dugger said, as I began to walk toward the cloudy glass door. "That didn't matter. I liked standing on the sidelines."

I turned halfway back.

"I could make out Brendan, even way off on the bank. Red, you know, his strings. They called out from real far away. Called, lolled. Don't spell 'em the same, but they still work."

A car drove into the lot on a wave of slush.

My reply took a moment to form. Because that last thing Dugger had said made a strange sort of sense. "Are you talking about laces? Skate laces?"

The car honked, a rude blast, and Dugger, still coatless, turned toward it.

"Dugger? Do you mean that Brendan wore red—"

"Sorry, Missus," Dugger said breathlessly. He flung open the door. "I got to see to this customer. The boss gets mad if anyone has to wait."

I was left to stare after him, and try to untwist his words.

CHAPTER TEN

The pharmacy would have to wait for another morning. Right now there was something more pressing I needed to check on at home.

Dugger's words, slow and precise, were still trickling through my head.

Go, slow, row to hoe. Was it wrong— paranoid of me again—to take that as some kind of message? Wasn't the word *tough* usually inserted in front of the last three? It was as if Dugger had been warning me about what I might be in for.

The wipers slapped snow back and

forth across the windshield, and I blinked to clear my vision, trying to make sense of the road amidst the churning flakes.

I was behaving as if I'd come in contact with some kind of seer, when in fact Dugger was probably just an eccentric character about town, compromised in intellect or sanity.

Did Vern know Dugger? He must. I could ask the Chief about him.

In the meantime, something even wackier than this morning's encounter was waiting to be resolved: the notion that once upon a time Brendan had skated.

"It's a box. A yellow flannel box," I told Teggie when she came upon me in the bedroom, not having bothered to remove my coat and hat.

The box had been an inheritance from Brendan's father, and he always kept it in his dresser drawer. The fabric covering was worn as soft as rose petals, and the lid caught a bit as I lifted it off. My gaze skidded over the objects inside. Brendan never encouraged me in looking at these things, although he hadn't exactly stopped me, either, and so even though I was wont to give his past some privacy, I had caught glimpses of certain items from time to time.

I recognized Brendan's college acceptance letter. There was a Christmas card with a picture of two boys on it, one much younger than the other, almost completely concealed by a snowsuit and hat. Brendan's little brother, who had died as a child.

I pushed some other things aside. There was a bumper sticker with a distasteful logo—a meaty, red tongue splayed out against a rock—and the word *Stonelickers* on it, as well as a slim stack of letters and a bulbous class ring that Brendan never wore.

Finally, a pair of long strands, which I lifted out, winding them around my finger.

They were red.

"What are those?" asked Teggie.

I held out my finger, cocooned in red cotton. "Remember? My proposal?"

"Oh, right. Your ring was on them. Like a necklace," she said.

I nodded. "But I never told you why Brendan did it that way."

"Why?"

"Why didn't I tell you? Or why did he?"

Teggie lifted the twin knobs of her shoulders. "I don't know," she said impatiently. "Both. Either."

I glanced out the window. The snow had finally stopped and the opaque world was starting to clear. "I learned something today."

Teggie propped one foot on a shelf three feet above her waist, nodding that she was listening as she began to stretch.

I walked closer to the window. The glass gave off a frigid layer of air, but I shucked off my outer gear anyway, feeling stifled by it all of a sudden.

"I found these laces around the time Brendan and I first met. In his dorm room."

Teggie wafted a slim arm down to meet her toes.

"They were in with a whole bunch of stuff. Brendan always keeps—kept—important things around. Together, in special places. This box mainly. It was his father's."

"So the shoelaces were important somehow?"

"Not shoelaces," I corrected. "Skate laces. Although I didn't know that until today."

Scales of shivers ran up and down my back. My husband had lied to me.

"Brendan said he'd been a clown once for Halloween. His favorite holiday as a child. So he held on to the laces that went in his shoes." It had sounded plausible at the time, although now I felt silly for believing it.

Plausible, I heard as a distant echo. Not right for *risible,* either. That was cheating.

Teggie, now limber, slid into a split.

"I didn't see them—or think about them—again until his proposal." I held my left hand some distance away. The diamond needed cleaning. I couldn't imagine going about that small task, which I'd once attended to frequently. Chemicals from renovation work tended to dull the stone. "And then we had a fight."

"You fought? The day he proposed?"

My cheeks heated. Teggie had always coveted a relationship like mine and Brendan's. Most of the men she came in contact with were gay. She joked sometimes that she was destined to be a maiden auntie to our kids.

But that hadn't turned out to be true, had it? Not for either of us.

Tears crowded my eyes, and I turned blindly away from the window, dropping onto the bed. The quilt still smelled faintly of Brendan, and I started to cry.

Teggie leapt to her feet, squatting gracefully beside me. "Oh, Nor. I'm sorry. I'm sorry for asking. Who cares if you had a fight? What matters is the marriage that came after, right?"

I pressed my fingers into both my eyes, hard, forcing the tears back. "It does matter, that fight. It matters now."

"Why?"

I took a deep breath and my sobs shuddered to a stop. "I asked him why he had done such a silly thing. Made a necklace out of laces that once belonged to a costume. For a clown, no less. It felt like he was making a joke of asking me to marry him. I almost said no that day. I wanted him to do it—" A groan escaped me. "Do it over."

"Okay," Teggie said soothingly. "That's understandable. Every woman dreams about how she'll get engaged."

"But Brendan convinced me that he used them because the laces were special. A memory from childhood." I looked up at Teggie, my eyes suddenly arid, vision clear. "I think he was telling the truth. These laces *did* have to do with his childhood. But not with dressing up as a clown."

Teggie shrugged, clearly puzzled. "So he swapped stories. The laces are from a childhood memory that had to do with skating. What's the big deal?"

The laces, dangling near the edge of Brendan's desk, suddenly slithered off. I didn't stoop to pick them up.

"No, you don't understand," I said. "What's bothering me isn't that Brendan used to skate as a kid. *Everybody* skates in the Adirondacks. Or even that he lied about it later. It's that for some reason he . . ."

Teggie's loosened-up shoulders suddenly tensed. "Stopped."

Later that night, after we'd failed to eat much dinner, I crept back upstairs, where I'd abandoned the keepsake box. I'd noticed several items when I looked for the skate laces earlier. Now I was looking for something I hadn't seen, but knew should've been there.

Bill Hamilton's wedding present to us had been a small, homemade album. The album itself was pretty, with a hand-tooled leather cover, but what made the gift really special was that it contained the only collection of pictures of Brendan as a little boy. My father-in-law had brought us to his sister's house for the presentation.

It was an older home, built around the turn of the last century, and Jean tended this property with care. Unlike the non-attention Eileen had given her twin house across the road, Jean had lavished framed daguerreotypes, antimacassars, and needlepoint benches upon all of the rooms, decorating in a fussier way than suited the house, but still obviously taking pains.

"Okay," she had wheezed during that visit. Jean was a heavy woman, for whom just talking sometimes took effort. "If she stops by, you're not here."

It took me a second to realize whom Jean was referring to, and it was then that I began to get a sense of how close the two women were. Linked through Bill, they were the sisters-in-law Sprat: one no fat, the other no lean.

"Just for this once," Bill told his sister, leading us into a spare room, and handing Brendan a paper bag.

The little album that was in the bag contained no more than a dozen pictures, all taken before Brendan was eight. But my husband loved that narrow, almost barren scrapbook, studying the shots far more frequently than twelve photographs required.

I figured Brendan loved the album especially because it was the last thing his father ever gave him. One Saturday morning, two months after our wedding, Bill went out to the garage for something and never returned. Eileen found him there at the end of the day, dead of a heart attack. Sadder even than my father-in-law's premature demise was the fact of how long it had gone unnoticed.

Dropping my gaze back to the yellow box, I attempted to take in each item of my husband's collection.

The leather photo album was gone.

CHAPTER ELEVEN

Teggie left for her audition the next day. I took her to the bus station amidst the swirl of another winter storm, this one heavier and more lasting. The snow must've begun hours ago, for everything was buried by the time we woke up.

I had to lean close to the dash as I drove, squinting between flakes on the windshield.

The station appeared behind a curtain of snow, a long, low-lit building, nearly invisible in the blizzard. I rotated the wheel, and my back tires skidded before I gained control.

The bus was heaving in the lot, billows of exhaust combining with the clouds of snow.

Teggie got out of the car and went around to the trunk, picking her way carefully over the ice. She didn't have boots equal to the climate; the ones she wore were fashionable but flimsy.

"Bus is about to leave," I murmured, hefting the duffel out for her.

"Teggie standard time," she said, and I smiled rotely.

"Can't risk a turned ankle," she went on. "Here in the great frozen north."

I smiled again.

She peered closely at me, snow flying about her face. Her knit cap was already covered in white. "Hey, Nor, are you going to be all right?"

I jerked my elbow toward the bus, whose gears I could now hear grinding.

Teggie stood her ground.

"Yes." I heaved a sigh. "I'll be fine. Reassure Mom and Dad that I've gotten on with the business of living."

"Whoa, mocking Mom and Dad now, are we," Teggie said, finally heading toward the bus, duffel bag swinging in her surprisingly strong grip. Her next words were almost lost. "When am I going to talk to Dad?" She turned and began to walk backward.

"Teggie!" I shouted, not sure what I wanted to say. *Goodbye? Come back?*

"Whose life?" she called loudly, over the engine noise and storm. "Yours or Brendan's?"

It was a question only an unmarried woman, one who'd never even really been in love, could pose. Brendan's life wasn't distinct from mine, not entirely. They were linked. And if I didn't find out why Brendan had taken his life, then I would never be able to live my own.

"Go, Teg!" I shouted, and she ran, perfectly graceful, without a hitch, over the covered expanse of pavement.

I plodded back to my car, scraped off the windshield again, and drove out over the heaps of snow that the salt hadn't yet attacked, back onto the slippery road.

I was alone now. Really alone for the first time since Brendan had died.

✳   ✳   ✳

I stopped in town at a place called Coffee Rockets. I could sit there until the drugstore opened at nine.

The café was filled with its usual mix of customers, united by only one thing. Whether they were skiers in brightly colored, outrageously expensive gear, fueling up before their day on the slopes, or professionals whose footwear wasn't even up for the trek across the parking lot, buying breakfast-to-go before their workday began all of these people were foreigners in Wedeskyull. At the diner across the road, they would've received something close to shunning. The ladies behind the counter would've eyed them silently, and the customers who idled away most of the morning there would've snapped their suspenders or chucked dogs beneath the table, causing the animals to sniff and mutter at the unfamiliar scent in the air. Coffee Rockets had been built to house the encroachers, and that was why, for all its tech lighting and matte chrome finishes, the smells of roasting beans and buttery pastry, it had the feel of a prison camp.

I could've stopped in at the diner and

gotten a warm enough welcome. The girls who worked there were good to the cops. But just as I'd never gone to Al's, I always came to Rockets instead.

The kid behind the counter started preparing my tall as soon as I appeared. He didn't live in Wedeskyull—went to college near here and came into town to work—and wouldn't know my name or anything about me, but he recognized repeat customers. I pointed to a muffin behind the glass case and he handed that over as well. Then I went to sit down in one of the armchairs near the gas fireplace, a choice spot.

Today the coffee, usually so appealing, turned my stomach; I could barely take a sip. I concentrated on my muffin instead, biting it mindlessly, letting it crumble away in my mouth.

The clock on the wall, which managed at once to be artsy and not at all unique, finally showed nine o'clock. I shrugged into my coat, and hurried down the street to the pharmacy, pushing in against a warble of bells. An older man, balding and stooped, occupied the high counter at the back.

It was a dim, dusty place, but the heated air felt good. The aisles were sparsely stocked, a small selection of out-of-date shampoos, only one bottle per brand; a short stack of soap cakes on the shelf. The candy aisle smelled stale, the colors on the bags no longer bright. This place was to the CVS several towns over as Al's was to the Mobil. But it was the one the police preferred.

The pharmacist looked up as I approached.

"Can I help you?"

I glanced down at the amber bottle. "Are you Donald Brannigan?" I asked, reading the name under the tab for *pharmacist.*

"Folks call me Donny," the man replied in a friendly way. Then he repeated, "Can I help you?"

Was I really going to tell this stranger that before my husband committed suicide, he'd drugged me so I wouldn't be able to stop him? How could the pharmacist dispute or confirm that Brendan planned his act a week in advance? I wondered if I would be better off trying to contact Doctor Bradley, although the man had a reputation for distance and remove, answering mainly to the Chief.

I extended my hand. "What can you tell me about this medicine?"

The pharmacist reached over the counter and took the bottle. "Sonodrine is a sedative," he said, before handing it back. "For when someone's having trouble sleeping. Also dulls aches and pains, although that's a lesser use. A hospital might administer it that way."

He wasn't telling me anything the computer hadn't. "Yes," I replied. "But more specifically?"

The pharmacist smoothed his strands of hair into place, an unconscious gesture instead of a vain one, which somehow lent it dignity. "I'm not sure what you mean."

I bit my lip, considering what to say. "I found this with—with my husband's things. But as far as I knew, he wasn't taking any medication. Can you tell me why it would've been prescribed?"

"Perhaps your husband was having trouble sleeping," the pharmacist suggested. "Or had some slightly more than minor ache or pain."

Which of course didn't tell me anything besides the indicated uses.

I breathed out a sigh of frustration, studying the bottle. And then I saw something on it that I hadn't noticed before. "Mr. Brannigan? Donny?"

The man nodded, delivering another finger swipe to his scalp.

"What does this little red mark mean on the label?"

The pharmacist reached across the counter again and took the bottle from me.

"I can't really say," he replied. Swipe, swipe. "Could just be a blotch of ink from our printer. Never did get the hang of using that thing. But Medicare says everything has to be electronic."

I nodded, though it didn't really look like a smudge from a printer. The mark wasn't quite even enough to have been made by a machine.

"Why don't you let me hold on to this for you?" said the pharmacist. "Technically, any kind of prescription meds, especially painkillers, are supposed to be turned over as soon as they're not being used." He gave me another friendly grin. "There's even a whole campaign about it. National Hand In Your Medications Month or some such. You have a good day now."

Clearly dismissed, I turned and walked out of the store, troubled by the feeling that in addition to being no closer to finding anything out, I had just lost the one clue I'd really had.

I ran between snowflakes, dwindling now, less driven in their assault. When I reached my car, I blasted the heat, hoping it might melt enough of the snow that I wouldn't have to get out and scrape. Where could I drive to anyway? Was there anywhere for me to go?

I had a sudden, compelling need to return to my house, take up some project that would let me dig and scrape and peel at plaster, real things, instead of the unknowables that were seeping in all around me. Maybe call Ned Kramer, get back to the paying kind of work I would have to rely on from now on. I poked around in my bag, pushing stuff around to locate my tools, testing their tips. My phone sat underneath. Until I'd started my business, I'd seldom had need of a cell, and this one had probably gone unanswered in the past week. I figured out how to scroll through the list of calls that had come in, seeing an unfamiliar number repeated. Almost idly I began to press *send,* wondering who would answer on the other end, when a glimpse through the windshield distracted me. There was a cop strolling around, his uniform a faint gray shadow between the remaining flakes.

And suddenly I decided.

The sixteenth. Even without the amber bottle to look at, that date was stamped in my head. Brendan had been working late all week, shifts running over.

I would go to the station. To Brendan's other home and family—Club Mitchell, and the men who might have been with him when this prescription was filled.

Making a turn onto Water Street, I drove out of town.

HIDDEN

Officer Tim Lurcquer looked on while Mitchell dragged the body.

No, he didn't drag it. He lifted it by the armpits, then skated it lightly over the top layer of snow. A hundred and eighty pounds of literal dead weight, give or take, and Mitchell moved it as easily as if he were hoisting a fishing pole. The composite, lightweight kind.

Tim grimaced.

He craned his head to look up at the snow sky, a solid fleet of clouds. Mitchell was now circling the enormous, mottled boulder, a stone whose surface re-

sembled faces. The faces changed all
the time, depending upon the degree of
light, how much lichen grew. In Tim's
younger days, the faces had seemed
benign. He and his buddies had broken
beer bottles against a grinning lip of
stone, made jokes about protruding
noses. But for some time now the faces
trapped in the rock all seemed to be
scowling.

It was brutally cold out, with occasional harsh blasts of wind that penetrated even the thickest coat, like the
hidden, deep cells of a lake you swam
out to in summer, sudden reminders
that warmth wasn't ever the true condition of the north woods.

Tim had been born to it, but he'd
never get used to it. He pulled the
earflaps on his hat a bit lower. No uniforms today. Chief's orders.

**No grays today, boys. Street
clothes. I don't want anybody recognizing you.**

No one's even gonna see us, Chief,
Mitchell had said.

The Chief had also made it clear that

Mitchell was in charge, with Tim assisting.

Tim didn't object. If this had been his job, the brute force required would've made him look bad. But it'd be the psychological weight of the task he really would've struggled with.

"Lurcquer?" Mitchell grunted, the only sign he'd shown of exertion. "You mind?"

Tim looked around. What was he supposed to be doing?

He always felt like this, two steps behind, while the others were like some rarefied elite. The damned starting lineup on the varsity hockey team. He'd played, of course, but he hadn't started. Even Gil—whom they all called the rookie, because he'd only recently joined the force after getting back from the service—had it over Tim. Back in high school, Gil had spent more time in the box than on the ice, the enforcer who broke opponents' teeth and bones.

Brendan hadn't played, but off the ice he wasn't as bad as the others. Brendan had been a good-natured sort, full of fun ideas for what to do when their shifts were over. He'd smashed his share of bottles. It'd been Brendan who started the annual polar bear dunk for the cops. And once in a while he'd ask Tim to ride along with him and Club, and they'd spend most of the shift laughing and complaining about the job.

There were also the times when Brendan went solo or stayed behind in the barracks. It'd always baffled Tim how much the Chief seemed to love Brendan, given what a slacker the guy could be. He was a good cop, though; he really cared about people. Tim didn't want to speak ill of the dead. Maybe Brendan wasn't slacking after all, just didn't want to be quite as close to things, this deep in the muck.

Tim could relate to that.

"Look at the hole," Mitchell grunted again. He supported his burden with one hand, pointing with the other.

Tim turned around on the patch of recently dug-up earth, his boots packing down new snow. Now he saw. Snow had already partially filled in the trench.

He used both hands to fiddle with the mechanism on the shovel, open it to its full length. Then he started to scoop out the fresh accumulation. As he dug, he registered how shallow the grave was.

But hell, it was amazing they had a burial place at all. The Chief had had equipment from Paulson's available to him. He and Lenny Paulson went way back, which was lucky. Only heavy machinery could break up the ground this time of year.

Trench empty, Tim turned to face Mitchell.

The other cop gave a massive bellow of preparation and tossed the body in.

"Well," Mitchell said, breath emerging in even white gusts. "There goes number two."

Both looked down at the rift in the ground, then around the whitened woods. They did it as one, gazes falling, heads turning to check.

And Tim experienced a brief, fleeting link of connection, the reason he had stayed on the job for so long. He could do it. He could be just like them.

They were two men sizing up a problem, assessing their location and the likelihood of its being discovered. Two

men deciding to work with what they
had.

Tim threw Mitchell a second folded
shovel, and Mitchell flicked it to its full
length as if it were a match.

They worked to conceal what they'd
done here today.

CHAPTER TWELVE

The police station was housed in a squat building high up on Roister Road. Its best feature was a view of Lake Nancy, now a silver mirror. Its worst was a sheath of vinyl siding, which I used to ask Vern if he would let me take down.

My car crunched over the combination of salt, pebbles, and grit that served as a parking lot. I avoided the gas pump, pulling into a space a fair distance off from the row of gray cop cars. Their shadowy forms made my red car look like the afterimage of some alien sun.

The room I entered was overheated

and spare. Brendan had always complained about sweating in his uniform in
winter. A mean fluorescent glow made
the space even starker than it might
have been: two chairs pushed against a
wall with a new sheen of paint on it, and
a sliding glass window that was always
kept streak-free. I'd never seen a cop
occupying this space, though, summon-
ing visitors with a look or a word.

It shamed me to think of it now, but
I'd never paid that much attention to
what Brendan did at work. The life of
the police force, efficient and well
equipped for such a remote region, had
always proceeded in a rather vague blur.
Sometimes Brendan was what he called
up to things: domestic problems that
occasionally escalated, and recently
there'd been a spate of thefts. But usually he led the life of any cop who worked
on the perimeter of great wilderness. He
made sure black powder season stayed
that way, kept an eye on bored kids
whose families all owned guns, assisted
with Search and Rescue.

I hadn't known what black powder
was until Brendan explained it to me.

And even then, I could never understand why some hunters preferred to act like frontiersmen, pouring gunpowder into their rifles and tamping it down, when Chance at the Bait and Ammo had forty different weapons that would kill a deer with a lot less fuss.

Then again, I couldn't imagine killing anything at all.

A metal door led into another room, gleaming and sleek. This was where the real work was done. Flat-screen monitors dominated five desks, the phones had LCD displays, and the gray cubicle walls were thickly padded.

Brendan had complained when the office had gone paperless, which was more the norm for big-city departments. The programs were hard to learn and cumbersome to use, and incident reports that used to take him five minutes to fill out now required a half hour of arduous clacking.

Vern Weathers sat on top of one desk, his back to me, fleshy body displacing a case or two of CDs, instead of the usual straying sheets of forms. A half-moon of men in gray uniforms perched on chairs, stares presumably fixed on the Chief's face.

"No partner patrols for the next few weeks," the Chief was saying. "You boys can divide up. I don't want any down-state assholes in those woods with their cross-country skis."

Someone chuckled. "Like we groom those trails."

Laughter mingled with his, the Chief's included.

Then Tim Lurcquer looked up and saw me standing in the doorway.

I had never really liked Tim, with his snub features and flat, humorless smile. He didn't quite seem to fit with the other guys, always attempting to squash the raucousness that ensued when all the men got together, Brendan's jovial sug-gestions.

Dave Weathers stood up. "Chief."

The Chief turned around on the desk. "Nora, honey." He glanced at Club and Tim. "Into your grays now, boys," he said. "Don't report in civvies again."

He began to walk, indicating that I should follow. "Got that taillight fixed?"

"Dugger Mackenzie took care of it for

me," I replied, trying to match the Chief's stride.

There was a pause, and I went on, selecting one of the many questions competing for reply. "Do you know him?" The Chief glanced back without answering, and I felt compelled to continue. "Do you know how old Dugger is?"

Vern touched some buttons on the keyless lock on his door and led the way into his office. He placed himself behind his desk and gestured for me to take a seat.

"Dugger? Thirty and change, I guess." He eyed me. "A couple-three years older than Brendan."

I couldn't believe it. Dugger was our age? The crazy thought occurred to me that the Chief might be lying.

He glanced at his computer screen, and the movement spoke more loudly than words.

I went on hurriedly. "Do you know anything about Brendan and skating?"

The Chief leaned forward, folding his thick hands on his desk. "I know that he hated it. You know that. How many times did the boys try and get him to take a spot on the team?"

"Right," I said. "I know. But Dugger told me he used to skate as a kid."

The Chief chuckled then. "Well, you can't trust much of what Dugger says, honey. He isn't right in the head. Been that way since he was little."

"Right," I said again. I had known that right away. Only in this case at least, what Dugger said turned out to be true.

The Chief shifted on his seat. "Anyhow, what does it matter either way? Kids grow up, their likes and dislikes change."

That sounded so reasonable, I knew I would seem crazy if I pursued it. But this did matter. If only because Brendan hadn't given me such a sound reason himself.

The Chief must've seen something in my eyes. "Look, Nora, can I offer you a piece of advice here?"

I nodded uncertainly.

"Time to time, I've had to make a call. You know the kind I mean? Where you deliver news to someone, knowing it's the last thing they're ever in their lives gonna want to hear."

I nodded again, this time with more understanding.

"It's the worst part of the job. I know Brendan thought so. Person like Brendan, sorrow just didn't fit." For a moment, the Chief glanced toward his window. Then he turned back to me, and his face looked smoother, more composed. "But we learn from those times. Boy, do we learn. And one thing I know is you're going through something like a war right now, and the battle's not gonna be lost or won for some time."

It was my turn to look away, to hide the tears running quietly down my cheeks.

"This isn't a time to be poking around, asking questions, coming face-to-face with—"

"With what, Chief?" I broke in. "With answers? With the truth?"

"Naw," he said fiercely. "That's what I'm trying to tell you. With the lack of answers. With how few answers there ever are. Why did someone take that last drink before he crashed his car?

What made him stay the extra hour in the woods and wind up freezing to death?"

The Chief stood up behind his desk. "Honey," he said. "It's the lack of answers that make a person die all over again. Why would you do that to yourself?"

I shook my head. For the first time since the funeral, I couldn't say.

"This is a time to hunker down," the Chief said. "Mourn. Join with your family. I met your family the other day. They're good folks."

I wiped my face, and the Chief dug into his breast pocket for a handkerchief.

"Will you think about what I've said?"

I nodded.

"Good," he said. "No, you keep that," he added, as I halfheartedly held out the scrap of sodden cloth.

The Chief came around and opened his door.

When I walked out, Dave Weathers angled his body away. Vern's brother was built like him, a bit softer and looser, but just as large. Dave's arm accidentally brushed against his desk, sending a few items sliding to the floor. He was stooping, sweeping them together, as I reached the door.

I exited against a wall of icy wind, zipping up my coat, then saw Club come out behind me. His face was chapped and raw, angry-looking, as if he'd spent time outside without wearing his mask. He flexed gloveless hands as I greeted him.

"I'll be salting later," Club remarked. "We're in for a big one."

I glanced up at the snow-blank sky. "Can I ask you something, Club?"

He didn't answer right away, fingering his holster, a steady—if apparently mindless—gesture. "Cold out here," he said. "Want to sit down in my truck?"

I looked at him. "Sure."

We crossed the buried lot. After we'd closed the doors, Club fired the ignition and turned on the heat. "What's up?"

I swallowed. "Do you have any idea why Brendan might've been taking painkillers?"

"Painkillers?" Club echoed. "Nope. I sure don't."

"Or sleeping pills maybe."

Club shook his head.

I stripped off my gloves and held my hands out to the blowing air. "You guys were working late a lot the last few weeks."

"Sure," Club replied. "Happens. You know that."

A sneeze overtook me, and I looked down. The seat I was occupying was thickly coated with black fur. I smiled, sneezing ferociously again.

"God bless," Club said absently. He was staring out the window. "The only thing I can tell you about Brendan's last days is he was doing a lot of talking. More than usual even."

"Talking?" I said. "About what?"

Club shrugged. "You know. How it's hard to do what we do. Protect the good when there's scum all around. Pardon," he added.

I sniffed in deep. "Yeah. That sounds like something Brendan used to talk about." Brendan's face—his whole stance—used to change when he did, become stiffer, more intense. I would attempt to humor him out of it, make jokes about small-town intrigue, who would mow the town square this summer, but Brendan lost his customary wit during those times.

"Mowing is big business up here, Chestnut," he told me once. "Goes along with snow-plowing." He'd spread his hands against a pane of glass, whitened at the time with frost and flakes. "Enough said." But clearly it hadn't been enough. "Bills can run to hundreds of thousands of dollars in these parts. When that kind of money is in play, the gloves come off. Anything can go."

I'd thought about it later, the various interpretations of that phrase. Had Brendan meant "anything goes"? Or "any corner can be cut"?

I gave another sneeze.

"You know?" Club was turning down the heat. "Maybe it would be a good idea to go see your family. Get a little time away."

"Yes," I said, something in his words bothering me. "Maybe."

It wasn't until I'd returned to my own

car that the question took shape in my mind. Did Club come to the same conclusion about a needed family visit on his own? Or had Vern asked him to pass the advice on?

CHAPTER THIRTEEN

Driving home, it occurred to me that Vern's suggestion could be taken another way. Well-intentioned advice aside, I had no interest in leaving Wedeskyull right now, let alone visiting my parents. But didn't Eileen fit the definition of family? Because my mother-in-law might know whether Brendan had some experience on the ice that turned him off skating for life.

I would just heat up something for lunch first. Facing my mother-in-law would require strength. I was hungry again, and plus, I had a call to make.

The nurse practitioner at the doctor's I went to clearly knew about Brendan. Her voice was thick with sympathy. "Of course, dear, I'll phone that right in," she said, when I asked for something a little stronger than Claritin. I hadn't stopped sneezing since leaving Club's truck. "We don't want you to be uncomfortable."

"Thank you," I said, and sniffed.

"Gosh, you do sound miserable," the nurse went on. "I'll make sure this is ready right away."

"Thanks," I said again, then hung up.

As I was cranking up the furnace the phone rang, and I answered it, anticipating some glitch with my insurance or prescription information.

"Nora?"

A male voice, neither the nurse nor the windless vacuum that had come with the other calls I'd received lately, the hang-ups on my cell.

"It's Ned Kramer."

I was reaching for my memory of how to conduct a business call when Ned went on. "I wanted to call and express my condolences."

I still couldn't come up with words,

but Ned continued as if there wasn't anything unusual in my silence. "I have a—a casserole for you. Maybe I can bring it by."

"You cooked a casserole?" I asked.

"I did," Ned replied easily. "Crumbling plaster wall above the stove and everything. I've learned to compensate."

"So this is about your house," I said.

Ned didn't seem offended by my tone. "Well . . . if you're ready to get back to work. Believe me, this place is a lifelong dream of mine, but there are days when I'm tempted to move back to the cabin I stayed in when I first came up here."

"That bad?" I responded.

"Only if you want to call rotted-out floorboards, four clogged fireplace flues, and mildew strong enough for chemical warfare bad."

"Music to my ears," I retorted, and Ned laughed.

"So you *are* ready to start on the job?"

I snuffed out the brief flame of kinship kindled by our exchange, walking over to the stove and emptying a can of soup into a pot. "Can you give me a few days?"

"I can give you whatever you need," Ned replied. There was a depth of understanding to his words.

"This not-working thing isn't good for me financially. Or otherwise," I added.

"Gotcha." He sounded as if he really did. Get it, that is.

An easy rapport existed between us that didn't quite compute. I had met Ned only once or twice, when he interviewed me for that article, an occasional quick hello in the places newcomers tended to congregate, like Rockets. "I shouldn't have said all that. I apologize."

"No, please don't. Apologize. Please do, I mean. Say all that. Even though it wasn't really very much."

Something about his awkward shamble of words prompted me to go on.

"I miss working," I said. "And that's the worst part of all. Because it's the last thing I should miss."

"You don't get a choice in what you miss, though, do you?" Ned replied, low. "That choice was taken away from you."

The pot I'd lit a flame under started to sizzle. I burned my fingers grabbing the handle.

"Nora?" Ned said. "Are you there?"

"Yes!" I cried, waving my hand in the air. "No! I can't come! I can't do your house."

Then I hung up. Even my mother-in-law would be better than Ned Kramer right now.

I drove through town, heaped white from the plows, then wound down Patchy Hollow Road for a mile or two before coming to the dead end where my mother-in-law's house stood. It was a foursquare that had been in the Hamilton family for generations, along with its companion across the road. One belonged to Bill, the other to his sister, so this had been Brendan's childhood home. But Brendan hadn't been over here much since his father had died.

I braked behind my mother-in-law's ancient Ford, kept alive by Al Meter. Eileen's clothes were two or three decades out of date, and her car was, too. Struggling to mount a smile of greeting, I got out amidst stalks of grass tall enough that their tips pierced the snow, and a faraway gleam of frozen lake.

Eileen came onto the kitchen stoop, a coat draped over her housedress. She brimmed her eyes with one hand, squinting and wrapping the coat around herself for warmth.

I called out a hello that got carried away by the wind, then headed across a blown-bare patch of grass. It crunched under my boots like thin bones.

My mother-in-law stepped back, allowing me inside.

The avocado appliances and yellow Formica weren't old enough yet to be fashionable. I used to long to put in a period kitchen here, Shaker cabinetry, a real Hoosier.

My mother-in-law had been making tea. The electric coil on the stove glowed like an angry wound. Eileen reached up for a second cup, clattering the contents of the cupboard, making even this simple gesture look begrudging.

When she sat down at the battered tin table, I did, too.

"You'll forgive me, Nora," Eileen said, taking a sip from her mug. "But you've never stopped by for tea before."

I blew on my drink. This woman and I

shared a dreadful loss. Why couldn't we come together over that? It struck me anew that Eileen had already experienced the death of another child. She was embittered long before I ever came along.

"I'm just—I'm so sorry, Eileen."

Her face changed, drawing into lines.

I snatched at something to say. "I wanted to talk to you about—about a payment schedule for Jean. Brendan handled the financial stuff, and I'm afraid I'm really at a loss."

Eileen inclined her head. "Well, I'm glad you're asking."

"You are?"

She nodded once, a jerk of her pointy chin. "Brendan wasn't paying Jean enough, you know."

"No. I didn't know."

Eileen lifted her bony cups of shoulders. "I'm not saying he was deliberately taking advantage. But a hundred and fifty more—that's nine hundred a month—would be what's fair. Folks coming up from that city of yours would love Jean's house."

Nine hundred was abjectly impossible, but I nodded anyway. "All right."

She eyed me over the rim of her mug. "By check, first of every month. Was that all?"

It wasn't. I lifted my gaze to hers. "Did Brendan—did he used to skate?"

I thought I heard Eileen take in a whistling breath before I realized that the kettle had been left on. My mother-in-law got up to fiddle with the stove knob, answering me with her back turned. "Did he what?"

"I mean, I know he hated skating, I do know that," I said. "Now. As an adult. But when he was young, did he used to skate?"

"What could you possibly want to know that for?"

"I'm not sure," I muttered. An expression on my mother-in-law's face made me flinch, and I worked to speak louder. "I met Dugger Mackenzie. Do you know him?" Without waiting for a reply, I rushed on. "He told me about watching Brendan on the ice when they were boys. I just wondered why Brendan developed such a loathing for it later on."

Eileen's gaze darkened. "You don't know anything, do you?"

I started to shake my head, but realized it might come across as agreement instead of protest.

"What did you and my son share?" she asked. "What kind of marriage could you have possibly had?"

Outrage filled me, hot and lethal as smoke. I rose from the table, careful not to knock over my cup. My vision blurred as I looked around for the door. I had lost my bearings, and made a circuit through the small room adjoining the kitchen.

There was the door. I bumped against an end table making my way toward it. The table was one of the few pieces of furniture in the room; the other, a stark, unpadded chair. The sole object on the table fell to the floor with a *thunk* and I stooped to pick it up.

Brendan's missing photo album.

CHAPTER FOURTEEN

Eileen shut me outside without a word of goodbye. I'd wanted to get a look at her face—see what her reaction might be to my learning what she'd done—but she was instantly concealed within her spare and dingy home.

I hadn't even had a moment to ask for the album. I would have to come back for it.

Had she taken the album out of Brendan's yellow box the day of his funeral? I knew Jean had been upstairs, but hadn't seen Eileen go up.

She'd clearly never cared much for

pictures of her son; that was why Brendan had only the minimal collection from
Bill. Where were all the other shots that
parents usually took?

Suddenly there seemed a whole world
of things I had never asked Brendan
about, and the weight of them threatened to crush me.

The snow blowing across the road
obscured someone's form, made even
more indistinct by the muffling and padding of a pink coat. I lifted my hand in a
wave, and walked over.

"Nora," Jean said, taking me into an
enveloping hug. "Here to visit Mother?"

Only Jean would act as if that were a
reasonable prospect.

"I stopped in," I said.

"Well, stop in with me right now," Jean
said. "I'll make you some lunch."

The prospect was tempting after the
meal I'd scorched before running out of
my house. "Thanks. That would be nice."

Jean led a slow mount of her porch
stairs.

Her kitchen was warm and steamy;
something smelled fragrant on the stove.
I took a cushioned seat by a table, and

let my eyes wander around the room. There was an old-fashioned pie chest and a china cabinet with glass doors that shone in the muted light. Jean ladled soup into a bowl and served a roll alongside it, placing a butter dish before me.

"Thanks," I said again.

"I'll just have one more myself. Since you're eating."

She was moving the butter knife in thick strokes across the bread when I burst out, "Oh, Aunt Jean, I don't know how I'm ever going to pay you!"

She looked up with as sharp an expression as I'd ever seen on her face. "Pay me? For what?" The skin around her eyes and mouth relaxed into folds. "Lunch comes pretty cheap at this joint."

The sound of my own laughter surprised me. "The mortgage, Aunt Jean," I said. "Or rent, however you think of it. Brendan's salary was really carrying us—"

Jean stood up and maneuvered around the table. She leaned down, wrapping both arms around my shoulders. I felt as if I'd been swathed in a luxuriant cloak.

"I'd better never hear a word about this again, dear heart," she said. "You pay me what you can, or don't pay me anything at all. That house will be yours one day, sooner or later." Jean straightened, using me for support. "I don't have any children of my own. Brendan was like a son to me."

"What about Eileen?" I found myself saying.

Jean let out an oddly high laugh. "Well, yes, of course. She's—she was his mother. I didn't mean otherwise."

"I know, but that's the thing," I began, trying to fuse words from the jumble of impressions I had. They'd never made sense before, but now they were taking on form. "Eileen doesn't seem as if she was that much of a mother to him."

Jean frowned, her eyes disappearing into wrinkles. "What do you mean?"

I looked down at the table, then all around the pleasant kitchen. "Why did we see Eileen so rarely? Why did we never go over there?" When Jean didn't answer, I added almost desperately,

"Why doesn't she have any pictures of Brendan?"

Jean reached for another roll, holding the basket out to me. I shook my head. My newly returned appetite had disappeared.

"There may be a few," I said. "On the end table in her sitting room. I'd like to see them." It occurred to me that Jean might know if her sister-in-law had taken the album, although she didn't say anything. "I have a feeling I won't be welcomed back, though." I lifted my head, attempting to find Jean's gaze. "I'm just trying to make sense of what happened, Aunt Jean. Something went horribly wrong."

"I know it did." She pressed her hands together until one was nearly hidden by the cushy flesh of the other. "But you're talking about things from a long time ago. And Eileen is like my very own sister."

"Yes," I whispered. "But you just told me Brendan was like your son."

There was a long silence. Jean tore off a bite-sized piece of roll without getting any butter on her fingers, a swift, competent gesture. At last she said, "Well, you're welcome back here. Any time for lunch," and my heart sank. But then she went on. "Sunday might be good. Eileen goes out that day. Every week, she meets Dorothy Weathers at noon."

I drove too fast down Patchy Hollow Road, braking abruptly when I hit the one light in town. The road had been recently cleared and I had to mount a hummock of snow as I got out in front of the pharmacy.

The pharmacist had already left for the day, but a clerk trailed me to the counter.

"Here you go," she said, lifting a white paper bag.

I was considering whether to pop a tablet, noting that my sneezing had already tapered off, when I saw a little red dab on the label.

"I'm sorry," I said to the clerk. "Can you tell me what this red mark means?"

The clerk paused as she stepped out from behind the counter. "Oh, Donny must've filled this as a rush job."

"That's what the mark means?"

The clerk nodded. "We have regular monthly prescriptions we fill on a schedule," she explained. "Or things to be sent over to the doctor's office for a patient to pick up. But if something is more urgent, we're happy to make it up for you right away." She pointed to a basket. Each of the bottles had a tiny red strike on them.

Why would the pharmacist, who clearly had a system for his prescriptions, have kept it from me? Donny Brannigan's words returned, and there wasn't any doubt. He'd acted as if the red dot on Brendan's Sonodrine were a mystery to him, maybe just an accident. It was a stupid lie, one bound to unravel sooner or later.

And what did it matter if the Sonodrine had been rushed? What did that say about whatever had happened on the sixteenth?

Arriving home in the early-winter dark, I pulled up the calls that had come in while I was gone, and spotted the same number I'd seen on my cell. This time, I had no impulse to ring it back. Some acquaintance who couldn't bring herself to record her condolences maybe, or else a creditor Brendan once would've taken care of. I dialed my sister, hoping to hear how her audition had gone, and feeling disappointed when I had to leave a message on her machine.

I climbed the stairs to bed, settling in for a night of scattered rest. It was impossible to know how long the hours between bedtime and daylight could be until you'd lost the one you loved. Night noises became entirely different things, not warm or comfortable, the tickings of an old house, but ominous and creaky, signs of decay. Outside, branches banged, and the deep cold of the dark caused things to snap, thunderously loud. If the temperature hadn't been so deadly, I would've thought I was hearing somebody's unsanctioned arrival, footsteps in the night. Was it any wonder I hardly slept? I was tired these days, exhausted with a solid feel that pulled on me and dragged.

Tonight there was something else

keeping me awake, too. The prospect of what was going to happen when I stole into my mother-in-law's house three days from now.

CHAPTER FIFTEEN

Sunday dawned with the promise of more bad weather. The weathergirl trilled that it was thirty-five below with wind chill, and gray cotton batting lined the sky. My stomach seemed to lift and toss with the rising wind. I was hungry, but nervous, unable to get much down.

By eleven-thirty, needles of snow had begun to fly, and a thought just as sharp pierced my head. What if the weather kept Eileen home?

I wanted to get Brendan's photo album back. He'd loved it. And no matter what Jean might say about Eileen's adequacy as a mother, I didn't think my husband would choose to leave that cherished gift in her possession.

Before donning my boots, I put on a pair of rubber-treaded socks for creeping around Eileen's house. My mother-in-law was a lifelong resident of Wedeskyull. A little snow and ice wouldn't keep her housebound.

Securing my outer gear until not an inch was exposed, I opened the front door and ducked beneath the ribbons still dangling limply from my wreath. I prodded huge shards of ice off my car with the pieces of broken scraper. I would have to pick up a new one before too many more storms blew in. Snow scoured my face as I worked, and my fingers were clumsy in the thick gloves I wore.

Climbing into the frigid vehicle, I swung out onto the icy road, overcorrecting as my tires spun. The metal flank of my car rattled against a wall of frozen grasses.

When I reached the matching four-squares, both drives were empty. Eileen's ancient Ford was missing from the long stretch of gravel, a skim of new snow atop the old, packed stuff. Jean's roomy Buick, a rather ridiculous vehicle for these parts, was also gone from her driveway across the street.

So Eileen had kept her lunch date with Dorothy Weathers, despite the thickening storm. And Jean, who almost never left her comfy abode, had scurried out into the snow, too. There were forces afoot in this family that didn't breach the surface.

At least I was alone for my venture. I parked at Jean's, figuring that seemed the more likely place for a visit, in case anyone returned. Of course, if anyone came home while I was still at Eileen's, my intrusion would be immediately discovered. But there was nothing for it. I took the keys from the ignition and got out.

I kicked my way through the mounting drifts—Patchy Hollow Road wasn't plowed very often—noting that my tracks would be covered almost instantly.

I started to sweat inside my coat as I grasped the doorknob. I imagined sidling through the door, and encounter-

ing the unforgiving length of my mother-
in-law's body, twig arms folded across
her chest. Hearing her desert dry voice,
all life sucked out of it.

**Brendan's dead, Nora. And even if
he were alive, how dare you enter my
house on your own? I can hardly
stand for you to be in it at all.**

Residents of Wedeskyull seldom
locked their doors. I paused to stow my
snowy boots behind an old receptacle
for milk bottles outside, then slipped inside.

The house had the feel of recently re-
linquished occupation.

I was just about to pad over to the
end table when something caught my
eye. I had thought there were only two
pieces of furniture in this room, but I'd
been wrong. Back in a shadowy corner
resided a small three-tiered stand. Its
shelves were covered with closely clus-
tered objects, a strange counterpoint to
Eileen's Spartan approach.

I crouched before the stand. Each
item seemed strange somehow, out of
place. Paperback books, wrinkly with
wear, pictures of horses on their covers.

Some odd-looking stones. A battered but lovely metal dish.

I glanced over my shoulder, feeling my mother-in-law's presence, hearing her voice as I picked things up. *Oh, and one other thing, Nora. I'm glad Brendan's dead, did you know that? Glad, I tell you, I'm glad.*

But why? Why would I think something like that? How could such a ghastly thing be true?

I sat back hard on my haunches, breathing audibly. Eileen wasn't some cold, merciless demon. She was just a sad, empty woman who'd suffered too many losses. By the time I came into her life, she had little love to spare.

For me or her surviving son.

And what I was doing right now shouldn't faze me so. I was used to poking and prodding around old houses, although I'd always had permission before.

At Phoenix Home Corp., we do your home, whether you like it or not.

Giddy laughter blossomed in my throat. I turned back to my task. On the second shelf stood a row of tin soldiers, surrounded by a scatter of playing cards, and then I finally made sense of what hadn't been right all along.

My mother-in-law couldn't abide clutter. Her house was practically bare. This array of objects didn't belong to her.

They had been Bill's.

Confirmation arrived in the form of a policeman's badge with the name *William Hamilton* etched on it. My throat closed as I studied the piece of metal, familiar right down to the lettering of the last name. Bill Hamilton seemed to have done so little of note for his son to emulate. My father-in-law had retired by the time I met Brendan, but this badge had influenced my husband's career choice, once he'd decided against law school and asked if I would accompany him back to Wedeskyull.

"It's different in a small town," Brendan had explained when we discussed it. "Not like where you grew up. Suburbs are dispensable places. Or maybe *interchangeable* is a better word. But small towns—they call you home."

It hadn't occurred to me to be offended. He was right—I didn't feel much attachment to the suburban town where I'd been raised. Part of me wondered if Brendan's home could become my own.

Perhaps the album did belong here. Bill had made it after all. Maybe Eileen stole it back in her husband's honor, put it on his stand of shelves, and had been glancing it over the day I arrived. Who had more of a right to the album—Eileen or me?

I stood up, crossing the room to the end table.

I was still trying to decide when I heard a scuffing of boots on the sill outside. All thought fled my brain. I lunged forward, snatching up the small album and stuffing it into my coat pocket. Then I backed out of the sitting room, which was clearly visible from the kitchen entry, and flattened myself against a wall.

I heard the sound of feet upon old boards. Creaks that meant whoever it was no longer stood in the linoleum-floored kitchen. Whoever had arrived— Eileen, it must be Eileen—was walking through the sitting room now and would soon pass right by me.

I flung one arm out and my hand

landed upon a knob. Relief stabbed me. This had to be a closet; there were no rooms with doors on the first floor of a foursquare. And a closet, with its winter layers of outerwear, would be the perfect place to hide.

I twisted around, praying that the ungainly movement wouldn't catch Eileen's eye, and slipped through a narrow crack in the doorway. I wound up at the top of a staircase, nearly toppling down the whole flight before I could catch myself, fingers crooking painfully as I dug them into a wall. Then I eased the door shut behind me.

This wasn't a closet. It was the basement.

CHAPTER SIXTEEN

The basement was so dark that I had to stand balanced, still teetering on that first step, as I let my eyes adjust.

Then I heard the sluggish grumble of a car engine igniting outside in the cold, and knew Eileen must be driving her old Ford away. She'd just forgotten something.

It would be best if I went now, too. While I could be sure of leaving unspotted. The photo album was a solid rectangle, distorting the shape of my pocket. I'd gotten what I'd come here for.

But then my eyes picked out something from the darkness. A slit of light below. Was there a sealed-off room in this basement? I couldn't think where a line of light like that, faint and far away, would be coming from except underneath a door.

Eileen might spot my car on her way out, and come back, intent on finding me. I could imagine the exact sequence unraveling, and yet I was drawn like a moth to that light, one of the few turned on in this unwelcoming house.

I made my slow, careful way down the stairs.

The dark got thicker as I descended, as if black sludge had settled toward the bottom. I followed that splinter of light like a beacon. When I reached the last step, I put one foot out in front of me, then swept it all around, in case I was simply standing on a landing, poised to fall as soon as I started walking again.

The blackness was complete, like space, or the bottom of the sea. Stumbling forward in the murk, I kicked out my feet and fanned my hands around to prevent falls and avoid knocking into something. My mind conjured up im-

ages of basement things: tearing cobwebs; roosting beetles; hulking, covered
objects.

I knew houses with more than my
eyes, though, and could sense the size
of this space. A long series of steps
later, my outstretched palms scraped
against the wall.

That line of yellow lay at my feet. I
blinked to make out a doorknob, protruding a yard or so above. With no idea
what I might find on the other side, I
twisted the knob.

It was locked.

A locked, lit room in a basement. Yes, it
was like something out of a horror
movie—mandating instant flight in the
real world—but in the real world there
was also a good reason to stay. With no
obvious explanation for such a place, I
thought its existence might possibly reveal something essential.

My fingers traced the keyhole beneath
the knob. Whatever this room withheld,
the lock warded off only the least deter-
mined of intruders; any rigid object
should force the mechanism to unclick.

There were half a dozen tools in my bag that would make short work of this task. Despite the near total lack of light, the correct one all but sprang into my practiced grip. I'd never used a flathead screwdriver to pick a lock before, but it worked as well in the keyhole as it did installing a quarter-inch screw.

The room I entered was so bright that a spear of pain instantly penetrated my head. I shut my eyes, leaving afterflashes of white. When I opened them again, I took in the walls, which were papered, but not with flocking or flowers.

Instead, all of the pictures that didn't adorn the rest of this house had found their way down here. Eileen had made a mosaic on the walls of her hidden room, a mural of all the moments it was a parent's deepest desire to chronicle.

I stepped closer to look.

There were a few shots of Brendan as an infant, Eileen and Bill as brand-new parents. But the bulk of the photographic journey seemed to begin when Brendan was older, and a new baby had been added to the family.

I had to back up a few steps to study

a picture of Brendan on a couch—its fabric a stiff, shiny gold—with a telltale white bundle positioned rigidly on his knees. Someone hovered in the foreground, only her arm showing, to keep the baby from rolling off.

The Hamiltons had taken a few vacations that had been immortalized in film. There was Brendan at the beach, digging a sandcastle, with the smaller boy dumping out a pail of sand on top. They'd gone skiing, Brendan waving a pole, his little brother beside him, no poles and concentrating fiercely on staying upright.

But pictures with Brendan in them were relatively rare. By far the lion's share featured the younger brother. Captured in the photos was a side of Eileen I'd never seen before, one that seemed alien to the woman I knew. She wore that universal expression of maternity, the same look exhibited by everyone from celebrity to welfare mom, as she gazed down at her baby. How I'd longed to wear it one day: a certain positioning of the face and crinkling of the eyes, a smile that held something un-stoppable.

There were filler shots, too, nobody in them, just vistas of sky and leaves and lawns and lakes, the seasons rotating by until the basement lathing had been almost completely covered.

I pivoted at the corner and began on the last wall. Here the time captured by the photos seemed to slow down. No more progression of seasons; all was winter, snow and ice. There was a photo of white fields behind the two four-squares, then a shot of the distant lake, but from up close, its surface ridged and humpy when it froze.

Then came Brendan dressed in win-ter gear and dragging a sled up a hill, his little brother now capable of holding on, but so padded that he couldn't bend at the middle to sit properly. He was tip-ping backward on the sled, almost hor-izontal, and Brendan had twisted around to look, stilled forever in the moment that he laughed.

Then the photographs abruptly ended.

There was a long slice of wall that Ei-leen had left bare.

A lone picture had been tacked up in the middle of that strip. It was of a man with red hair, taken as he crawled across the ice, his face pressed to its scabby surface. My father-in-law, with his cheek glistening black. Was that blood? I studied the picture, making out other men gathered in the distance. A hockey game Bill had been part of? I knew those could get pretty rough. But why, of all photos, had Eileen chosen to display this one?

Very few shots of Bill were included on this wall. It was as if the elaborate collage represented the standings of each family member.

Eileen, the baby, Brendan, Bill. No. The baby, Eileen, Brendan, Bill. And most of the shots of Brendan also included the baby.

The cessation of photos must mark the time of his death. Brendan's brother had died so terribly young.

Shame engulfed me. I hadn't known *anything*.

He didn't want you to know, came a voice.

I was carried along on a wave of nausea, staring into space, unseeing, until a few other shapes before me took form. In addition to obscuring the walls, Eileen had also topped a long table, something like a workbench, with an array of objects. A frost of dust lay on every surface.

The fact of the passing time hit me like an electric shock. How many minutes had been eaten away, looking at those photographs? Eileen could be on her way home by now.

But she got off to a late start, I reassured myself, delayed by whatever she'd come back here for. I'd just take one more quick look. Who knew if I'd ever get the chance to come down here again? And the things in this room held answers—partial answers at least—if I could understand them.

One part of the table was concealed by a large sheet of paper, the kind torn off a roll. Someone—Eileen, of course—had penciled a series of quick sketches along its length. Eileen had been an archeology student once, before coming back to this cold place, which turned out to be filled with so much tragedy. In her studies, she'd probably learned to draw, to document her findings.

Here on the length of paper were captured a small form running, then a shed or little shack, and finally a black oval, violently scribbled in with pencil to provide shading. Arrows had been scrawled between the oval and the shed. Beneath the arrows were numbers. Three, seven, ten, and a question mark. Two, five, eight, and another one.

I had no idea what the numbers meant, nor what I was seeing elsewhere on the table.

Canceled checks in a neat stack. I flipped through them rapidly, then replaced the pile. They were all made out to cash, and appeared to be starter checks, without Eileen's name or address printed on them. On each memo line, the same word had been jotted over and over, in the sharp quills of my mother-in-law's handwriting. *Resurrection.*

A consignment shop, or cutesy antique store was my first guess. Then my thoughts turned wilder. Some kind of service aimed at parents who'd lost chil-

dren? The worst kind of scam artist tar-
geting desperate people, driven all but
insane by grief, with some life-after-
death fantasy?

The time. Great amounts of it being
gobbled up in questions and confusion.

I scrabbled at the flaps of two cartons, both of them stuffed with tiny,
folded outfits as out-of-date as Eileen's
own.

Then I picked up a rag doll that looked
as if it might dissolve into dust at my
touch. But the thing remained intact,
and I raised it, wrinkling my nose against
sour smells of age and sorrow. Around
the doll's wrist, Eileen had attached a
heavy stock card that bristled again with
her handwriting. *Pooky.*

Nearby, a clump of coarse hairs had
been bound together and shellacked.
The spiky letters on its label read: *Rascal.*

Dog hair? Was I touching fur from a
dead dog? The tuft singed my fingers
and I let it plummet, not caring when it
missed the desk and fell with a stiff
crackle onto the concrete floor.

Here were my mother-in-law's aborted

career dreams. Poured into a ghoulish museum exhibit, an archeological dig that chronicled her second son's fore-shortened life.

I stared down at my hands, clenched into rocks, then squinted into the main part of the basement. I would have to use the light from this vile shrine to memorize my way back to the stairs before closing the door. Jointed tubes of ductwork hung from the ceiling like some multi-limbed beast, but otherwise my path was clear. Just as I was about to sink into the bath of darkness, one final object lying on the table gripped my gaze.

A splintery snake of rope.

It matched the piece Teggie had dug up. Another tag had been secured to the end. With savage strokes of her pen, the cardstock torn through in places, Eileen had scrawled two words this time.

Brendan's idiocy.

CHAPTER SEVENTEEN

I stabbed my feet into the boots I'd hidden on the porch, and raced down the steps.

There'd been no need to worry about anybody spotting my car. It was fully covered by snow, indistinguishable from Jean's Buick. She hadn't returned yet, and neither had Eileen.

But there was a gray police car parked several yards away. My heart began to thud.

Dave Weathers got out.

I trudged toward him across the still-unplowed road, stumbling over a drift.

Dave thrust one gloved hand out, tripping a bit himself as he tried to steady
me. His chest heaved in his police-issue
snow gear. He leaned over for balance,
breathing hard. "What are you doing
here?"

I offered up my first lie stupidly. "I
came to see Aunt Jean."

Dave stared at me. He seemed the
bumbling brother—certainly he had
none of Vern's paternal strength—but
that didn't mean he was dumb. Groping
for an explanation that would come
closer to the truth, I said, "And I thought
Eileen might have something of mine."

The storm was getting sparser; it
would tease us with a brief extraction
from its hold. Dave looked up, shielding
his eyes against the remaining whirl of
flakes. He didn't say a word about my
decision to look for this item when Eileen wasn't home, and when he spoke
his voice was kind. "So did she?"

"No," I said quietly. "I don't think so."
I turned and began sweeping at the accumulation of snow on my car.

"Let me do that." Dave withdrew a
brush from his holster, clearing the glass

with waves that scattered snow upon our boots.

I decided to ask a question of my own. "What made you come all the way out here?"

Dave scuffed through the snow to my hood. "Just checking on the state of this road. Chief's worried it don't get plowed out very often."

Well, that was certainly true. I thanked Dave for doing the clearing. He was looking down, brushing snow off his coat, as I climbed into my car.

Surely a mother who sequestered herself in a dungeon of relics and testimonies, more than twenty-five years after losing her son, was at the very least disturbed. The light was on in the basement; Eileen must've been down there today. And now Eileen's other son had killed himself. Was death the only way to get his mother's attention?

My clumsy attempts at psychoanalyzing made me wince. Brendan and I had been in love. He'd lived only a few miles from his mother for most of his life, and never displayed any particular conflict about it, nor any great longing to see her more often. Brendan hadn't wanted for attention.

As I drove, I became aware again of my booty, poking into my lap.

Teggie's voice, clear as glass in my head. *You're not even going to look at it, are you?*

The album belonged in Brendan's box, back amongst his things. After today's immersion in the past, Eileen-style, I had no desire to see the few pictures his dad had been able to put aside.

The answering rebuttal was wordless, but distinct.

I would never become like Eileen, lost in images forever gone, but how could I not at least glance through these shots that Brendan had so loved?

"One quick peek," I told the silent car. "Okay? And then no more."

Nobody replied.

I covered the last miles home faster than the newly plowed roads rendered safe, then turned into my drive. Someone had salted it for me. A small-town favor.

Inside, I shed my coat, scarf, and hat,

then walked over to the living room couch, where I withdrew the leather album. It felt clammy in my grasp. Maybe I'd only be able to stomach a glance at the first picture. I knew it well: Brendan in a diaper, all but lost in the folds of a garish, vinyl beanbag chair.

Flipping to the first page, I braced myself for a glimpse of the picture Brendan had examined so often. Then I brought my gaze down, the smile of appreciation I'd always worn sitting ghoulishly upon my lips now that Brendan wasn't here to see it.

It didn't matter whether I smiled or not.

Because the book I held wasn't a photo album.

CHAPTER EIGHTEEN

Nausea roiled my stomach. This time I knew I would really be sick, and raced to the bathroom, where I lost the remains of my scant breakfast.

I returned for a second look at the page that held no photograph. It swam before my eyes. I flipped it shut, making sure I had made no mistake in the shadowy corners of Eileen's house, that the book really was a twin to Brendan's.

The leather cover looked exactly the same; this one too was slim and spare. But it contained not a single picture.

Nothing but a froth of lines, dabs, and dots. Instead of photos, this book was filled with a messy sea of words.

I didn't recognize the handwriting. Certainly it wasn't Eileen's stark penmanship, the tops and sides of her letters clipped like hedges.

Two hand-tooled books, the first special enough that Bill had given it as a wedding gift to his son. Surely this one had belonged to him, too. I let the letters take on form and clarity before me. The first line was a date.

January twenty-fourth. It was the day after Brendan had killed himself. Twenty-five years ago, but nearly the same date. That couldn't be a coincidence. I began to read.

I never did this before, but if I don't write something down, I think I'll go crazy. Wind started up again yesterday afternoon. Why did the morning have to be so calm? If it hadn't been so calm, we never would've let the boys go outside.

Yesterday.

That would've been the day, twenty-five years hence, that was to be Brendan's last.

She hasn't stopped talking about what he did. No tears at all. I say, instead of blaming the kid, let's ask Franklin some questions about his own boys.

I calculated swiftly in my mind. Subtract twenty-five years and Brendan had been eleven. If he was eight when his brother had been born, then this journal had been started right about the time the last photograph of that little boy had been taken.

The next entry confirmed what I was reading about.

Coffin was so tiny. Nobody should ever have to learn how small they can make them.

My eyes filled, and the words blurred until they were meaningless, the way something gets when you say it over and over. *Coffin. Tiny. Coffin, tiny, coffin, tiny, tiny, coffin.*

You can't believe it when your eyes remember to open, that your heart still knows how to beat. They go on doing their things, so I have to go on doing mine. But still I want to ask someone, does time really not go backwards? If only just for a second or two? Is there no way to make it do that? I thought scientists had learned how. I can't believe the greatest minds at every moment in history haven't been put to this task. Because one day each and every one of us will need to give that wheel a spin in the other direction.

Every word felt as if it had been penned just for me. I knew what Bill was writing about with an ache so intense that my whole body crumpled. I sat down on the floor, pressing my fingers into my eye sockets until they hurt. Still, the tears flooded out. I went on reading through rivers.

I should have been there. She should have been there. We both should be struck down for not having been there.

And then a fragment that, despite reading twice, I couldn't understand.

Not him who was.

Only one thing was clear. I needed to find out more about Brendan's little brother. I needed to learn what happened to him.

Because Brendan had chosen to die on the exact same day of the year.

The phone jangled and the journal slipped in my hand. When I answered, I was greeted by a rushing sound, a sigh over the line. My recalcitrant caller, or the noise of the phones going down, another storm already on its way? I needed to plug in my cell, which must've long since run out of charge.

Something else struck me then with alarm. My back went rigid, and I looked down at the book. This hadn't belonged to Brendan after all. I'd better return it to Eileen's before my act was discovered; it seemed as if she might look the journal over quite frequently.

I opened it up again, skimming the rest of the entries. There weren't many of them, and they didn't offer anything but the same grief-soaked musings. Bill had written that he'd never before been a chronicler of his days or thoughts, and it seemed he had dropped the habit quickly.

The phone rang again, and I answered, expecting no reply.

"Nora? Are you okay?"

It took me a second to place the voice as Ned Kramer's. "I'm fine."

A pause. "Sure about that?"

"I'm sorry?"

Again, he didn't answer for a moment. "How could you be fine?"

His tone angered me, and I snapped at him. "It's a politeness, okay? You're not supposed to analyze it." We were bickering like an old married couple, and something inside me went brittle.

"I'm sorry," he said again. But then, "I just meant that you don't have to pretend with me. If you don't want to."

"I don't want anything," I muttered.

There was another careful pause, Ned picking his way around the grenades I had scattered. "Nothing you can have, right?"

"What?" Tears filled my throat, a salty, nauseating wash. "What?" Ned didn't answer for so long that I burst out, "Right! That's right. There's no way I can get what I want!"

Ned gave a sigh I could hear, and I exhaled a shuddery breath as well. He didn't say anything, and I didn't feel the need to, either, although neither of us made a move to hang up. After a while, I began pacing around, thinking of what I knew about Ned. "You work at the paper, don't you? You must know a lot about this town."

"I guess so," he said. "Anyone who works at a small-town pub has to prove familiarity with the things newsworthy there. Or what passes for newsworthy."

I let out a laugh, at the same time thinking fast. Surely familiarity wouldn't extend all the way back twenty-five years. But just because Ned might not know offhand what happened didn't mean he couldn't find out.

"Why?" he asked. "Something I can help you with?"

"I think so," I replied. "That is, if you have access to old copies of the paper."

DROPPED

Ned Kramer reversed out of his long driveway with a feeling at once strange and familiar. It was like finding a friend online whom you hadn't seen since childhood. *Hey,* you wanted to say. *I know you.*

When you first started working on a story, everything was scattered. Just pieces here and there that you hoped one day would turn out to form a cohesive narrative. It was your job as a journalist to find ways to link the pieces together. That was what Ned was trying to do now.

His tires cradled by ruts of snow, Ned backed up and entered the road.

Nora Hamilton wanted something from him that suggested she might be asking some pretty hard questions. And if she was asking those questions, it was possible that some piece of information had come her way. It was also possible she knew something without even knowing she knew it.

But somebody else had contacted him first, and set up a meeting. Just to talk, this person had said. Feel you out about some things.

Shades of Ned's former life. There were times before when he'd had to decide between two pressing leads.

He had moved up here because in a small town everything would be more manageable, on a smaller scale. He'd wanted that to be so anyway, although it was proving less true than he had anticipated. Of course, in the deepest sense, everything would always be small potatoes, no matter what happened from here.

When the measure was your family,

entire kingdoms could topple and you wouldn't even feel the thud.

He stared down at the directions he had scrawled. He wouldn't rely on the GPS, which still got confused way out here. Not for something as important as this had the potential to be.

Two o'clock exactly, his contact had said. *I won't be able to stick around long.*

Out of the way, had been another condition. *We can't be anywhere*—anywhere—*someone might see. Are you okay in the snow?*

Ned had said that he was.

Ten minutes later he slowed to a crawl and began wending his way along a narrow backcountry road. These roads weren't plowed very often, and the Subaru was having a bad time of it. Ned actually had doubts that the car—purchased just for his move north—was going to make it. He was tabulating the risks of getting out and completing the trip on foot, when a gray body appeared in front of his windshield.

"Shit." The word escaped him as he jammed both boots on the brake.

Lucky he'd been going slow.

The Subaru bucked to a halt, snow flying up in waves. Then the cop was there to one side, indicating with a rapid roll of his fist that Ned should let his window down.

"This road is closed, sir."

As Ned studied him, another cop appeared, the tense, twitchy one who always seemed to be riding a wave of adrenaline.

A curveball. No one else was supposed to be here.

That had been the final condition.

"All right," Ned said after a moment.

"Turn yourself around," his contact said. "Just take it nice and slow."

"Right," Ned said again. He was craning his head to try to, windows fogging up from the differential between the heated air within and the frigid temps outside.

The cop let a hand fall to his side. He could've been reaching for something, radio or gun, or simply giving his leg a scratch. The gesture held no hint of intent. He gave the lowered window two hard raps, telling Ned to go.

Ned shifted into reverse and began to execute his turn.

He was a quarter mile up the road before he noticed that something had been dropped into his car.

A wedge of paper, tightly folded. Ned opened it to reveal a hand-drawn map.

CHAPTER NINETEEN

These days, entire afternoons often gave way to sodden sleep. It didn't matter where I was, which room I happened to be in, although the naps mostly took place on the living room couch instead of upstairs. I figured I was sleeping in the daytime for the first time since childhood because my nights were so restless and uneasy. These naps offered no more refreshment than the nighttime did, though. I awoke as if I'd been hit over the head and was just coming to. For hours afterward, I stumbled around, the threat of sleep still tugging at my heels.

During the latest of these, I was disturbed by a series of knocks on the front door. When I finally blinked awake, squinting in the low, dull end of daylight and scrubbing at my face, I had the feeling that whoever was here had been knocking for some time.

I got up, wrapping my arms around my shivering frame. I gave the furnace dial a tweak as I went past and was rewarded by the rumblings of heat throughout the farmhouse.

There came another loud knock, and I pulled open the door.

Ned Kramer stood there, a dusting of snow on his cap, which he shook off on the porch while stamping his boots. Then he looked down at me. "I brought you some old papers to look at."

He was a tall, lanky man, probably five or six years older than I was, but with a tousle of red-gold hair that gave him a boyish appearance.

Still fog-brained, I frowned at the sheaf of papers he was holding. It occurred to me to right my sleep-twisted shirt.

Ned stepped inside, switching the papers to the other hand as he struggled to shed his coat. "Here," he said, holding them out. "Not one to let sleeping dogs lie, are you?"

I was reaching for his coat, not the papers, but I stopped. "Why do you say that?"

Then I began to laugh.

Ned looked at me curiously.

"I'm just laugh—laughing," I told him, more laughter bubbling as I spoke. "Because I'm the ultimate enabler of sleeping dogs. I usually put them to—to—"

Ned smiled a bit awkwardly.

"—to sleep myself, if they seem to be—" I was trying to stop. "—stirring."

Finally I was able to taper off.

"Can I fix you something to drink?" I asked at the same time he said, "So why are you poking at this one?"

"Anything you've got," he answered swiftly.

I turned to attend to his request. I didn't have as ready a response to his question, beyond the obvious.

Coffee still made my stomach dip and founder. The pot made that horrible morning had been my last. I spied a jug of cider in the fridge and thought to heat it, but that idea didn't seem too palatable, either. I settled on tea, setting out sugar and milk as the water boiled.

We sat at the pine farm table.

"This is nice," Ned said, planing his hand over the wood. "My parents had a table like this. Did I ever tell you the house I bought looks a lot like the place I grew up in?"

"You *can* go home again?"

Ned inclined his head, acknowledging the remark. "Maybe. I hope so."

"You need something a couple of decades newer," I said. "More refined."

It took him a second to realize I was talking about the table. "This is a primitive," I explained. "You live in a Queen Anne." Then I remembered the papers Ned had shown up with, and I rose, heading back to the entryway. The sheaf on the sideboard was shiny and slippery. The pieces nearly slid out of my grasp as I tried to get a hold on them.

"Microfiche printouts," Ned explained.

He had come up behind me. "Slick stuff."

I frowned, staring down at the tightly packed lines. The date leapt out at me. January twenty-fourth, twenty-five years ago. The first day Bill wrote in his journal. I looked at Ned, then again at the pile. Headlines appeared out of a garble of words, and with them the answer I'd been looking for.

TWO-YEAR-OLD BOY DROWNS IN FROZEN POND

Red Hamilton Falls Through Ice on Patchy Hollow Lake, Drowns

Ned steered me into the living room, keeping the papers straight so the pile didn't slither to the floor as we made our way over to the couch.

"You knew right away, didn't you?" I choked out. "Was it that obvious? Am I that pathetic?"

"It's not obvious, Nora," Ned said roughly, helping me to sit. "And you're definitely not pathetic." His gaze met mine for a second, then slid away.

I continued to look up at him, tears streaking my cheeks.

Ned glanced around the room in search of something. "Bathroom," I muttered, "under the stairs," and he walked off, returning with a handful of tissues.

I swiped at my face.

"I'm a reporter," Ned said, indicating the papers that now lay in a curl on my lap. "And even so, I didn't put it together at your husband's funeral."

I looked down.

"When you told me you were looking into things," Ned went on gruffly. "That's when I started thinking about the dates. That day . . ."

He trailed off and I waited silently.

"What happened twenty-five years ago is still one of the worst tragedies this town has ever known. I'm not from around here, but you can't work at the paper and not know about it. The old salts at the desk still talk about that day sometimes."

I placed the pile beside me on the couch, then lifted the first page. Ned settled down on a chair, and I began to read.

January 24th. Wedeskyull, New York. Gregory (Red) Hamilton, the two and a half year old son of Bill and Eileen Hamilton, drowned yesterday afternoon while in his brother's care.

According to Police Chief Franklin Weathers, an ice-fishing hole had been cut and not properly sealed off when the unknown fishermen took a break. "Brendan and Red Hamilton were out together in the worst place at the worst time. The ice is three feet thick right now. Once the little fella went down, he would've been sucked right away, then trapped.

"We plan to locate the culprits, although it's not likely they come from around these parts. A charge of negligent homicide would be in order. Our town will have a hard time getting over a senseless tragedy like this."

Suddenly I was back in Eileen's basement, in that sealed-off room, studying the one lone photograph pasted on an empty strip of wall. When Bill had been crawling along the ice, face pressed down hard enough to draw blood, he'd been looking for his son.

The futility of his search assailed me: how many miles Patchy Hollow Lake was across, how dark and mottled its surface would've been as my late father-in-law blinked to clear his vision, hunting any streak of color going by in all that leaden gray.

The question occurred to me only belatedly. Who had taken such a ghastly picture—observed Bill in his anguish, held a camera, and clicked?

"There was a manhunt," Ned said, watching me. "For whoever had abandoned that hole. They blocked every road leading out of town. The police extended their search across all of Franklin County."

I didn't answer. The articles that followed began to blur together. One after another, citing leads that fizzled out, all boiling down to the same tragic repetition of facts: two brothers alone together. One little and clumsy on the ice.

184

Falls through an unprotected ice-fishing hole. Drowns.

No arrest was ever made. No one was even brought in for questioning.

"You've lived here long enough to know this is sport country," Ned said.

I looked at him. Brendan had been the one who mostly engaged in athletics. Not ice-fishing, though. Never anything that had to do with the ice.

"Rock-climbing on bald peaks. Bear- and moose-hunting. Skiing or boarding in avalanche regions." A deliberate pause. "Ice-fishing may seem pretty innocuous, but it's really not. A hole isn't big enough for a man to fall into, but even if he just accidentally dunks a foot, if no one's around and he can't get to warmth fast, he'll die. The water will seep up his leg and he'll freeze. And needless to say, if someone small slipped through . . ."

I closed my eyes against the scene my mind had already played out, that thick shelf of ice, impenetrable to tiny, beating hands.

"My point is that people up here take this stuff very seriously. They have to.

They know what nature is capable of, and they have procedures in place to prevent it. In the case of ice-fishing, buddy systems. Lean-tos within so many yards of a hole. How big the sheets of plywood to cover those holes must be and signage up to flag them." Ned paused, the mental tickings of a man who put his facts together methodically. "For someone to come along and flaunt those safety rules—well, this town was beaten senseless over it. Angry. And it stayed that way for a very long time."

His words were a toneless tune in my ears. They didn't matter. Or rather, they weren't what mattered to me right then.

"How did I not know?" I asked numbly.

Ned looked down at his linked hands.

"Something this awful—a wife should know." I heard my voice rise, but seemed to have no control over it. "Maybe I could have kept Brendan from—"

Ned rose from his chair. His eyes blazed. "There's no way you could've prevented anything." He leaned down and I reared back. "No one can prevent a suicide. Except the person doing it."

The slimy pieces of microfiche print-out threatened to slide off my lap, and I grabbed at them. A few more sentences jumped out from the rivers of text.

Although details are sketchy, due to the shocked condition of Brendan Hamilton, it appears that the older boy left the lake to get some rope from a nearby shed just after his brother fell through. States Eileen Hamilton, "Instead of coming for us, Brendan thought he might pull little Red up. While he was gone, Red drowned."

My heart beat at a furious clip, and I blinked to bring into focus Eileen's scroll of paper, the one with the series of sketches on it and the numbers written underneath. That furiously scribbled-in oval, a small building that must've held rope, the running boy. Those numbers represented guesses as to time. Eileen had charted how long it would've taken Brendan to leave his brother, go in search of rope, and return to the ice-fishing hole. How long Red lay beneath the ice, no help forthcoming except in the form of another terrified child.

Everything in that sunken room made sense now. It was a tribute, testimony to a mother's crazed love of one son, sacrificed to sainthood as a toddler. And to her hatred of the other, who in Eileen's desolate estimation had committed the final, fatal mistake.

CHAPTER TWENTY

Ned left sometime in the unknown hours after that. I didn't remember seeing him out, nor even saying goodbye.

I'd thought things were as bad as they could get, that the worst had happened. But that was the thing about the worst, wasn't it? You never quite got there. The worst was a horizon, moving farther and farther away as you approached it.

How could my husband have carried the incendiary coal of his brother's death inside him for so long? What I wouldn't give to have been able to sizzle cool water over that guilt, tell Brendan it wasn't his fault, only a tragic accident. But he'd never let me know.

My sister's voice again: *You never tried to find out.*

"Shut up!" I screamed aloud, words reverberating throughout the house.

Why did Brendan propose the way he did? When he wound my engagement ring on that pair of old skate laces, was he trying to tell me something? Get me to ask? Ned's refutations aside, I couldn't suppress the thought that had I asked, had I been more of a questioner when faced with things that didn't add up, Brendan might be alive today.

My mother's voice began speaking on the machine, the words faint, disembodied, from another room. I hadn't even heard the phone ring.

"Mom?" I said, snatching up the cordless.

"Yes, honey," she said quickly. "Oh, you're there. What's wrong?"

What's wrong? I suppressed a bolt of laughter. What was right? "I don't know what to do, Mom," I said brokenly. "I didn't know things could get any worse."

"What do you mean, sweetheart? How could they be worse?"

"That's a good question," I said.

"Nora?" my mother said. "You sound funny. What's going on?"

"Do you really want to know?"

"Do I—" My mother stopped speaking abruptly. "Sweetheart, I'm not sure what you mean by that."

Then ask, I thought.

"I called—I wanted to see how you're doing for food. Can I send up some more dishes?"

"Food," I echoed.

"You're eating, aren't you?"

I wasn't sure what to say, how to explain the complicated relationship I had developed with my stomach these days. It never felt steady. Hunger, when it arrived like a straying lover, was savage, impossible to appease.

"Mom?"

"Yes, darling?"

"When you said—remember when you said Dad was better with scrapes than cuts?"

"I said . . ." My mother sounded as if

she couldn't follow, had no hopes of following. "*What* did I say?"

"You meant—you meant that he liked to skate along the surface of things, didn't you?"

"What?" my mother said again, but the word was less of a question now.

"Because . . . because, you see, I think I got a little . . . some of that from him, too—" And then my voice broke, I had to fight to keep control.

"Nora," my mother murmured. "Oh, Nora. This is so hard. So . . ." Her voice trailed off.

My dad got on the phone. "Baby? How are you doing?"

A sob lurched inside me, but I quelled it. "Not so good, Dad—"

"No, well, how could you be?" he replied. "You need any supplies—salt, that kind of thing?"

I blinked my eyes. They felt dry. "No," I said. "Thanks. There're people here— Brendan's friends—who will take care of that."

"Okay then," my father said. "Your mother and I will plan another trip up.

Soon as we get a break in the weather. We go online every night to check."

Next he was going to be telling me which Internet weather site they pre-ferred.

"Okay, Dad," I said, defeated.

When I tried to place the phone in the charger, it slipped back out, and I flung it down with an awful *thwack.* "How could you?" I cried to my absent hus-band. "How could you have kept this from me—"

The phone squawked in anger at be-ing kept off its base.

In a smaller voice I said, "How could I have let you?"

What had drawn us to each other? Brendan was a man of secrets, and I was a keeper of them. What kind of marriage did we have, Eileen had asked me. Maybe the only one that either of us possibly could.

Tears filled my mouth with the sting-ing water of oceans. I was going under, diving, drowning.

"Who were you, Brendan!" I wailed. "Who were we?"

* * *

After a long while, my sobs turned into hitching breaths. In a fetal position on the floor, I snaked my arm out to the phone. Like me, it had given up in silence. I pressed the button to hang up, then pushed a series of numbers, my fingers weak and trembling.

"Nora?" Teggie asked when I made an audible croak.

I pictured my sister sliding gracefully to the floor, the phone cupped between her swan's neck and the shell of her ear.

"I should've stopped," I murmured. "You were right. I didn't find out anything I needed to know." I was quiet for a second, confused. "No, wait, I did need to know. But not now. I found out too late." There was a stunned, bewildered edge to my voice; I sounded like someone who'd just survived a shelling, or the fall of tall towers.

"You don't sound good, Nor. Want me to come up?" The barest of pauses. "I'm coming up. Tomorrow."

"Oh, Teggie, are you sure? Let me know which bus. I'll be there."

"No," she replied. "I don't—I won't need a ride."

I didn't bother to find out why. Tears were seeping out again, silent, but impossible to stem. You could drown by a trickle as well as by a flood.

"Shhh," Teggie said, although she couldn't have heard me crying. "This has got to get better. It will get better, I swear. This will all be over soon."

"That's the problem!" I cried. "It *is* all over! It's over, and I can't stand the ending!"

CHAPTER TWENTY-ONE

I fell into another one of my heavy, logy sleeps, and when I woke up it was with the awareness that something had changed. It was like finally throwing up when you knew it was coming all day. Or confessing a sin that had been plaguing your soul.

For some time now, I had been suppressing a dawning understanding, a growing sense of guilt. If I hadn't been the person I was, someone who squinted and shrank and turned away from hard truths, Brendan might have shared whatever he was going through. And then maybe he wouldn't have done what he did. But I couldn't change that now.

No more crying. No more regrets. All I could do was move forward. Make sure I was the wife now to Brendan that I should've been all along.

I did regular things then. Heated up a lasagna someone had brought by, ate half a helping. Sat down in front of the television with a cup of tea.

And I thought, or tried to.

The day passed with little of note to mark it.

I had never been big on conspiracy stories. They always seemed contrived. Real life was not only more mundane, but also more haphazard. Things happened without any plan or order. But Vern knew why Brendan didn't skate— he had to know. Ned had said that Red's death was the worst tragedy this town ever suffered. And Vern's father had been police chief at the time.

Suddenly his well-meaning suggestion made at the station, and Club's seconding of it, took on a darker cast. Not *go home,* but *get out.*

Why would Vern not want me to know

about Red's drowning? Had he been trying to protect Brendan, or if not him, his memory?

When the front door opened, I jumped.

"Hello?" I called out, getting up and striding toward the entry. "Ned?"

"Who's Ned?" asked the person coming in.

"Teggie!" I cried, and threw my arms around my sister's narrow body, which seemed to have taken on substance, become even more of a force to be reckoned with, in the short time she'd been gone.

Maybe I had strengthened, too. Look what I'd done without her.

Broken into a home. Stolen property. Learned the secret my husband had kept from me our entire marriage. "How'd you get up here so fast? I didn't think there was a bus until—"

Someone else had entered behind her, and was stripping off his coat.

It was a man, not tall, but powerfully built, with a dozen muscles distinct upon him. He had a swell of blue-black curls, and eyes as dark as coffee beans. The T-shirt he wore, through which all those muscles were visible, read *Gabriel Deacon Dance Company.*

"Nora," Teggie said, one slim arm outstretched. "Meet Gabriel Deacon."

I looked from the beautiful man to my sister, and spoke stupidly, trying to resolve it all. "This is why you didn't need me to meet you at the bus."

"We drove," Gabriel Deacon said. "My car doesn't get much of a workout in the city."

"I'm impressed," I said, and I was, for more reasons than their confronting the snowy Northway. I had never been given a glimpse of my sister in the company of a man. The ones she had known, briefly, furtively, she'd kept sequestered away, in a late night corner of her life into which our relationship didn't extend.

I offered them some lasagna.

"That'd be great," Gabriel answered. "Nothing but fast food on the highway."

I went and turned off the TV. We sat at the table.

"I'm sorry I haven't said . . ." Gabriel began, his Adam's apple gliding up and down in his throat. Even his hesitation looked studied. "That I'm sorry. I never met Brendan, but I wish I had."

My God, this guy was smooth.

"I wanted you two to meet," Teggie began, digging into her meal, a sight whose shock value I barely had time to register. "Since Gabriel has decided to make me his—"

Because I knew my sister, I knew that she wasn't about to make a sappy declaration. I glanced at the words on Gabriel's T-shirt. "Oh, Teg! Principal? Did you get the part?"

"No," my sister said. "Better than that." She glanced up at Gabriel; they exchanged smiles. "Gabriel thought that I had a real feel for the female roles." He was nodding along with her. "He's offered to make me co-choreographer."

I stared down at the table. Teggie had been debating—resisting—this change in roles for years, ever since she entered her late twenties and parts started getting harder to come by. If Gabriel Deacon had talked her into it, then he had to be more than the muscled smooth talker for whom I'd taken him. A wave of nausea lifted my stomach. I felt ashamed for underestimating Gabriel; I felt ashamed for wanting to underestimate him.

I tried to shape a response. "Congratulations, Teg. I know you'll be great." I didn't know, though, not really, not the way Gabriel Deacon must. "And thank you," I added to him, "for coming."

His eyes smiled along with his mouth.

We went up to bed not long after that.

"It's okay that I brought him?" Teggie said, holding both of my hands in hers as we stood in the hall. I extricated myself, pulling down a stack of towels from the closet.

"Yes," I murmured, "sure."

"Is that a Nora sure?" she asked. "Or a real sure?"

"It's a you've-met-the-love-of-your-life-and-didn't-bother-to-call sure," I replied, and Teggie let out a harsh bray of laughter, covering her mouth before glancing over her shoulder.

"I did better than call," she said. "Here I am."

We exchanged another quick smile, but even while doing so, I felt as lonely as if my sister had stayed back in the city. I sighed, dreading the open maw of my bed.

I teetered on the verge of sleep for what felt like a long time, but in reality couldn't have been more than a few minutes, before I started to hear noises, the rustlings of people moving about in a strange room, their hushed chatter. The prospect of sleep was yanked away like a cloth snatched off the table in one of those parlor tricks.

A murmur.

"Nice, right?" Teggie responded audibly.

I wondered what was nice.

A thud. One of them had bumped into something. My bedroom and the spare room shared a wall.

Gabe's voice, low. "Nice is as nice does."

A laugh that Teggie quickly muffled. Some kind of private joke between them.

There was the sibilant movement of sheets, two people getting settled in bed. Then a couple of murmurs I couldn't make out, followed by one I could.

"Good night, sweetheart."

My chest hollowed out like a vacuum; for a moment I couldn't summon breath.

There came the unprecedented sound of my sister responding in kind, before voices from the other room began to subside, give way to the stirrings of sleep.

I rolled over on the vast, smooth spread of my own sheets. The down cover settled on me like a deflating balloon. Our bed used to be so rumpled and worn. But there were only so many wrinkles one person could make.

CHAPTER TWENTY-TWO

Gabriel appeared while I was making toast the next morning. He was already showered, dressed for the day. I indicated butter and a row of jam jars whose lids were stuck fast from disuse.

He smiled at me. "Sit down. Let me fix you a piece."

Smooth, I thought again through a yawn. *But I'll take it.* I sat.

"Teggie still out?" I asked when the silence slipped from companionable to awkward.

"Like a light," he said. "She sleeps heavily, huh?" He set a plate down before me, then lowered himself lightly into a chair.

"Always has," I agreed. I let the tea steam my face.

"Quiet up here," Gabriel said after a moment. "I keep wondering what's missing."

"Sirens, horns, yelling, curses," I ticked off.

He grinned. "You miss them? It?"

"The city?"

He nodded, using one finger to lift a blob of butter back onto his bread. Somehow he managed to make even that gesture look appealing, no greasy mess or need of a napkin.

I glanced away. "No."

He looked up, his response unspoken. *Not even now?*

I shrugged. "This is home, I guess." *Wake up, Teggie.* But my sister didn't come, there wasn't a single noise from upstairs, and so almost helplessly, I began to speak. "Although some things are strange, I have to admit."

Gabriel flexed his arms. "Like what?"

I stared out the window. The gray air was motionless; there'd be snow again today. "People in small towns are secretive," I said at last. "New York's like this open book. You meet someone on the street and she's telling you about how she's trying to get pregnant."

Gabriel laughed. "Then the guy behind her offers to help."

"Well," I said, "yeah. It's crude and it's loud and it can be mean even, but there's something less threatening about that. Everything's on the surface. You know what you're dealing with."

"You feel threatened here?"

I stared at him. I hadn't said that, but Gabriel seemed to have a way of cutting to the heart of things, teasing out their guts. He was good for my sister, I realized. He matched her.

He stood up to refill my cup.

From behind me, Teggie spoke. "Who's threatening you?"

I jumped up from my seat. "No one!"

I was ready to offer Teggie breakfast, although she rarely ate any, but she pressed me back down as Gabriel took the bread out of my hands. He crossed to the counter, Teggie stepped out of his way, and before long she was sitting with a buttered slice of toast.

There was nothing sharp or askew or unfitting between them. They anticipated the other's gestures, knowing when to pause for each other and make room; there was no bristle or resistance, the cautious curbing of anger that comes at the beginning. You looked at the two and expected to see wrinkles forming in response to each other's laughter, and life. It was as if all the rough surfaces had already been buffed away, leaving only burnished metal behind, and yet, how could that have happened? How had they been together long enough to bypass all the sticky grittiness of newbies? Teggie hadn't even had time to call Brendan with the news that she'd met someone. He always got her tidbits first, before passing them on to me for deeper excavation.

I had to make them stop looking at each other. To stop *not* looking at each other, on my behalf, studying me with generous, understanding eyes.

I opened my mouth and began to speak.

I revealed facts to them that Brendan had kept hidden from me, his wife. Everything that had happened since my husband's final act, linking events like beads on a string. Then I spoke of Red's death, and the role Eileen felt Brendan played in it. Finally, the miserable story wound down, my words petering out in the chill air of the kitchen.

"Can we get some heat on in here?" asked Teggie.

I pointed to the thermostat, and Gabriel went to adjust it.

Teggie watched him, a smile on her face that slowly faded. "You found all this out just now, Nor? Recently?"

I studied my empty plate. "You can say it. How did I not know before?"

Gabriel cleared his throat, elbowing a lock of hair from his eyes. "Don't we always keep things from the people we love most? Especially from them?"

His response was like the rush of heat from the furnace, a blanket on my soul, and I suddenly knew why my sister was falling in love with this man.

Teggie looked at him—*We'll never*

keep secrets, her eyes said—and I turned away.

"And the police chief didn't want you to find out?" Teggie asked. "He suggested you go home when you asked about it?"

For once, she wasn't saying anything I hadn't thought of already. "Well, it wasn't quite that linear. But yes. I think he might've been trying to protect Brendan. His memory anyway."

Teggie was glancing at Gabriel.

"What?" I said.

Teggie lifted knobby shoulders. "That's kind of presumptuous. Even for a police chief."

I shook my head. "You don't understand. Gabriel was just saying how different it is up here." I looked at him, he nodded support. "Vern loved Brendan." Teggie raised her eyebrows, and I tried again. "The Chief is like this mother bear, and all Wedeskyull his cubs. He's—"

"Protective," Gabriel said, using my word. Teggie let out a snort.

"What?" I cried.

"You're trying to play along," Teggie told Gabriel, "like it's all *Little House on*

the Prairie or something, when you know
this place is creepy as hell."

"Teggie!" I said, and again Gabriel
echoed me.

"This is your sister's home," he added.

"A mother bear is fierce when it comes
to it." My sister faced me across the table. "She'll kill on behalf of her cubs."

"So?" I replied. "I'm sure the Chief
would kill if he had to. That's kind of
what cops do." I heaved a sigh. "And
you know, he also might have thought
he was protecting *me.* It's not like this
was fun to learn. He was wrong, though,
I will say that. I needed closure."

A terrible smile appeared on Teggie's
face. "I hate that psychobabble crap.
Closure."

My shrug felt effortful, requiring of
muscles. "At least now I know."

"Know what?" she asked, as if speaking to a small child.

I frowned, looking to Gabriel for help.
"Well, why Brendan did it."

"Why did he do it?" she asked, still in
that I'm-sorry-you're-so-goddamned-
slow tone.

Only it was Teggie who seemed to be

the slow one, at least as far as I could tell. "Because of his brother drowning while in his care. I told you. Brendan made it so they both died on the same day of the year. And he used the rope he'd brought to try and save Red."

Teggie settled back in her chair, laying whip-thin arms across her belly. "Ah. So you've figured it all out."

It was my sister's sharp voice, her I'm-about-to-throw-something-in-your-face challenge, and as usual I had no idea what was coming.

"Well . . . as much as such a sense-less act could be figured out," I whispered. "Yes."

Gabriel stood up, beginning to clear the plates, and I felt a surge of gratitude for his gracious exit. Stage left. Enter the unwitting sister.

"What's that cute, country bumpkin moniker again?" Teggie demanded. "Red? And he's been dead twenty-five years. *You* just told *me* that. So why this particular January twenty-third? Why not any of the twenty-four years that came before it?"

I felt the skin on my chest pucker with cold. The snow was holding off for now, which meant the temperature would drop.

"Or make that fifteen, if you want to say a kid can't off himself very easily?"

My entire body shook. It wasn't Teggie's harshness, but the loss of the level ground I'd only just recently staked out. Stumbling around in Eileen's basement, reading Bill's journal and then Ned's clips, I had been so sure. Now the surface was tilting again.

"Anyway, you're forgetting something," Teggie continued.

I stared wordlessly down at the table.

"Something happened that you don't have the slightest inkling about yet. And it happened a whole week before the anniversary of Red's death. Right?"

I looked up, damning the haze I always let myself inhabit.

"The dope, Nora? The meds that were prescribed, not on January twenty-third, but on the sixteenth?"

My body wouldn't stop shuddering.

"So you'll say Brendan was preparing. A week in advance. Because this

January twenty-third was the one he'd decided to do it on."

"Stop it . . . please," I begged.

Was the anniversary of Red's death the least of it? Had something even fouler occurred on January sixteenth?

Gabriel stepped forward, settling one strong hand on my sister's shoulder, but she paused only to muster breath. "Except remember what you told me, Nor? You called and left a message on my machine."

I jumped up on trembling legs, while Teggie freed herself from Gabriel's grasp so that she could hold me back.

"This wasn't some well-thought-out suicide plan. What did they use? A red dot? Everything's flipping red up here." Teggie settled back, patient in her triumph. "It was a—"

I spoke the words through chattering teeth. "Rush job."

VISITS

Vern Weathers shoved his chair back and tugged a cloth napkin from the collar of his shirt. "That was some good meal," he said.

"Nothing I haven't made a thousand times before," his wife replied. She was nibbling at a forkful held aloft.

"Your chili mac is famous," Vern said, polishing off his glass of water. "You could make it ten thousand times, and I wouldn't complain."

"Just because folks around here like something doesn't make it famous."

Vern looked across the table. "Something happened on one of your shows that's got you all upset? Someone got voted off or voted down or voted under?" He smiled at the question, figuring Dorothy would smile back.

But she didn't. "I'm just saying that Wedeskyull isn't the whole world."

There was silence for a minute or two.

"Will it be a late one tonight?" Dorothy asked.

"Might be."

Dorothy set down her fork with a trembling hand. "Maybe you should stay home."

"You telling me how to do my job now?" Vern asked. "Maybe you've been watching the cop shows. You wouldn't be the only person in America who thinks watching TV qualifies him to be on the job."

"Stay home," Dorothy said suddenly. "Oh Vernon, stay home. I'll fix coffee, and we can watch a show together. There's one on at eight o'clock. You wouldn't believe what the people get up to—"

Vern dropped his napkin on the table and rose to his feet.

Dorothy stopped speaking.

Squaring his hands on his hips, Vern took a look into the dining room. The kitchen had a pass-through for platters to be handed in. They'd never done much entertaining and the pass-through usually collected mail and other clutter. Tonight it held snakes of Christmas garland and assorted other holiday frippery that hadn't been boxed up yet.

"Take care of this, will you?" Vern asked, gesturing. "I don't want to be looking at bells and ribbon come Easter." He paused. "It'll give you something to do besides getting all riled up looking at TV."

"Yes," his wife murmured, clearing the plates. Hers was still laden. "Of course."

She walked around him to the kitchen, her movements slow and deliberate. Dorothy walked as if she had an ache somewhere deep inside her, a little hunched over. By the time Vern had finished with his coat and mask, she was busy coiling up a dozen strands of lights, which had gone dim long ago.

Vern got into his Mountaineer and headed out. He'd been looking in on

Nora Hamilton at least once a day. Making sure she was all right. Checking through a window if he didn't want to bother with a visit. She'd been out and about a little much for his liking. It didn't do to go running around the North Country when your head wasn't on straight. A person could get into trouble that way. Brendan had found trouble as bad as it got; Vern would be goddamned if the wife had to suffer any more. And what she was looking for could only lead to suffering. So if he had to make a few calls, ask Donny at the pharmacy to take it easy on the wife, not tell her anything about a night best left forgotten, then he would. These were his people, and he knew best.

He'd thought that with Brendan gone, the wife would go, too. Leave for where she came from, go back to *her* people. But that didn't seem to be happening.

Vern drove into the Melvilles' driveway. Nora's next-door neighbors spent part of the winter in Florida. The Mountaineer was dark gray; it would stand out against the snow if he parked on the road. He left the engine running so the interior would stay warm as he back-tracked to Jean's place, the one she kept in town.

Any luck, Nora would be sleeping. In addition to parading herself about, she seemed to do a lot of sleeping these days, too.

Vern decided that since he'd already been to one of Jean's houses—dim and quiet the whole time he was there—he might as well go see the other one.

There'd been a second car parked in the drive alongside Nora's little red number. Some pansy-ass German model. Vern had called in the plates, but there hadn't been anything on its owner besides two parking tickets, racking up fines. A Gabriel Deacon. Someone else to keep an eye on.

It wasn't that Vern hated outsiders—that wasn't it at all. It was just that they made things more difficult, harder to manage, with their questions for the real estate agents, their observation of problems once their kids started in school, and the upgrades and new things they wanted for their different forms of fun.

Snow-surfing and wind-boarding? Life was recreation to these people. They had grills the size of a pickup truck bed—and the men were the ones who cooked. Hot, bubbling water to soak in, out on their decks in wintertime. One thing Vern knew was that life and sport were two different things.

All Vern had ever wanted to do was maintain the peace in his town, let the men work, have their play come week's end, keep folks safe and warm in a land that was hard on people. Like his daddy had done before Vern took control, and his granddaddy before that.

What civilians didn't understand—and never would—was that a few shortcuts, some corners cut, created *more* safety for the people the police were charged with protecting. All those rules and regs slowed an officer down, kept him from doing what was right, or else they dragged out the trouble in a situation already gone wrong. Civilians didn't get why or when the rules needed to be bent, but they benefited when they were. So sometimes you just had to keep people from seeing.

Vern radioed for a plow as he drove down Patchy Hollow. He couldn't stand the way this road narrowed over the winter months till it was no better than a single-laner come April. Lurcquer could take care of it, or better yet, the rookie, back less than a year from Coronado. Gilbert Landry. His mother was from away, her folks had moved up when she was a baby. And Paula Landry was raising her son on her own, another count against her, no matter what Vern had to pretend for modern minds. He'd been glad when Gilbert had come back home, though. Boy with his training knew more than a lifetime on the job could teach.

Vern pulled up in Jean's drive, tires flattening the recent coating of snow.

"A visit from the Chief," she said, once he rapped on the door. "This is an occasion."

"Take a walk with me, Jeannie," Vern said, and waited while she went for her boots.

They crossed the road, giving Eileen's dimly lit house a wide berth, as if by silent consent. Vern had carried on a brief but heated affair with Jean back when he was first married, and just beginning to feel the crush of Dorothy's shortcomings. It had been more than just physical relations, despite the short duration of their time together. He and Jean understood each other, always had. Vern harbored more than a few *could've beens* where Jean Hamilton was concerned.

They never referred to it, though, their shared past. One day, decades ago, Vern stopped coming to see her for stolen wedges of time. He realized that a scandal—or worse, a divorce—would make what he had to do as Chief impossible. How could you father a land when you couldn't even father your own—well, of course he and Dorothy had never had any kids.

She'd never been able to, the cavity of her womb vacant for some reason, nothing for a baby to latch on to, as the doc put it. It was a failing Vern hadn't signed on for, but which duty compelled him to accept.

Their childlessness made it even more important that he serve as a good role model for the wider group of people he oversaw. And once Vern understood that, he never allowed himself to meet Jean privately again, although there were times when they ran into each other, many times, this town being what it was, and a powerful storm of regret always surged through him.

He and Jean neared the lake, hardly distinguishable from the snowy fields around it. No one cleared this lake anymore because no one ever used it. They stuck to other smaller and inferior bodies of water for winter recreation, though in summer it was like people forgot, and Patchy Hollow would again sport bright figures and shouts of laughter.

"So many of us are gone now," Jean said, each word so heavy it seemed to be pulled by gravity to the ground. "Burt . . . Bill . . . Brendan." She raised her eyes. "It's bled into the next generation, hasn't it?"

Vern gazed out over the expanse before them. A falcon sat in a high-up branch, tawny against all the white, hunting. Vern watched the bird find something and dive, its beak an arrow aimed at a spot Vern couldn't detect on the ground. He looked away before the bird could seize its small, unsuspecting prey.

"I don't know about that, Jeannie," Vern said. "You might see it that way. But I look around, and I'm glad for how many of us are left."

Jean's hand hung limply at her side. Vern allowed his to drop, brush Jean's glove for just a moment. Even thick padding couldn't muffle the charge it ignited. Vern's heart started pounding, although he suspected the conversation was as responsible for that as the touch.

Jean pretended not to notice what he'd done. "Sometimes I wish we'd sold the houses after everything happened."

Vern kept silent.

"I tried," Jean went on. "I bought the place in town, moved in for a while. But it didn't matter. Eileen was never going to leave this spot."

"That's what I admire about you, Jeannie," Vern said at last.

She raised her face toward his, but Vern looked away.

"You were always willing to put the past behind you," he continued. "Not like your brother or his wife. For them it just went on and on. It never stopped. But you were always ready to be done."

Jean lifted her tired eyes again. Vern wondered when they had come to look that way, the valleys beneath them so creviced and deep, and whether his own appeared anywhere near the same.

"Yes," she agreed. "That's right, Chief. I'm ready to be done."

The twin ways Jean's words could be taken occurred to Vern as he was climbing back into the Mountaineer, accompanied by an uneven thunk in his chest that made him realize he wouldn't be around forever, overseeing this land. Dave was younger by only a few years, and in worse shape than Vern. Who would the job fall to, now that Brendan was gone? Gilbert had the strength, the brains, and the conviction, but Vern would be goddamned if anybody whose family had barely lived up here two generations was going to step in as Chief.

He let his heart rate slow, then got out and stamped back up the walk to Jean's.

"Been a while since Burt Mitchell's name came up," Vern said when Jean opened the door. He gave her a smile that crinkled his eyes. "Takes me back to old times."

Jean didn't smile back.

"There's not much left of those times, is there?" Vern went on. When Jean didn't reply, he forced another statement out. "It's probably safe to say there's nothing left."

Jean wrapped her arms around herself, and Vern saw her, many years younger and many pounds thinner. What a looker she had been. But tonight she was even more beautiful.

"That's right, Chief."

Vern took off his hat, holding it down by his gut. "You're sure now?"

Jean looked up at him.

Their eyes held.

The weight of all that wasn't said—all that never could be said—hung between them.

"My God," Jean said. "Do you ever think back? Seems like in my memory all we did was laugh. Everything was cause for fun. Remember us then?"

Vern nodded. For just a second, he did remember.

"How could there be anything of that left?" Jean asked.

Then she rose on tiptoes, overcoming her height and the added girth, until she was almost as tall as Vern. His chest cramped again as Jean brushed her lips, so much softer and more lush than his wife's, across the corners of his mouth.

CHAPTER TWENTY-THREE

Vern hadn't wanted me to know about Red's death, and he didn't want me to know what happened on the sixteenth, either. What had he done as soon as I told him I was going to the pharmacy to ask about the medicine? Sent me off to replace a taillight. Giving him time to call—what was his name, Donald Brannigan—and instruct him to play dumb.

Talk about conspiracy theories. And even if I was in the neighborhood of right, what could I possibly do about it?

The next day, I took Teggie and Gabriel out to breakfast at the diner in town, then accompanied them both to the Northway, following Gabriel's BMW in my Honda. We stopped at the entrance and I climbed out to see them off.

The ground was uneven, humped with snow, and drifts were getting stirred up by a fast wind, cat-high and screechy.

I screened my face, leaning down to the driver's-side window. Gabriel lowered the glass. "I'm really glad we met," I said, and he reached up to squeeze my gloved hand.

Teggie opened her door and got out.

"I'm sorry I was such a bitch yesterday." My sister lowered her head to mine so that her burnished curls could mingle with my unattended strands. I couldn't remember washing my hair lately, let alone having it cut. "It makes me crazy when I think you're fooling yourself."

I leaned in for a hug. Despite Teggie's puffy coat, my arms still fit all the way around her, but she was gaining weight, I could tell. For some reason, I said as much.

My sister laughed. "I think you might be, too."

"Me?" I tried to get a look at myself through my layers of outerwear. "Bereavement. It's a real appetite enhancer."

Teggie cackled. "Hungry, and suddenly snide, too."

My smile waned. "I love you, Teg."

"Oh, Nor. Me, too."

"And I'm happy for you," I whispered, and she held on until something made her turn toward Gabriel in the car. He was looking significantly at the clock on the dashboard, and she gave him a quick nod, me a final squeeze, then ran lightly over the rutted ice before jumping inside so they could drive away.

When I started my car and wheeled around on the empty road to get going back north, an engine light came on. It was wild and flashing, orange with an unintelligible black symbol in the middle of that glowing eye. I switched my gaze between it and the road, making sure no cars were coming just in case mine decided to do something unpredictable. The light continued to blink on and off at a pace rapid enough to induce seizures.

Some kind of glitch in the electrical system?

I had gone a few more miles when the engine stopped altogether. I heard everything go off. It was as discreet as a jet airline powering down at the gate.

"Oh, damn," I spoke aloud.

This wasn't a glitch; it was massive, catastrophic failure. And my car had been driving just fine. For years.

With the remaining momentum, I steered—heaving, effortful; the power gone from the wheel—to the snow-banked shoulder and let my car coast to a stop. I gave an automatic twist of the key, but there was nothing to turn off.

I looked around. No cars on the road.

I reached for my pack, praying my cell had held its charge. Too cold to be out here for long in this situation. I was about to dial AAA when I spotted a white rectangle of paper lying beside the phone. I drew it out, hitting keys in rapid succession, suddenly aware that there was no one I would rather have help with my car.

When Dugger drove up in the tow

truck, it was clear he hadn't understood who I was by my greeting on the phone, nor did he recognize me now. I tried to mount a smile, but it trembled on my lips. Dugger off-kilter was a startling—if not scary—sight.

"It's me, Nora," I said, then forced myself to add two words that still caused pain. "Mrs. Hamilton? I was at the garage last week—"

Dugger was lowering himself from the cab, a wild expression in his bright eyes. Only when he reached the ground did his breathing finally start to slow. "Missus?"

The nod I gave was a bit frantic itself.

"Something wrong with your car?"

I barked a short laugh. "You could say that."

He lifted the hood and took a look underneath, coming up with his forehead furrowed, his brows drawn down. "I'll have to hitch it," he said.

The announcement seemed to be as much for his benefit as mine.

I waited in the truck while Dugger got to work, slow and patient, the wind yowling around him.

At the garage, he put my car up on a lift, and took out a device that looked something like extra-long pliers, only computerized, trailing wires. The tools of his trade had gone digital. Refinishing wood or walls still required caustic chemicals and the repetitive motion of your own hand, and I was taken aback by a fierce wave of longing.

"Missus?"

I lifted my head from my reverie.

"Engine's working fine."

I hadn't even heard it come to life, but I registered the steady rush now. I started to frown. "You mean . . . it wasn't broken?"

Dugger's face split into a grin. "It was broken. Just wasn't hard to fix." He held up a battered metal box. The piece of equipment he'd started with lay abandoned on a stool. "Had to get out my old tools."

He slammed the hood down.

I felt a frown building; my habitual state when accompanied by Dugger seemed to be one of confusion. "Your old tools? How come?"

From the expression on Dugger's

face, I could tell he wouldn't be able to explain it to me, whatever had gone wrong, the machinations of which he was capable. And I guessed it didn't really matter, so long as my car was in working order.

Plus, he looked like he was getting upset, and I didn't want that. So I hurried to change the subject. "You were right, you know," I said. "About Brendan skating."

Dugger gave me a beatific, gleaming smile as he climbed into my car and rode it, door open, one leg hanging out, through the bay to the lot. Then he came back inside, circling over to me. "I know I was, Missus."

"You used to go with him?" I picked up the thread as if there hadn't been any interruption. Hungry now, on a hunt for the past, I felt almost as crazed as Dugger had looked when we met by the side of the road.

"Not me, Missus," Dugger said calmly. "Told you already, I wasn't allowed out on the ice. But I watched. I always like to watch."

"Were you there . . ." My voice trailed off. How far could I push him?

He was watching me with those vivid eyes, no hint of his earlier trouble or distress.

"Were you there the day Red died?" I asked at last. Someone had to have been there, not running or helping or doing much of anything. Someone had taken that horrid picture of Bill.

"Red dead," he answered in a casual tone. "Red head."

"He had red hair, you mean?" I said, thinking of the rusty shock topping the little boy in those pictures. "That's how he got his nickname."

Dugger lowered his face toward mine, and I had never seen his gaze more limpid, or his voice so clear. "It probably would've darkened," he said. "If he had lived. Most folks do, time they get older, especially when they start out such carrot-tops."

"Right . . ." I said pointlessly.

"Not everyone, though," Dugger went on. "Some folks stay redheads."

This had been a bad idea. Dugger's eyes were still placid pools, but I didn't know what potential lay in their depths. And we weren't getting anywhere. I couldn't make sense of his circles. "I'm sorry," I said. What did it matter if Dugger had been there when Red died? I already knew what had happened. And knowing more about that long-ago day wouldn't provide any information about the other January twenty-third, the most recent one.

"Red hurts," Dugger said suddenly, and I looked up. "*Lynn lurks*—no! That doesn't work!" He punched himself swiftly in the chest, a hollow, rapping sound.

"Dugger, stop that!" I cried. Then I paused. Who was Lynn? "We don't have to talk about Red anymore—"

He was fidgeting with something beneath the counter. Then I heard the sound of my own voice, urgent and driven. "Were you there the day Red died?" And Dugger's airy, disconnected response: *Red dead. Red head.*

"What is that?" I asked. "Dugger? What are you doing?"

He lifted his hand. In it was clasped a slim silver rectangle, part of its front speckled with dots. An audio recording device. I frowned again.

"You recorded us talking?" I asked. "Dugger? You record people?"

"Be quiet, Missus!" he said, not threateningly. "Talking, walking, balking—"

The crash of a glass door startled me as much as the onset of Dugger's rhymes.

"Mackenzie!" Al Meter barked. "I can't figure this thing out." He seemed to be muttering half to himself. "Can't fix an engine now without a goddamned computer. It's lucky I got you to—" Then he broke off, taking a good look at Dugger.

His voice was still rising beside me.

Al peered through rheumy eyes at us both. "Miz Hamilton?"

"Caulking, mocking—no!" Dugger struck the counter with one balled hand. The other still held the recorder. "Stalking—"

"Aw," Al said. "He's gone and gotten all upset."

Al thrust a thick, oil-smeared hand against my chest. I stumbled backward, not sure if I'd just been assaulted or simply shunted aside. Al was scrabbling around in a cabinet that stood near the counter. He came out with an amber medicine bottle. No red dot on that one, I'd bet; Al was used to what he was doing.

As if in confirmation Al grumbled, "Now he'll be tired out the whole rest of the day."

"Why?" I said in a whisper. "What's wrong with him?"

Al hardly looked up. "Don't matter what fancy name you put on it. But his ma says he's artistic. He takes one of these when he gets excited and it sets him right."

Autistic, my brain corrected. That must be what Al meant.

Al got the lid open and shook two tablets out. He held them up to Dugger's mouth and he gobbled them right out of his boss's grease-blackened palm, like a beast who'd learned to love his master. I backed away toward the door, letting in a freezing column of air. Neither man seemed to notice when I left.

CHAPTER TWENTY-FOUR

I stood panting in the lot outside, fresh, new flakes of snow flying at me, and my thoughts in a whirl, too. Why had Dugger recorded us? And why had he shown me that he had?

Not to mention the talk about redheads. More than guilt over upsetting Dugger, or indecision about whether he had anything relevant to say about the past, his strange speech concerning hair stayed uppermost in my mind. Teggie had called Vern presumptuous, trying to tell me what was best. But there was somebody else who suddenly had a whole lot to say to me too, wasn't there? And the word *redhead* applied to him as surely as it did to a little boy twenty-five years in the ground.

The entrance to Ned Kramer's old house near Queek Pond was indicated by a yellow hidden-driveway diamond. The drive was over half a mile long, rutted and buckling from years of freezing and thaw. But the house itself was grand, three stories clad in clapboard and fish scales on a turret that poked up high over the slate roof.

Much of that clapboard was rotting, its paint long since faded, and I could spy at least ten heavy roof tiles ready to fall, all of which clutched at my restorer's heart.

But none of that was why I had come to Ned's right now.

I took in his tousle of hair as he opened the door.

"Nora?" he said, a question, although the look of recognition, of knowing, in his eyes was so strong that I flinched from it. "Are you okay?"

I didn't answer.

"Come in. You must be cold," Ned said.

He ushered me past gaping, unfurnished rooms, cluttered with sealed-up boxes, toward the kitchen.

"Coffee?" he offered.

I shook my head, trying to hide a grimace.

"You okay?" Ned asked again.

"A little—queasy," I began. "It's been kind of an upsetting morning."

"Tea," Ned said, remembering. He filled two mugs with water and stuck them in a microwave. This room looked to be the only really functioning one in the house, on the first floor at least, although it seemed most heavily dependent on a microwave and toaster. The surface of the stove was pristine.

"Upsetting how?" Ned asked, handing me a cup.

I studied him again, then asked abruptly, "Do you know Dugger Mackenzie?"

"Guy who works at the garage?" Ned said. He was straddling the edge of a counter. There was no table or chairs.

This space would look good with a built-in island, some stools.

I took a sudden gulp of tea, letting the liquid burn my mouth, stun me a little.

"Why are you asking me about Dugger?"

I raised my gaze to his. "It's more that he was talking about you. At least, I think he might've been. Maybe he wasn't. Oh, I don't know!"

Dugger hadn't used the word *Ned* in the string of rhymes he'd recorded, and it would've fit. *Red dead. Red head.* What did Dugger call it when a rhyme didn't work? Cheating. But *Ned* wouldn't have been cheating. I began to wonder why I had come here. Because I was trying to answer a question, fill in one of the maddening holes that were causing me to stumble? Or was I after another thing altogether?

"Can you just tell me straight out what Dugger said?"

I barked a laugh; it sounded harsh and unlovely in my ears. But Ned didn't seem repelled; he continued to stare at me from not quite far enough away. "I don't know if I've talked to anyone straight since Brendan died." I paused. "And not often before that, either."

Ned eyed me in a way that made me go on.

"It always seemed easier not to. Only now I'm starting to realize—that the easiness is false. All the stuff you never look at just lays there, rotting, so when you finally start to poke around, it's even harder to see." Another pause. "Might be better just to talk straight all along."

Silence for a moment. "Well," Ned said at last. "That was a good start."

A smile tugged at my mouth. Ned set down his mug, contents untouched, on the counter behind him. He did it without looking, gaze still focused on me.

"Someplace we can sit?" I asked weakly.

"Not many," Ned said, and we both laughed.

He led me to the space that would one day be his living room and threw back a sheet from a couch. The cloth gave off a cloud of plaster dust as it landed.

I glanced down at the black floor-boards—paint that probably covered up pumpkin pine, and the equally paint-smothered woodwork, which might be no longer obtainable chestnut under-neath—taking a moment's respite in finding the house's bones and guts.

"I need to find out more about Dug-ger," I said at last. "He seems to know things. Some things at least."

Ned thought for a second. "I think Dugger sometimes spends time with Dave."

"Dave Weathers?"

"Right," Ned said. "Dave's a nice guy. Not as—remote as the rest. He's a big hunter, and I remember he said once that Dugger likes to tag along with him. Apparently Dugger will never shoot any-thing, but he's a hell of a good tracker."

I imagined the conversation I might have with the Chief's brother, and sud-denly shivered. Ned's house was cold, draughty, its furnace unequal to the enormous spaces contained within.

We would have to install a more mod-ern system.

"I think you might be on the wrong

track here, though," Ned said. "If you're looking to learn more about Brendan."

I glanced at him, shadows falling between us through the tall, undraped windows.

Ned looked away, and his lips compressed. He had a generous mouth, I realized, used to talking and laughter. But just now it looked tight.

While I was studying him, Ned went on. "You want to know about Brendan's last days on duty, right?"

I nodded.

"So read the records," Ned said. "One thing cops do is keep logs. They'd probably share them with you. That'll at least give you a place to start."

CHAPTER TWENTY-FIVE

When I got home, there was a carton on the front porch. I glimpsed it from several yards away. Everything was white, the snow mounded three feet up the walls of my house, so any patch of color appeared like a brazen splash. This was beige, a box similar to the ones all over Ned's house, only its flaps were unsealed. I picked it up warily—it was light, the contents surely able to have fit into a much smaller container—and brought it inside.

My house was as chilly as Ned's had been. I cranked up the heat before shedding my outerwear, listening to the rumbles of the furnace while I studied the carton. *What are you waiting for?* Teggie's voice demanded. Finally I dropped one hand inside, coming out with a small plastic device, and a note with a single word on it. *Missus.*

Dugger had left me one of those drives for extra memory. I trudged upstairs to Brendan's study.

Brendan had had the use of a computer in his patrol car, and since all I'd done was make files for prospective clients and order supplies off the Internet, one machine had been more than enough. One day, if Brendan had lived, perhaps we would've needed to get another, and a moment of longing assailed me, for the squabbles and bickering that occurred when a single resource was drawn tight between a couple. I was about to flick on the computer, and insert the drive, when something else grabbed my attention.

Brendan's yellow flannel box.

Had I brought it down here? I'd looked over the contents with Teggie, and one time afterward, but I had returned the

box to its drawer in the dresser. At least,
I thought I had.

I seized up the lid—it hitched again
on a corner, which I hadn't ever noticed
being a problem before—and began
combing through the items. They all appeared to be present and intact. Had
Dugger come inside before leaving his
offering for me on the porch? Maybe he
wanted to make sure I had a computer.
But why would he have touched Brendan's box?

I made a quick search of the rest of
the house, glad to find nothing disturbed.
The closet door in the bedroom was
open, but I might've done that myself.
Perhaps I'd moved the box without remembering it as well.

It was Dugger's device that required
attention now.

Dozens, then hundreds, of files
streamed by on the screen, impossible
to make sense of. They were all identified by a single date from a couple of
years ago, and hadn't been given de-
scriptive names, *Al Meter talking, Hunting with Dave* or anything like that. Instead Dugger had used a single word,

many of them abstract, to label each file. *Time*, said one. Another was called simply *River. Window, Petering, Upside down, Hard.* The strangest combination of words I had ever seen in one place. Like a poem your Lit professor in college tried to convince you made sense.

And there were so many of them. I stared at the list, extending above and below the section of screen now displayed. The only way to figure out what he wanted me to hear would be to go through all of them, one by one, in a slow, arduous search. And there might not be anything on them that would help me at all.

On the other hand, it wasn't as if there were a whole lot of things competing for my time right now. Going to the police station could wait. Maybe I'd find something in Dugger's files that would direct me there, give me some questions to ask.

I sighed, scrolled to the top of the list, and began.

Hours later, I was lost in the entrails of Dugger's recordings, the scraps and

parcels of life he had seen fit to preserve. Not because each one was inter-
esting. To the contrary: I found myself
listening to the minutiae and mundanities of life. Tools clanging at what must
be Al's garage. Dishes being rattled and
the strange birdcalls and cries of meal-
time in a diner. I kept listening, concentrating to some degree, because at any
moment I might happen across the one
key file Dugger had deemed important
enough for me to hear. *Then why didn't
he identify it,* I asked myself, ears buzz-
ing and brain watery from trying to make
sense of the sounds, attempting to put
a visual overlay to the audio scenes being brought to life here in Brendan's
study. Maybe there was nothing significant on this device at all, just further
manifestation of Dugger's autism, or
else him trying in his stumbling way to
occupy me somehow, offer me something to do.

Hunger had come gnawing again.
Cooking meals was perhaps the least
tolerable way of filling my time now;
each step and task reminded me of do-

ing the same things with Brendan. But I couldn't ignore my appetite. Unlike those widows who wasted away in their desolation and their grief, I seemed unable to skip too many meals in a row, much less stop eating altogether.

My fingers were still fiddling with the mouse, scrolling from one file to another. *Reserve, Carpeting, Bottled, Nice.* Some nonsense words: *Oodle* and *Lade.* I clicked on them, but their sounds were even less distinguishable than the others. *Barn.* I tried that.

Noises that were almost violent filled the recording. Grunts, thumps, a crash or two, then a groan of pure release that confirmed I wasn't listening to a fight or crime taking place, but instead the illicit sounds of somebody's overheard lovemaking. I slid the mouse around frantically until the cursor found the little red x. When I finally clicked on it, I was breathing as fast as the people in the recording. And I was wondering, who was Dugger Mackenzie really? How far would he sneak into other people's lives, and why did he do it?

*   *   *

I knew what it was time for now, what I had better do. Head back outside into the snow that was mummifying Wedeskyull and drive up to the police barracks.

I slapped together two pieces of bread in the kitchen, a wedge of cheese between them. Gobbling it down like a wild thing, I fixed another, and ate that, too. I drank a tall glass of juice. Then I grabbed my sack and went out.

The world was quiet and calm, snow falling in a gentle cascade. My car slid through it like a body between blankets, whispery, rustly, still. It climbed Roister Road without mishap, and I turned into the lot. Then I got out amidst a sweep of pillowy flakes.

The barracks were steamy with artificial heat. Only one cop was inside, which, although a plus for my errand, made me wonder what might be taking place. The Chief's door was shut and Club wasn't in his cubicle.

Tim Lurcquer rose from his seat and came forward. His squinty eyes got even smaller as he identified me. "Nora. Hi."

I returned the greeting.

"Looking for someone?"

"Club?" I suggested, then was struck by the obvious alternative. "Or Dave?"

Tim shook his head. He wasn't much taller than I was; I could look right into his eyes.

"Is something going on today?" I began to glance around the streamlined department, the gleaming silver computers. The place was spare in its efficiency, no forms in triplicate or overflowing filing cabinets.

"There's always something going on," Tim replied.

I decided to play it straight. "Tim, do you have a log for shifts?"

He sat down on a corner of desk. I was struck by the difference between Tim in that position, and Ned, who had assumed it a few hours earlier on the counter at his house. Ned was taller; Tim's legs would've dangled in Ned's kitchen. But it was more than height that lent Ned an appearance of surety and strength, someone who could get things done, while Tim simply looked bland, uncaring.

"A shift log? Sure," he said. "State requires us to keep a paper record."

"Could I look at it?"

"Why would you want to do that?" Tim began tapping stubby fingers upon the desk. I was suddenly sure that he was toying with me, for his own fun, that despite his flat manner of speaking, he was perhaps the least straightforward of any of the five cops on the force.

"I just—I want to know what Brendan was doing. In the time before he died."

Tim got to his feet, idly, looking around. Then he crossed the room so slowly that I wondered whether he had any intention of coming back. But he did return, carrying a book that looked out of place in this updated shop, as old-fashioned as a rotary phone. The faux leather volume was awkward, overlarge, in Tim's grasp. He tossed it down carelessly, as if nothing inside could possibly be of interest or importance, and the *thwack* it made caused me to jump.

I flipped through the thin sheets of paper, the all-but-illegible notes, until I found the sixteenth. There was information there, and it stung my eyes with tears, but not because it was especially significant. Instead, the few lines were mundane, referring to things Brendan used to complain about, the nuisances and wrinkles of a cop's everyday life. There'd been an accident on the Northway and—if I was reading the rapid squiggles correctly—the driver had posed something of a threat. The cops had been called into town at a late hour for a Drunk and Disorderly. I was no better off, no more informed, than I'd been before being granted access to this. If I'd hoped for some stark, dramatic line of text pointing to a felony or other obvious event, then I was in for a letdown.

Tim remained beside me. I was going to ask him about either the accident or the D&D, for sheer lack of any better thing to do, when the door to the inner room of the station banged open, and the newest addition to the force strolled in.

"Two-oh-one's just about clear," he said.

Tim reached down and slid the log into a desk drawer.

Gilbert saw me then.

"Nora here was just looking for Club," Tim said. "He on his way?"

"Few more minutes maybe."

I had never bothered memorizing the codes. "What's a two-oh-one?"

The cops exchanged glances. "There was a fire today."

"Oh no. Where?"

Another quick exchange of looks. "Five-twelve Queek Pond Lane."

I jumped to my feet, wondering if Tim or Gilbert would know that I knew.

It was Ned Kramer's house.

CHAPTER TWENTY-SIX

Everything was still chaos when I arrived—having driven too fast along snow-strewn roads—but the fire appeared to be pretty much over. Black plumes of smoke gusted out of the shattered first-floor windows of Ned's house, like the breath of some hellish beast, and long strips of clapboard had peeled away, exposing the core. The fire seemed to have been contained down there; the second and third stories appeared to be untouched.

Two neon yellow fire trucks stood close to the house, with firefighters walking around, checking for hot spots. A generator was running, plus the Hotshot, used for thawing outdoor pipes. In wintertime, lack of ready water was the number one reason for a fire blazing out of control.

I braked to a halt at the end of the long drive. Tim and Gilbert had followed me from the station; they joined Vern and Dave in a ragged cluster of grayclad bodies.

There was also a runner, dressed head to toe in a second, blue skin, and jogging in place.

Where was Ned? At work? Did he know what had happened?

A single, hard thump sounded against my window. I jumped, turning toward it. Club's thick fist still lingered on the glass. I started to pull at the door handle, and he stepped back, asking before the door was even fully open, "What are you doing here?"

I raised my head. "I'm working on this house." It was almost true. About to be true.

He raised his eyebrows. "Yeah? You've been here recently?"

This perhaps inevitable reaction hadn't occurred to me. I nodded.

"Step over here then," Club said, all cop now, not a friend, even though I noticed he wasn't in uniform. "Let's have a word."

I stood patiently for his questions: the last time I had been here, what I had done, whether I'd seen anything. I volunteered that the only appliance we had touched was the microwave, then asked, "Does Ned know what happened?"

Club frowned. "We don't know what happened," he replied.

At that moment Weekend bounded up, frolicking about his master, poking his moist snout into my palm. I rubbed him absently. "You brought your dog?"

Club shrugged large shoulders. "I wasn't on duty. We were on our way back from an outing when the call came in." In a moment of solicitousness, he explained, "Week likes to listen to the police channel in the car." Then he pointed somewhere off in the white, smoky distance, and I spotted his civilian car, a Jimmy. The dog gave a bark of assent, and Club lowered a hand to quiet him.

I glanced toward the house again. It was smoking as it cooled, and the sight brought about an almost physical pain. The house was like someone recently admitted to the hospital, once hulking and imposing, but now laid low, vulnerable. Another board fell away, offering a glimpse to the structure's maimed insides.

Dave Weathers walked up. He extended the hand that had been depressing a button on his radio, letting forth a blurp of static before he could fumble it silent. His face stained red, and he looked like he didn't know what to do with the offending hand.

I took it.

"Hi, Mrs. H.," he said in a friendly tone.

"You get a statement from that jogger?" Club asked. There was derision in his tone, but I couldn't tell if it was meant for the runner or Dave.

Dave jutted his chin up and down.

"Let him go then," Club commanded, and Dave began to back away, still nodding.

Weekend had abandoned Club and come to sit by me, upright on his haunches, silky ears perked. Drenched stalks of grass that had been washed clean of snow were already beginning to ice over. The firefighters were rolling up flat lengths of hoses, shouting instructions, stepping back from the drifts that billowed up when the hose nozzles hit them. Someone was nailing sheets of plywood over gaping holes in the exterior.

Club was watching his dog. "Can you look after him for me? For a few hours?"

"You want me to take Weekend?" I responded, becoming aware of something then. Weekend was close enough for me to feel his heaving flank, but even though I hadn't yet cracked open my new medicine, I hadn't sneezed once. I wiggled my nose, testing it while breathing in the smell of damp dog, but didn't feel so much as a single sniffle.

"Can't stay off duty now," Club said, while one gloved hand checked that his gun was in place. "There'll be things to do."

And then Club's eyes narrowed and

he folded his arms across his chest. He was so well-built that muscles could be seen through the thick coat of his uniform.

I turned in the direction he was staring. Ned Kramer had just driven up.

Ned got out of his car and crossed the broken plains of snow. "What the hell is going on?"

Club stepped forward and I backed away with Weekend, listening to Club's low rumbling explanation, and Ned's louder rejoinder.

"Nothing, nothing," he said. "Go see for yourself, if there's anything left to see. I'm hardly living in this place. I don't even have a fucking stove." My heart squeezed at the raw pain in his voice. He scrubbed a hand across his face.

The Chief had arrived at Club's side. "Mr. Kramer, I wish I could say your situation was unusual," he said. "But we see this from time to time. Folks move up, occupy these big old houses, wired back in a different age. A circuit gets overloaded, and *boom,* before you know it you got . . ." The Chief extended an arm toward the smoldering house.

Ned was staring at him. "I just said I'm not even using the stove."

The Chief looked back levelly. "Craig McAllister, the fire chief, wants to talk to you, sir. I'm afraid me and the boys got work to do at the station."

I hadn't known if Ned realized I was there, but as he turned and went in search of the fire chief, he paused. "Hold on for a bit, Nora, will you?"

I flinched at the brokenness in his tone.

"Take good care of my dog," Club said, as he headed toward his Jimmy.

The other cops were dispersing as well.

Vern rolled down his window as he got into his car. "You get out of here now, honey. There'll be other houses for you to decorate. This place is unsafe in a dozen different ways."

I promised, and Vern gave a single wave of his hand, his face creased with worry as he drove off.

I struggled to lead Weekend away by his leash. Club had said he should visit a tree before we left. A shallow perimeter of field, now snow-veiled, had been mowed around Ned's house. Once it ended, thick woods encroached upon the land. We entered them, Weekend eager for his break, sniffing one tree trunk after another.

His hind and forelegs were soon buried. The snow in the woods was deep. Weekend was still looking for a tree that pleased him when he let out a loud bark. I looked up to see Ned stomping through the snow after us. We had come quite a ways.

"I'm so sorry," I said, as Ned neared. Weekend seemed to have abandoned his search for the perfect tree, twining himself between my knees.

"I didn't have this in me," Ned replied, his voice low, and rough with something like anger. "I didn't have this in me to lose."

"I understand," I said softly, "when a house is hurt. I think I feel the injuries myself."

Ned accepted that with a nod.

Weekend was starting to move a bit agitatedly, and I bent down. "Go on, boy. It's okay." He turned liquid eyes on me—you could've sworn he was making sure—before trotting off.

"You haven't lost it, you know," I went on. "I think the structure is all right. And it's not like it didn't need some pretty major attention before this."

"There were hard copies," Ned said after a moment. "That burned. Nothing I don't have backup for. But still—my office suffered the worst damage."

Vern's words returned on a gust of wind, overloaded circuits, houses not upgraded for their new purposes. I considered the flammability of paper. Could this have been Ned's fault after all? In some ways, the untended nature of the house made it more vulnerable. There must've been whole rooms he never even entered. But not his office.

Ned was looking off into the distance. I heard some faraway banging. There came the heaving sound of fire truck engines departing, and a car engine gunned as well.

"What did the fire chief say?" I asked.

"A lot of stuff while saying nothing at all. You know? How it is when there's nothing to say?"

I couldn't stop tears from welling up. "Yeah," I said. "I do."

Ned was starting to turn. "I'd better go check if my old cabin is rented this week."

"Look," I called, hearing my voice pitch and yaw. I didn't want Ned to leave like this. It didn't matter who was to blame, if anyone even was. "I can match the remaining clapboards. We could do a real painted-lady exterior."

Ned paused while mounting a drift of snow.

"I'll make some calls," I shouted. "Disaster repair first, there must be a lot of water and smoke in there. And someone to come seal things up better."

"Yeah?" He was still clambering upward, but at least he was calling over his shoulder, engaged in our exchange. "You really think this could still turn out okay?"

"Better than okay!" I shouted, beginning to laugh as Ned skidded down the embankment, one hand raised, giving a thumbs-up, as the rest of him disappeared.

I opened my sack and jotted a few

notes, people to call, materials to order. I was getting back to work, for real, and I thought Brendan would be glad.

Then I huffed on my hands, drawing my thick gloves back on. I had gotten cold suddenly; the warmth of the trek out here had worn off. I looked around for Weekend. I could see soft mounds of snow he must have kicked up, but no sign of the dog.

"Weekend?" I called. "Week?"

The dog's coat was pure ebony; he should've been easy to spot. But I didn't see him anywhere in the winter woods. I started to walk, scouting for paw prints in the deep drifts. When I found some, I followed their trail.

The tracks ended abruptly at the perimeter of trees that formed a moat around Ned's house. I stopped, using one hand to shield my eyes against the few flakes that flew, and squinted at the scene, which had cleared out. All was still, cold, and blankly white.

I looked about for Ned but he had beaten me out here and taken off. Probably couldn't bear to remain for one minute longer than necessary near his house.

"Weekend! Come here, boy!" I shouted, wondering if the tremor in my voice would scare him off, or summon him. If he was here to be summoned. Had Club taken his dog after all? And then I heard a whine. It came from the direction of Ned's house.

The house was steaming in places, with a few tendrils of smoke curling up. I took another look around, hunting for a last, straggling fireman to ask if it was safe to approach. But no one was left.

And still that high whine persisted, almost a yipping.

The house didn't look in danger of collapsing; the fire's reach hadn't extended to the support beams or outer walls. And it didn't matter anyway.

I set off at a run, boots clumsy in the snow, sending up clods. Relative to the frigid air, you could still feel heat coming off the house, and everything was a sodden mess, shrubbery trampled, dirt that wouldn't normally have been exposed for another three months turned to mud.

"Weekend?" I called, tramping through the muck and debris.

A floor-to-ceiling window had either blown out or been shattered to gain access; someone with a more astute eye than mine could probably have said which. A sheet of plywood had been hastily nailed up in place of the glass, and as I neared it the whining grew louder.

"Weekend!" I shouted. Still he didn't bark, which somehow frightened me most of all.

I started to attack the nails. Gloves made my hands less precise, but at least their padding was able to withstand the slit of the nail heads. The nails hadn't been that well secured; I was able to tug them out without a claw. Once I had freed all but the lowermost ones, I tore off the sheet of plywood, and left it dangling.

An overwhelming smell of smoke and char assailed me. I had to reel away, momentarily dizzy, scrubbing at my eyes. The second my vision cleared, I peered into the house.

Weekend crouched as close to the outer wall as he could get, a length of rope drawn taut between his collar and a heavy table that had partially burned. He had been able to drag the table some ways, as evidenced by marks on a ruined rug, but had apparently reached the limits of his endurance, or else given up.

The dog was terrified. He was trembling, fur rippling as his body quaked. When he saw me, he immediately ceased whining, gazing up with dark, confused eyes.

"Oh, Weekend," I murmured. "Oh, you poor thing. Who did this to you?" I continued clucking words of reproach meant for someone else, which seemed to soothe him, as I stripped off my gloves and picked at the knot in the rope that bound his neck.

And then I saw a note tucked under the cruel collar.

The scrap of paper held three words: *Stop asking questions.*

Weekend stared silently as I extricated the piece of paper. It was evidence, wasn't it? I could show it to someone. But who? The police? And evidence of what?

Weekend's chest was quivering beneath my fingers. I hadn't realized I was stroking it.

"I'm sorry, boy," I murmured, getting back to work.

My hand stung with the cold. The plywood had been a slap job, but this rope had been well knotted.

When he was finally loosed, I led Weekend through the frame of the window, shielding him from its jagged glass teeth. His flanks were heaving in uneven bursts, but he didn't lope away from the site of his imprisonment. Something in him had changed. He huddled by my side, and I couldn't tell if he was offering me protection from some unnamed threat, or still too scared to make a move.

CHAPTER TWENTY-SEVEN

I thumbed buttons on my cell as I drove home, Weekend silent in the backseat. I had to send a crew out to Ned's house immediately now that I had opened that makeshift barrier. I hadn't spent a moment fiddling with it once I'd freed Weekend—I didn't even stand the plywood back up. I had simply gotten the two of us away from there.

Turning the car into my snow-slicked drive, I parked and got out. Then I opened Weekend's door. The dog moved in his new, hesitant manner, setting his front paws on the ground, before easing

the rest of his body out and trailing behind me slowly.

I had just begun to twist the knob on
the front door when a low, deep rumble
started in Weekend's throat. I wasn't
sure if it was the aftereffects of his en-
trapment, or something else.

I placed my hand on his neck to calm
him. "It's okay," I murmured. "You're
okay now."

The dog's black lips rolled backwards,
exposing a fierce V of teeth. I could feel
the vibration of his growls against my
palm. I let go, and Weekend scooted
back a little, but didn't leave my side.
"Week?" I said. "What's wrong?"

I must've loosened the latch just
enough that when the wind gusted, the
front entry swung open. Weekend's
snarl split into a volley of barking, so
alarming that I yanked the door shut and
began to back away, down the porch
steps. "What is it, boy?" I whispered.
He was sliding after me, claws scrabbling on the snowy steps. "Is there
someone in the house?"

I saw a shape appear behind the curtain at one of the windows.

Teggie and Gabriel—they'd come back—was the thought in my head. No one else had the right to enter my house without permission. Not even Club, returned early for his dog.

But that shape didn't belong to my sister or her boyfriend—or to Club, for that matter. It was shorter, and tousle-topped. I looked again, and my shoulders slumped in relief. I should've known; I'd had cause to consider this possibility earlier today.

Weekend was huddled close to me on a hump of snow, and I reached down and patted him. "It's all right, boy. That's Dugger Mackenzie. It's just Dugger."

"You scared us," I said, when both the dog and I were safely ensconced inside.

"Sorry, Missus," Dugger said calmly. Then his face split into a grin. "That's Club's, right? Club's pet?"

I nodded. "Club's working, so I'm watching Weekend."

Dugger's face changed. "Something happened." I was wondering how—or what—to tell him when he said, "Cloak, smoke, poke," and I realized how Weekend and I must look, and smell, how badly we both needed baths.

"There was a fire," I said, and Dugger's glance slid away.

"Did you get my present, Missus?"

Weekend gave a shuddering shake, and Dugger looked at him.

"Yes," I said, suppressing my own shiver. "I did."

"Dog needs water," Dugger said. "Food, too."

I glanced up.

"He had himself a fright."

"He was scared when you were in the house—"

"No," Dugger broke in. "Worse than that."

As my eyes narrowed—how did Dugger know these things?—he went on, "You want to get him back to normal quick. Quick, lick—"

"Okay," I broke in. The advice made sense. But I wasn't sure how to follow it. I didn't have any dog food, and the grocer in town was about to close up for the night.

Dugger ducked away behind me, a sudden, graceful move, occupying a space I wouldn't have thought big enough to hold anyone. Then I heard the suck of the refrigerator door. Dugger returned with a package of hamburger my mother must've supplied. Not the freshest, then, but the first barks I'd heard in hours began as Dugger tore away the cellophane, and placed the pound of meat on the floor.

"Okay?" he asked me. The dog had lowered his snout, and was ripping pink coils apart. I nodded, and Dugger went on. "Now we can go and listen?"

Something inside me winced at the idea of being upstairs alone with Dugger. I felt shame for my reaction, then dumb for being ashamed. I hardly knew this person. And one thing I did know was that his brain didn't work in the usual way. But I also feared saying no. Dugger had never been anything but kind to me. But if I made him angry—or even if he simply got upset again and had none of that medication along with him—then things might truly go bad.

Weekend was here, I reasoned. He'd shown the ability to watch out for me. If anything went wrong, the dog would be upstairs in a flash, fangs bared.

I added a bowl of water to his meal—still far from a dog owner, but figuring things out—then led the way to Brendan's study.

The computer was still booted, with Dugger's device attached. He slid into Brendan's chair and brought up the long list of files.

"Which ones did you hear?" he asked, with a white flash of teeth.

"Um . . ." The sound came out tonelessly to my ears. "This one." I pointed, so as not to touch Dugger's hand on the mouse. "And this—this—all of those." I traced a row of file names with my finger, deliberately failing to indicate the one called *Barn*—I didn't want to reference that—but too late I realized it would've been better to say I had already heard it.

Dugger began playing it without a trace of hesitation or embarrassment. I closed my eyes as the now familiar sounds started—the thumps, that crash, the rhythmic huffing—cringing while I waited for the recording's final, universal noise of fulfillment. No flush suffused Dugger's cheeks as he listened until it was over, then quietly lifted the mouse and started scrolling through the files again.

I leaned against the desk, tired of standing. I felt as if I'd been on my feet for a very long time. Weekend seemed to be okay downstairs, although he must've finished eating, for I could hear him pacing around. I wondered when Club would come. Dark was rapidly descending, and I returned my focus to the monitor.

With Dugger at the helm, the search was focused and concise, whereas mine had been aimless. There was no clicking or false starts. Canned noises and voices came to life, only to be deemed the wrong ones and abruptly aborted. Dugger made the mouse leap over whole lines of titles, circling the cursor as his mind seemed to chug, remembering, then landing precisely on whichever file he'd been seeking. The one he decided on now was called *Seconds*.

Second servings? Seconds of time? I

couldn't get a handle on Dugger's naming scheme.

Before I could conjecture further, I heard the click of running footsteps on a floor or maybe it was pavement, then a woman's high-pitched call. "Wait! Baby, stop!"

Images of Baby leapt into my head—he was tall, good-looking, the woman was chasing after her departing lover—before the next bit of recording almost made me smile.

"Not in the street! Baby, slow down!"

A child's gurgle of laughter confirmed that the woman had no reason to caution her boyfriend about cars. There was a tangle of unintelligible sounds, then the rush of an engine, and behind it, muffled words as if the speaker held a small body up against her face. "Don't scare me like that again, baby. You have to hold my hand," she said, and the child let out another burbling laugh.

I looked down at Dugger. His face was bland, expressionless, his hand immobile on the mouse. "Who are those people, Dugger?" I asked at last. "When was that recording made?"

An explanation for the identical dates on the files crept up on me. If the recordings had been made on an old technology, and only recently rendered digitally, all the time stamps would be the same. Could "baby" have been Brendan or Red, the only two possibilities that seemed relevant enough for Dugger to want me to hear them? But the loving mother in the recording didn't sound like Eileen, although I supposed life events could've changed her voice along with everything else.

Dugger was studying the screen again. He clicked. And a file called *Heart* began to play.

These sounds too were violent, and my own heart began to hammer. What was Dugger interested in, where did his tastes run? A thick swell of nausea lifted my stomach. I realized I hadn't eaten since those slapped-together sandwiches.

The woman in this recording was screaming. "I can't! *I can't!* Don't! Not there, don't touch me there, don't make me move, no! Oh, no!" A moan with no pleasure in it, only pain. Then thrashing, and the unmistakable rasp of tearing fabric.

It was sex, but not consensual sex this time. I was listening to a rape.

"Dugger, stop it," I muttered. "Turn this off."

"Please, don't make me—don't make me do this—" she sobbed. Despair as drawn out as taffy. I had never realized before how intimate were the sounds of suffering. I had no right to be listening to this, to be overhearing.

I started to turn, walk for the door, but Dugger extended his arm. His fingers settled onto my wrist, as lightly as falling snow, yet the touch compelled me to stay.

On the recording came a bustle of people moving around, a low murmur of excited voices, unclear sounds of objects being moved. Things thrown across the floor. Wheels rolling maybe. There were more than two people on this recording. With a jolt of horror, I realized that there had been other participants, watching, or waiting to join in.

"No screaming," ordered one man,

while another echoed him in a kindly tone that was somehow worse than all the cries: "Try not to yell, honey."

"Oh, ow!" A shriek of pure pain, then an otherworldly howl. "Noooooo!"

I began, silently, to cry. Forced to listen, I felt violated in some small way myself.

Dugger looked at me, then at the numbers flashing by on the screen, tiny beacons in some countdown to hell. "Fifty seconds, Missus."

"No—" I said, forcing my voice down from the bellows I was hearing in the recording, aware that pushing Dugger had its own risks. "I can't take any more. Stop it now."

The woman had finally gone quiet, but a series of moist, slippery sounds had replaced her screams. I clapped my hands against my ears; that had to be body parts, slapping and mashing together.

"She's nearly through," Dugger said calmly, and I hated him then, for speaking of this poor woman at the same kind of remote remove that allowed the men to do this to her.

"Almost. Ah—almost. Almost there now. We're almost done."

Incoherent, guttural cries. "Uhn, uhn, *uhhhn!*"

"You did it!"

Impossibly, a woman began speaking, in a tone that could only be described as jocular. "That's the first time anyone's gone and ripped the sheets!"

Then came the high, thin wail of a newborn baby crying.

CHAPTER TWENTY-EIGHT

Tears flooded my eyes, too. I had already been crying out of fear and shock, but these sobs came for a whole other reason.

Dugger finally seemed unsettled, scrabbling around in his pockets. Of course he hadn't been frightened before; he knew what he'd recorded. My fear had probably seemed inexplicable to him. With a branding stab of guilt, I recalled the momentary hatred I'd felt toward Dugger for subjecting me to something I was all wrong about.

"Missus?" Dugger said.

He was cupping a silver rectangle, aiming its round black eye at me.

My ears were so clogged I could hardly make out the sound of Dugger's voice; it was as if he were speaking to me through water or after a suddenly steep airline descent. I had no idea why I was being photographed.

He must've recognized my confusion. "Nobody takes pictures then."

The moment of lucidity sliced through the muddiness in my head. "What?" I cried, then lowered my tone, afraid of losing him. "I mean, when? When don't they take pictures?"

"The worst," he said softly. "The cursed, the ones about to burst . . ."

It was a rhyme, but not only a rhyme, more of a description.

I peered at him, frowning. There was meaning here, some import to the photos Dugger chose to snap, the things he saw fit to record.

Suddenly, he pitched forward, stooping over Brendan's desk. His hand began racing across buttons on the keyboard, so fast that I couldn't believe he would accomplish anything. But a series of photographs began to appear on the screen, conjured up by his flying fingers.

A car wreck, the vehicle accordion-folded, its occupant being lifted into an ambulance on the corner of Water Street.

The kitchen of a dilapidated house on the outskirts of town, its refrigerator open, empty.

A man standing in a lot near the consolidated school, where a new foundation was being poured, holding a cold pack to his head with an obvious grimace of pain.

Someone staring at a shattered figurine on the floor, tears rolling down her cheeks.

Photographs kept scrolling by, Dugger's fingers slipping, more careless now, closing shots before I really got a look at them. Gray faces, and tired, sloped bodies, caught in places throughout Wedeskyull and poses that seemed to have no connection.

And then I finally saw the link. All of these people were hurting in some way.

I raised my face to Dugger. His eyes had gone wide and wild; there was a frenzied look in the whites of them.

Weekend entered the room at a run, skidding to a halt before his body could bang into either of ours. His hind quarters brushed against a shelf and two books fell over. As I stooped to stand them up, I saw a tiny volume lying between.

The twin to Bill's journal. Brendan's photo album.

I took it out and checked to make sure. The pages wafted by, a rainbow of years. I closed my eyes momentarily. The album had never been taken at all. It had stayed right here in this house, paged through by my husband, perhaps on the last night he was alive.

There came a low, throaty rumble, and I looked to see Dugger stroking Weekend's head blindly. He was staring straight ahead, but his eyes were losing that crazed expression. After a moment, I approached them both, bending to bury my face in the dog's fur. Dugger was calming down, and Weekend also seemed back to normal now. It was I who had changed. I didn't sneeze as I breathed in warmth from the dog. I wasn't allergic anymore. It was the only good thing in this whole fathomless mess, the one thing that could distract me from the glimpses of my husband in years gone by, and everything else that I'd just heard and seen.

Dugger left in the time it took me to lift my head from Weekend. I hadn't even noticed. How many times had Dugger slipped away unheard, unseen? He seemed to have a gift for such sleight of form.

I went downstairs, spent, alone except for Weekend, but still hungry. The hamburger meat had been consumed, its Styrofoam tray licked clean. I freshened the dog's water bowl, then fixed myself a sandwich, which I ate listlessly, one bite after another. The raging in my stomach began to quiet, although my spirit remained unstill.

I had to get out of here. For a few days at least. I couldn't stay in this house, concealed by snow, the echo of that baby's first cries in my ears. A shadowy sense of loss that I couldn't identify plagued me.

There was only one place I could think of to go.

I looked down at Weekend, sniffing for scraps on the floor as I finished off my hasty meal. "Okay, Week," I said. "Let's see if your master's gotten home." The dog lifted his head. "Just have to throw a few things together first," I went on. Mentally planning, I added a quick phone call to my list of to-do's.

Ned wouldn't be at home, of course, but the number for his cell might be in the business folder that I'd begun putting together on my computer. I could hardly stand to approach the machine again, sidling over to it as if there might be real monsters contained within, rapists, madmen, unknown others. I forced my eyes to zero in only on my own sparse list of files, ignoring anything imported from Dugger.

Weekend stood patiently by me, tongue lolling, sides rising and falling as I phoned.

"This is Ned."

I felt an almost irresistible urge to tell him everything, break down in the comfort of his response. We were going back and forth, the two of us, consoling each other. But I just said, "It's Nora. Did your cabin turn out to be free?"

"Nora?" he said. "No. It's occupied till Saturday." He hesitated. "A group of ice fishermen actually. I'll be at the inn in town tonight." Another pause. "Why?"

I hesitated only a second. "I'm going away for a few days. Out of town. You'd be welcome to stay here."

There was silence again over the line. "Any particular reason you're leaving town?"

"No," I said honestly. "I just feel the need for a little time away."

"Straight?" Ned said, and it took me a moment to get what he meant, recall the conversation we'd had in his house, but then I responded, "Straight," and he said, "Well, then, thanks. I'd appreciate that."

Weekend didn't leave my side as I finished my preparations. In addition to my pack, weighed down with the usual, plus enough clothes for a getaway, I took one other thing from home. Brendan's box. Something about Dugger's recordings told me it was time to go through the relics of my husband's past as well.

The task might be a little easier away from the home that we'd shared.

With Weekend straining to get out into the cold night air, I lingered for a moment on my porch. I had left two lights burning for Ned, and the rooms were neat and tidy. They'd always stayed on the spare side, and had only become more so in Brendan's absence. I had hoped that a tangle of kids would introduce some disorder and chaos one day. Still, they provided a warmth and familiarity I knew I would miss. For a beat of time, I regretted my momentary impulse. This was my home now, and only in the leaving of it did I realize how bereft I would be to live anywhere else.

Weekend's claws dug into the porch floor as we emerged from the house. Someone had come by and shoveled off today's accumulation. Another small-town favor. I wondered if whoever it was had seen Dugger inside, witnessed any of the tumult tonight, and I realized that I didn't really mind if they had. Somewhere along the line, I'd come to rely on the way people in a small town worried, nosed, and cared.

Maybe the warning I'd received at Ned's house was a small-town favor, too, albeit one that had frightened the hell out of an innocent dog. But in any case, it wasn't one I could heed any longer. The ability to look away had been stolen from me. Or maybe a need to examine had been bequeathed.

I descended the porch steps, and crunched with the dog over a wide expanse of snow.

Club lived on the far side of Wedeskyull, hardly in town at all, but for a scatter of houses around his. They were all of a piece, a hundred or so years old, too nondescript despite their age to inspire any urge to restore. Boxy frames, stumpy porches, a plain smattering of rooms. Lights blazed throughout Club's house and his Jimmy sat in the drive. I wondered why he hadn't come by for his dog.

Weekend started barking excitedly as soon as I parked. The drift at the side of the street stood well over my head. I leaned across to open the passenger door, and Weekend bounded up and over the hill of snow, paws sending down a spray of white. He stood at the top, waiting for me as I made my slower way around.

Snow frozen hard as concrete had begun to clot in the ruts of Club's driveway. Usually he scattered salt thickly enough that winter-skinny deer braved the outskirts of town to lick it. Weekend went slowly, seeming to hold himself back from the porch light that beckoned, while I reached down to his collar for support, skating and skidding my way up the drive.

I didn't recognize the lady who pulled open the door. She was buxom, with thick arms folded over pendulous breasts. Club had always been single, although according to Brendan, he took home a succession of hookups. Weekend greeted the woman with neither a growl nor a brush against her stout body.

"Club's not home," she said.

"Oh," I replied, patting Weekend's back. "I brought—I mean, I'm on my way out of town—I'm a friend of his," I finally concluded my string of inane fragments.

"I know who you are," the woman replied flatly. She reached out. "I'll take the dog."

I looked at her, not letting go of Weekend. "You know who—" Then I broke off, not sure why this plain, middle-aged woman inspired such idiocy on my part.

"Nora Hamilton, right?" she supplied. "The widow."

I waited for the inevitable *I'm sorry for your loss*, but it didn't come. "I don't think I know—"

She broke in brusquely. "I'm Ada Mitchell. Club's mother. I live upstairs."

These types of blunt bungalows made decent two-family residences, and I knew the historic society—comprised almost entirely of newcomers—often went head to head with the owners over doctoring their homes for extended families or extra rental income.

Since this lady didn't seem the type for pleasantries, I didn't bother extending my hand. "Is Club still at work?"

"Still, always," Mrs. Mitchell replied, lifting the twin stumps of her shoulders.

"That boy never stops working. Just like his daddy."

"Club's father was a policeman?" I couldn't remember if I'd ever known that.

"Good job for someone who likes to shoot," she replied, no spark or life in her eyes as she spoke. "In his case, it got him killed. They called it accidental, but when my husband discharged his weapon, it was never any accident." She peered out into the blackness. "Hope my boy fares better." But she didn't sound optimistic.

I was getting cold standing on the porch. I stamped my feet in their boots, and Weekend pressed closer to me, his big body lending warmth. Club's mother didn't appear to feel the temperature, even in her thin housedress.

"Mrs. Mitchell?" I said. "Would it be all right if I came in for a few minutes?" I was trying to drum up some explanation as to why, but it turned out to be unnecessary.

"No, I don't think you want to do that," Club's mother replied, easing her plentiful shadow over so it eclipsed the front door. She reached out a hand and bundled up Weekend's leash in a leathery knot so that she could pull the dog in without slack. He went to her obligingly, but upturned his face, chocolate gaze meeting mine one last time.

"I'm sorry?" I said, stalling. All of a sudden, it seemed a bad idea to have come here, to be dropping off the dog, or leaving town at all.

Weekend rushed at me, and I bent down, receiving a wet faceful of fur. Mrs. Mitchell stepped outside into the frigid night, drawing the dog back with neither gentleness nor aggression, just a simple, stolid tug. As she moved to do so, I caught a glimpse inside.

What I saw made no sense. Club was on duty now, using his department-issued car, and department-issued weapon. So why would his gun cabinet, displayed in its prominent place by the door and containing his private collection of arms, have been left ajar?

WARNING

A few days ago, the Chief had given Club an assignment.

"I'd like you to pay a visit to Jean Hamilton's house this morning," he'd said. "The one in town. Nobody's home."

Club had looked levelly at the Chief.

"Jean made a trip upstairs the day of the funeral," the Chief went on. "Saw her go myself. Might be she was just getting a little peace and quiet. Might be she wasn't. So I want you to take a look around. See if there's anything that stands out. Looks awry."

"Isn't that a little vague?" Club had said, holding the Chief's gaze.

"You're a police officer, boy," the Chief replied. "You know how to pick something out that don't belong?"

Club had felt his jaw muscles clench and his vision grow shady. He'd said that he would go, turning back only to ask how the Chief could be sure that Nora wouldn't return while he was looking. The Chief promised he would take care of that part.

At the end of the week, the Chief summoned Club into his office. "A report should've come in," he said. "I want you to take care of it."

Club nodded.

The Chief walked behind his desk. "Might've been made by someone at Ay-Ay-Ay, might be the grease monkey over at that flashy Mobil. Could even be Al. Somebody fancying himself some kind of detective."

Club crossed his arms over his chest. He wasn't sure where this was going, and he never liked to be in the dark where the Chief was concerned. The

Chief used him as a battering ram, always had, but Club knew he was capable of much more than that.

"Whoever it is suspects intentional damage to an engine," the Chief continued. He was tapping idly with one hand on the keyboard, not hard enough to depress any keys. "Red Honda Civic." The Chief paused again. "Alpha kilo golf, one niner four seven."

Then Club understood how the Chief had given him the time he needed at Nora's house.

But when he went looking, there was no report.

Would an obvious tampering job go unnoticed, especially with that same car now driving around perfectly fine? Club knew it was being driven—he'd seen Nora in it.

The pieces clicked together. Club figured out who else might have had his hands on Nora's car. Someone who, even if he did put things together, wouldn't go to the police.

Club felt relief seep into him. His father had brawn without brains, but Club possessed both. He'd never make the same mistake the old man had.

Club took the Mountaineer. When the Chief went off duty, he left it parked in the lot by the barracks.

Just the other day the Chief had gone from shift patrols—one man on at a time, round-the-clock—to partnering them and daytime-only coverage. Club wasn't entirely behind him on it. Lurcquer had objected loudly as well, the day the Chief paired him back up with Landry, and Club had been glad for the support, though he didn't generally side with Lurcquer on anything.

But the Chief wanted things back to normal.

"We've had a bit of a shake-up," he'd said. "And we've dealt with that well. But there are civilians to think of. They're going to start wondering what's wrong. I don't want people feeling scared in their beds at night."

The SUV tolerated Club's driving—no, more than that: it welcomed it. Its tires pulverized banks of snow when he rode up too high and took every bend without sliding. Too bad there was only one such vehicle. Maybe Club would be granted it officially someday.

Once the Mountaineer would've gone to Brendan, along with everything else. Club had accepted that, even though Brendan wasn't cut out for the job the same way he was. Both their fathers had been cops, but Brendan's old man had been pretty lackluster, while Club's had been a pitbull, ready to face off with anything. His father's ways were a legacy to live up to, even if his end had to be avoided at all costs. And now Brendan's end had come about prematurely as well, which put Club in an altogether different position, and he wasn't sure how he felt about that.

Could you miss someone like hell and still be glad they were gone?

Club steered around the huge boulder, which used to be such an obstacle when they drove out here in high school to get wasted. When you were stoned, the rock seemed to have faces in it, to look at you with eyes. Now Club was glad for the rock. For a while it had served as guard, as sentry, preventing sight of the torn-up patches of earth. No adult was likely to drive way the hell out here, especially in winter, but kids just might. And now it would be okay if they did. The holes were covered with snow, the ground blank and white as a sheet. Come springtime, when the dirt thawed, they'd have to redo their work by hand, deeper into the woods. But it'd been hard to get Paulson's bucket loader in even as far as this.

Club made a full circle around the looming boulder and drove out.

Time for the real purpose of the night.

When he knocked on the door of the first-floor apartment, one of only a few such buildings in town, Club was met with wild eyes. "Whoa," he said, extending both hands, palms up. "I'm just here because of Dave. He wants us to meet him."

"Dave?" Dugger repeated. "Save, pave, cave."

Club waited patiently till the rhymes petered out. Then he said, "Come on."

Dugger noticed the loaded gun rack on the Mountaineer as soon as they got outside. "Dave's gone hunting?" he asked.

Club nodded. "When he's got the urge, he's got the urge."

Dugger didn't respond to that.

Club opened the passenger door, stopping himself from buckling Dugger in, but only just. The rest of them had grown up, found women, jobs, lives of their own. Dugger never had, though he was older than they were. He had Al, and he had his mother. That was about it.

Club drove in the opposite direction of the woods he'd just come from, heading into other desolate wilderness.

"Not much out in the dark," Dugger said, his voice steady. "Lark, spark—"

This time Club cut him off. "Maybe he's after coons."

He swiveled the big wheel with one arm and pulled up hard beside a ditch. The woods spread out all around them, nothing visible besides snow and limbs.

Club opened his door and jumped down. He reached above him to take down his gun, cocking it, and locking.

Dugger joined him on a high-drifted heap. "Where's Dave?"

This was almost too easy. Club pointed. "In there." He led the way.

They had gotten half a mile in when Dugger finally made the connection. His mind didn't work like other people's did; sometimes he failed to take logical leaps at all.

"Didn't see Dave's car."

That was when Club swung.

He used the rifle to knock Dugger to his knees, bashing him in the shoulder, deciding to avoid the head for now.

Dugger's face was hanging, spittle drizzling out onto the snow.

"Dave?" he said in a whimper.

Club stood over him. "You always did like to track, kid," he said. "But tonight you tripped and fell into me. My rifle discharged. I can make it look like an accident. That's if anyone would miss you enough to report you gone."

His voice was a harsh rasp by this point, emitting labored puffs of white into the dark night. He had the feeling Dugger didn't understand a word of what he was saying.

His head was still dangling, and he'd started to bring one careful hand to his shoulder.

Club jabbed him again with the butt of the gun, hard enough that Dugger screamed, a high, pathetic scream, like a mountain cat or a woman. Not a woman. Dugger was more like a kid, forever surprised that anything could hurt this much. His head dropped so low that his bare face brushed the snow.

"You're helping her and I want you to stop," Club ordered. "Understand?"

"Grand, stand, lend a hand—"

"Cut it out!" Club yelled, louder than he'd intended, frustration a fever inside him. By sheer will, thinking only of his old man and what happened when he'd lost control, Club forced his voice to drop. "You get me, you retard? You know what I'm telling you to do?"

Dugger lifted his face, partially flecked with white and dripping. He was trying to rub his shoulder, flinching every time he did, then bringing his hand up again as if he'd forgotten what effect it would have.

Words came to Club with a blinding

jolt. The guys on the force thought he was loyal to Nora for Brendan's sake. But Club wasn't loyal to anyone.

"Leave her alone. Or I'll hurt her next."

Then he left Dugger there in the snow.

CHAPTER TWENTY-NINE

There were guns missing from Club's case, at least one, I was sure.

The lights had been on in the foyer. When Club's mother stepped forward, I had seen yawning space, an empty column where something usually stood. The cabinet was tall, built for rifles. Club would keep his handguns somewhere else, just as Brendan had kept his official weapon in a lockbox in our closet.

Club's need for a rifle while on duty made less sense with every mile I covered.

The wilderness receded little by little,

acres of snow and stalks of white woods giving way to the occasional shock of dull green or brown. I'd forgotten how in other places it sometimes ceased to snow for a while, and sporadic thaws melted the accumulation.

I stopped for a sandwich at the first rest area, many miles south. The packed rows of cars and streaming bodies stunned me. It was almost 11:00 p.m. and I could've bought a burger or a doughnut or sunglasses in a building lit bright as day. I had to pause for a moment in the whirlpool of people circling me. Then I returned to my car and drove on.

My parents lived ten miles from my sister, in the suburbs before the bridge, but in addition to determining that it'd be better to show up at this hour in the city that never sleeps, it was always Teggie I was headed for, Teggie I needed to see. No one else could soothe me like my sister, make me feel I was still tethered by something to this planet.

She lived in an apartment on one of the anonymous, unbeautiful blocks south of Lincoln Center. It wasn't the most upscale area, but it wasn't bad, either. Teggie said she felt safe coming home late at night. I circled for ten minutes before finding a spot a few blocks away.

There was no doorman in the building, so I'd have to ring up despite the hour. I took everything out of the car, and remembered to lock my doors, before climbing the single stone step and pulling open a door that led into a vestibule. My hands and even my legs trembled with exhaustion. It seemed like months had passed since I'd almost lost Weekend at the fire, or glimpsed Club's missing gun.

A male voice answered my brief, cautious tap on the buzzer. It sounded sleepy and annoyed. He was expecting either a mistake or careless exploitation: somebody stabbing buttons randomly, hoping the desire to get back to sleep would prevail over good city sense.

It hadn't occurred to me that my sister would no longer be living alone.

"Gabriel," I said, softly into the speaker. "Hi. It's Nora."

* * *

Teggie was brewing coffee by the time the old, creaking elevator opened on her floor. I had to remind her that I no longer drank it. She put water on for tea instead.

"Are you hungry?" she asked, and I shook my head. For once I wasn't. The rest stop sandwich sat in my stomach like a ball of paste.

My sister wore a T-shirt askew on her shoulders, and nothing else; Gabriel had pulled on jeans, but his muscular chest was bare. I had interrupted something, or else they were just sleeping naked, but either way, their sudden slide toward partnership baffled me. How could my sister be there and I here? It was a total reversal of the hemispheres, the earth shifted on its axis.

As if reading my thoughts, Gabriel straightened from where he was slouching by the fridge. "I need something a little warmer. Teg?"

"My robe?" she said, and he left the room.

I couldn't stop my head from spinning. They would have children, Gabriel and Teggie, the ones I'd so longed for. My sister's lithe body would swell and distort, pushed in ways she hadn't made it go.

This was why Dugger's recording had hit me so hard. Not because of the shock, after being so sure that I'd been listening to an appalling crime, but because it reminded me of everything I had lost, everything I would never have. Brendan hadn't wanted kids—I'd known that even before we married—but I never doubted that eventually I'd either convince him or there'd be a mishap, some spontaneous burst of passion that got the better of both of us.

For the first time I realized that it must've been Red's death that had made parenthood such a dread prospect for my husband. He believed—Eileen had led him to believe—that he would not only fail at the job, but destroy it completely. I pressed my eyes shut, but couldn't stop the tears from falling, a dike giving way beneath too much pressure.

Teggie squeezed my hand. She

pushed a cup of tea across her small square of counter.

I drank.

Gabriel reentered the room, dressed, although still in bare feet, a faded blue drape of terry cloth over his arm for my sister. "Want me to take the couch?" he asked, looking at Teggie. "You guys can sleep in your room?"

I never would have asked or even accepted aloud. But when my sister said, "If you don't mind, G," a tidal swell of gratitude rose inside me. To sleep in the warmth of another—someone who loved me in her own way as much as Brendan had—was almost too much for me right now, and at the same time, exactly the right thing. I met Gabriel's gaze, nearly on the level of my own, and tried to come up with words.

Gabriel found them for me.

"That terry-cloth number's pretty hot, Nora," he said, and I laughed. "Try to resist."

"He's funny," I told Teggie, as we lay curled in her bed, and I saw her nod in the dark. Then she must've said, "I don't know how I ever lived without him," or something like it, because I remembered thinking as I finally dropped off to sleep, *I felt that way once.*

CHAPTER THIRTY

Teggie and Gabriel were both gone by the time I woke up the next morning. There was a stack of folded blankets on the couch. I padded around, finding Teggie's hastily scrawled note of explanation, her whereabouts for the day, then made tea and fixed breakfast from the groceries Gabriel now kept the kitchen stocked with. My sister's refrigerator used to contain nonfat yogurt and Vitamin Water.

Brendan's yellow flannel box sat beside my sack on the floor, and I knew I was putting off the task at hand. The apartment was warm, heat coming up through the radiators, hissing reproach. I slid a palm across the worn fabric covering, then shimmied up the lid where it stuck, and looked inside.

I set aside the first item I came across, a thin stack of letters. First I flipped quickly through them to make sure they were in fact letters, as opposed to printed-out emails. But no, here was real stationery, some of the sheets still in actual envelopes, and the sight seemed such an anachronism, weighty for its rarity today, that I couldn't stand to look more closely yet.

Several of the objects I'd caught glimpses of before: a toy soldier identical to the ones Bill Hamilton kept on his shelves, a water-polished stone, a key ring. I picked each one up to give Brendan's collection of trinkets its due—the collection of a lifetime, as it turned out—then put them all down on the comforter that covered Teggie's bed. The coil of red skate laces went near the rest of my accumulation, as did the photo of Brendan and Red.

There was another photograph of

Brendan, not as a child but in the full flush of manhood, and the sight of it stole my breath. I had to work to take in air, seeing my husband again, out of the blue like that. Someone stood to the left of Brendan's broad shoulder, but whoever it was had gotten mostly cut out of the shot. I could make out only a slice of face, its features indistinct, and a spill of pretty hair to indicate the person's gender, as well as one hand lying on Brendan's arm.

A few receipts clipped to a business card came next. A Second Empire Victorian mansion had been sketched on a cardboard rectangle, to the right of some dignified script.

The Looking Glass Inn
Cold Kettle, New York
Come get away

I'd never heard of the place. The bits of paper attached to it were room bills.

I began to grow warm. This apartment was getting overheated. I stood up and

made my way over to the bedroom radiator. I spun its rusty dial all the way
down, but the steam continued to *tsk-
tsk,* and I suspected that I wasn't changing anything at all.

I snatched up Brendan's box and
dumped the remaining items out on
Teggie's bed.

That bumper sticker for Stonelickers
with its graphic logo. It looked as if it
might be a bar. I slid my finger up and
down the shiny rectangle

The final item was another photo,
identical to the one that had laid me flat
a few minutes ago. Brendan standing
tall and proud, most of his companion
lopped off cleanly. Except this second
one had *In Wedeskyull* jotted down on
the back.

And something else.

Across the top was a rust-colored
smear, dried dark, like oil paint.

Why did Brendan have two copies of
the same poorly posed photograph?
And how did one come to be blood-
stained?

* * *

I stalked around Teggie's apartment, still shrinking from the one thing I knew might shed some light on that picture. The constant soundtrack of noise was making it hard for me to think. Horns, sirens, squealing brakes, the clank of a garbage can being overturned. Voices, shouts, spitting, curses. All of it audible, or else conjured up by my over-fevered brain.

I pulled my unbuttoned shirt off, leaving on only a tank. My efforts with the radiator hadn't worked; Teggie's bedroom was as sweltering as the cramped rest of her apartment. I went back to the bed, crawled across it, and tugged at a window. It opened with a sticky separation of paint, and the volume of the city instantly increased.

Then I picked up the stack of letters, leafing through them, directing my gaze toward the bottom of the pages.

They were all signed by someone named Amber.

Hi! began what seemed to be the first, judging by its placement in the stack. The writer hadn't included dates at the top of each page. *I hate it here, you were wrong, it's not any warmer, but I'm learning a lot. Miss you like crazy, though. When will you come down?*

The next letter referred to a visit. *Everybody's jealous of me now that they've seen you. They always said I'm way too serious—now it's* we're *way too serious—like we're thirty-year-olds or something.*

That made the corners of my mouth lift momentarily. Thirty. That old.

Then again, they're all scrounging dates at the dining hall or fooling around at parties. They're just posers, trying to act like real college students. And then there's me. I know everything about you and always will. I used to hate having no one to tell my secrets to. Remember when you first told me about—I won't even write it down?

Was the girl referring to Red? Did Brendan used to talk about his brother more freely?

I scanned the rest of the letters, but they were more of the same, references to how lucky Amber was to have Brendan, especially since she was studying

so intensely and had no time for anything else. Had this been a college romance? I'd thought I was the only girl-
friend Brendan had in college.

And then something changed.

**We always said we couldn't live
without each other. But maybe we're
not as similar as we think. What I
want most when it comes down to it
might not make you happy.**

How articulate and well spoken this
girl had been. I couldn't help admiring
her a little.

**And I think Tell Spring might be
good for me. I really do. I know I said
I didn't want to go at first and I know
it's far away. But I can establish resi-
dency and have a good chance of
getting into one of the best state
schools in the country.**

Amber hadn't even been in college
yet. A high school romance then. Had
she been in some kind of accelerated
residential program? That would fit with
how she described herself as serious,
and loving to learn.

**You could come, too. We could still
be together. But I know you never**

would. I know you'll never leave the Dacks, not for very long anyway. And maybe it's better that you don't.

I had no idea why. Why Amber was moving, abandoning her program if that's what it was, nor why she thought Brendan wouldn't have come.

The final letter contained a poignant, heartfelt plea.

I just want the normal things, the things every girl wants. I want you to meet my parents. Why haven't you ever? I want you to describe our future to me, nights when we're lying alone. And I want—I want to be able to say the last thing I want.

I wondered what it was. I reread this girl's words and tried not to exult in the fact that Brendan had given at least some of those things to me.

The script on these letters—simple, graceful—was the same as on the photograph. I scrabbled around amongst the disarray on the bed, lifting the photo with the dark red smear.

The words *In Wedeskyull* had been written by Amber. It didn't take a handwriting expert to tell me that.

And so it must be Amber who was cut off in the picture.

I tossed the papers into a fragile heap. There was nothing to be gleaned from them.

Nothing besides the fact that my husband had been in love with someone long before me.

CHAPTER THIRTY-ONE

To a lot of people this discovery wouldn't have been such a hammer blow. Most couples had an unspoken rule: anything that happened before the two of them didn't count. But Brendan and I weren't like that. Rather than the free pass of that-was-before-our-time, Brendan and I had a rule of firsts. We were each other's firsts. We'd done this and that for the first time together. Said I love you. Met the family. Gone on vacation.

Or so I'd thought. Been led to believe.

If Brendan had been involved in some fiery teenage romance, one he'd traveled for, one that made other kids jealous with its apparent seriousness, one to put in the offing a long-distance move—where was Tell Spring anyway?—then I should've known about it.

How often had I said that by now about Brendan and me? The thought brought on a queasy swell of nausea. I stumbled to the kitchen for another bite to eat.

Then I let myself out of Teggie's apartment, securing it with the spare ring of keys she'd left on top of her note. I walked down Tenth Avenue in the kind of daze the city doesn't take kindly to. People cut around my slow, halting pace, their bodies sharp as blades. Tires sent showers of yellow-black slush onto my jeans whenever I wandered too close to the curb.

I made my way to Gabriel's studio. He and Teggie looked up as I entered through the heavy metal door, but a sound system continued playing, and the assembled dancers kept leaping and turning across an acre of wood.

Gabriel clapped his hands together. "That's it for this morning, ladies. Take an extra thirty on me." He strolled over and stopped the CD.

There were a few whoops amidst scattered murmurs of disappointment. As they toweled off and shimmied on sweats, the dancers looked like I often felt when my eyes were tearing so badly I couldn't scrape away another inch of wallpaper; or my legs started wobbling, high up on a ladder, and I simply had to climb down then or slip a few minutes later from exhaustion.

I couldn't imagine ever looking or feeling that way again.

I still hadn't said one word.

Gabriel was steering Teggie toward me, tossing her a hoodie to put on over her low-slung sweats. "Come on," he said to us. "Let's go get some lunch."

We walked to a hole in the wall for Chinese.

Gabriel ordered a lunch special, but Teggie left it at steamed wontons.

She smiled at me. "I'm not dancing as much these days. I've gained weight for the first time since ninth grade."

I tried to smile back. I ordered soup.

After the waiter had walked off, my sister handed me a printout of a Web page.

"What is this?" I asked, without looking.

"Read it," Teggie said, a patient tone in her voice that I didn't like.

I looked down. The black copy read simply: SOS. SURVIVORS OF SUICIDE. LOCAL CHAPTERS. And an 888 number to call. "Great, Teg," I muttered. "Thanks."

"There's a regular meeting in Troy," she said.

"Only a hop, skip, and a jump," I responded, and she rolled her eyes.

"It's near enough," she said before going on. "Look, Nor, I think this could be good for you."

"You know who you sound like?" I said. "Dad."

The sharp plains of Teggie's face reddened. The waiter brought our food. Steam billowed up from my soup. I lowered my nose to it to conceal my own flushed cheeks.

"I don't sound *anything* like Dad," Teggie said, ignoring her dish. "I'm saying this'll give you a chance to talk. Go over things with other people who've been there."

"Maybe I don't want to go over things anymore," I said, slurping up some broth.

"Well, that's not exactly surprising. And look who's calling who *Dad*." My sister glanced at Gabriel. "You're the one who came here, you know. You came to us."

I couldn't stop myself. "To you," I said. "I thought I was coming to you."

Teggie looked at Gabriel again. "You can't have it both ways, Nor. If I'm the one who customarily makes you *go over things*"—her voice lilted in mimicry—"then presuming you'd find me alone and ready to do just that doesn't exactly help your case."

Gabriel must've touched her on the leg because her own hand dropped beneath the table.

"Did you say 'have it both ways'?" I asked mildly.

Teggie shrugged at me, a sharp lift of her shoulders.

"I don't have it any way, Teg," I said, still mild. "No way at all. Don't you know that?"

Teggie thrust her white china plate away.

"Of course I know it," she said. "How could I help but know it? How could anyone help but know about the pity party for Nora? Help but try and comfort her, commiserate, and conceal their own happiness—"

"Oh yeah," I interrupted. "You've done a great job concealing your—"

"Ladies." Gabriel set down his pair of chopsticks. "You know you're both going to regret the vitriol—however well scripted—so why don't we all just take five?"

I turned on him. "Is that dancer speak?" I asked, while my sister snapped, "Save it, G."

I looked at her. "Don't be mean to him."

She started to smile. "See? You can't help but like him."

It was a rare peace offering from my sister, but I didn't take it. "T-E-G-I," I muttered.

Gabriel looked up. "Why are we spelling?"

"Shut up, Nora," Teggie said.

Swallowing a last mouthful, I lifted my head and stared at my sister.

"And aren't we missing a few letters?" Gabriel went on.

Teggie sighed.

"I'm sorry," I said brightly. "Does he not know?"

"Know what?"

Teggie flicked a graceful hand in Gabriel's direction. "Go ahead. Tell him."

But suddenly I was tired, deflated. Teggie and I had done this routine together often enough before, and it was usually amusing, a memory shared by siblings of their parents, taking aim at the most furious or ludicrous things as if they were all fodder for humor.

"Go on," Teggie urged, in control again.

The waiter appeared and dropped a scrap of yellow paper on the table.

"It's not her real name," I said at last. They were so close. How had this never come up?

He looked at us both, a question that quelled my sigh.

"Temperamental," I began, feeling absurdly grateful when Teggie joined in, and the two of us finished in singsong. "Excitable, grouchy, irritable."

Gabriel still had a question on his face. He ignored the check.

"They're all traits my parents said she had as a baby," I explained.

"Nora was calling me Teggie before she ever learned to say my real name," my sister added.

"Wow," Gabriel said, laying a few bills on the table. "That's kind of . . . awful."

Teggie and I both laughed.

"I guess your real name must be hard to pronounce," he said, after a moment. "Or else really ugly. Scheherazade? Myrtle?"

Teggie gave him another laugh, then nodded in my direction.

"Lora," I supplied. "Her name is L-o-r-a. Nora and Lora, like a little twin-set or something, when we're fifteen months apart."

"Yeah," Teggie said. "At least this way I have my own identity."

"Some identity," Gabriel said.

Teggie looked at him, and I watched her perception shift. From something accepting, almost pleased even, to troubled. She was seeing things as he did now. They each held the other's gaze, and I walked out, leaving them to it.

After this morning, I couldn't stand to bear witness to the coming together, the knitting and pairing that takes place between a couple who are falling deeply in love.

CHAPTER THIRTY-TWO

I spent the rest of the afternoon uptown on campus, meandering along the same paths Brendan and I used to walk, grateful for the weather, which was mild. I was thinking about how Brendan had become intent on our returning to his hometown, after deciding against a career in law. Becoming a cop was partially an homage to his father. But I wondered if the motivation might also have been that Brendan of all people knew that before crimes could be tried, they needed to be solved.

The temperature was starting to drop

by the time I approached the concrete stoop that flagged Teggie's building, and fumbled for her ring of keys. I wondered what kind of plunge was happening back home.

Teggie and Gabriel met me at the door to the apartment.

"Someone's been trying to reach you," Gabriel said.

"There were twelve hang-ups," Teggie added. "From a 518 number."

I frowned.

Gabriel handed me the phone with the number already set to redial, but before I could press the button, the phone rang in my hand.

"Nora," Club said, his voice a low rumble. "I'm sorry to have to call with this."

For one crazy second, I thought of Weekend, left alone with Ada Mitchell, and I asked if his dog was all right.

Club ignored my question. "There's been another fire."

The firemen must have left something smoldering, ready to ignite. Or had somebody in fact set the fire at Ned's house, and returned to finish the job?

Maybe the same person who had warned me off by imprisoning Weekend.

"At your house, I mean," Club said, as if reading my thoughts. "Jean's house is the one I'm talking about."

It took me a while to determine that Club was referring to the farmhouse Brendan and I had shared, not Jean's foursquare out by Patchy Hollow.

By that time, Teggie and Gabriel were both standing close by, Teggie mouthing, *What?* and Gabriel silently urging her to wait.

There was a high, hysterical note in my voice when I finally stopped mumbling that I didn't know which house he meant. Then I said, "Ned! Ned's staying at my house! Is he—"

Club cut me off. "He's fine. Wasn't there at the time."

Something in me seemed to settle.

"Okay," I said. "Okay, then. I know what to do." I went on, thinking out loud in a way that should've told me all was not well. "I can work on two houses at once, that's all. Things at Jean's were never quite done anyway." I let out a trilling laugh that made Teggie flinch. "After all, this is what I do, right?"

There was silence over the line or cable, whatever it was that crossed the distance between the sparse and frozen Adirondacks and this crowded, melting city.

"Nora, I don't think you understand," Club said at last in a grief-clotted voice. "Jean's house didn't just catch fire. There's nothing left to fix up. It burned to the ground."

My knees bent robotically, and Gabriel was beside me, guiding me over to the sofa, phone still clutched in my hand. "Why didn't you call my cell?" My voice sounded muffled, indistinct. I couldn't think of anything besides this to ask. "How did you find me here?"

When Club's answer came, it contained neither comfort nor threat, just a simple, matter-of-fact reply.

"Your cell's dead. We're the police, Nora, don't worry. We can find you anywhere."

I had nowhere to go.

But I couldn't remain with Teggie and

Gabriel in their tiny apartment. New York City wasn't the right place for me anymore, if it ever had been. And my parents would be the worst people to be around right now, as much as it pained me to think so.

"I'm asking you to stay," Teggie said for the fiftieth time, crouching gracefully beside me the next morning, while I assembled items in my pack.

"Remember you accused me of wanting to have it both ways?" I said.

Teggie shrugged sharply, then nodded.

"Well, now I think you're the one wanting that," I said. "For me."

"Is this the part where I'm supposed to say naïvely, *What do you mean?*" Teggie asked. "And then you startle me with your clarity and insight?"

Gabriel reached down and gave Teggie's shoulder a squeeze. It looked as if it hurt. Muscles rippled beneath his shirtsleeve. "Ow," Teggie muttered.

I stood up, hoisting my sack. "You want me to face things," I said. "Deal with the cuts, however deep they are.

But now you're encouraging me to run away."

Teggie followed as I headed out of the room.

"Okay, okay," she said, giving me a hug at the door. "I guess I was wrong." She paused to offer a grin. "You did surprise me."

I managed a smile back. Then I went out to my car and drove away.

It is a strange and terrible thing to head back to a place you've never felt entirely a part of, knowing that now there is nobody there you can trust. Ned, who'd been living in both residences when the fires started, and whose hair color once sent Dugger into a spate of rhymes. *Red head, Red dead.* Or Dugger himself, with his recordings and riddles? And finally Club, whose missing rifle had made me suspicious only two nights ago.

The roads out of the city were clogged with traffic. Cars hitched and halted before me. I avoided the gas pedal, rolling forward through a toll plaza, slowly making my way north.

There were questions I had promised

Brendan I would answer, and those answers resided in Wedeskyull. Besides,
despite having no sure place to go,
somewhere along the line the town had
become my home.

There were things that were mine
there now. Not only the house I'd inhab-
ited, Jean's house, but also Ned's. He
needed me to transform it. Already I
could picture the multiple colors of exterior paint that would cast their reflection on the land, and a new, soaring
roof. When you change something like
that, a small piece of it belongs to you.

Miles passed in a meaningless blur.
An hour later, I noticed an abrupt change
from washed-out color to nothing but
white, and the temperature gauge suddenly dropped on my dashboard. But
little else registered. I rode with the window cracked to keep me sentient. When
I became chilled enough and hunger
grew pressing, I stopped for some tea
in a Styrofoam cup, and a tasteless egg
sandwich.

I had changed my ringtone after
charging my cell last night, so as to be
more alert to its intrusion now that I was

utterly dependent on it for contact with the outside world. The strategy worked, and I jumped in my seat when the first cacophonous lyrics blared. As I snatched the phone out of my sack, which lay across from me on the passenger side, the car wove. Someone honked, loud and long.

I straightened out, sailing past an exit. Then I glanced down at the screen, expecting Teggie, or possibly my mom, if she'd heard what had happened. It wouldn't be like her to initiate a call about it, though. Club again, with more news?

Instead I saw the phantom number that had appeared several times before. Impatiently, I hit the green icon and said hello. A silent exchange while driving seemed pointless, if not risky.

Only this time somebody spoke.

BURIED

Ned wore Zamberlan boots with snow-shoes, and a coat that was rated at twenty below. His only exposed skin was a millimeter circumference around his eyes and mouth. The hand-forged map he carried was almost impossible to grip in his gloves, and worse, hard to follow.

"They're patrolling this spot," his contact had said. "Frequently. You'll have to come around from the other side. If you get to a big, granite boulder, stop immediately and go back half a mile. You could be seen."

Ned climbed the sheer white wall of a hill, puffs of snow rising up every time he took an awkward, lunging step. He'd never been good in these things.

The sky was the same color as the hill. No color at all. Ned blinked a few times, disoriented, which he knew could happen out here. He shielded his face with one arm and took a look around. The hill was a clean, bare slope, completely free of trees, and he had an unobstructed view into the woods below. He was looking for the loud, synthetic colors that would signal a person, out of his true habitat and dressed to fight the elements, but he didn't spot any such flash. Ned began to suspect a trap, or at least another wild-goose chase. The battering in his chest pointed to the former, and Ned unclenched his gloved fists, breathing hard.

Two houses had caught fire, but because he hadn't been in either one at the time, Ned had to conclude that hurting or killing him wasn't the goal.

What was, then? The simple burning of his notes, when he'd obviously have computer backups? Not that there was very much to destroy. Any savvy member of the public should've been able to learn what Ned had. He was still collecting background, although he hoped that would change today.

A report of an industrial accident at Paulson's, the concrete plant in town, had come over the police channel, but was later revealed to have been a mistake. And suddenly an idea of Ned's for a story, the flouting of OSHA regulations, had snowballed into something potentially much larger, which Ned didn't yet have a handle on at all.

Snowballed, he thought. Appropriate out here.

Cold radiated off the whiteness all around, so that the snow seemed to emit cool, white breaths. Ned felt uncomfortable prickles descend beneath his coat.

He fought an impulse to turn, difficult in the snowshoes. Instead he launched out on another succession of slow, clumsy steps, making progress up the hill.

The map said he should come to a cave. His contact had described it as more of a rock overhang, piled so thickly with snow that walls had been formed. Ned squinted, shuffling ahead, and making a visor of his arm again. He thought he saw something and lurched toward it. The toe of one snowshoe got caught in a drift, and he went down.

Ned did an immediate push-up, lifting his torso from the snow. On his knees, he rested a moment, searching for that cave. If he had even seen one. It was impossible to make out detail amidst all the white.

A streak of color appeared. Something blue rose up from the spot where he'd imagined the cave to be.

Ned got to his broad, webbed feet again and resumed the arduous climb.

Now that he was nearing the top of the rise, he could see a road snaking up, maybe a hundred yards off. If you could call that white plateau a road—his Subaru wouldn't have been able to handle it. The road ran parallel to the woods barricading this immense sweep of white.

He arrived at the entrance to the cave, and somebody ducked out.

His contact.

"You made it," he said.

"What do you have for me, Lurcquer?" Ned asked.

Ned had encountered the cop a half dozen or so times before, at car accidents, or other orders of business relevant both to local reporter and cop. On each of those occasions, Lurcquer's face had been smooth, so expressionless that it looked painted. Now, however, he was frowning. Even the mask couldn't hide it.

"I hear you've been looking into conditions at Paulson's," he said.

"Who told you that?"

"Doesn't matter."

Ned took out an audio recorder, but Lurcquer reached down and folded his fist over Ned's. "Nothing with my voice."

Ned glanced at him. "Little hard to take notes in this weather," he said. "But okay." He used his teeth to remove one glove, then substituted a notepad for the recorder.

"Things there are worse than you've heard," Lurcquer continued.

Ned nodded.

"You want to look for a Melanie Cooper," Lurcquer went on.

Ned jotted down the name.

"She's going to tell you something people have other explanations for. But hers is probably closest to the truth."

Ned stopped scribbling. His hand had gone numb and he tugged his glove back on, putting the pad away for the moment. "Mind being a little less cryptic?"

Lurcquer looked at him. His bland stare had come back. "I gave you a name. Isn't that a good enough start? Look, you think I'm in the business of talking to reporters?"

Ned knew when he had pushed a source far enough. "I appreciate your talking to me."

"You've got plenty," Lurcquer said shortly. "You've got maybe more than you think."

Ned stared at the cop. He was out of practice, and had to remind himself that sources sometimes required cultivation, like rare plants. "Yeah?"

"Yeah."

Ned took a look around. "What's the cave like?"

Lurcquer glanced away briefly, then extended an arm. "It's a free country. Especially out here."

Ned ducked down to enter. Inside the roof was low, and he had to hunch over nearly in half. But the cave was at least ten feet in depth. And plenty light.

"Big place," he called out.

His voice, eerily displaced, echoed back off the walls of snow.

When he emerged, Lurcquer was already clomping off, a faraway streak of color against all the white.

The granite boulder Ned had been supposed to avoid was only a half mile away, according to Lurcquer. There must be something important there. Otherwise, why would the cops be patrolling so frequently? Why would his being spotted nearby be so bad?

Lurcquer had all but dared him to find out more. Deep in his reporter's gut, Ned knew he'd been given the biggest lead of all by being left alone out here.

Disparate pieces, requiring links. The

fires. Paulson's. Lurcquer's potential source.

Ned decided to head for the road that led up here—the one Lurcquer hadn't wanted him to take—and thus hopefully the rock. A landmark like that might be possible to locate. If it wasn't, Ned would simply retrace his steps back to his car.

He checked his compass from time to time, noting that he was walking roughly north/northeast, and keeping his eyes peeled. His head started to ache from the glare, and he had to fight to operate in the snowshoes. The road was icy and actually harder to traverse with the apparatus on his feet. Plus, Ned was trying to peer into the woods on either side, looking for a large rock. He decided to head for deeper snow.

There was a rock several yards off, between two trees, but when Ned clopped over to it, the thing was too small to be of much note. And there was nothing unusual here so far as he could detect—just winter-brown trees sticking out of drifts of snow.

Ned pulled up the cuff of his coat with his teeth and looked at his watch. Twenty minutes had passed. More than enough time to cover half a mile, even given his decelerated pace. He glanced to the right, deciding to return to the road so he could double back to the cave. He still had the walk to his car, and overdoing it out here could be dangerous in fifty different ways.

Except that he didn't see the road.

Stupid, idiot, city-slicker mistake. One Ned never would've made if he weren't on the hunt for a story. Out here every expanse of white blended into another. You went snow-blind, thinking you were seeing one stretch of land, when really it was something else altogether.

Ned got out the compass again. He would walk roughly south now, although he knew it wasn't as easy as that. Topography was a lot less linear than the grid on a map.

He continued to curse himself to dispel a mounting charge of panic. From the moment he'd moved up here, Ned hadn't underestimated the north woods, especially not in winter.

A gray police cruiser cut like a shark

through the shadows. Lurcquer coming back for him? Right about now, Ned would be grateful to see any of the cops. He clomped in the direction he thought the car had gone. But he came to no road, nor did he see any tire tracks, and Ned blamed his snow-fooled eyes for an illusion created out of the dim light in the woods.

At least the snow was shallower here. Ned reached down to unclip his snow-shoes. They were slowing him down, and he couldn't afford that. Ned considered leaving the snowshoes behind altogether, but told himself he'd give it another fifteen minutes.

Then he struck off again.

He passed only identical, snow-clotted trees. If the compass hadn't assured him he was walking straight, Ned would've been sure he was going in circles. His cell wouldn't pick up a signal. Sweat lathered his body, which posed the biggest danger of all. He could build a snow cave of his own, and given his gear, probably last out the night, if it came to that. Although nothing would be very different tomorrow, except that he'd be hungry, and tired.

He would miss his group this afternoon. Ned always tried to get to a weekend meeting. Would any of the members report him missing? Did they even know where he lived?

Ned forced himself to calm down.

And then he dropped his snowshoes and began to run.

What was the saying? God favored the young and foolish? It was sheer, dumb luck when Ned spotted the hill he'd mounted what felt like days before. The hump of the snow cave drew his eye. Keeping his gaze focused, Ned headed toward the edge of the woods, wishing he hadn't lost his snowshoes in such a foolish, impetuous move. But it was easy to regret that now, with panic already ebbing away.

He might make it to his meeting after all.

As he hooked left toward the final barrier of trees, Ned spotted another set of boot prints. They wound back as far as the eye could see, in the direction he had come from. They were recently made, freshly sunk into the snow. The entire time he'd been out here in the woods, someone had been following soundlessly and invisibly alongside.

CHAPTER THIRTY-THREE

"I've been trying to reach you for some time," said the woman on the other line.

"You might've tried saying hello." It was my sister's voice, coming out of my mouth.

There was a long silence, during which I studied the road.

"I was afraid to," the woman said at last.

There was something in her voice. My body grew awash in chills, and I had to raise the heat in the car.

"I read about what happened to your husband," the woman said.

This time I stayed quiet.

"I'm sorry," she added.

"Thank you."

"It might—what happened to him might have something to do—I mean, I might know something about it."

My hands on the steering wheel tightened into vises. I felt the imprint of ridged plastic on my palms. Suddenly the call I hadn't even wanted to take became the one I couldn't let go.

"What do you mean? What do you know?"

Whitened trees streamed by, flanking the highway, and cars fanged with ice dropped back as I sped up.

"I can't tell you—not here," the woman said.

The meaning of her words penetrated instantly. My brain was on accelerate, making sense of things I once would've refuted. I crossed two lanes of traffic, hunting the next exit.

"In Wedeskyull, you mean? That's okay! That's fine. I'm not there now anyway."

"Where are you?"

A big green sign appeared.

"Troy," I said instantly, and swung onto the ramp.

The bars on the phone informed me that the call had dropped. As I tried to get it back, something sticking out of my bag caught my eye.

The sheet of paper my sister had given me at the Chinese restaurant. I smoothed it out, scanning the information. It'd be just Teggie's luck if there was something scheduled today. Sure enough, the flier announced that meetings were held on weekends and Wednesdays.

My car seemed to wend through streets of its own accord, no intention on my part. This place had seen more bustling and productive days. The houses were old but untouched, any work done on them the slapdash kind intended merely to keep a structure standing. The city's scattered restaurants and stores were largely unappealing. A river moved sluggishly past the center of town, unevenly frozen in shades of yellow and ivory.

The call finally went through, and the

woman picked up as if there'd been no interruption. "Troy would be good," she said. "Where?"

I read the address off the sheet of paper. It was one way to kill time. I guessed I'd be going to an SOS meeting.

The GPS took me to a steep street not far from the polytechnic institute. My tires clutched for purchase on the ice-slick incline before I thrust on the emergency brake.

I zipped my coat and tied my muffler, then emerged into the freezing afternoon sunshine. A series of decrepit nineteenth-century houses sagged against one another. I longed to stop, observe paint-choked details despite the cold. But I hurried along toward number 61.

The front door was unlocked. A makeshift penciled sign—SOS *meeting today*—pointed the way to a room down the hall.

I'd expected a funereal gathering of members dressed all in black. But when I peered into the ground-level room from the doorway, it was streaked with silvery winter light, and clumps of men and women stood chatting and laughing, drinks in hand.

Someone appeared beside me. He was young—terribly young—and held a can of soda in one fist. I noticed that his nails were bitten.

"First time?" he said, offering a smile.

I nodded.

"That's the hardest," he said. "Come on."

I followed him to a table. The people hovering around it crossed the age spectrum and other spectrums as well, their clothes both designer and brand-less, hairstyles chiseled to ragged.

A few people smiled at me, then an older woman, small and hunched over, indicated that everyone should head for a circle of folding chairs.

I sat down beside the boy.

The shrunken gargoyle of a woman took the lead. "Why don't we start with introductions while we wait for any late-comers?" She looked around the circle. "We're still short one regular." There were nods all around. "And I see we have someone new with us today." More nods.

I wasn't sure what to say—if I should say anything at all—but luckily someone else began to speak. He was heavyset with a hairy froth of beard. He wore overalls, and his hands were hidden, thrust into the pocket on his front bib.

"I'm Gary. My daughter, Emily, killed herself two years ago. Swallowed pills, we still don't know where she got 'em, her stepmother and me. My wife Judy already done it, twelve years before, when Emmy was just a little girl."

Silence spread over the last of the chitchat.

Two family members? This man had been through it twice?

A tall, glamorous woman spoke up next.

"I'm Peggy," she said. "My son, ah, came out to the family. It was about a year ago, I think. And my husband had some trouble with the news. He had a young lady he wanted my son to meet, the daughter of somebody he worked with, really quite lovely. But my son— our son . . ." Peggy half turned in her seat, pressing two sharp, jewel-tipped fingers against her eyes. "He shot himself the night that was to be their first date. Before he'd even met her." Tears ran freely down her made-up cheeks now, but she no longer tried to stop them. "My husband still won't come to these meetings, but I find they really help."

A woman touched Peggy on her cascade of hair.

"I'm Betty," said a stout lady in a plain dress. She was crying without seeming to be aware of it. "I still haven't said why I'm here yet."

A second reassuring soul patted that speaker's arm, and I swiftly shut my own eyes. How much pain could one room hold?

The door banged open, and from the way everyone immediately looked up, you could tell they'd been waiting for this person to arrive. I looked over, too.

It was Ned Kramer.

CHAPTER THIRTY-FOUR

We left the meeting early. A bereavement expert had come to speak about how the five stages of grief are altered in cases of suicide, and Ned and I were able to sidle out.

I stopped as soon as we got out to the street. "So much for being straight with me."

Ned had the courtesy to look away. "Yeah," he said. "Right."

"Yeah, right?" I echoed.

"Maybe there've been some things I wasn't straight about."

"*Some* things?" But then I sighed.

"Don't worry, I'm not going to be the pot, or the kettle. This business of being straight isn't the easiest."

Ned laughed. "No. It's not."

A truck went by, spraying twin waves of salt. Ned and I both jumped back.

"Remember I told you how my house is a twin to the one I grew up in?"

I nodded.

"Well, that's only one of the reasons I bought, on my own, a seven-bedroom home in need of a massive overhaul."

"It's true you're not exactly the proto-typical client," I agreed.

Ned eyed me. "It's also almost an ex-act replica of the house my wife had her heart set on in Connecticut. We couldn't afford it there. And then she died."

I sucked in my breath. "Ned, I'm—"

"—sorry," he said. "I know."

"Sorry," I said again, and we smiled wryly.

But then Ned seemed to gather breath. "Five years ago, my wife and four-year-old daughter joined a church," he went on. "It was supposed to be re-ligion for a different age, liquid, gather-ings online, all of that. I stayed mostly on the outskirts, I've never been one for organized religion. But Sue got very involved. She'd lost her father young, and this guy was charismatic, I'll give him that. He began preaching about the rapture; he identified a date from Scripture. When he got it wrong, he had another revelation." Ned paused. "They had to give the punch to the children first."

"Oh, Ned!" I was dislodging a clump of snow with my boot. Another clump followed the first, a small avalanche begun with my foot.

He ducked his ruddy head. "That was my first big story—an exposé of the pastor who called himself Pater Iesus. I rushed it to press after the mass suicide. I think that's all I did for the first three months—investigate and write. That's right—I'm a reporter, but I didn't sense the story under my very own roof until it was too late."

I opened my mouth, then shook my head. There wasn't a single thing I could think of to say.

Ned went on, his voice sharp as a blade. "The good pastor didn't drink anything himself, by the way. But he did get convicted on thirty-seven counts of fraud and extortion after my story ran. He's serving sixteen years."

I continued to stare at Ned through the brittle air. The cold scarcely penetrated in the wake of his words.

"Shit, I'm sorry," he said finally.

"You're sorry?" I said. "What for?"

Ned angled his head back toward the building. "One of the first things I learned in there is to stop elevating my tragedy. It doesn't matter how many people died with Sue and Tracy, or what kind of attention the event got. Your husband's—Brendan's death is just as important, even if it wasn't part of anything larger." His mouth compressed in a way I'd seen it do before.

"Maybe Brendan died as part of a larger thing, too," I muttered.

"What do you mean? I thought—are you talking about the ice-fishing accident?" Ned took a step forward, his eyes alight. "Did you find something out?"

"No!" I said. "No. I don't know anything about what happened twenty-five years ago besides what you told me.

And I don't know much of anything else, either. Except that I might not have been quite straight with you myself."

Ned stared down at me. "Look, I've had a really shitty day so far. I didn't think I was going to make it to this meeting." He scrubbed his gloved fists together. "Do you think we could go somewhere and warm up? You can tell me anything you have on Brendan."

"Anything I *have*?" I repeated, distracted from what Ned had said about his day. "My husband's not a source, you know. His life wasn't material for a story. And neither is his death."

"No, of course not—" Ned broke off. "I'm sorry. I told you, my day's been from—"

"And why do you always look like that when you talk about him anyway?"

Another frown transformed Ned's features. "Like what?"

I pointed. "Like that. Your eyes do a funny thing, they kind of drain. And your mouth gets all tight."

Ned didn't answer and it occurred to me how closely I must be examining him to see all of that. Unaccustomed heat filled my face, a strange partner to our surroundings.

Ned turned around on the sidewalk. "Look, Nora, I don't speak ill of the dead, especially when the dead person was married to someone I happen to—to someone I'm with right at that moment. But Brendan and I didn't get along especially well, okay? He just wasn't my favorite person, and I'm sure he'd have said the same of me."

"Why?" I asked smally.

He gave a hard jerk of his shoulders. "The few times I had questions to ask him—a story to do—he just didn't seem all that interested in helping. Onward and forward, he told me once. Don't look back. It was hard to get information out of him."

"He didn't like hashing over the past," I said, still in a small voice. "I guess his work and yours are kind of at odds."

"Right," Ned said. "We clashed a few times, and that's probably what you were reading in my face. So I'm sorry. I'm sure he was a wonderful husband to you."

Before I could figure out how to answer, someone ran up and grabbed my arm.

"Nora?" the woman said as I swiveled.

I instantly recognized the voice of my mystery caller.

Ned took a step back, observing the two of us.

"There's a coffee shop over there," she went on hurriedly. "Can we sit and talk?" She was already heading in the direction she'd indicated.

Ned held up his hand in a wave. "I'll, uh, see you. Or I could wait—"

"Yes, do," I said, the words awkward and stupid on my tongue.

I turned to follow the newcomer along the sidewalk.

She paused as soon as we were alone.

She was dressed in the sort of long wool coat I had dispensed with during my first winter in Wedeskyull, after learning they were no better than a windbreaker against the cold. The one this woman wore was slightly threadbare, its hem frayed and a piece of lining torn at the collar. A dull brown muffler snaked around her neck and lower jaw.

"I don't really want any coffee," she said. "Mind if we just walk?"

I was beginning to feel the cold, but I turned in the same direction she did, and we went down a side street.

"Sorry I interrupted you with your friend," she said, from several paces ahead.

"That's okay," I replied. "He's not ex- actly a friend."

She stopped and looked back at me. "Who is he?"

I was unsure how to describe Ned. "Well, he's a reporter—" Before I could go any further, the woman's face blanched and she started walking again.

"I was told not to talk to reporters. That they wouldn't help me. But it didn't seem like friendly advice to keep me from wasting my time, if you know what I mean," she added darkly. She drew me forward with a pull of her hand. "And it's not like anyone else has helped, ei- ther."

"Helped with what?" The woman was starting to sound a little paranoid.

She continued urging me along, away from the lighted houses. The weave of her silver gloves was ratty, threads springing loose, like a woman's first gray hairs. We traversed two streets and came to stand by a lone copse of trees at the edge of some woods.

"Look," I said, before we could go any farther. "It sounded like you might have some information about Brendan." At the woman's blank look, I added, "My husband."

Understanding crossed her face. "I hope I didn't mislead you," she said, and I felt something plummet beneath all the heavy layers of gear I wore.

"I'm not positive I know something about your husband," the woman went on. She raised her shrouded face to mine. "But mine has disappeared."

CHAPTER THIRTY-FIVE

A halfhearted snow had begun to fall, ceasing periodically as if even the weather lacked the will to collect itself into a storm. I felt thick with disappointment, movement coming only with great difficulty. I realized I'd been holding out hope—for what I didn't know.

"I heard about what your husband did," the woman began. Then she paused, moving forward into a denser stand of trees. I noticed she was no longer saying *what happened to your husband,* instead making Brendan into a far more active participant. "And it seemed like there might be some connection."

"Why?" I asked. "Why did it seem like that?" Then I burst out, "Who are you?"

Now that we were hidden away, the woman turned and faced me. Snow dusted her bare head. "My name is Melanie Cooper," she said. "We moved up here four months ago."

She still wasn't telling me anything— certainly nothing to justify my abandoning Ned on a sidewalk and walking off into the woods with a stranger as a storm was taking root. But maybe she did have something to offer. Maybe bringing things down a notch, speaking easily and congenially, would get this woman to open up.

"Ah," I said. "Newcomers."

"And you are . . ." she responded.

I gave a laugh of assent. "Slightly less of a newcomer."

God only knew when I'd earn any other status. Maybe after three generations of my family had been born here? Sadness shifted over me. There'd never be another generation of my family now, in Wedeskyull or anywhere. Not without Brendan.

Melanie and I began to walk apace, into the deepening woods.

"Moving up here was the worst mistake of our lives," she went on. "I'm afraid—" Blindly, she reached for my hand. "Oh, Nora, I'm afraid it was the last mistake we made!"

I stopped on the path we'd been forging. "You think your husband's dead?"

Stupid, I told myself, or Teggie did. Of course she thinks that. Was that the connection she saw between her husband and Brendan? That wouldn't help me at all.

Melanie's gaze twitched, taking in all sides, although dark was beginning to descend and the falling snow added a curtain of concealment. Bare, black branches swept over our heads, and Melanie was shivering much as they were, her body trembling as if it were being jolted by electricity.

"I don't know what to think," she said, starting forward again. "John went to work one day and never came home. He didn't answer his cell. Eventually it must've run out of charge, because now it just clicks right to voicemail." She glanced sideways at me. "We have kids. Can you imagine how hard it is to come up with something to tell them?"

I couldn't really imagine that, and I looked away.

Melanie's head was ducked low, droplets of water making tiny divots on the new layer of snow.

"What kind of work does your husband do?" I asked softly.

We stepped between more trees into a few lilting snowflakes. They were disorienting; I didn't know where the street was anymore.

"That's why I thought to contact you, after I heard your husband was a police officer. Because of the work my husband does," she said, and I nodded, thinking, *antiterrorist plant near the border, organized crime spy, drug mule.*

"He's in concrete."

I almost laughed. The draining of tension, the pinnacle of anticipation I hadn't even realized I'd been on, then the sudden skid back onto my plateau left me weak in the knees. For a moment I forgot the cold, that I was out here in a burgeoning blizzard with a woman I had no good reason to meet.

Melanie noticed my reaction. "Seems pretty mundane, right?"

The echo of Brendan's voice far away. *Mowing is big business up here, Chestnut.*

"There's a lot of work here, though. All those big-box stores going up on the Northway. John saw an opportunity to get in by taking on some of the overflow. But he didn't win a single bid. In the end he had to give up and go to work for Paulson's."

Lenny Paulson was the only show in town, as far as I knew, the only one I ever used anyway. If the foundation on a house was bad, I'd have to get it reinforced first off, and Lenny was a good friend of Vern's.

I remembered something then. "On the phone," I began. "You said you were afraid to meet in Wedeskyull." In the way of storms in the north country, which disappear as quickly as they start, the snow had suddenly become sparse, and the woods had gone very dark.

"The policemen I spoke to—" Melanie looked down for a moment, and I saw she was crying again.

"It's okay," I said softly. "You said they weren't very helpful?"

"I wasn't allowed to file a missing persons report for two days. That might be protocol, but once I did file one, I wouldn't swear that report was put where it was supposed to go." She paused. "I wouldn't swear it was put anywhere at all."

"Who did you talk to?" I asked.

She hesitated. "An Officer Mitchell and one named..." Her gaze flit away briefly, then she handed me a small gray card, its paper slick and familiar. *Gilbert Landry* was the name on it.

I wondered why Brendan wouldn't have been with Club when they spoke to Melanie. Gil was ex-military, a firecracker, always ready to go off. Brendan had said that he'd never liked him, even as a kid, and that he was worse once he joined the force.

"They were more than not helpful, Nora," Melanie went on. "They gave me instructions. What I should and shouldn't do. And while he was talking, Officer Mitchell kept reaching for his gun. Not taking it out, of course, but it was—" She broke off, leaving me to think what that gesture would look like to someone not accustomed to it, to someone who was looking for help.

"What do the police think happened to your husband?"

Melanie averted her gaze. "They say he must've run off. Just left me and the kids."

I was trying to tease out the possibilities of her story, the things she wasn't saying from what she was.

"But he wouldn't have done that, Nora, you have to believe me!" Melanie cried. "If John didn't come home, it means something terrible has happened. And they must know about it! Anything that goes wrong, at the plant or on a job, has to be reported!" Her voice disturbed the silence. "And then I learned your husband killed himself!"

Her words were as stark as a splash. My mind instantly shot to the night of January sixteenth. "When did John disappear?"

"Only two days before," she said, her gaze burning into mine, eyes like two embers, red-rimmed and fierce.

"Two days before what?" I asked.

A bird took flight, releasing a branch. Snow plummeted, but Melanie didn't bother to duck. The spilled flakes melted upon her face, making slow, teary rivulets. "John disappeared just two days before your husband's death."

And then her head jerked up, gaze rising as if she were tracking the sight of something.

It was behind me.

CHAPTER THIRTY-SIX

Melanie turned and fled. For a second, the tails of her coat could be seen flying out behind her while the drumbeat of her footsteps sounded dully against the terrain. Then all trace of her was gone.

I revolved slowly, instinctively beginning to back up.

Ned Kramer stood before me, hands held out appeasingly.

Pent-up breath escaped in a *whoosh.* "You scared me to death." The draining of adrenaline added a bite to my tone. "You always have that effect on women?"

Ned's gaze followed Melanie's retreating form. "They've been known to turn and run." Then he explained. "I was worried about you. You hadn't said anything about meeting someone, and then you ran off into the woods. So I figured I'd try and tag along. Took me a little while to find you."

Ned was a reporter; I'd known him first in conjunction with a story. Had I become the potential story?

He was peering at me closely. "You need to get someplace warm."

It was suddenly all too much to think about. Everything was too much to think about.

Ned seemed to sense my state of mind. "Let's drive back together and talk," he suggested. "I booked a room at the inn in town last night. But I have to be in Albany tomorrow, and I can take the bus down, pick up my car then."

"Are you sure?" I asked. "Wouldn't it make more sense just to stay here?"

"Come on," he said, beginning to lead me away. "You can tell me all about your friend."

✳   ✳   ✳

Melanie had said she would've liked to talk to a reporter, so I assumed it was okay to reveal what she'd told me. But still I hesitated as we began to drive, my car pegged toward Wedeskyull as if it knew where it was going.

I didn't have a good handle on Melanie. Was she a bereft woman, projecting her abandonment outward—running from reporters in the woods and elevating normal police procedures to the level of a cover-up? Or was there something dreadful and unexplained going on here, a missing man, and police who failed to take notice?

"She's not my friend," I began. "I just met her. Her name is Melanie Cooper."

Ned twisted sharply in the passenger seat.

"What?" I asked. "Do you know her?"

Ned was staring out the window, his mouth set in that clean line again. "No."

I forced myself to focus on the road. "You sure?" I tried to get him to look my way. "Are you being straight?"

Ned didn't crack a smile. "How did someone you didn't know come to be talking to you a hundred miles from home?"

It was a good question. "Her husband . . . I guess he's disappeared. Or left. And Melanie found that the police didn't help her very much. When she heard that Brendan died . . . she thought there might be a connection."

"Because Brendan happened to be a cop?"

I spoke sharply. "She's reaching. You do that when you're bereft. Right?"

Ned didn't reply.

The road was a dark river before us. The contrast between it and the wild whiteness flanking the highway made the eyes blink, do funny things. "Maybe I shouldn't have told you all that."

"Why not?"

"Well . . ." I felt suddenly silly. "Why're you so interested?"

"I'm a reporter," Ned said. "I'm interested in everything. You could describe your last trip to the grocery store and I'd be taking notes."

"What about the fires?" I asked bluntly. "You were there at both houses. How do I know you're not behind them?"

Ned was still staring out at the glistening scenery, the night sky. The stars were blanked out by remnants of the earlier storm. "How do I know you're not?"

"What?" I took my eyes off the road for a moment, and with the glare of the headlights lost, the lightless sky overwhelmed me.

"Look, all I'm saying is that you were going to work on my house and it caught fire. Then you let me stay at your house and it burned down. Maybe you're trying to kill me."

My lips quivered. "You're kidding, right?"

Ned twisted around in his seat. "The fires are a false road, Nora. Or at least any connection I have to them is."

"What?" I couldn't follow what he was saying. "What does that mean?"

"If you focus on the fires—try to track down where I was when they started, if there were accelerants used, what the reports say, who made the 911 calls, that kind of thing . . ."

He was handing me a roster of ways to go about it, an investigative reporter's approach to the matter. And then Ned finished his thought.

". . . you might be giving some pretty powerful people enough time to cover their tracks."

Everything seemed to go quiet around me. I was flying down the highway at seventy miles an hour, temperature plummeting and moon racing across the planet to make its appearance in the north, yet all was suddenly still. I couldn't hear a thing, not the blast of the engine nor the rush of tires against the road. Not even the steady, quiet rhythm of Ned breathing.

He had just confirmed—for me, for Melanie—that forces were at work here we hadn't yet begun to comprehend. That the one thing I'd held on to, ever since finding my husband's lifeless body dangling from the ceiling, was true.

"Do you want to pull over?" Ned asked, and I nodded soundlessly. He pointed to a swath of shoulder up ahead, helping me steer the car, while looking behind us to make sure there wasn't any traffic. He leaned over, chest brushing my arm, to shift into *park.*

"Which powerful people?" I asked at last.

Ned stared out the window, but the dappled globe of the moon still hadn't appeared. I followed his gaze, hunting some spark of light. We both seemed to give up at the same time.

"You think of Wedeskyull as a town, the place you've made your home."

I was about to tell him that wasn't quite the whole story when Ned looked over at me, planing his hand across the seat.

"I've come to think of it as a tiny empire."

His use of the word made me laugh, and he jumped on it. "You think we're a country, Nora? A democracy, one nation under God?"

"Well, you make me sound a little naïve, but . . ."

Ned gave a definitive shake of his head. "Power-hungry people want to control." He swept his hand across the seat again. "Before my wife and daughter died, I was trying to write a book. If I ever get back to it, that's what it'll be about."

"So who are you saying has control here?"

Ned looked out the window. "Look, I'm just beginning to be able to answer that myself. And I can't tell you every-thing—protection for sources and all that."

I nodded slowly.

"But I can say this: I had cause to start looking into things, matters of pub-lic record. How this town is run, how it's always been run. And that opened up some questions that didn't have an-swers, not good ones anyway."

"Like what?"

Ned grinned at me, but the look was devoid of mirth. "Did you ever wonder how the police force came to be so well appointed? The barracks, computers in the cruisers, all of it?"

I shrugged. "It always just seemed a plus for us. Brendan's job was secure, and he was well paid, especially for these parts. It's what allowed me to start my business."

Ned gave a snort. "Well paid for sure."

He was staring at some far-off point, impossible to see. "The chief of police—

and his father before him, and grandfather before him—have always made sure they have plenty of funds, and they aren't overly scrupulous about how they procure them." Ned refocused his gaze on me. "And of course, there's always something to use them for."

I frowned. "Do you mean—are you saying that the police manufacture crime?"

Ned gave me a look I'd seen before, but only in my sister's eyes. "I'm saying they're the criminals themselves."

My mouth went chalky and I couldn't speak. Denial crested up inside me, but just as quickly Ned's likely refutations crashed down. "That's impossible. Brendan wouldn't have been part of anything like that."

Ned hesitated. "Look, why don't we go to my office? There's stuff there that will make what I'm saying seem a little more plausible."

CHAPTER THIRTY-SEVEN

The *Daily Record* was housed in an old brick building on the far side of Lake Nancy, parallel to the police department. Where the barracks stood high on a hill—an imposing location for such a small building—the *Record* sat in a valley. The rear of the building lacked a plowed path, but Ned told me to park in the lot there anyway.

I looked at him, brows raised.

"No reason to let anyone know we're here," he said.

Snowdrifts around the lot had grown tall; it was lucky they had frozen over.

We scaled a mound, boots hardly breaking through, then slid down its other
side to the back entrance.

Ned took out a jingling bunch of keys,
and unlocked the back door. I followed
him inside. He flicked on a set of switches
that illuminated a long length of hallway,
and pushed buttons on a thermostat. I
heard the dragon's breath of some distant furnace.

"This way," Ned said, still speaking
shortly.

I felt fingertips press upon my back.
We were alone in a darkened, after-
hours building, and as Ned had worked
to ensure, no one else knew we were
here. Why was I trusting this man I hardly
knew over the police force, who had become almost like family? Over, in some
terrible way, my own husband? Because
Ned had lost family members to suicide,
too? Because he had *told* me that he
had?

Ned unlocked another door, then
stood in its opening, waiting for me. I
took a step forward. Ned's face relaxed
and the customary crinkles appeared
around his eyes. I noticed how blue the

orbs were in the light cast by the fluo-
rescents of the hall.

He entered the room, and I watched
him disappear, then heard a rustle of
papers. I covered the last leg of hallway
to catch up.

His office was neat and spare. It had
one window that looked out onto the
snow-heaped field and the black, star-
pricked sky. All trace of the impending
blizzard was gone.

The room contained a desk with a
flat-screen monitor on it, as well as
shelves of books. File cabinets flanked
one long, bare wall. Ned had assembled
a stack of neatly slit articles, and he slid
the pile in my direction, gesturing to a
wheeled desk chair.

I took a seat.

Ned dropped down on a corner of
desk. He watched as I began to read.

Some of the events described in the
more recent articles were familiar to
me—things Brendan had sketched out
briefly over the years—but this stack
also contained sheets that were brittle
and yellowing, the dates moving back-

ward in time, headlines becoming more quaint.

Chief of Police
Franklin ("Lin") Weathers
Honored at Charity Dinner

That one caught my eye for some reason, made me pause, before I continued on.

There was a story about the cops solving a string of local robberies—then being awarded a grant to keep kids out of trouble—and another featuring a Wedeskyull family that was honored at the statehouse with the cops providing escort. A teenage runaway had been brought home. Club's opening season kickoff was extolled in an article about the high school football team; Tim's sauce placed first at the annual rib-off. The mundanities of small-town living, writ just a little large. There were some posts from a blog called CopShop, which I also glanced at.

"Let me make us some coffee," Ned suggested. "Or tea for you, right?"

I nodded gratefully, laying the first

page of a feature facedown on Ned's desk, and picking up its continuation. Engrossed, I added, "And do you have anything to eat?"

Ned smothered a smile. "I'll see what I can do."

The scents of tea and something else—soup—signaled his return. Ned was carrying three steaming Styrofoam cups. I started to sip and spoon, the hot liquids traveling straight to the teething emptiness in my belly.

"So?" Ned asked, when he saw that I'd finished. He drank deeply from his cup.

The aroma of coffee still turned my stomach and I slid the chair away from the desk. "Um . . ." I was attempting to smooth out the pile. "We have a pretty active police force?"

Ned took another long draught, then tossed his cup in the trash, walking over to the window and laying both palms against the cold, black glass. "I'll say," he answered dryly.

I tilted my soup for the last.

Ned repositioned his hands on the glass. "The Wedeskyull Police Department is like this well-oiled machine, every cog turning. All of them know where and when to go, and what to do when they get there. It's a regular hive of activity. Or at least, so it looks from here."

"Well, what would you expect? Barney Fife just because we live outside the city?"

"Not to mention how nice it is up there," Ned continued, his back to me. "The Chief's office is the size of my first apartment. He drives a sixty-thousand-dollar SUV. There's a late-model patrol car for every two men—with computers in them, no less. Those cops had computers in their vehicles before I bought my first laptop. There are police departments in major cities that still run on carbon copies. And don't forget the fleet of ATVs and snowmobiles for wilderness work."

Taken all together, it did amount to quite a list. Briefly, I let my mind flick to what Brendan's life—and my own—might've been like if he had worked someplace else, say a drug-riddled ghetto back in New York.

Still not facing front, Ned asked, "But did you notice anything else?"

"Sure," I replied. "I noticed how good they are."

"Yes," Ned said. "That's what I wanted you to see."

Silence draped itself over the office, and finally he turned.

"In every story where the police are mentioned, they've done a great job. They have a ninety-five percent solve rate for homicides—over sixty years' worth of coverage." Ned gestured to the pile of cut-outs. "Even allowing for the fact that there aren't that many of them and almost all are DV—that's still too high." Ned raked his hair out of his eyes. "And amongst all these tales, nothing bad is ever written about the police. No one ever questions their actions. Everything they do is justified and it always—*always*—works."

"This is Wedeskyull," I said, for what felt like the hundredth time. "Domestic violence, yes, we have plenty of that. But police brutality, corruption, those things are for the city. I don't think there's even an IA department here."

Ned began tapping his fingers on his desk. I watched them move in a strong, steady rhythm. "The police are untouchable, Nora. And you know, nothing bad ever happens *to* them either. In all that reading, I couldn't find mention of one single mishap. No cop has ever been harmed on the job or in the line of duty—"

I interrupted him. "No, that's not true. Club's father was."

Ned's fingers stilled. "What?"

I nodded, faster now. "Mrs. Mitchell told me. He was killed, actually, not just harmed. And she said that they—the police, I guess—called it accidental."

I recognized the look on Ned's face. It was one I wore—Brendan had described it to me several times—when the final layer of paper or plaster or paint fell away, and a house at last began to give up the secrets it had kept.

"Never made it into the paper," Ned said. He snatched a pad from his desk and began scrawling bits of things— short, choppy notes, his mind obviously moving fast. I caught the name *Burt Mitchell,* a letter paired with numbers that I was pretty sure meant some kind of gun, and a couple of dates with question marks.

"There's someone who's begun talking to me," Ned said, almost to himself. "I wonder what he knows about this."

"You mean, like, an informant?"

He hesitated. "Maybe. I can't say anything more yet. I just wanted you to know . . . how essential you've been. What you've told me could make this whole thing come together. But listen—" Ned paused again. "I don't want you to do anything now, okay? People won't look kindly on you asking around. I have some leads to follow, and I'll keep you in the loop as much as I can." His face broke into a grin as he looked down at his pad, then back at me. "I'll be straight. I promise I'll be straight."

A chill took hold of my whole body; I felt rocked by its force. "You used me."

"What?"

I clenched both hands. "This is why you've been so friendly to me. Not because we both lost people to suicide." I felt a sob roll up my throat. "But because you knew I could help with your story."

I spun around, the office seeming suddenly small to the point of claustrophobia. "You knew I would drive, and drive, and drive, until I found out what happened to Brendan. And you knew that was exactly the information you would need!"

"No, Nora, what are you talking about?" Ned shouted over my cries. "I just told you to *stop* searching, remember? I just told you I would do it—because I don't want you to be in any danger—because I couldn't stand it if you ever got hurt!"

The bare emotion in his tone made me start to turn away, but then our eyes locked. I began shivering convulsively, the tremors so extreme that Ned tugged me forward. I went to pull free, but as I did, I lifted my face and that was when Ned's lips seized mine, or did I move my mouth to his?

Either way, we were kissing, his mouth the only true source of heat in the universe, and I entered that warmth, took it in, drinking so deeply I thought I might drown. His lips moved over mine like heated silk, then to my neck, igniting the skin there, before traveling back again to my mouth. The wind started keening, moaning outdoors. It was Ned who stopped first, taking his hands from my face and holding me bodily away, and when he did, I screamed, a raw, un-checked sound, torn from the depths of me, as loud as the wind.

"Oh Nora," he said, so hushed I could hardly hear him for the clatter of branches knocking against the window in the sud-den gale. "It's my fault. I'm sorry. Please don't blame yourself. It happens. It can happen to anybody—"

"To you?" I burst out. "Would you have done this after your family died?"

He was staring at the floor. "I might've done anything in the days—weeks, months—after they died," he said roughly. "Anything. And it wouldn't have mattered. If I did do something like this, I might not even remember it." He raised his face, meeting my gaze. "Which is the biggest reason I wish we hadn't let that happen just now."

It took a moment for the meaning of his words to sink in.

And then something happened, maybe the only thing that could've made Ned look up, and me look away from him, both of us with a start.

Outside, in quick succession, two car doors slammed.

CHAPTER THIRTY-EIGHT

Ned paused for just a second, slapping his pocket, plunging his hand inside.

"What are you doing?" I whispered.

"I can't leave this room unlocked," he hissed. "My laptop's in here." He lunged for a desk drawer, yanking it open. A shadow passed over his face, a look that made the one he'd worn when he discovered his house burning appear pacific. Ned fisted his hands, and he spoke in a low growl. "Stay here. I'm going to take a look outside."

I tiptoed over to the drawer he had opened. It was empty.

I couldn't just stay behind in Ned's office, or hunched alone in the hall. If I went out the way we'd come in, the back way, then I could conceal myself.

I retraced our steps and eased open the door.

Images of coming face-to-face with a mask played like a movie in my mind. At the least there'd be a gray patrol car, maybe a circle of them, surrounding the building like a pack of wolves. Hugging the side of the building, I began to inch forward.

Snow swarmed around me, stirred up by the wind. The rear lot was empty but for my car. The road that led to the brick structure looked clear.

Ned stalked up to me. "My laptop's gone. Goddammit, all the notes for my book were on it. Not to mention this article."

Surely Ned had backups: a flash drive, such as Dugger had given me, or hard copies somewhere. Then I recalled. He'd had hard copies inside his house.

Ned was staring out across the snow-heaped lot. "We both heard those doors close, right?"

I nodded.

"But no one was inside the building. We would've heard them. My computer must've been taken before we got here." Ned took a slow, dawning look around the parking lot. Gooseflesh broke out on my skin. "Did someone just get here?" he asked. "Or did they just leave?"

"Nobody's here now. We can see that." I shrugged helplessly, and then it hit me. "Oh, Ned, if someone stole your laptop, I wonder if they might also have gone for—" I took off at a run for my car, Ned at my heels.

I tugged open the car door. The dome light came on, and I took a quick look inside, then one more to make sure. The second look was unnecessary: I could see my bag was gone.

I had no house, and now no phone, or money. If I hadn't stuck my keys in my coat pocket, I'd have had no car, either. I would've been stuck. Trapped.

"Hey," Ned said from behind me. "What's going on? What happened?"

Before I could answer him I recalled the one possession I had that mattered more than anything else.

It couldn't have cost me more than a minute to hunch down, hunting the last thing I still owned in the world. *No one even knows it's here,* I told myself, searching the floor. *And the things inside don't mean anything to anybody else.* Still, my fingers trembled as I leaned over, sweeping beneath the seat where it must have slid during my journey, until my hand finally brushed the soft flannel of Brendan's box. I could lose my wallet, my cell, even my tools. But the items in Brendan's box were the last things he had to give. Awash in relief, I stood up.

"Well," I said to Ned. "Your laptop wasn't the only thing that was stolen."

I turned around on an uneven hummock of snow, scanning the lot for him.

There was nobody anywhere around.

Ned was gone, too.

SECRETS

Jean was as nervous as a sixteen-year-old getting dressed for a date. She wanted to look not only nice, but important. Like someone you had to believe.

Although she never forgot to be grateful that she hadn't suffered like Eileen, her sister-in-law's life was in truth the fuller, containing all the normal features of womanhood. Eileen once had a husband, children. That made her worthy of consideration in a way Jean never would be.

The most Jean had had to lose was a house. Lifeless boards and bricks that, once cooled, would be cleared away as if they had never stood or sheltered a soul.

Maybe that wasn't true. Jean had known love, it just hadn't led to marriage or a family. It couldn't have. How could two people live together with a secret as sharp as a blade between them and never speak of it? They would spend their lives avoiding being sliced to shards. It was better that Vern had married someone who didn't have any idea, even if that someone was plain, thin Dottie Miller, who had dried out to a husk over the years.

Jean felt tears prick her eyes. She'd been crying a lot lately.

She checked the mirror to straighten her skirts and make sure her powder hadn't gotten disturbed. Then she tugged on a hat and made the trip across the road to visit her only real companion in the world.

Eileen fixed tea, while Jean tried to hide the fact that she was looking around for something to go with it. Eileen's counters were so bare, and her cupboards and fridge were always empty as well. She had nothing to offer, and Jean felt stung by sorrow again. In some ways Jean had passed through life untouched. She might leave no footprints, but she was also largely unscathed. While Eileen had been dragged through every bit of her life, and the violence of it had simply worn her away.

Jean gathered breath. "Dear heart?"

Eileen lowered her sharp chin to her cup.

Jean's tea tasted bitter; Eileen hadn't added any sugar. She only bought the fake stuff anyway.

Jean fought to make her next words distinct. "There's something I need to tell you."

The sip of tea Eileen had taken started to dribble from her mouth. Her face went slack; it looked like she was having a stroke.

"Dear heart, what's wrong?" Jean struggled to rise.

"Don't," Eileen commanded.

Don't what? Jean wondered. *Get up? Or tell you?*

Jean sat back down, watching her sister-in-law warily. "I might not have. I might never have said anything. But now with Brendan—"

The cup rattled as Eileen set it on the table. Jean reached out to assist her, and when she did, Eileen caught her wrist in the strong winch of her hand.

"I've told you never to speak about him."

A sound escaped Jean's mouth, something like a mew. But she forced the words out. "I wish you'd known—been able to see how much fun Brendan was. Even afterward. Oh, could he make me laugh—"

"Stop it." Eileen's voice had hardly risen, but her grip was like a vise.

Jean abruptly closed her mouth.

"Don't ever bring him up again." Eileen bore down on Jean's arm, squeezing the flesh around the bone.

"You're hurting me!" cried Jean.

"Understand?" Eileen hissed. "And nothing to do with him, either."

Jean was stricken by an altogether alien sense of pain. She hadn't let anything come close enough to hurt her in a long, long time. Her wrist blanched beneath Eileen's strong fingers. The relief when her sister-in-law finally freed her was so great that Jean couldn't imagine how she had ever dared consider unburdening herself, far less speaking her mind.

CHAPTER THIRTY-NINE

One thought stabbed my brain like a shard of glass. *Get out of here.*

For a moment, though, my body wouldn't obey. I spun in a clumsy circle, noting that the door to the building was still cracked, just as I had left it, and that not a single boot print or slide mark interrupted the swaths of snow we ourselves hadn't disturbed. It was as if Ned had been pulled up into outer space.

He'd been right there, just behind me, a moment ago. I was about to shout his name when I stopped as abruptly as if someone had clapped a hand across my face.

High on the hill, on the opposite side of this valley, stood the police department. It sat in shadow now. All looked motionless there, but Ned's description of a hive of activity came back to me on a cold current of air.

Anything that had come so swiftly, as silent and skillful as a sword, was capable of making me disappear as well. I couldn't help Ned right now. If he had chosen to go, well, that was further indication of the way he'd do anything for a story, even leave me behind on a frozen, deserted lot. And if the more likely scenario proved true—that something terrible had taken place—then the farther I got from the scene, the more I could help him.

How? By calling the police?

I dove into my car, igniting the engine. Swerving wildly, I reversed out of the parking lot without once looking over my shoulder or into the rearview mirror.

My chest was still rising and falling in uneven gasps as I headed down the empty, snow-banked road. The State Police, I realized. They were the ones to call. But I didn't have a cell phone anymore, nor a house with a phone to use. I had to get out of Wedeskyull. It wasn't safe.

And then a thought occurred that made my breathing even out.

Something had happened to Ned. But I had been standing not twenty feet away from him and nothing had been done to me.

I began to assemble the pieces of a plan. I would report Ned's disappearance using a pay phone. Wedeskyull still featured a few; many of the residents still used them.

It had snowed while I was gone; a foot or more sat atop the rock-hard drifts. I wasn't aware which way I was driving. Or maybe I was, maybe I'd needed to come here. Because I'd chosen to head into town via the street my house sat on.

The street my house used to sit on. I hardly slowed as I went past—imagining someone sent to watch and wait for me to do exactly this—but that didn't stop the sight from registering.

Club hadn't begun to hint at the devastation I would find, the accumulation of snow rapidly laying waste to a smoldering ruin. Here and there on the ash-heaped plot of land, smoking black stalks stuck up through the drifts, like shards of decaying teeth. Studs. The farmhouse had burned down to its 150-year-old studs.

All the hours I had spent there, prying at paper till my fingernails peeled, stroking on paint with a horsehair brush, ignoring my stinging eyes, were gone, as burned up as the house. All of the time Brendan and I had spent living here. The loss of that past hit me harder than the destruction. It was as if it had all never been.

I entered the intersection that made up the center of town. A fresh onslaught of tears blocked out the sight of familiar things—Al's garage, Coffee Rockets, the pharmacy—as I drove down the recently plowed streets.

I pulled up in front of the movie theater. I had to dial information for the

State Police, using a credit card number I'd memorized over the years. I told my story to the person who answered.

"Ma'am, we don't take missing person reports for an adult until forty-eight hours has passed," said the man on the other end. "And unless this occurred on the interstate, it wouldn't be a matter for us. Where are you located? Where did the incident take place?"

A pause. "Ma'am?"

Hadn't Melanie Cooper just been through this? What had I thought would happen?

"Ma'am?"

I pressed the silver lever as silently as I could to disconnect the call.

CHAPTER FORTY

The patrol car stopped me on Patchy Hollow Road.

I was headed toward the only person I could imagine seeking shelter with now, the one person who felt like family in Wedeskyull now that Brendan was gone.

I opened my door and got out, a brute breaking of protocol. Any civilian knew to stay in the car while the police officer walked around. But if I had sat there, the cop would've seen me trembling, legs vibrating on the seat. Getting out was a show of strength.

It was Tim Lurcquer.

"Nora," he said, flicking his light to my face, then damping it, along with a note of surprise in his voice. "You came back."

Tim hadn't been at Ned's office, then. Not unless he was a damn good actor.

"Going to your mother-in-law's?"

I didn't answer. There was a mad thrum in my head. There was no feeling of danger about this encounter, and yet a man had disappeared virtually in front of me, and I wasn't telling the police.

Tim's face was mostly hidden behind his mask, only small, close eyes, and a thin, ungenerous mouth exposed to the elements. I pulled my hat down, too.

A flock of bats took off, skittering, disturbed from hibernation by something. I watched until they became scarcely visible miniature black rockets against the sky. Then a second gray car appeared, just a shadow in the night, and Club let down his window. He shone a flashlight in my face for longer than Tim had; I had to blink and shield my eyes. "Lurcquer, we're needed."

"Yeah?" Tim said, touching the radio on his belt. "Nothing came in."

Club looked at me again. "Say hello to Mrs. Hamilton."

He meant Eileen; Jean was simply Jean, and sometimes Aunt Jean, to everyone. I decided it was just as well if no one knew where I was really going.

Club drove away, and Tim got into his car and took off after him.

Jean's drive had been recently cleared by whichever service she used, but she didn't seem to have bothered shoveling the day's accumulation off her porch. I mounted the humped steps unsteadily, holding on to the railing, then tapped on Jean's door with a gloved fist. She could be heard approaching slowly before she opened up. A dry gust of heat hit me.

"Oh, Nora," she said. "I'm so glad you came back."

"I'm sorry, Aunt Jean," I said after a pause. "I'm so sorry about the house." I leaned forward awkwardly, and Jean enveloped me in a hug.

"You have nothing to be sorry about," she whispered fiercely. "Nothing."

She led me inside. Jean's foursquare had always been a pleasant, homey place, but today nothing fragrant came from the kitchen, and the holiday lights she still had entwined around her staircase hadn't been turned on.

"I'll fix us a snack," Jean offered. "Where are your things?"

All I had left in the world wasn't even really mine, but I realized that it shouldn't be left in the car. I gave her arm a quick squeeze, then turned for the door.

"Go over and say hello, why don't you?" Jean called. She meant to Eileen, and I didn't have the heart to respond.

As if she'd been summoned, Eileen was emerging from her house when I came out of Jean's. My whip-thin mother-in-law was coatless; the energy with which she was moving must have helped to combat the cold.

"Nora!" she shouted as she strode forward.

I began to shiver. My hand shook as I tried to locate my keys in my coat.

"I know you've been in my house!" Eileen's arms pinwheeled as she advanced across the snow-heaped field, refusing to slow or find her footing. "Rascal's hair was on the floor!"

I felt that lacquered clump again between my fingers. It seemed a long time ago that I had invaded my mother-in-law's lair.

"Calm down, Eileen," I said, when she drew close. Couldn't a draught have accomplished the thing she referred to so plainly, as if it weren't the slightest bit odd to keep a dead dog's fur lying around?

"Don't tell me what to do, you thieving witch." She made a brutal stab at my face. I flinched instinctively, but my mother-in-law didn't so much as falter. "And stop going after things that don't belong to you." Did she mean Bill's journal? "You never know, Nora. Someone might do the same to you."

It was a strange comment, especially when you considered that I had recently lost just about everything I had. "What do you mean?"

Eileen didn't seem aware of how cold she was, her thin frame snapping back and forth like a line in the wind. There was silence over the twin lawns and roadway that bisected them. Nothing flew or cracked or rustled. The sky was still almost lightless, just an ivory hint of the coming moon.

She turned on me. "All your poking and prying will get you nowhere," Eileen said. "Leaving well enough alone is a skill."

Words came to me unbidden. "Like you left Brendan alone after Red died?"

There was a cold, pure silence then. The air seemed to settle around us, heavy, laden with unfallen snow. "You've got that backward," Eileen said at last. "It was your precious husband who left someone alone."

"Because he was trying to *help*," I replied, almost panting. My own vision was fiery now. "In the only way a child could think of. Has it occurred to you that neither of them should've been on their own?"

My mother-in-law looked at me, and in that moment I was more frightened of her than of any of the cops. Eileen's fists were folded and in her eyes was a look of sheer loathing. If she'd had a gun, she would've shot me. No, something hotter, more intimate than a bullet. She would've dragged a knife along the skin of my throat.

"I'm sorry," I began. "That was out of line—"

My mother-in-law turned around on the uneven ground. She walked off, stumbling once and going down on both knees. Before I could get to her, she had risen and started forward once more, back bowed so that she wouldn't fall again.

CHAPTER FORTY-ONE

Don't feel bad for that bitch, stated the version of Teggie who lived in my head as I walked across Jean's lawn toward my car. *If it weren't for her, none of this would be happening.*

But that wasn't precisely true.

I had just reached the driveway when a hand dropped onto my shoulder from behind, all five fingers splayed. At first I assumed it to be Eileen's—proof that she had felt every ounce of the rage I had seen in her eyes—but even as I was held in place, my brain threw up a string of facts almost too fast for me to parse.

This person was tall. The hand had landed from above. Whereas my mother-in-law and I were almost exactly the same height. And he was strong in a way no woman could've been, at least no past-middle-aged woman who had spent her life collecting relics, not black belts.

I fought to twist around, but the powerful hand kept me facing forward.

One finger found an area in my shoulder that I hadn't known existed, a spot that produced such pain that I went still and silent. I was in a place beyond protest or screams. The next thing I saw was the snowy driveway underneath me.

The hand was in my pants pocket. Not pulling my pants down or groping me. It was searching for something.

I tried to get one word out—*coat*—but my ability to speak had been lost.

He must've found them. I didn't feel anything when he did. Some unknowable time later, maybe no time at all, I heard the sound of the locks and my car door opening.

My body twitched on the frozen

ground. What was making it move? Aftershocks from my shoulder, which felt as if it had been passed through a meat grinder.

My head happened to be facing Jean's house and I squinted at it. Jean had said she was going to make us something to eat. She should've missed me by now. An image took shape before my blurred gaze. A wavering glow of color. Jean had the television on.

Feeling began to return. As if it were detached, I spotted my arm, lying across the snow. I watched my palm appear and disappear as my hand began to open and close.

I was about to try to lift my head when a boot stomped onto my back, pressing me to the drive. The voice that spoke came at the far boundaries of my consciousness—I would've been able to place it if not for the state I was in.

"I can shut you up," the voice said, the truth of his statement made clear by my mouth, which gaped open and closed like a fish. He got closer, replacing the boot on my back with his knee, so he could speak right into my ear. "And tell the old bitch to shut up, too."

I had no idea how long it took me to get up. First the pain began to recede from my shoulder, then feeling started to return to the rest of my limbs. Only then did the throbbing bruise on my back awaken, along with my raw, frozen cheek, which had rested on the ground.

I went immediately for my car, crawling across the snow.

All it held that could've been of interest was Brendan's box. And if that had been taken—because it had value beyond the sentimental unbeknownst to me—I wouldn't care about the shoulder-grabbing ninja move, which had temporarily crippled me. The cops could steal my things, destroy my house, and ruin my burgeoning career.

But if they messed with my dead husband's box, I was going to figure out whoever had taken it, and I was going to hunt that person down and kill him.

Every item in Brendan's box had been taken out and dropped or tossed about dispassionately. I found the Stonelickers bumper sticker on the floor of my car, patting my hand around and locating by feel. The letters had been torn from their envelopes, while the toy soldier and red skate laces wound up on the snow. But nothing was missing. I reassembled everything inside the box, then replaced the lid, jiggling it over the side that stuck.

I hobbled across the lawn like an old woman.

Jean was in front of the TV when I let myself in. She peered at me in the low light. "Nora?"

I gave a single nod.

"Oh no!" Jean got to her feet with surprising alacrity. "What happened? Why is your cheek so red?" Her cushy fingers probed the tender side of my face.

"I—I was pushed, Aunt Jean."

"Pushed?"

I nodded. "Someone was searching for something inside Brendan's box. The one that used to be Bill's."

Jean took the yellow box from me, frowning. "You mean something's missing?" She cradled the box in her hands, absently stroking one side.

"No, nothing," I replied. "I don't know what they could've been looking for. Brendan just has keepsakes in there. They wouldn't mean anything to anyone besides him. Or me."

"Yes," Jean murmured. "I understand."

Given who her sister-in-law was, I supposed she did. Surely Jean had stumbled upon Eileen's dungeon at least once in all these years.

"Come into the kitchen," Jean said. "Let me take a look at that cheek."

She cleaned it gently, then doctored it with ointment. The fire began to subside.

I looked up gratefully.

"I must've been making sandwiches," Jean said apologetically, "when you were . . ." She trailed off. "Would you like one?"

My appetite was returning, and I accepted Jean's offering. She stood by while I ate, though she didn't pick up anything from the platter herself.

"I'm worried about you, Aunt Jean," I said, swallowing my mouthful.

"About me? Whyever for?"

I gave a little shudder, recalling the sound of that voice in my ear. Then I set down the rest of my sandwich and looked at the soft creases around Jean's eyes. "Do you know something?" I asked. "That somebody could be afraid you would tell?"

I recalled Ned's fleeting conviction that I had learned something about the first January twenty-third, the one that took place twenty-five years ago. The police investigation had seemed so thorough, according to the articles Ned had brought me. And yet—look what Ned suspected about the police. It must've been one of the cops who assaulted me. Not Club. And affable Dave couldn't have aped that tone if he'd tried. It had to have been Tim, or possibly Gilbert.

I couldn't stand to hear that awful snarl again in my mind, and spoke to blot it out. "The man who attacked me outside said something."

Jean was staring at me steadily.

It occurred to me that although she knew at least one crime had been committed tonight, Jean hadn't suggested calling the police. I took a breath and uttered the poisonous words. "He said, 'Tell the old bitch to shut up.'"

Her reaction surprised me. Jean let out a laugh, feeble and not all that far from a croak, but still a laugh. She sounded like somebody coming off a long illness maybe, or else someone just waking up. Something sparked in her eyes and caught mine.

"Is that right? Because I'd say this old bitch has been silent long enough."

I frowned. "About what, Aunt Jean?"

She reached over, squeezing my hand between the folds of her own. "Tomorrow, dear heart, all right? After I figure out the . . . best way to do this. In the morning," she said. "We'll talk."

I was about to protest, ask something further, but Jean switched her gaze then, staring out the kitchen window. The moon had finally risen in the sky, and for a moment the view was blinding.

CHAPTER FORTY-TWO

Not long after that I went up to bed. My shoulder still hurt, and my back ached enough to force me onto my stomach for sleep. The spare room was the coldest in the house, and Jean had plugged in a space heater for additional warmth. While I slept, the room grew close and overheated, and I began to dream.

For the first time since he'd died, I dreamed of Brendan. In the dream chestnuts were heaped on a city street all around us and we were trying to gather them up, but Brendan kept getting fistfuls of my hair instead.

His hands on me felt wonderful, and then the dream changed—we were back home, making love, as we did that last night. It was just as it had been, Brendan coming and taking me with none of the usual preventions or pause, just raw, relentless passion.

I remembered he was dead, but that was impossible, because he was moving inside me, as potent a force as ever. I wanted to cry out—did start to cry out—with pleasure and pain, saying that I had so many questions, what happened on the sixteenth, how much had he known about the police. But then I realized I couldn't ask Brendan anything ever again.

I looked down to see him on top of me.

His body was cold, and soft in some terrible way, the flesh beginning to slide from his bones. His weight was dead weight and I couldn't get him off me, although I thrashed and bucked, throwing my arms up so that my fingertips dragged against the walls. I woke with a start, the feel of grit beneath my nails, and a moldering taste in my mouth as if

I had come into contact with something that'd been lying deep in the ground.

I sat up in bed, heaving and panting, brushing off my hands. My gaze tore around wildly. It wasn't only the dream that had woken me; I'd heard something, too. Something sudden and loud, a noise I couldn't quite place. And I was continuing to hear sounds, not as alien as the one that had startled me awake, but still not as quiet as nighttime should have been.

My heart tripped through the logical possibilities. Heat ducts contracting and expanding, wood buckling as the cold intensified, branches batting against the glass. Gooseflesh rose on my skin. This wasn't any of those. One thing I knew was old houses, and what I was hearing was the unmistakable sound of floorboards sagging beneath somebody's weight.

Jean? Just after we had said good night, she'd added that she rarely slept all the way through the night. "You don't anymore once you're my age," she'd explained. "A little snack sometimes helps."

But the methodical thunks coming

from below didn't sound anything like Brendan's soft-footed aunt padding around.

It was warm in the spare room, but as soon as I got up and walked to the door, a rush of cold air met me, and I began to shake. Midway down the hall, I saw why it was so cold. The front door was ajar.

"Jean?" I called out. A stupid thing to do, betraying my location.

I reached the flight of stairs and began to descend, wending through the hall and parlor and into the kitchen. Then I stopped and sucked in my breath.

This room had been ransacked, drawers yanked out, contents spilled onto the counters or floor, table pushed to one side, cupboard doors hanging open. The stove burners sat askew. A toaster was overturned and even the appliances had been breached—fridge, dishwasher, oven.

The front door, flung wide enough that icy air was rapidly filling the house, gave a view of bare tree limbs splitting the starless sky.

Someone had rushed out in a hurry

after doing all this damage. When he had heard me? Or *she* had heard? Briefly, I recalled Eileen's rage, the slap of her voice. Where was Jean? Was it possible she had slept through all this? I supposed that I had missed most of it myself, only awakening at the end. But I had been sleeping particularly deeply, pushed under by the artificial heat, as well as by the weight of my dreams. Jean said she slept lightly.

I was heading back for the stairs to check Jean's room when I saw her.

She knelt on the floor, leaning over a low bench that stood behind the staircase, which was why I hadn't spotted her on my way down. The first thought in my head was that she must be checking on some especially cherished possession, hoping it had been spared from the demolishment, because one of her hands was outstretched. But the expression on her face was too peaceful to be guarding against great loss; she actually wore a slight smile.

If it weren't for the small, black hole in the midst of her hair, I might've missed the fact that she was dead.

CHAPTER FORTY-THREE

I called 911, forgetting that in Wedes-kyull 911 calls were routed through to the Chief. I'd known it when I used the pay phone to call about Ned, but the sight of Jean's fallen form had erased all lucid thought. When Vern answered, my mind went completely blank.

"State your emergency."

I couldn't speak.

"State your emergency. This is the chief of police. Hello? Jeannie, is that you?"

"My bag was stolen, Vern," I said non-sensically. And then I started to scream.

*   *   *

The police cars arrived in a kaleido-scope of red and blue lights. Vern exited his vehicle first, mounting Jean's porch stairs with the speed of a much younger man. Dave emerged from the same car, but he stumbled on the last step, squaring his fists on his hips and taking a look around as if there might be something outside to be seen.

Vern came upon me in the entryway, then took several fast steps in the direction of the staircase. When he spotted Jean, he let out an animal howl.

It was a bellow of shock and despair, long, drawn out, hollow, and it told me that no matter what else the Chief might be responsible for, he wasn't the one here in the house tonight.

His fists were clenched as he roused himself from studying Jean's body on the floor.

After that, everything happened quickly.

The Chief ushered me outside, and the rest of the cops descended. Tim Lurcquer arrived with his kit; a while back he'd been sent downstate to study crime scene investigation. Eileen dashed out of her house, mouth a gaping O of puzzlement. When the Chief spoke to her, her body went rigid, throwing off the Chief's hand as if an electric shock had been exchanged.

A spasm shuddered through my whole body as well; it was too cold to wait out here on the lawn. I got into my car, turned on the engine, and wondered how long the gas would last.

Vern stationed himself on the front porch, barking orders to the cops and pointing a gloved hand to direct them. In their uniforms and masks, they looked like nothing less than a troop of robots.

An ambulance drove up, along with a state vehicle whose driver looked barely awake. Both vehicles parked on Patchy Hollow Road, and the occupants got out and walked across Jean's lawn, wheeling a gurney. The gurney emerged from the house, and I wrenched my gaze away from the sight of the black body bag on top. Half a roll of yellow tape was haphazardly affixed to the rails of Jean's porch, ends immediately torn down and whipped about by the wind.

There was a reporter speaking into a tiny recorder. I scanned every face in the crowd for a glimpse of Ned, miraculously returned.

A rap shook my window.

I opened the car door and got out on the snow-clotted driveway. The Chief stood there, appearing a little more composed. "Planning on going somewhere again?"

"Just trying to keep warm," I said, wondering if he would notice anything in my abbreviated reply.

"We'll need you to give a statement." Vern gestured toward one of the cops, and the moment Gilbert opened his mouth, suggesting a place we could go, I knew.

My gaze shot down to my feet; I had to fight to remain standing.

I could feel that finger digging into my shoulder, hear the cur's rumble of his voice in my ear. Gilbert had told me to shut the old bitch up, and I hadn't. Had he killed Jean?

I raised my face to the Chief's. The man I had just been fighting to avoid, or interact with only in the briefest possible way, suddenly seemed my one hope of salvation.

"Vern—Chief—can you do the questioning?"

But the Chief was already marching off to meet Club across a snowy field. It looked like he was yelling at him. Club's finger started a jig against his holster. I caught a snatch of words.

"—even have the guts to look 'em in the—"

Gilbert was just starting to take a step forward.

Dave shambled up to me. "Mrs. H.?" he said. "I can ask you the questions."

Gilbert left, then Dave drove off after getting the scant information I had to give. Instinct kept me silent about anything besides the basics. Maybe I was wrong. And if I wasn't—and Gilbert had killed Jean after attacking me—then voicing that suspicion to the police was far from a safe option. No IA up here. Hadn't I just told Ned that?

Tim Lurcquer stood on the porch, arms folded across his chest, hat pulled down low as he gazed around methodically, right, then forward, left, and right again.

Club was also still there. Approaching me, he said, "We'll put you up in a hotel tonight."

"What?"

His reply was grim. "Where did you think you would go?"

Brendan never had to deal with a murder where the suspect wasn't obvious and locked up right away. Tim was going to stay here, all night probably, on the lookout for anything that might happen, someone who might return. Did I really think I would just cozy up in the spare room of a woman who'd just been murdered?

Something plugged my throat; I had to gulp back tears. I turned and headed for my car.

"I'll drive you," Club called.

"No," I said. I swiped a gloved finger across my eyes. "That's not necessary."

Club strode toward me, slowed down not at all by the heaps on the ground. "You want to take your own car?" he said. "Fine. It'll be the Super 8. I'll have Dave meet you there. You seem to prefer him lately." Club huffed a cloud of white. He reached for his radio, speaking into it between crackling bursts of static.

CHAPTER FORTY-FOUR

Dave pulled up behind me in the Super 8 parking lot. "You're some driver," he said, getting out and slipping a bit as he crossed the lot. "That ice was bad."

"How does this work?"

Dave shrugged genially. "Not much to it. Police have an account. I'll go in and tell whoever's there that we need a room for tonight. Then you get a key." Dave looked down at me, and I saw a hint of something sharper than the usual in his eyes. "You can stand next to me the whole time. It's not like I'll get a dupe."

"I didn't think that," I said, and he patted me companionably on the arm. He pulled open the door, started to enter, then stepped backward in a hurry. But Dave was too bulky for me to pass in front of, and when I signaled that it was okay, he shook his head in protest before going forward, so that we got confused and tripped over each other again.

After that, registration went smoothly, and I let myself into room number 12, keeping the door open an extra few seconds despite the cold.

Dave lifted one thickly gloved hand, waving goodbye as he clomped across the lot.

I waited to leave until he had driven off.

I thought of Ned's sudden, soundless disappearance. The police could do pretty much anything, but their tactics seemed to involve subterfuge and misdirection. Fires that might've been accidents. A death that could've been a bungled robbery in a dark house in the middle of the night. Here at the motel where the cops had stashed me—where

they might stash everyone who was giving them trouble, for all I knew—I was a
sitting duck.

How had I gone from considering the
police my husband's second family to
suspecting them of arson, abduction,
and murder? The thought that this whole
thing was some sort of grief-induced
psychosis beckoned like a warm quilt.
And Ned is suffering the same delusion?
demanded the internal Teggie.

Better safe than sorry. I wouldn't let a
desire to turn away get me killed.

But it wasn't as if alternatives
abounded. My own house was gone,
and the house Ned had just hired me to
work on wasn't in a much better state.
Jean had been the only member of the
family who could stand me, and now
she was gone, too. And I'd never really
made any friends of my own up here. I
took in a choking gulp of air as the fact
of my aloneness descended, as deep
as the cold that encased this part of the
world, seeming permanent by now, as if
spring would never come again.

There weren't other motels, not anywhere nearby. And you couldn't exactly check into one of Wedeskyull's quaint inns at this hour.

The temperature precluded trying to last out the aborted remainder of the night in my car. I'd be dead by morning.

And then a possible place occurred to me.

Ned had never given up his cabin on Squall Lake. He'd been going to occupy it himself after the first fire. If it wasn't still rented, then I might just be able to hunker down there for a night. Decide tomorrow what to do.

I hadn't been to the cabin before, but Ned had mentioned its location, and it was easy enough to find. The road had been kept clear by a private service used by vacation residents and owners of rental units. No vehicle sat in the drive, and the cabin was lightless. Its door was locked, but a window opened without difficulty, and I hoisted myself up and crawled through.

It was almost as cold inside as out. The rough wood walls gave off vapor, and I stared longingly at the logs criss-crossed by the stove. But I was wary of revealing my location even by as unlikely a hint as smoke curling up from a distant chimney.

I realized I was starving, and entered the kitchen. The last renters had left it in pretty good shape, except for a few cabinet doors hanging loose on their hinges. But those cabinets contained tins of ready-to-eat food, and I gobbled their contents gratefully.

A closet held blankets, and once I got settled beneath them, with the food in my belly, I didn't even feel all that cold.

I fell asleep.

I awoke with a stunned sort of sense of well-being. Aunt Jean was dead, and Ned had gone missing. I had no home and no belongings. And no one to turn to for help with any of it. But I had eaten, and I'd slept.

And I had figured out what to do next.

A gap in the blankets exposed me, and frigid air bit my neck and arms.

My tools were lost, but I was fairly sure, given the well-stocked nature of this cabin, Ned would have a screwdriver somewhere. Trusting that he would be back one day to see, I straightened every one of those sagging cabinet doors.

TACTICS

Gil Landry was the only cop on the force without a family connection. He wasn't the Chief's fucking brother. His old man sure hadn't been on the job. Gil didn't even know his old man. For as long as he could remember, it had been just him and his ma.

Which was okay. They were a team, always had been, except when Gil had enlisted. He didn't know what would've happened if he hadn't washed out. The look on his ma's face when he came home—well, it made the whole fucked-up situation worth it.

The day after the fat lady's death, the Chief called Gil into his office. Early, before anyone else had come in. Thick snow was falling outside. Gil hated snow, he always had. The snow got you in a chokehold and didn't let go for seven months. But no matter how cold Gil got, he always stood staunchly, body straight as a rifle stock, refusing to shiver.

That had been the best part about being on a carrier. No snow in the Gulf. Still, he was glad to be home. Turned out things in the Navy didn't work like they did in Wedeskyull. And frankly, Gil thought they had it wrapped up better here.

"I got word from McAllister," the Chief said from behind his desk.

The fire chief. Gil kept his hands locked behind his thighs, face expressionless.

The Chief's face looked heavier than usual this morning, and his big body slumped in the chair. Too bad it had been Mitchell in that house last night, not him. If some old broad had started giving him trouble, he would've done exactly what Mitchell did, but he would've done it better and cleaner. If he'd been there, no one ever would've found out what had happened.

Silence hung over the office like a haze. Gil waited patiently.

"He suspects accelerants on the Queek Pond job. Says if they hadn't gotten there as fast as they did, the whole place would've gone up."

Gil's hands, which had been hanging by his sides, clenched into fists. "The whole place didn't go up because there was nothing in there worth burning. It was empty as a fucking warehouse. We ignited some papers on a desk and left."

"What papers?" the Chief asked. But he was looking away and didn't really seem to care about the answer.

"We didn't take time to read them, Chief," Gil said.

The Chief looked at him. "You talking back to me, boy?"

"No, sir." He drew a breath and went on. "Whatever they were, they're gone now. And we took take care of anything else there might be, too."

"Yeah," the Chief responded. "Seems

like there's a lot being taken care of lately."

Gil's vision fuzzed for a second. He was trying to keep up and the effort made his head throb. The Chief was talking, but he wasn't saying what he meant. That must've been a reference to the second fire. But Gil wasn't to blame for how that had gone down. He knew explosives, a little, but this wasn't somewhere in towel-head-istan. Torching a private residence was a whole other deal, and he'd told the Chief he was no firebug. Hamilton's house had to be destroyed anyway. They'd torn every inch of it apart before striking the first match. The reporter who for some reason was crashing there had been out, but who knew when he might return? No way could they have gotten it back in decent shape in time.

Gil didn't get the feeling from Hamilton's old lady that losing her house— losing any house, even though she worked on them, if you could call that *work*—would make her run away, though. Hamilton had never talked much about her, he was good at keeping his head down and his boots out of the muck. They had hated guys like Hamilton in his class. But his wife wasn't the same. She kept messing and pushing. Luckily she had no idea what she was looking for.

There'd been nothing in her house, and nothing in her car. Whatever they'd been trying to find didn't exist. And maybe the Chief was finally coming to accept that. At least, he sure looked today as if he'd given up.

"I'll deal with McAllister's report," Gil said. "No one will ever see it."

"You're forgetting the insurance company."

Gil's hands were still clenched. "I have a feeling no claim will ever be filed."

"You sure about that?" the Chief said, his tone changing so imperceptibly that at first Gil hardly even noticed. "No surprises?"

He raised his head, and Gil saw that as slow and plugged as the Chief seemed to be this morning—the same look had deadened Gil's ma the day Gil left for boot camp in Great Lakes—he was still sharp as an ax.

"No surprises, sir."

"Like you and Lurcquer were surprised by Mr. Cooper?"

"Cooper didn't fucking surprise us," Gil said, working to restrain himself.

"No?" the Chief said, voice gleaming with understanding. "I thought you were taking him to get medical treatment."

Gil felt a cord start to pulse on his forehead. "You know the state that poor bastard was in? His lungs were fucking barbequed. Charred meat, man. He didn't stand a chance."

The edge disappeared from the Chief's voice, and his shoulders suddenly sagged. "Look, boy, I don't care. I don't care what you did. Just make sure I never hear another word about it." He paused. "Or about the reporter, either."

The Chief gave Gil a look that said he was dismissed, and suddenly Gil wanted nothing more than to lodge his elbow in the Chief's fleshy neck and break his windpipe. Elbows and knees: the best weapons man would ever possess to extinguish a close, personal threat.

"What are you waiting for, boy?"

Gil turned and left the office. He strode to his desk, suppressing an urge to sweep the surface clear of all its fancy gadgets, plastic flying like shrapnel.

Whatever was about to happen, he was still on the job. He still had his freedom. And a Chief who knew—better than any lieutenant ever had—that if things got bogged down, you had to climb out of the bog using any means available. You didn't wait around to see if someone was going to lower a hand.

He wished the other seamen had understood that back at training. He would've made a good SEAL.

Gil Landry knew how to appear out of nowhere, and disappear the same way, so that nobody ever had any idea that he'd been there.

He knew how to hurt a man so badly he couldn't draw breath.

And he knew how to make sure a man never knew that the breath he had just taken would be his last.

CHAPTER FORTY-FIVE

Eileen would be gone this morning. She'd have to be; there was no one else to arrange for the funeral. Jean's last words, about having been silent long enough, came back to me. Silent about what? What had she been intending to do?

If I let myself think now, I would be paralyzed. I shook my head with a willful jerk.

When I arrived at the bottom of Patchy Hollow Road, it was clear that I wouldn't have to do any sneaking around. The emptiness was total. I'd driven up at a crawl, ready to drop back the second I caught a drab glimpse of gray, but not one police car was parked anywhere nearby, and although I circled the perimeter of Jean's house, no cop was stationed outside.

I climbed onto the porch, ducking beneath a swag of yellow tape, and peered through the windows into the deserted rooms.

The lookout and investigation had been pro forma, put on for whatever media coverage Jean's death drew, or maybe even for me. Nobody was looking into her murder.

I descended the porch steps and made my way across the snowpacked road to Eileen's.

As I had expected, my mother-in-law was gone, too. I had taken two things from Ned's cabin after deciding on a plan. One was a flashlight. Answers had been found in this house once. Maybe there were others I'd missed.

Something brushed against the back of my coat as I pushed open the basement door, and began my descent. Stifling a yelp, I barreled down the rest of the steps, the basement less forbidding than the prospect of my mother-in-law behind me.

Hitting the concrete floor, I whirled around and aimed the flashlight at the top of the stairs. The beam illuminated a rope of dust, swinging from a ceiling light. I went back upstairs on trembling legs and shut the cellar door, closing myself inside.

What had been a perilous blind-man's bluff without the light was an easy stride now. I used Ned's screwdriver to pick the lock, then pushed open the door to Eileen's cavern. I'd have to search with precision. I had no idea when she might return.

But what was I looking for this time?

Surely if Eileen had anything here of value to be found, her house would've been burned, too, or its occupant menaced. Maybe she had been; I had no way of knowing. Yet unlike Jean, whose final words had held such portent and intent, Eileen seemed perfectly content to keep things concealed.

The furnace stood only a few feet away, breathing right outside this room.

Sweaty and hot, I stripped off my outer gear, and left it in a pile by the door.

Something was different. I took a slow look around, considering. The first time I'd come everything had been frosted with dust. Now all the surfaces were clear, swept clean.

I resisted the urge to throw things around in a desperate hunt, as somebody had done in Jean's kitchen. Instead I approached it the way I would a job, conducting a methodical examination of all the objects I recalled to make sure nothing was missing, then seeking anything hidden, much as I used to find ceiling medallions beneath asbestos tiles, plaster under wallboard.

There were the photos, of course, several walls' worth of them, including one that leapt out: Bill searching beneath the ice for his son. Those canceled checks, made out to cash, but with that baffling word on the memo line. *Resurrection*. The long paper diagram, rag doll named Pooky, a carton of minuscule clothes. Eileen had replaced Rascal's fallen clump of hair in the precise spot in which I'd found it.

I crouched down, but there were no hidden relics under the desk. Standing on tiptoes to locate any concealed spots by the ceiling yielded nothing, either.

Helplessly scanning the walls once again, I took in a picture I hadn't spotted before. The unquenchable horror of it glued my eyes, made me forget the time pressure I was under. Someone had taken a shot of the place where Red must have died. An enormous expanse of scabby ice, and the Cyclops eye Red had dropped through at its center. This was a monstrous-sized lake, a body of water of such volume that its frozen three-foot covering might be nothing more than a cap on a giant's head. I couldn't stop staring at that hole.

And then I saw another photograph high up on a corner of wall. If I'd seen it the first time, I hadn't dwelled on it because I didn't recognize the person in it. A boy, perhaps fourteen or fifteen, with longish, almost flaxen hair. Something about him was familiar. It was his T-shirt.

I boosted myself onto Eileen's desk, and walked a few paces down, not caring when I disturbed her displays with my tread. I squinted at the picture, then reached up one hand, picking at the paper's slick edge. Eileen had used some kind of indomitable glue; I needed my tools. One corner came free and I peeled off some more, standing on tiptoes to look again, be sure.

The letters on the boy's shirt spelled out the word *Stonelickers*. There were a couple of beer logos on the shirt, and beneath them, an address. It was in Cold Kettle, New York.

The picture came free and I pocketed it. Then I jumped down.

I had no idea if this was all that was here to be found, but I knew it was important, a link between Eileen's archeological dig and the contents of Brendan's box. And I knew one other thing. I was out of time.

Through the thick, muting walls of the cellar, there came the gust of a car engine.

I crept up the basement stairs and into the parlor, clicking off my flashlight. Pulling a narrow flap of curtain aside, I peered out into the yard. Eileen's car was still gone. But a gray vehicle sat in her drive.

I let the curtain fall and whipped around, breathing hard. I couldn't tell which cop had come. The possibility that it was Gilbert triggered fear so great that it nearly aborted all motion, the way a child will grind to a halt when she is being chased. Gilbert was about to climb the steps and knock, or more likely he would just enter. And then he would come and get me and do that thing to my shoulder again. Sense memory returned, those fingers grinding down to meat and muscle, and panic threatened to overtake me.

There was a thud of boots on the walkway outside.

Withdrawing the photograph from my pocket, where it made a telltale outline, I slid it down past the waist of my jeans. Then I backed away from the window.

Upstairs seemed both the most risky and least detectable place to hide. It surely contained numerous spots for concealment. But if the one I chose was discovered, I'd be trapped. I dashed up the stairs anyway. I knew foursquares. I

should be able to locate someplace un-
apparent to the casual seeker.

Except this seeker wouldn't be casual. He'd been sent to find me.

HURT

Dugger stood in bare feet, wearing only his undershorts. He was looking for something in his room. He picked things up and set them down one at a time. He could only use one hand, so it took him a while. When he had nothing left to pick up, he took a look around. He liked this room. It cost him three hundred dollars every month and Mr. Meter always gave him precisely triple that, so he had no trouble paying for this room.

He had a few other places in the apartment he could check, but he had to get dressed first. He'd almost forgotten to get dressed. Clothes on, he lifted up the shade on his window and looked out. He never did that before, but now he had to. His arm reminded him.

He wished that he might see Brendan, driving up, looking in on him. But he knew that wouldn't happen anymore. Brendan had been a good kind of friend, sometimes standing along the sidelines like Dugger did, making a joke or, since Dugger never laughed, just listening to what he had to say. Dugger wasn't friends with the other ones, but still, he hadn't known one of them would hurt him. He never thought someone would do something like that.

It was funny—funnier than the jokes Brendan used to tell—but even though Brendan came to check on him, really it was Dugger who looked out for Brendan. He had ever since Brendan did something he got into terrible trouble for. Not the punished kind of trouble. The worse kind, when no one even needed to punish you.

And with Brendan not here anymore to look out for, Dugger would do the next best thing. He would watch out for the person Brendan had loved.

He opened up drawers in the kitchen, but they were mostly empty. One held a fork, a spoon, and a dull knife. Another held just a bright rubber ball. There were some old candy wrappers. What he was looking for wasn't there, although he did come across a ribbon of negatives. Dugger held the strip up to the too bright ceiling light, blinking. This light always hurt his eyes.

There was the lake with the hole in it. And Mister Hamilton crawling across the ice, looking underneath. Dugger had developed these pictures for Missus Hamilton a long time ago and left them under her doorsill. He could still remember her face when she found them. She looked like Brendan and his friends did when they had drunk too much beer by Big Rock and were going to be sick.

He'd been spying on her, watching while she looked at the pictures. And then she stopped looking at them and pressed them tightly to her chest. And Dugger knew Missus Hamilton wasn't going to be sick after all and that he had done a good thing. He had been crouched behind a bush, still small enough to fit, even though people didn't seem to notice him much more even after he got big.

And suddenly Dugger remembered where the thing he was looking for must be. He had been small when he had hidden it away. He hadn't lived here yet, in this room that he liked.

But now he was bigger, and so was what had happened.

He lifted up another shade. Everything outside looked quiet. Dugger turned on his car, using the remote control. Now he had to wait precisely six minutes until the car would be warm inside, and the engine would hum like a busy hive of bees, every part doing its work. Listening to the beautiful song of the engine, Dugger forgot the pain in his arm for a while.

Finally he went out to the street. One-handed, he started to drive.

The roads were twisty. He had to go a long ways. Dugger had forgotten how far he had come on his own. His other arm, the one that didn't throb and ache and scream in a voice Dugger had never heard before, was getting tired from doing all the work.

He stopped and got out in front of the house he had lived in a long time ago. He was supposed to knock, but one hand was too sore to make a fist, and the other felt too weak.

Someone heard anyway and came running. Dugger could hear the tripping of feet inside the house. She opened the door. She started to spread her arms out, but then she stopped.

"Momma," Dugger said. "I think it's time."

Words spun together in his head, a candied, sticky web. *Grime, lime, mime. Rhyme.* Words that fit together like the pieces of an engine.

His mother raised one hand and the words broke into bits before they could leave his mouth. She stepped out on the stoop. "Welcome home, baby."

CHAPTER FORTY-SIX

Toward the back of Jean's foursquare was an attic crawlspace she had never bothered to finish. I figured that if Brendan's aunt, who had lavished such care on her house, didn't do much with that space, then there was a good chance Eileen had left hers alone as well.

Aware of the thud of boots on the porch, I raced down a threadbare length of rug along Eileen's hallway. I got down on the floor in a crouch and pulled open the little door. People stowed cartons or vacuum cleaners or buckets in here; it wasn't sized for a human. I lay on my belly and wriggled into the dark, gritty channel. Squeezing myself into a ball, I pulled the door shut.

I blinked a few times, willing my eyes to adjust to the dark. Then I army-crawled along the strip of dirty subfloor so that I would be as far away from the opening as possible. I scooted ahead a few final paces, hitting the wall hard with the tips of my fingers, and stifling a bark of pain.

I could make out other noises now. The creak of stairs sinking beneath someone's heavy tread, a steady pace of footsteps down the hall. The sounds ceased just outside the low door that concealed me. I lay there motionless, not daring to blink.

The door opened and a column of light shot in. I remained on my belly, breathing hard as my thoughts contin-ued racing forward.

How had he done it? Whoever stood outside now had tracked me as surely as if I'd left a trail of bread crumbs. His stride had been loud, methodical; he'd made not a single wrong turn or misstep, nor taken any effort to conceal his approach.

"What the fuck are you doing?" asked a voice that was faintly recognizable.

Not the voice of my attacker, and scared as I was, something in me blossomed with relief.

Still, I had no idea what to say. Part of me wanted to throw my arms over my head and play possum. Maybe he was bluffing; didn't know anybody was in here at all.

"Get out of there, Nora," Tim Lurcquer said. "Now."

It was humiliating to slide out of the crawlspace on my stomach backwards, like some errant hide-and-seeker, and even more humiliating to be terrified as I did it, limbs rattling like loose pipes so that I fell forward and smacked my nose once, bringing tears to my eyes.

When I reached the entry and started to rise, Tim loomed above me, an implacable wall of gray. He reached down and grabbed my arm, yanking me roughly to my feet.

"What are you doing here?" He spoke

through gritted teeth as he dragged me down the hall.

"Nothing," I stammered, mind scrambling. "I mean, I wanted to see if I could find my mother-in-law." Maybe playing the family card would buy me something. "Offer help with the arrangements for Jean."

"You were looking for her in the crawlspace?" Tim said.

We had reached the stairs. He was still gripping my arm, but he had relaxed his hold a little now that he had me. What was he planning to do? I had to skip a step to keep up with him, and I lunged awkwardly, twisting my ankle. Again, I stifled a bleat of pure pain.

Then I gave up all pretense. I couldn't deceive Tim; obviously there was no good reason for my having been where I was. And if he wanted to hand me over to the Chief—or to somebody worse—then I couldn't stop him. All I could do was fall back on the thing that'd been hanging me up ever since Ned told me his theory about the police. I knew these men. They'd been both friend and family to my husband.

"What happened to Jean, Tim?" I asked, low. "Do you know?"

He glanced at me. I looked at his small, pressed-together features, searching for a hint of kinship or kindness in his narrow eyes.

"We're questioning a vagrant. He's been staying in one of the unwinterized cabins nearby." Still holding on to me, Tim pulled me toward the front room. He yanked the curtains apart and squinted outside.

I stared at him. Even I could discern the difference between a robbery and an execution. "Jean was shot in the back of her head," I said. "From the look on her face, she had no idea what was coming at all."

"That's right," Tim replied blandly, still looking outside. "Also, in all the years Jean Hamilton occupied that house, no one ever thought she had anything worth stealing." He dropped the curtain back into place. "So we gotta ask ourselves, what's changed? Who was she spending time with, what was she doing that was different before she got killed?"

He looked at me significantly, eyes narrowing till they were almost shut.

I gave an experimental tug to try to free my arm. Tim's fingers bore down. My voice came out small, choked. "Am I under suspicion?" If the police were wondering about my role in things, then Ned had it completely wrong. Far from being the overlords of Franklin County, these cops were idiots, with no clue what was really going on.

Of course, the best defense was a good offense.

Tim was still regarding me, the familiar, appraising look of a cop.

"On the other hand," he continued, "Ms. Hamilton was coming into a large insurance payout. Or maybe she kept cash around. And this asshole went looking for it."

Jean did keep cash in the house. She'd given me some before we went to bed, to replace the lost funds in my wallet.

The radio let out a crackle of static at Tim's waist. I heard some codes, a whole combination of numbers, and watched Tim react. Something in his face changed, or maybe it was his stance. I felt his grasp loosen. And in the split second he gave me, I tore away. I ran for the front door and pulled it open. My car was a red beacon. I heard the steady thump of Tim's boots behind me, but kept running. I stumbled in the deep snow, and realized as I threw my arms out to protect myself, and icy chunks slid up the cuffs of my shirt, that I had forgotten my coat.

But my keys were in my jeans. I had learned never to let those off my person.

The temperature in the car had to be hovering around zero, and my entire body spasmed with cold. I could die out here like this, but I didn't have a choice in the matter right now. Tim was standing on the buried lawn, just feet from his patrol car.

I twisted the key in the ignition once, then twice, the second try followed by a startling screech from the engine. I lurched into gear and reversed onto the road. Patchy Hollow was empty, an unfurling ribbon of white between woods. My car hurtled down the middle of it, avoiding the snow flanking both sides, keeping to the plowed center.

And then it wasn't empty anymore. Before the roar of the motor could reach me, I caught a faraway glimpse of Club's Jimmy barreling down the road. I saw the black slash of Weekend's snout thrust out as if he were scenting something.

I glanced left and right. Up ahead was an opening in the high wall of snow, a snowmobile trail carved through the leafless trees. I wrenched my wheel to one side and jolted onto it. The trail was narrow and twisting; my tires rose up against snowdrifts, causing the body of the car to settle back down with a jaw-cracking bounce. I slowed abruptly, inching forward until I could be sure that no spot of red would be seen.

Then I sat and waited for the sound of Club's engine to dissipate as he raced by.

CHAPTER FORTY-SEVEN

The first thing I did was check my jeans for the photograph. It had slid down my leg and gotten slightly crumpled during my maneuvers; a white crease bisected the boy's T-shirt now. But the word on it was still discernible, and so was his face.

The cops had found me at Ned's office. They'd found me at Eileen's. Wedeskyull was their land more than it would ever be mine. I needed to go where no one would ever think to look for me.

But first I had to buy a coat.

The sun was rising in the sky, blinding

against the vast vistas of white, when I reached the road into town. I took my foot off the gas and pulled over to the shoulder. My car was too recognizable to stay put for long, but I needed to assess my options. The blowers were finally emitting hot enough air that I had stopped shivering, and an uncertain sun had emerged. I reached up, squinting, to pull the visor down, and a piece of paper dropped out.

I looked around to make sure the road was empty, then unfolded the sheet.

My heart immediately started an uneven thronging in my chest as I beheld the scrawled signature.

Ned.

He was alive. I realized only as my vision started to swim that I had been convinced he wasn't—and what a second gap of loss this had left.

I'm all right, and if you're reading this then you are, too. I won't be able to surface for a while, and you need to go somewhere as well. I would come for you, but it would only make things worse. They'll be looking for me now.

Those last six words clanged like a bell. I took a rapid look around, then read the rest of the note.

I had no idea they would go this far. Next time we see each other, I promise I will never say you don't look at things straight again.

Next time we saw each other. Swallowing hard, I checked the road, then pulled out and headed into town.

A stack of maps sat in my glove compartment. One was of New England, one was of New York State, and the southeastern region was spottily covered by a road trip Brendan and I had once taken to Disney World. But I didn't own a single one addressing the cobweb of roads that made up Franklin County. My explorations here had been limited. And without a map, I didn't stand a chance of finding the tiny spot of habitation amidst a blowing world of white that would be Cold Kettle.

It was probably only twenty or thirty miles from Wedeskyull, but they were miles best left alone in the dead of winter.

I would simply have to find a road that stayed open, meaning the plows went through every few days. Because I had a feeling, sure and pressing as a lump in my throat, that whoever or whatever was responsible for Brendan's death was now rallying forces, closing in. By winter's end, any hope of finding out the truth would be gone, too.

The best place to buy local maps was the Mobil station across from Al's garage. I didn't want to linger in town, but right now the need for a map was nearly as urgent as that for a coat. Just a brief stop, I told myself. Nothing could happen to me in broad daylight, out in plain sight.

If the Chief, propelled by Gilbert or Tim, decided to identify my whereabouts, how easy would it be for him to do it? I imagined gray patrol cars, leaving their barracks like insects, swarming out across the streets of Wedeskyull.

I entered the everything-store in town—junk food, soda, hardware, small appliances, cleaning supplies, toys, paperbacks, and music, in addition to clothes—and began jogging through the aisles, snatching winter gear off the racks. I gave a longing thought to the tools, just one row away, but no time for that now. No time even for a toothbrush.

"Hello, Mrs. Hamilton."

I stopped in my tracks in the middle of the aisle. I didn't turn around. The silence grew thick and dense behind me.

"Need help finding anything today?"

I glanced over my shoulder at the clerk in her pink smock. "No. Thank you. I'm done."

The clerk took my items out of my hands and carried them up to the register. I shifted from foot to foot as I waited, looking out the broad windows along the front of the store.

"That'll be forty-seven dollars and six cents."

I paid, using a chunk of Jean's cash, and the clerk began to bag my items.

"I can just take those," I said, reaching for the winter gear and pulling it on as I continued to steal glances outside.

"Nora." A hand settled on my arm, and the zipper I was yanking up gave a high whine.

"I've been meaning to drop by ever

since we came home. I'm so sorry we were away for the funeral. And then we got here and saw your poor house—"

It was my neighbor.

"Thanks, Mrs. Melville," I said, beginning to back toward the automatic doors. One opened behind me.

"Is there anything I can do for you?" the woman went on in an imploring tone. "I just feel so dreadful."

"No, thank you, there's really—"

"Here, step in," she urged. "You're letting in all the cold."

"Mrs. Melville—"

"Where are you staying, dear? At least I could bring some dishes by."

Someone entered the store, and my heart jumped when he had to steer around me, bumping my arm.

"And you know we do have a spare room ourselves—"

"Mrs. Melville," I cried. "I really have to go!"

And I ran out of the store, clutching my new hat and scarf.

The Mobil On the Run smelled of old coffee, and I suppressed a ripple of nausea. I was hungry, though, despite my apprehension, and still chilled, so I filled a cup of tea and grabbed a fistful of chocolate bars. Then I crouched down before the bank of registers and fanned through the selection of maps. I pulled out the ones that covered Franklin County and the surround—some of this area extended upward to Canada—and plunked my purchases down on the counter.

"Pump number?" asked the bored clerk.

"I didn't get any gas," I said, flicking my gaze out to the parking lot. My red car sat there like a traffic light, a stop sign. But the rest of the cars in the lot seemed innocuous enough, mostly SUVs with skis or snowboards atop their roofs.

"What's in the cup?" the clerk said in the same monotone.

"Tea," I answered, a little frantically. I dug around in my pocket and laid a twenty on the counter. Without my pack, I felt as if something had been amputated. "Look, I think this should cover it," I said, turning for the exit.

"Ma'am, your change!" the clerk called, finally with some intonation, but I was already at the glass door, its electronic *ding* as loud as the crescendo of a symphony as I raced across the salted expanse of asphalt, clumsy in my boots but moving fast.

When I got to my car, Dugger was sitting in the driver's seat.

He was dressed entirely in white camo. I came to a sudden halt, drink, maps, and bars wobbling in my hands. Steadying everything, I started to walk around to him, but Dugger raised one finger and pointed to the other side of the car.

I saw his lips moving behind the glass. Then he raised his voice, loud enough to be heard. "Get in, Missus," he said, startlingly lucid before his normal singsong returned. "In, din, time for a spin—" He broke off, responding to something unseen, or at least something I wasn't seeing. "Now," he said. No rhyming. "Please, Missus."

I had been thinking to question him, if not refuse outright. But the tone of his voice changed my mind. I yanked open

the door and dropped onto the passenger seat.

Dugger drove out of the lot, cutting
cleanly in front of an SUV loaded with
brawling twenty-somethings out for their
day on the slopes, keeping their beast
of a vehicle looming to our rear, where
it blocked the sight of my little car, so
that I had to twist around to see the patrol car traveling in the distance behind.

BEATEN

In the feverish hours of his recovery, as he spoke in a sequestered location to federal officials, and worked on his story, Ned tried to recall the details of his capture and escape.

He had gotten dragged off from the parking lot outside his office. Either that or lifted somehow; his removal had seemed almost instantaneous. A hand had landed on his shoulder and then there'd been a blow to his temple—Ned did remember that—before consciousness was blotted away.

When he'd come to, his vision had

been blocked with a blindfold drawn tight as a vise, and his coat and boots had been removed. The floor beneath his feet felt gritty, and the temperature wasn't much warmer than outside. Ned fought to put together where he might be. Some kind of unheated shed? The basement of an abandoned building?

There were smells—a reek of perspiration and fear, the sweet stink of sudden bodily effluence—and an iron tang in his mouth that Ned couldn't wash out no matter how often he spat. He was scared at first that the blow to his head had left him bleeding internally, but after a terrified couple of seconds, bringing his fingers to his ears and his nose, he reassured himself that the damage must be relatively superficial. He was in pain—his head and face felt as if they'd been smashed—but his mind was starting to clear.

Then a voice crawled out of the darkness. Ned hadn't been able to place it, and he wasn't sure if that was because he didn't know the guy, or because his brain was still foggy.

"You're gonna lay off now," came the command.

Ned kept silent, hoping the person would give him something he could use.

"Say something, asshole," the voice continued. "Or are you too used to other people talking?"

Ned still didn't speak. The next thing he heard was a whistling through the air. Was that the whicker of rope, or reins maybe? Ned felt something streak past him, whipping his arm so hard and so fast that at first he didn't realize he'd been cut. His shirtsleeve was not just torn, but split apart. Blood spilled from the wound on his arm.

Ned howled, a sound that somehow seemed to belong with the appalling animal stink of this place.

That voice came again, low and terrible. "I can stay here all night. Or you can stop this right now."

Ned could think of only one play, one way he might be able to get himself out of here. And if it didn't work—Ned didn't want to think about that whip coming at him again. His insides cramped with fear as he forced words out. "Stop what?"

This time the silence came from his oppressor. There was a long pause before the voice spoke again. "What you're doing, asshole."

"What am I doing?"

Silence again.

The effort to speak had brought to life a pulsing in his head. Ned was going to be sick—Jesus, he couldn't be sick right now—

"The fucking story you're working on."

Ned knew the Chief's voice, and Lurcquer's. He'd spoken to Mitchell from time to time. This wasn't any of them. Landry, then. How much did he know? Had Lurcquer been made?

Ned forced out a laugh, dragging it past the nausea in his throat. "What's wrong with my story? What's it to you?"

This time nothing filled the silence.

Ned fought to speak again. "What's the big deal? It's a human interest piece. About ancient history."

The voice that returned was dreadful, but it also planted a tiny little spark of hope in Ned. Because it sounded unsure.

"You kidding me? What the fuck are you talking about?"

Ned aped patience. "I'm talking about my story. The one you saw fit to smack me around over." If he made light of what happened, he'd be in better straits. Landry might feel less threatened. "What don't you like about it?"

A pause. "It's—" The voice broke off. "What's the story about?"

Here was the moment. Here was his play. And it had to be done just right.

"See for yourself. You burned up most of my hard copies, okay? But there are a few things left. Look in my coat." He'd shoved these papers deep in his pocket after meeting with Nora, and as far as he recalled, never taken them out.

Good Lord, he'd better never have taken them out.

The effort of putting the words together had left him shaky and queasy. Ned leaned over, trying to lower his head, and a rush of air against his arm set it aflame. He stifled a groan.

Then he heard something that distracted him momentarily. Boots thumping, shuffling sounds, things being shifted around, the *whish* of fabric. Finally, a crackle of paper, which made Ned's heart give a strong, relieved beat.

He straightened up.

Landry spoke in a tone of total disbelief from where he had located Ned's coat. "That ice-fishing accident? Some kid died?"

"Right," Ned answered, a pulse starting anew in his head. If Landry saw through the bluff, he knew what awaited. He fought to get words out. "It's the twenty-fifth anniversary. Paper wanted me to do a follow-up in honor of it."

"Fucking A."

Ned kept his face expressionless beneath the blindfold. He had no idea which way Landry might be looking. It was easy to stay still anyway—motion started a three-alarm blaze in his head.

Then he heard the sound of papers being tossed down, and a queasy wave of hope rolled over him.

Landry didn't bother to return his coat or boots before pulling Ned out into the frigid night air. He opened a car door and kneed Ned into the backseat. This was a cruiser all right.

They drove for a long time. Then the rear door was pulled open, and Ned dumped out.

Seconds later, he felt the muzzle of a gun on his temple.

"If I ever see you in Wedeskyull again," Landry said, "you will wish I'd shot you tonight. You will wish that you'd begged me to shoot you. Got it?"

Ned heard a car door slam and realized that the cold bite of the gun had been replaced by icy air at the side of his head.

He waited until the engine noise had dissipated to pull off his blindfold.

The road was utterly empty. No houses were lit up in the distance, which left Ned no choice but to trudge along in his stocking feet. They had started to tingle and burn—which he knew was a far sight better than the next stage, when all feeling would be lost—by the time a pickup truck came along.

Ned flagged it down, watching as the truck rolled to a halt a quarter mile up the road.

The driver cranked down his window and leaned out. He frowned, taking in the sight of Ned's missing shoes and coat, the blood on him, and his torn shirt.

Ned finally pitched forward, and he began to retch.

CHAPTER FORTY-EIGHT

The unlit light bar atop the cop's car was the most ominous detail of all. He didn't want anyone to observe him coming for us.

The car sped up, a shadowy blur of gray.

Dugger pressed on the gas, turning a few corners and losing the SUV. But the patrol car remained, and it was gaining on us.

I tightened my seat belt across my chest. My car was doing speeds on snow-narrowed roads I hadn't known it was capable of. Dugger took a corner, spinning the wheel with one hand, and lodging the other arm in front of me like a barricade. He winced when he did it, and I wasn't sure why.

We made a turn that threatened to send us both flying across the interior, if not roll the car altogether, and only Dugger held me in place. I panted in gratitude but he didn't even look at me, setting both hands down on the wheel as the tires squealed. Whoever was behind us wasn't managing the turns as well. Dugger increased his speed, flooring it now.

The car crested a hill, and for a second I thought there was nothing on the other side, not anything a car could take anyway. The road was so steep that the rear tires rose off the ground as we plummeted over the top.

My body actually left the seat for a second, and again Dugger was bracing me, his own form miraculously steady. Then I slapped back down with a jaw-cracking bounce. My tongue tasted blood, and a steely pain pierced my head. At last my car seemed to be feeling the chase, riding low on one side, slip-sliding in the snow.

"Dugger," I gasped.

His brow was set in furrows of concentration and he didn't answer.

The tires caught with a zigzagging wave as Dugger raced around another bend. The rear of the car swung out as if it were on a hitch. I stifled a scream and clamped my hands against the dash, holding myself this time. Dugger's fists were wrapped around the wheel; he needed them both. But the other set of tires behind us was no longer squealing. It was the only sign I had that we might have lost him.

Dugger also seemed to be slowing minutely, another indicator. Then finally he spoke. "Sorry, Missus. I had to lead him this way."

I looked at him, trying to steady my breaths. "What are you talking about?"

He was glowering at the dirt and gravel spraying up beside us as he pumped the brakes.

"Lead him what way? Where are we?"

We had arrived on a stretch of unpaved road that dead-ended at a mountainside. The steep slope was glossed with white and studded all over by trees. I had no idea where we were, dense forest somewhere. There was another car parked across the road, a nondescript sedan.

Dugger came to an abrupt stop. He flinched again, undoing his belt, although there'd been no contact this time.

"Dugger?" I asked. "Are you okay?"

"My arm, Missus," he responded. His bright eyes momentarily darkened. "It got hurt."

"Hurt?" I echoed. "How?"

But he didn't answer, just opened the door with his other hand and got out.

I cracked my door and leaned sideways to thank him for helping me escape Wedeskyull. Saving me maybe. But he gestured me forward. "Hurry, Missus."

I glanced up at him.

"Your car is red," he said.

Red dead, red head.

"We can't take it."

"Take it where?" I asked.

Dugger got into the other car, and waited for me to follow.

✳ ✳ ✳

I stuck the maps and candy bars—melty now, and warm—into the pockets of my new coat. I got out Brendan's box. And then I approached the driver's-side door.

"Dugger," I whispered. "Tell me what's going on."

Dugger opened his mouth and closed it. I watched as a million words seemed to string themselves across his mind. He was fighting not to utter any of them, pressing his lips tightly together until he could finally get out what he wanted to.

"There's something you have to—I'm going to show you something."

I held his gaze. His eyes were light again and contained all sorts of things. The clarity he'd achieved began to ebb away. I nodded once. "All right."

Dugger drove us up the side of the mountain, then down again. We hadn't seen a single car since losing the police. The roads out here were empty, hardly roads at all, just cutouts with the snow tamped down upon them. The sedan was doing amazingly well, and when I frowned as we drove onto a long lick of unplowed trail, abandoning the last hint of civilization, Dugger responded to my unasked question.

"Chains," he explained. "Tires have chains, gains, pains."

I glanced at him, but he seemed steady. For now.

"We have to walk, Missus," Dugger said, pumping the brakes judiciously. "Can't go any farther."

We'd driven far enough off the road that the freshly fallen layer of snow hadn't gotten packed down; huge heaps and drifts lay ahead. "You mean we're stopping?"

Dugger looked at me. Then he opened his glove compartment and withdrew a fur-rimmed hat and gloves. He handed them over, and I pulled them on over the ones I was already wearing. But that did nothing about my only calf-high boots and lack of waterproof pants.

"Don't worry, Missus," Dugger said, still reading my cues. "This won't take long."

"What won't?" I asked, but Dugger was already out of the car.

The road behind us melted into the

vast expanse of white, before disappearing altogether. We came to an enormous boulder, cloaked with a fresh covering of snow. Dugger guided me around the stone, its surface mottled like the moon. Then we circumvented a stand of snow-laden firs and started down a path.

I craned my neck up to the sky. The sun was a cold, silver coin behind a bank of clouds. Even through my new layers of outerwear and the items borrowed from Dugger, I felt gooseflesh rise. It wasn't just Dugger who was strange now, but the whole environment we were in.

I took a slow, revolving look around. Tree limbs, those that weren't skimmed with snow, looked bare as picked-over bones. There were no hoofprints or tiny tracks, not a single bird took flight. It was as if all life had fled this place.

"See," Dugger said urgently. "Tree, key, free—"

"Okay, okay, I'm coming," I said. Dugger couldn't get upset. Not out here.

"Now, Missus," he said, beginning to kick through the snow.

"Nora," I called out, and he turned around. "Call me Nora, okay?"

"Okay, Missus," he said.

I had to hurry to catch up.

One of Dugger's loops of hair snagged some hidden pine needles, and a shower of flakes sizzled onto a bit of exposed skin on my face as we passed between another copse of trees.

It was quiet as a vault all around us. An almost undetectable shushing sound came when snow patties dropped from a tree limb onto the blanket below.

"How much farther?" I called out, hearing a tremble of cold in my voice.

Dugger came to such a sudden stop that I walked right into him. We extricated ourselves slowly. "No farther, Missus," he said. "We're here."

CHAPTER FORTY-NINE

I turned around, watching a flock of ancient ash-colored leaves flutter onto the frozen drift with faint, whispering breaths.

Dugger was looking around, striding forward, then back. "They check," he told me.

"Who?" I asked, seizing on the scrap of information. My voice got carried away by a gust of wind, and I spoke louder. "Who checks?"

"Checks, wrecks, decks," he chimed. "But not as much now. Not so often."

I frowned, slowly making sense of his words. One thing was clear.

We might not have much time.

Dugger's outstretched finger pointed to a heap of white between a skeletal stand of trees. The mound looked askew, higher than the drifts around it.

"That pile of snow?"

Dugger dropped to his knees. He placed his hands in the frozen heap and began to burrow, tossing chunks of white behind him. I dropped into a crouch, and began digging, too.

I watched his blue eyes glisten, and wondered if Dugger Mackenzie might be crying.

It was like clawing at boulders. After an untold number of minutes had passed, devoted to the seemingly im- possible task, I noticed Dugger periodi- cally leaning over to breathe on the mound. The snow loosened under his exhalations, and he was able to shift some around. I copied his technique, blowing and scooping.

How I longed for the tools that had been stolen along with my bag. My shoulders ached, felt like twin rocks themselves. I paused for a second to stretch. "Dugger, I don't know if we can do this without any—"

He halted my protest, taking both my hands in his and returning them to the mound. "Dig, Missus," he said. "Before someone comes."

We didn't have to excavate as deeply as I'd feared.

Still, Dugger and I should've torn our hands to shreds, even with our gloves. Somehow we budged the mound. It was frozen, but it had melted at some point after the deep freeze of the season. The hard-packed soil we soon reached shifted too easily as well.

I concentrated on scooping out brittle flecks of dirt. Soon I was sweating, working hard enough to unzip my coat.

Floating in the back of my mind was an explanation I didn't want to face.

Someone had come out here with power tools to churn up the earth. Heavy equipment maybe. Otherwise Dugger and I couldn't possibly have made the headway that we did.

And why would someone have gone

to such effort to delve into the ground in winter?

At first it didn't register when my gloved fingers rasped against something. But then it did, and I screamed.

"You found him?" Dugger began scrabbling at the remaining scum of soil.

I yanked my hands in their filthy gloves away so that I wouldn't have to feel the unmistakable roughness of denim again. Then I stood up shakily, unable to take a look at what we'd uncovered. The bony click of denuded tree limbs tapped out a refrain.

"Dugger," I said numbly. "What is this?"

No.

"Who is this?"

I thought I knew the answer. I'd known as soon as the question was formed. Whose disappearance had I just heard about, who had also recently vanished? Dugger must have led me to the body of Melanie Cooper's missing husband.

I'd been right that with spring would come an end to any hope of uncovering the truth. If not for the concrete earth, this secret would never have lain so shallowly, awaiting winter's thaw for a more thorough burial.

The body lay facedown in a rift in the soil.

But for contemporary clothes, he looked like a piece of statuary, the exposed parts of his skin turned to marble. He wore jeans my fingers would never forget. A few ropes of jewelry—gold and silver links—were knotted around one stony wrist.

My bleary eyes refused to focus on any of it.

Even the small, ragged sun in the midst of his coat.

Brendan's years on the force had taught me what the entrance wound of a bullet shot from some distance away looked like.

Like Jean, this person had been murdered while his back was turned.

"Dugger?" I mumbled. I wondered if he knew, if there was any such thing as guns in his rhyming, riddling world.

He didn't reply.

Were we supposed to heave the body

up, somehow carry him out, begin the
process of investigation? It wasn't as if
we could call the police. I let out a brittle laugh. It sliced the silence in the
woods.

"Dugger!" I cried.

Dugger screamed back. "Tree, key,
free, see!"

Bare branches whipped along with
our soaring voices.

I sat down on the ground, some ways
from the grave, heedless of the icy bite
of snow through my pants. We couldn't
drag the body out. Even if Dugger had
the strength—a supposition I could just
about believe—there was nowhere to
go with it. But I could do something else
to ensure future investigation.

He looked at me, the whites of his
eyes gone a deathly blue, like the corpse.

The groaning trees suddenly hushed.

"Do you still have your camera?"

His face brightened, skin stretched
taut and shiny. He reached into one
pocket and brought it out.

I circled the grave, framing shots as I
would on a job, preserving every angle.
When I had finished, Dugger reached

down without hesitation, and flipped the body over.

The last shot was already framed, but my finger froze on the button.

I had been wrong about the identity of the corpse. This wasn't John Cooper.

Instead it was the person in the photo from Eileen's basement. The golden-haired young man in the Stonelickers T-shirt.

CHAPTER FIFTY

I made it out of the woods, trudging along several paces behind Dugger. He checked to make sure I was there, then sprinted ahead. When I reached the road, the sedan drove up like a ghost car, Dugger surrounded by a billowing cloud of exhaust.

I got in and closed my eyes. The camera sat heavily in my coat. I couldn't return it to Dugger until I found someplace to download the shots, but I suspected he might have trouble functioning without it.

Could I ask him to take me to Cold

Kettle? Dugger seemed to be driving with intent, turning around on this road that led nowhere, and heading the other way down it. As the miles streaked by, it became clear that what lay ahead was town.

"Dugger," I said, emotionlessly, "I can't go back there." I paused. "And maybe you shouldn't, either."

He gave me a humorless grin. "Nothing will happen to me, Missus."

"No," I responded, thinking that however the body had gotten to its makeshift grave, Dugger had obviously learned about it without reaping any punishment or constraint. He learned about a lot of things, for that matter, didn't he? "I guess not. Why is that, Dugger?"

"Can't do anything," he responded. "I'm useless, dumb. Dumb, crumb, piece of scum. So why would they do anything to me?" One hand traveled to his arm and for a moment his face seemed to change; then Dugger replaced the hand on the wheel.

"Your arm?" I asked. "What happened to it?"

But he only flashed that loveless smile again and kept driving.

"You're not dumb," I said slowly. "You put pieces together as if they were a puzzle. You're one of the smartest people I've ever met, Dugger."

He still didn't look at me, but a shine adorned his eyes.

"But I'm afraid it might've been dumb to show me what you did today," I said, and then I began to cry. "Because I'm not smart enough to do—to do anything about it."

Dugger steered the car so abruptly over to the side of the road that the tires rode up on one bank. "Don't do, rue, construe," he said.

I tore my gaze to his, trying to get him to look at me. I answered the rhymes as if they were a conversation. "Why then, Dugger? Why did you show me?"

The lids of his eyes settled shut. He answered without opening them. "Because now we both know."

Dugger didn't go into the thorny knot that was the center of town, instead driving down one of the streets that abutted it. Closely packed houses spread themselves out as they got farther away from the buildings and the stores. The house Dugger stopped at was the last on the street, its neighbor a quarter mile away.

"What are we doing?" I took a look at this working-poor section of Wedeskyull, which my business had never given me cause to enter.

"It's time, Missus," he said. "I've known it for a while."

"Time?" I echoed. Dugger sounded so lucid. "For what?" But I got no answer. "Do you live here?"

Still no response, but when Dugger got out of the car, he came around and opened my side. Heat from the blowers had thawed my pants, and with the fabric damp against my skin, I started shivering convulsively. It didn't matter whose house this was; I needed to get inside.

Dugger mounted a set of concrete steps that had heaved and cracked with each winter's coming and going. He took out a loop of keys and opened the front door. I supposed that keeping doors unlocked was a privilege relegated to the more expensive areas, a rural fantasy of what country life should be.

A woman met us in the narrow rectangle of hall. She was slight like Dugger, but older, her hair chalked with gray, blue eyes beginning to dim. They assessed me without blinking.

"There'll be a change of clothes in my room," she commanded Dugger, who trotted off obediently. "Coffee or tea?" she asked, no less abruptly.

"Tea," I said, my teeth chattering so hard they clacked. "Thank you."

She added a hefty dollop from a liquor bottle to the mug she filled. I drank the whole thing down, welcome warmth suffusing my body. Dugger had returned with an armful of clothes. The woman eyed me again. "You have a few pounds on me, but they should fit," she said, and pointed. "Powder room by the back door."

I nearly laughed as I headed to do her bidding. Only minutes ago, laughter would've seemed a less likely prospect than my flying to the moon. Or than

dredging up winter hard soil in Wedeskyull. My smile faded.

I crossed a stained but recently
mopped patch of linoleum, then wedged
myself past a rusted washing machine.
No dryer. There must be a line outside,
which meant a Laundromat in winter. I
pulled open the door to a tiny bathroom.
I had to bend into all sorts of awkward
angles to strip off my sodden garments
and pull on the clean, dry ones, but the
effort was worth it. I felt the events of
the morning drop off with my clothes.
Both my calves were a pale, chalky
white, one step away from frostbite. I
slapped and rubbed them with curious
disinterest, which faded as soon as the
porcupine quills of circulation started
returning to my skin. Sucking in breath
to button the pants, I realized that the
woman had been right in her assess-
ment of my size, and almost laughed
again. She was skinny, though, knotted
and hard as a tree branch.

When I came out, she had gone. Only
Dugger stood in the kitchen.

"Momma said to tell you to have more
tea."

"Thank you," I said again. My mind was whittling away at possibilities, wondering what would come next. "I'm okay though. Now."

"Okay?" Dugger echoed, and I nodded. "Then come."

I frowned, but didn't argue. In this small, shabby house, obedience seemed to be the order of the day.

Dugger led me up a skinny crook of stairs to a room tucked beneath the eaves. This house had charm. He had to duck to pass through the door, then crouched even lower and pulled out a bin from under his bed. The bed was a single, made up neat and flat with a wool plaid blanket. Otherwise the room was almost bare.

I stooped a little going in.

Dugger pried up a lid to reveal a whole electronics store—no, more like an electronics museum—of tape recorders, microphones, and other audio devices. The biggest amongst them was scratched and dented, a flurry of holes like BB pellets across its prow, and a fat orange button lying at one end of a row of plastic levers. It looked like what I'd used in sixth grade Social Studies when we had to interview old people about their lives.

Dugger had begun sorting through a carton of tapes, focusing intently, his matted head bent. I realized that he must've gotten wet in the woods too, but he hadn't bothered to change.

He was mumbling while he searched. I leaned closer to hear.

"No, Missus!" Dugger stuck one arm out in the direction of some shelves. "Go stand over there."

Once again, I obeyed.

But I had caught Dugger's rumblings as he hunted the tape. He'd been sing-songing with a more fully elaborated rhythm than usual, almost like verse.

As I huddled by the stand of shelves he started up again, a dreadful poem, clotted with meaning. The meter filled my ears, growing louder, roaring like a wave rolling onto the beach, until Dugger stuck both arms into the air. "Found it!"

He held a cassette, circa thirty years ago, its shiny innards spilling down around his wrists so that it didn't seem the thing would ever play.

I was still hearing his rhyme in my head. Or maybe he was still chanting it.

"Ice, slice, pay a price. Ice, slice, run like mice."

He pushed the *eject* button on the big recorder and the flap on top swung open. Dugger snapped in the cassette, which he had patiently wound.

A rising whistle sounded, with the steady mew of tape spinning beneath it. It took a couple of arduous turns of the cassette player for me to perceive that I was hearing screaming wind. Wind that must have been blowing decades ago.

"Dugger? How old is this—"

"Shhh!" Dugger lifted one finger.

The rush of wind competed with other noises as the tape continued to roll. Voices hollering to be heard, *"Hurry, hurry, there, stop,"* a few sudden, loud barks. Then banging. Thuds.

A rush of wind drowned out everything. Dugger continued to squat on the floor, his finger depressing the button, pale head tilted in concentration.

I couldn't make out what I was hearing besides the roar of the outdoors.

A crack, loud as gunfire in this en-
closed space, boomed off the walls,
and I jumped. Dugger eased the cassette out of the player. The clatter had
been the *eject* button popping up.

Without looking up, Dugger held one
hand out to stay me. "Just have to turn
it over."

Why? This was nothing but an ancient, wheezing collection of gibberish.
His other recordings had been far clearer.

The tape had spooled out again. With
meticulous care, Dugger wound the glistening intestines back into their plastic
casing, then inserted the neatly coiled
cassette.

A burst of voices, clearer with no wind
roaring over them, crackled to life. One
gruff, commanding, the other arrogant
in its youth.

I took one step forward, then another.

Dugger watched as I walked, his irises
specks in snowy fields, lips moving
along with the words, or to his own in-
audible rhymes. He hobbled closer,
thrusting the tape player out, the better
for me to hear.

"Dugger," I whispered. "Who is that? Is it . . . ?"

But there was no reason for me to finish the question. I doubted he would be able to answer in this state anyway. And I didn't need him to.

The gruff voice sounded awfully familiar. Dugger had finally recorded something important, or at least something whose relevance I could imagine. He had caught Vern Weathers on tape.

CHAPTER FIFTY-ONE

As soon as I placed the identity of the speaker, I realized I had to be wrong. How could Vern speak in the exact same voice twenty or thirty years ago? He would've been a young man then. In case I doubted my ability to date the cassette, the next words crackled to life.

"—heard what I said, Vernon."

It was the gruff voice again. He was speaking *to* someone named Vernon. And it was Vern who answered him, younger and reedier, but unmistakable.

"Far as anyone knows, we were at the Dugout all day, Pop. I got twelve

witnesses can attest to us watching the game. All too drunk to know exactly when we got there.”

The tape rolled for a quiet second or two.

“We’re supposed to go out on Packey Lake with Mike on Tuesday. How’m I gonna explain bowing out on him?” the same voice continued. **“It’ll be worse if Davey and I *don’t* do what we always do.”**

Davey. Dave.

“You boys,” said the gruff voice in a tone that made disagreement sound threatening, unsafe, **“ain’t never going fishing again.”**

Silence on the tape, more telling than words.

“This isn’t like the others.” That was another voice, young, too, but containing less bravado. **“This time they’ll keep looking. They won’t stop. You already promised not to stop, Pop—”**

“And we won’t,” said the older voice calmly. **“We’ll keep trying to solve this. We’ll keep looking into it forever. Right, boys? Forever.”**

There came a sharp bray of laughter.

Then a sound that could only be the slapping of feet.

"Go get your brother," intoned the gruff man. **"Make sure he does what he's supposed to. And you do it, too."**

Agreement ominous in its wordlessness.

Another gunshot boom, and the tape popped up.

I looked at Dugger, but his eyes wouldn't meet mine. He thrust the cassette at me and I took it.

The articles Ned had brought over told me that the police never found out who left the fishing hole uncovered. The one that Red fell through.

Bill had written in his journal about a man named Franklin. He'd pleaded for a chance to ask him some questions about his own boys. Franklin Weathers, chief of police when Red Hamilton died. Twenty-five years ago, Franklin had told reporters that he would do everything in his power to find the people who left the hole unbarricaded, although he lacked hope because he was sure the "culprits" weren't from Wedeskyull.

An unprecedented manhunt had been launched.

When the criminals were his own sons, under his roof all along.

Red hurts, Lynn lurks, Dugger had once rhymed. I'd heard the word as *Lynn* anyway. But what if Dugger meant *Lin*, the nickname given to the chief of police in a headline Ned had snipped?

Franklin "Lin" Weathers.

His sons had left the hole untended, and he had lied to protect them.

Had Bill, a cop on the force, suspected the truth?

Once I had wondered why Dugger would record scenes of suffering, snap pictures of the things no one else wanted to see. All the moments better off *not* set down in memory. But now I thought I understood. For an autistic person, cut off from emotion as if he were living through glass, were all these peaks and valleys a way in?

A tree limb began to snap back and forth outside. Dugger's eyes had gone snowy. He was still crouched on the floor, staring at the wall without appearing to see a thing.

I knelt down to try to help him, to thank him. Even if I still wasn't sure what to do with the knowledge he'd given me. But Ned was alive somewhere. Together we would figure out a way. I just had a few pieces left to fit together, picking up where Dugger had left off.

Mrs. Mackenzie appeared in the doorway. Her hunched form didn't have to bow to enter, and her gaze flew straight to her son. "Oh no," she said.

"Where's his medication?" I asked.

"That medicine don't do a thing." She transferred her direct stare to me. "What happened? Who *are* you?"

I fought to rise. "I'm sorry, Mrs. Mackenzie. My name is Nora Hamilton. Dugger was—he's been trying to—"

She cut me off. "Nora Hamilton?"

I nodded.

"They're looking for you," she said. and I frowned, heart beginning to hammer. "All day today, it's been on channel six."

The local channel.

"Come here." Mrs. Mackenzie extended a hand and led me.

We went back down the stairs, into a living room with one sofa, and a TV on a stand. Mrs. Mackenzie clicked on the news.

A few stories came on that contained no meaning or relevance—fluff pieces, winter sports, school events—and I had time to wonder if Mrs. Mackenzie might be as confused as her son. Except Dugger wasn't confused at all, was he? He knew more than anyone.

And then the coverage changed. An anchor announced breaking news.

The reporter was blond and trim, standing in front of a white winter scene that looked fake. "Police Chief Vernon Weathers had this to say," she chirped.

Vern appeared on the screen, mask removed, gray hat pushed back, his face reddened by real wind and weather. "New developments have raised questions about the recent death of a member of our force."

My heart began clip-clopping in my chest. Not to be alone in this anymore—not to be the only one who believed Brendan's death demanded answers! Or even more—the possibility that it hadn't been suicide at all, just made to look that way! That was a wish I had never even dared give voice to. I could hardly breathe.

Mrs. Mackenzie was watching me closely.

"Officer Hamilton was a hero and we will get to the bottom of this," Vern continued. "I only hope that Officer Hamilton's wife—who is now missing—is not in any danger herself."

The scene cut and the reporter came back into focus.

"So today Wedeskyull residents may be asking this question: When it comes to local police officer Brendan Hamilton . . ." She paused for a dramatic beat. "Suicide or slain?"

My palms had dampened with sweat. I wiped them on Mrs. Mackenzie's pants without thinking, then glanced at her self-consciously.

"They want to talk to you," she said, turning and walking a little ways out of the room.

A second reporter flashed onto the screen. "Police are asking Mrs. Hamilton, or anybody with knowledge about

Mrs. Hamilton's whereabouts, to come forward immediately, in the hope that she is able to shed light in the matter of her husband's death."

Mrs. Mackenzie had fetched a cordless phone.

I don't know what exactly tipped me off. This was the biggest lure Vern could've dangled in front of me. And it was as false as the wintry scene the reporter had delivered her lines before.

Brendan hadn't been a hero, never did one thing in all his time on the force to earn that appellation. But it wasn't only that. It was Vern's implication that my safety was in question, when in reality his words had been a call to arms. They were setting up a manhunt.

CHAPTER FIFTY-TWO

In the act of reaching for the phone, I let my hand drop.

"No," I said, and started to back away from Mrs. Mackenzie. I had to find my car. I didn't know where it'd been left, though, and I couldn't make the trip on foot.

"You have to do what the police say." Dugger's mother frowned. She aimed the remote at the television set and silence fell over the dingy room.

A set of words jumped into my head. *The long arm of the law.* The police had control of the news, enough friends there that a totally concocted story hadn't gotten questioned, fact-checked to death. How could I outrun such men?

"No," I said again.

Someone else said it, too.

Mrs. Mackenzie and I both turned. Dugger had appeared in the doorway.

His eyes were crazed, almost pupil-less, and his hands couldn't stop moving, twisting his hair into loopy knots.

I had to get out of here. Walking, not sure of my direction. I had my keys, and money. Maybe I could act the part of damsel in distress—that wouldn't require much playacting at all—find someone who didn't watch the news, and call a cab from his or her house.

Mrs. Mackenzie lifted the phone. It was on speaker. We heard the trio of tinny beeps it made as she pushed the buttons, just three of them.

"No, Momma," Dugger said, his voice suddenly strong and sure.

A V of wrinkles deepened between Mrs. Mackenzie's eyes. "Baby? You all right?"

Dugger stepped out of the shadows,

coming farther into the room. "I've always been all right, Momma."

"You are by me, baby," his mother said, and the weight in her voice seemed enough to crush it. She looked at me. "It's just the world who cares he's got the autism." She pronounced the term as if it were two separate words, as if she were expressing regret. *Aw-tism.*

"This is the Chief," came a bass rumble over the line. "State your emergency."

Dugger turned to face his mother, and a moment of complete and total understanding passed between them.

Dugger let the whites of his eyes roll up.

"Shine," he whispered. "Sign, mine, hand me a line."

That V appeared on Mrs. Mackenzie's forehead again, a question, a pulse. "You sure, baby? You sure about this?"

Dugger bobbed his head.

I fought to keep up, to understand.

Mrs. Mackenzie took one deep, hitching breath. "It's my boy," she said into the phone. Her voice broke. "Oh no." She looked from me to him. "He's taken ill again."

"Keep him there," said the Chief. "Mrs. Mackenzie? Don't let him get away."

"Yes," Dugger's mother whispered, watching her son pull his hair and rhyme and nod her on. "I mean, no. I won't."

Dugger moved very quickly after that. He was as clearheaded as I'd ever seen him, pulling back the curtain from the window with intent, then glancing in my direction.

Mrs. Mackenzie was pacing back and forth. "He's been in before. Three times, four. Last time he said he wasn't never going back there again."

Understanding struck.

"No, Dugger," I said. "You can't be locked up. You don't have to do this for me. We'll find some other way—"

"Hush, Missus!" he hissed, tilting his head to listen to something outside.

His mother sat down on the sofa, face in her hands, mumbling a string of utterances almost as disconnected as her son's rhymes. "I'm sorry," she said. "He's special. My boy has always been special. I didn't know what to do with him. I always trusted my boy."

I couldn't tell what she was apologizing for, if she thought she was doing the right thing in allowing him to protect me, or making the biggest mistake of her life.

"Everyone made fun of me, Missus," Dugger said, his voice so lucid that my gaze snapped up. I leaned forward, blinded by tears, groping for his hands, which seemed the safest thing to try to touch.

"Said I couldn't do anything right. They always said that. Even after they grew up." He paused, and I thought I had lost him. "Everyone except Brendan."

Somehow, without my feeling it, he had pressed a set of keys into my hands. I sniffed in raggedly, looked down.

"Your car?" I asked, but he didn't reply. He patted a pocket on my coat, and I thought he might've stuffed something in there, too, though he could also have been returning my touch the only way he knew how.

Dugger tugged me to the door, and pushed me out onto the stoop. He left the door ajar as I finally gained some of his urgency and ran for the vehicle he had given me. I had just dropped down inside when the sirens started to wail.

The gray patrol car came first, followed by an ambulance from Wedeskyull Community Hospital. I fell sideways on the seat, then scooted into the cramped space beneath the wheel.

I stayed there, huddled, breathing hard, as metal doors clanged, and voices began to yell.

Dugger's voice filled the still air, so frantic and undone that it seemed he must really be having a breakdown, and I had only misread his intent, construed a kamikaze act, self-sacrifice where there was none.

I dared a peek at the paramedics. They were snapping lengths of brown leather, pierced with holes, and studded with cruel metal buckles. Dugger's legs smacked against the stairs as they brought him down, and he fell heavily, letting out a high-pitched, wounded scream.

The men descended upon Dugger.

He was still chanting, a string of words that seemed tied together somehow, as meaningful as the best of his rhymes. "Steal, kneel, make no deal."

Tim Lurcquer stepped into view, his gray form sinister, deadly. He eyed the other men, and then with some unspoken, preordained exchange of motion, the medics moved forward. They tightened the binds around Dugger's wrists, chest, and ankles as they laid him on a gurney.

I threw myself back down below the seat, moaning protest.

"Snow, no, I'll go, don't show!" Dugger screamed.

So I didn't.

CHAPTER FIFTY-THREE

It took me a while to get a feel for Dugger's car. The weight of what he'd done for me made my foot heavy on the gas, my hands clumsy at the wheel. As soon as I'd placed some distance between myself and town, I unfolded the stiff, new map I'd purchased. Its vast gray-green areas were riddled with faint lines. Cold Kettle appeared to be every bit as out-of-the-way as I'd feared. Twenty miles from here, a thick rope of road gave way to a thinner whip called Rural Route 701, and finally to a series of wisps nearly too narrow to make out on the paper.

Those roads were well nigh impass-able in winter. Every year Brendan used to have to dig out at least one frozen car that went off such a road as the one I'd be taking. Once in a while, there was a body inside. Sometimes more than one body: the worst tragedy I could re-member happening in Wedeskyull in-volved a family of four freezing to death after getting lost on their way to a lodge. They'd come from Pennsylvania and I could still recall how a collective breath had been heaved, and interest seemed to fade, when the out-of-state license plates had been revealed.

Some of the roads had CLOSED FROM OCTOBER TO APRIL signs nailed up at their starts. But since the true beginning of such a stretch was a hard thing to sort out amidst the tangle that crisscrossed Franklin County, often you were already on a road that would prove impossible to follow long before you were warned. And that was if the sign wasn't too snow-covered to read.

But there wasn't any choice. I was a pretty good driver in the snow, and I would have to rely on that to get me through.

I filled up the tank as well as an extra red canister at an anonymous truck stop. The food smelled good when I paid for my gas, so I purchased lunch as well and sat in the car to eat it. Gobbling a sandwich, I remembered Dugger's tape of the Weathers boys, and was thankful I still had somewhere to stow it.

That tape was twenty-five years old. It contained information that didn't exist anywhere else. The dim fear nagged at me that the words on it might not be evidence enough to bring about proper punishment for Red's death, but still. The cassette couldn't be lost.

I bunched up the paper wrappings of my lunch, then leaned over the seat to get Brendan's yellow box. The lid stuck again as I went to lift it. Annoyed—I didn't have time for this—I tugged hard at the cover.

And then I saw.

If you hadn't known to look, you never would've noticed it was there. Not unless your hands were used to planing over wood all day long, knew how it felt and moved and breathed. One side of the box shifted just a little. It wasn't secured like the others, at least not anymore.

With silent apology to my husband, I began to pull at the yellow flannel covering.

Now that I was looking so closely, I could see that this particular piece of fabric had been peeled away at some point, then smoothed back into place. It came off as I picked at it.

I knew exactly what I needed—a small putty knife, some kind of shim—but I didn't have either. The job I did was brute and crude; everything in my restorer's soul railed against it. But I didn't have a choice. Using the sharp tip of Dugger's key—thank God his car wasn't a late model, with a blocky remote or keyless ignition—I separated the dovetailed joints.

This box had a false side. A hollow side, composed of two panels that fit cleverly together. When I jiggered them apart, something fell out.

A Polaroid photo.

Horror scalded my eyes as I took in the scene and constellation of people.

I held the Polaroid between trembling fingers.

Off in the background you could see the twin roofs of the foursquares. This picture had been taken on Patchy Hollow Lake. Three people were walking away from a black hole in the ice. A younger, less shuffling Dave held up a fish with pride. Beside him was Vern, stocky, but more built. He had a beer in one hand. His other arm was slung around a slim and pretty Jean. Vern was looking down at her, and the expression in his eyes contained a youthful blend of things. Cockiness, abandon, lust.

I laid the photo facedown on my lap, unable to look at it a second longer.

Some words were penned in girlish handwriting: *Vern, me, and Dave, with Burt on the lake.* And the date. January twenty-third, twenty-five years ago.

There in the rest stop parking lot, the sounds of car doors slamming and engines thrumming faded away, as I took in the meaning of the picture. Jean and Vern had been in love, or something close. And she was there the day they abandoned a fishing hole for two little boys to find later that day with deadly results.

The guilt Jean must have carried as this secret was kept. It made my stomach heave.

But she'd been planning to tell. This had to have been what she was talking about the night she was murdered. At some point, perhaps long ago, perhaps recently, Jean had hidden this photo away, irrefutable proof that the Weathers boys had been on Patchy Hollow Lake when a hole was bored in the ice and left uncovered.

Who had taken the photo? Dugger again? The other person named on the back? That had to be Club's father. He would've been Vern and Dave and Jean's age, just another teenager, drinking and making sport on the winter lake.

According to Club's mother, Burt Mitchell had been killed while on duty.

The snow that had threatened all morning started to fall. Great, soft flakes of it starred the car window. When it was big and puffy like this, it didn't pose much of a threat. It would come down slowly; accumulation would take time. Worse were the tiny crystalline granules that bespoke terrible, windswept cold. I shifted into drive and left the rest stop, hoping to beat the impending storm.

By the time I reached the exit for route 701, the lovely ski-slope powder had given way to icy bits pelting the windshield. I had gone too far to turn back, though, even if there had been somewhere to go. With the wipers turning the windshield opaque, glass frosting over before it could be swept clear again, I squinted and headed west.

Twenty minutes later, I was checking both the map and the gas gauge repeatedly and fighting to remain calm, speaking out loud, almost chanting in the silent cave of the car.

"Still more than three-quarters of

a tank, plus the refill. My stomach is full. I have directions, I can't lose my way."

The third at least was untrue. A map was no artillery against this vast, untrammeled land, whitened over and free of landmarks I wouldn't have recognized anyway. All the stories I'd heard of naïve downstaters, and residents who'd gotten cocky, began to take on a sickening reality. I understood how small was the space between survival and giving up. You could cross from one to the other without even knowing it.

Route 701, as empty as it had been, was a wide, generous swath compared to the knife blade of road before me now. Two hunched-over trees stood on either side of a steep run that I had to descend before it would level out, bisecting a stretch of seemingly endless, snow-covered fields. The chains on Dugger's tires bit into the pitch, keeping me secure. Then I was down and moving along slowly, the front of the car pushing aside snow that had risen in places as high as the grille.

This road was so narrow that stands

of frozen bushes rattled against the side of the car as I inched forward, the noise shotgun blasts in the unrelenting silence. Since there was no room for two lanes of traffic—and not a car in sight anyway—I steered cautiously out into the middle.

I glanced again at the map laid out on my lap. My next turn was coming up, but despite how slowly I had been going, I passed it. I swore aloud. Focus was essential now. I was going to have to turn around, and doing so on this skinny, snow-laden stretch would be no easy feat. I pulled to a stop, setting the emergency brake with my hand. Then I got out.

Snow whirled in a crazy cyclone. I drew my hat down and tried to measure the room I would have. I walked from one side of the road to the other, kicking for snow-draped obstacles. There was nobody out here. Whatever house was associated with a run of barbed-wire fencing that poked out of the snow must sit hidden acres away. The snow was flying too fast for the glare of a porch bulb or window light to penetrate.

Seeking shelter, I would stumble around until lost beyond finding.

I got back into the blessedly warm car. When my hands had stopped quaking enough to grip the wheel, I succeeded in making my turn.

The road I'd been seeking was wider than the last. An occasional home stood along it, and relief blew hot inside me. I sat higher on the seat, my face some distance from the windshield, and drove with a feeling of having made it. Every once in a while, twin cones of mist signaled the approach of another car, and I was forced to a halt, allowing it to pass. I didn't dare risk edging along the buried shoulder of the road, which threatened to suck the wheels down to their axles, quicksand-style.

If the map was correct, then Loon Lane, possibly paved, possibly just dirt, and dangling precipitously around a large lake, would be my next right.

The road was as promised: curvy as a skein of yarn, nearly obliterated by the storm. It took another painstaking five-point turn, tires spinning against a bank of snow, to make the all-but-invisible turnoff.

The only hint of a lake gaping below my turtle-slow car was a gray circle on the map. Otherwise, the empty air to my right might be nothing but a dizzying cacophony of flakes, a deceiving pillow to plummet down on.

As soon as I started driving, I missed the cars that had slowed my way back on that last road. Everyone who might come to these woods knew to stay inside during the storm. No one lived way out here anyway; there were no houses. Perhaps a smattering of seasonal cabins around the lake, but like the circle of water, they were invisible, too.

When another car finally did appear, though, it wasn't as reassuring as I'd imagined.

I heard the engine rumbling somewhere behind, volume increasing too quickly. It was gaining proximity. Rather than try to remain ahead, I pulled to the far right and stayed there, hazards twitching. I realized how stupid that was and switched them off, turning off my headlights as well. My car was concealed now, hugging the side of the road.

But no one came.

I couldn't hear the baritone rumble of the motor anymore. I'd just come from a ways down Loon Lane. I would have seen if there was a turnoff, even a driveway, for some car to take.

I unrolled my window to listen, which only deafened me further. The storm roared louder than any engine.

Drive on? Was someone waiting for me to do just that, knowing that if I built up too much speed, I'd lose control of the car? Despite the blizzard, I opened the door and got out. More risky would be continuing to creep through the snow in a four-wheeled tomb.

Snow flew horizontally, embedding itself in my face like glass. Squinting between the flakes, I could make out a wall of shale behind my car, thickly bearded with ice. A mountain that had outlasted many a winter storm, as stable a rampart as I could hope for. For a moment, I wished that I could just stay here, sit with that motionless, unwavering rock at my back. But I remained on my feet, boots crushing fresh clumps.

Hooked fingers of trees clawed the stormy sky, and snakes of snow undulated over places on the road blown bare by the wind.

A ways off down Loon Lane, far enough that it may have been only a shadow, or an optical illusion brought about by the snow, I saw the gray tail of a vehicle. It hung off the bank, buried up to its flanks in snow.

I raced back to the car, my boots flailing in the drifts.

There couldn't be a police car back there. How would they have figured out where I was going?

I pulled the door shut soundlessly, then took the remainder of Loon Lane as fast as I dared. I didn't want to suffer the same fate that had befallen whichever car had been tailing me. My map said that the lake would funnel into a brook, crossed by a one-lane bridge, and then I'd be on Main Street.

A straight run into the center of Cold Kettle.

CHAPTER FIFTY-FOUR

The single traffic light in Wedeskyull was quaint, the complete absence of any such beacon in Cold Kettle less so.

The only thing that signaled my arrival was a sign, swagged with snow, announcing the name of the town. There was also one stop sign, so riddled by BB pellets that the "S" had been obliterated, and the "T" turned into a "C" so that its face seemed to read COP instead of STOP.

Ironic.

I decided not to risk any more unplowed streets. I pulled over on Main

Street, guessing at the lines to park between. Then I emerged into the swirling
sea of snow. It flew up, down, and sideways like corn in a popper.

Brendan had been here. I could feel
him all around me; this was a place he'd
been a part of. But Brendan was Wedeskyull, born and raised.

For a second I actually scanned my
surroundings, imagining my husband's
tall, lanky form appearing amidst a cloud
of snow, both of us rushing to reunite.
Where have you been? I would cry. *Right
here, Chestnut.* A pause. *I've always
been here.*

With a start, I realized that I'd better
find my way inside quickly. I was chilled,
my mind showing the effects of the cold.

The shops along Main Street had
been sealed up tight, closed early, not
due to the storm, which the residents
were surely used to, but because business in Cold Kettle moved like a trickle
of water in a winter stream, and there
was no reason to be out on a day like
today. The houses on the side streets
were warmly lit but also somehow shut
off.

The only sign of movement was scurrying snow, and a fluttering lamppost, cloaked in the detritus of small town announcements.

I walked up to it.

Lost kitten and dog signs, a tattered missing child flier, several torn advertisements for yard sales and church bake-offs that took place last summer. One particular scrap of paper whipping in the remnants of wind snatched my attention. Half of a poster for Stonelickers Tavern. THURSDAY IS LADIES NIGHT. HALF-PRICED SHOTS AND CHASERS ON FRIDAY.

My husband and the dead boy in the woods had both been to this bar.

Suddenly, the Looking Glass Inn appeared behind a curtain of flakes. It had a majestic mansard roof, and what looked like an original stained-glass transom.

Before I could head toward it, there came the squeak of fresh snow being trod upon.

I spun around, the movement nearly sprawling me on my feet. Nobody was there. Not Brendan. Not anyone. The inn would be a haven, a place I could both hide in and look for information about the many dead left back in Wedeskyull.

I rang the bell on a long, burnished desk, and a man emerged from a back room, scratching his head in a befuddled way and looking around. "I need a place to stay," I told him.

He didn't react to my abrupt tone. "Of course. Just for the night, then?"

"I'm not sure how long." I patted my pockets, feeling the wads of Jean's money, and also a prick of tears at my eyes.

He eyed me with concern. "If you don't mind . . . you look a little peaked, luv. Could you do with a cup of tea? You might get settled in your room while I fix it."

Now tears were really welling up. I turned away. "Tea would be wonderful. Thank you," I said, hoping a touch of formality would compensate for my sad display.

My room was papered in pink, and had a lofty bed with blankets upon it, the puffiest one matching the flowered walls. I had to work to remember the last time I'd spent a whole night in a bed. I found a small chest and placed Brendan's box inside, taking two photos from it first. Then I made the journey back down the curving staircase in search of my tea.

The innkeeper met me in the parlor, tray held aloft in his hands. "I'm Dick Granger, by the way," he said. "Dick, if you need anything tonight."

I tried to work up a smile. "Nora Hamilton."

Dick set the tray on a table and indicated that I should take a wing chair beside it. I sat down, squinting as he handed me a cup. The skin on his hands looked familiar, blotchy with paint, and so roughened and dry that shreds of paper stuck to his knuckles.

He saw me looking and blushed. "We weren't expecting guests this week." He gestured over his shoulder to some cans and tools stacked in a corner. "We've just arrived back in town, and I was taking the opportunity to go about some work." He shook his head. "The upkeep on this place—well, it's hard to believe."

I laughed, a sudden, spontaneous

sound. "Not as hard as you might think."
I looked around. "The whole house is beautiful. You've done a great job."

"Thanks, luv."

"May I ask you a question?" With a few warming sips in me, my manners had returned.

Dick nodded.

"Do you know this man? Or this woman?" I asked. I withdrew the picture of Brendan, with the sliver of Amber beside him. The one without the bloody streak on it.

Dick looked down at it, and shook his head. "I don't recall ever seeing him. And as for the lady, I can hardly make her out. Have they been to our inn?"

The question brought with it a charge of pain. "I think so. A long time ago. How long have you been here?"

Dick looked at me, perhaps just a touch less friendly now, and I imagined how close to urgent my tone must've sounded. "We took over three years ago."

Brendan and I were married by then.

Dick added, "I'm afraid that I'm one of the few people in town who wouldn't recognize everyone who's ever lived here or passed through."

I nodded, then withdrew the other photograph. The boy in the Stonelickers T-shirt. "Is there a chance you know him?"

A frown blossomed on his face, and he took a step back. "Did you tell me how you came to be here, luv? Do *you* know this boy?"

The silence of the parlor, the whole cavernous, empty inn, settled around us.

"Not exactly," I said in a small voice. "Who is he?"

Dick didn't answer my question.

"I'm looking for someone who knows him," I went on. "I know something about—I mean, I might have some in-formation—"

"Well, that would be a blessing now, wouldn't it," Dick said, his frown easing. "He comes from a town in Colorado, but he has family here in Cold Kettle. A grandmother. I can put you in touch with her."

"That would be great," I said.

Dick's hands rasped as he rubbed them together. "Perhaps you already know this, but he went missing while he was on holiday here a few weeks ago."

"While he was here?" How had the boy made it to the woods in Wedes-kyull?

"His poor grandmum, she's been a wreck. I'll go ring her right now. She thinks the sun rises and sets on the lad."

Sometimes a circle closes so seamlessly, you don't remember that it was ever open.

I posed one final question. "Can you tell me when he disappeared?"

Dick hesitated. "I do hate to keep the date in mind. The police say that the more time passes, the less chance they have of bringing the lad home safe. Do you know, the townspeople still search, days when it's clear. There's too much land to cover all at once. I've taken part in some searches myself when we haven't been booked."

I watched him steadily.

Dick let out a sigh, and began to tick off on chapped fingers. "Let me see. It was . . ." A pause as he calculated.

"Longer than I thought. It's unfair how quickly time passes, isn't it?"

I was gripping the photo so tightly that a corner of it slit my skin.

"It happened the day after we returned from England, so it must've been—"

A line of blood appeared on my hand.

"Yes, that's right," he said, more to himself than to me. "It was the sixteenth of January."

CHAPTER FIFTY-FIVE

"Do you want me to call Liv Peterson, luv? You can run over to see her in the morning," suggested Dick. When I didn't answer he added, "Greg's grandmother?"

I frowned. Fragments were flying, connections being made, faster than I could keep track of them.

"No," I told him.

"No?" he repeated.

"I mean, I'd prefer to see her today. If that's all right."

Dick glanced toward a large parlor

window. Early-winter dark was gathering.

"Please," I continued. "It's—I think it might be important." *And I might not have much time,* I added silently.

"All right, then," Dick said. "Let's see what she has to say."

It didn't matter what she said now, of course. What mattered would be what was said when I told her. I stood up effortfully. This town still held hope—probably Greg's grandmother most of all—and I was the only person who knew that he was dead.

The innkeeper said that Liv Peterson lived just a few blocks from the center of town, the center being the stretch of street with the inn upon it.

"Of course, in this town, everyone thinks he lives in the center," Dick added, and we shared a smile, mine brief. We both came from places bigger than Cold Kettle.

I decided to walk. Things seemed safer on foot, where I could take off instantly at a run. I hurried forward, fresh snow flying soundlessly in front of my boots.

From a glance over my shoulder, both the shoveled sidewalk and drifted street appeared to be empty. A shortcut the innkeeper had described came up suddenly on the left. The path bisected an orchard of apple trees, stripped bare and hunched like crones in the twilight, then wound into Mrs. Peterson's yard.

I climbed a wraparound porch and knocked on an elaborately carved door.

My mind flitted briefly to a day when all this might be over. Could I be happy in a place even smaller than Wedeskyull? The trouble was, whether I could be or not, I couldn't imagine what *over* meant. Which answers would I have found, what would be the status of the police, and how would I ever feel safe again?

The door opened and a woman appeared, looking many years younger than grandmother age. She was dressed in jeans and tall boots, and her slightly silvered hair was worn long.

"Nora," she said. "Dick Granger said you know something about Greggy."

She turned and walked inside the house. I followed, startled by the lack of introduction or invitation. It was as if the need for greetings, an exchange of names and pleasantries, didn't even register. It didn't, I realized. This woman's grandson had disappeared and that meant only one thing was on her mind.

Despite a growing sense of urgency— I could picture the cops descending in a gray mass out of the mountains—the words wouldn't form quite yet. Luckily Mrs. Peterson seemed to realize her manner might've been abrupt.

"I'm Olivia, by the way," she said. "And I'm sorry to all but drag you into my house, but the last month has been a nightmare. We've been given the runaround by everybody. I'm afraid I've lost all hint of social graces."

She strode over to a couch in a cluttered sitting room, jerking her thumb toward a chair. We passed a big table, covered with papers, and several framed photographs of the boy at different ages. First, a baby cowlick, then corn silk hair that deepened over the years to that leonine mane. I recognized one of the later ones from Eileen's dungeon. There were other pictures, too, of a woman with a spill of hair like golden syrup, whom I presumed to be the boy's mother.

"Yes," I said, taking the seat and finding it difficult to breathe beneath a sudden weight. "I understand."

Olivia's glance hardly seemed to take me in. She leaned over and flicked on a lamp. "I doubt that," she said, but then looked again, a little more closely.

I met her gaze.

"Jesus," she said. "I've become cruelly blunt. And unseeing. You've had your own share of trouble, haven't you?"

I swallowed, looking away. "My husband died last month."

Olivia brought a still-smooth hand to her face. "I'm sorry. This is why we have social graces. To avoid moments like this."

I almost laughed, but the impulse shriveled inside me.

And then Olivia frowned. "Your husband died," she said, and all strength seemed to leave her body. She aged a decade before my eyes, shoulders sagging, face crumpling into folds. Even her hair seemed to wilt. "Are you saying that there's some connection between your husband's—between your husband and Greggy?"

She had given me the opening herself, found it, and invited me in. But somehow I couldn't take it. Protest rose like a froth to my lips. "No, Mrs. Peterson, I don't know that at all." It was true, but only technically.

Olivia continued to stare at me with those keen eyes, the one part of her that hadn't seemed to lose its vigor under this new threat, and I felt compelled to go on.

"My husband—he killed himself."

Olivia Peterson was the first person I'd ever said it to. I hadn't even told my story at the SOS meeting. She seemed to sense her position, averting her eyes, allowing time for the words to float away in the air, lose some of their terrible power.

"Come," she said at last, and rose from the couch. "You poor thing."

She led me into a vast white kitchen. She poured juice and set a glass down on an island, then leaned into the fridge again. "I'm afraid I don't have much in the way of food." She paused. "See? My social graces are returning. The truth is, I don't have *any* food. The neighbors brought some by for a while. Then I asked them to stop."

"That's all right." It took a lot to make me lose my appetite these days, but this had done it. I was kicking myself. Not only had I revealed the truth about Brendan to someone I didn't even know, but doing so had brought me further away from the purpose of my visit. How could I now tell this woman that her grandson was dead?

"Sorry if we got off on the wrong foot," Olivia said, extending a hand to me over the countertop. She'd clearly chosen to accept my halfhearted reassurance for now. "You've been through the wringer yourself."

I wiped condensation off my glass.

"To be honest, in addition to worried half out of my mind, I've also been superbly ticked off for the last month. The police have been no help at all. They think just because Greggy's gotten in some trouble in the past that he must have run away. Afraid of getting caught having done something. Or up to no good somewhere else."

"What kind of trouble was he in?" I said after a moment.

"Oh, the usual. Driving without a license. Underage drinking, a possession charge or two. He's stolen some things."

That sounded like just about every crime under the sun for a minor, and Olivia seemed unbothered by it, but I chose not to press her. Dugger's rhyme wafted in on a current of air. *Steal, kneel, make no deal.*

Olivia was watching me, as if reading my response. "Kid with no dad." She shrugged. "A little recklessness is to be expected."

I gathered my thoughts together. "But you don't believe he ran away?"

Olivia met me with a stare. "Greggy would never worry us like this. That's what I keep telling the police. His mother thought he might've gone back home to Colorado early, but that's ridiculous. He wouldn't have wanted to cut his visit short. He and I have always been close.

Do you know he still visits every single Christmas?" She looked at me, then shook her head since, of course, I didn't know.

"But what he feels for me is nothing," Olivia went on. "Compared to how devoted he is to his mother." She paused. "Kat flew back to Tell Spring a week ago. But why wouldn't Greggy have told us if that's where he was going?"

Fragments still sorting themselves out, bits and pieces in my mind. "Tell Spring," I repeated. "It's in Colorado."

Olivia began to pace back and forth, paying no mind to my statement or the odd way in which I'd phrased it. "We've done everything!" she burst out. "I'm sure Dick told you about the searches, just in case Greggy is out there in the— in case he's still around."

The muscles in her face trembled, a queer, palsy-like effect. She knew what it would mean if anyone found her grandson in the woods more than a month later.

"They won't do an Amber Alert. We even met with a child exploitation expert. He showed us how to make up fliers." Olivia stalked over to a kitchen drawer, taking out a stack of papers and handing one to me.

Eileen had mounted this photograph in her basement, and Olivia had it framed in her sitting room. I wondered about the connection between the two women as I regarded those hazel eyes, that rumpled forelock of pure gold.

The boy's demographics were printed on the sheet, as were a phone number to call with information, and the final, stark pronouncement:

MISSING SINCE JANUARY 16TH.

"We posted them all over the place," Olivia said. She had poured herself some juice; now she tossed it back like a shot of whiskey. "Kat took some home with her, but we mailed them, too. Made them look like real letters. Something important so everyone would open them up. That was a tip from the expert. Otherwise, he said, most of them go right in the trash."

I shook my head along with her, two people recognizing how untouched was the rest of the world by our own personal tragedies.

Olivia left the room and I trailed her.

"We drew a circle around Cold Kettle," she said, continuing to speak by rote. "Troy on one side, Montreal on the other, and we've been sending them to as many homes as possible."

I nodded.

"We couldn't include Albany. It's taken weeks already."

Wedeskyull lay in that circle, well north of Troy. But I hadn't received the letter as far as I knew. Had mine been one of the addresses missed? Or did Vern have influence over the mail? While in the context of things, it might've been the least of his misdeeds, the idea that something as unceasing as mail service could be made to go awry chilled me.

I spoke casually. "You sent them to Wedeskyull, right?"

"Sure," she said. "I even went to visit someone in Wedeskyull. Just yesterday. A woman I thought might—" Then she broke off.

I nodded her on.

But Olivia had finally halted in her aimless wanderings. "I'm sure this is me forgetting my manners again, but weren't you supposed to be bringing me information? All you've done is ask questions."

She was right. I couldn't think of a single other excuse or delaying tactic.

But at that moment I happened to glance at a large pier glass on the wall, and those disparate bits finally slammed into place, taking on form.

Tell Spring. Greggy. The sight in the mirror of my hair.

CHAPTER FIFTY-SIX

In the very first article I'd read about him, Red's full name had been given. It was Gregory.

Olivia had chosen, correctly, not to resilver the antique mirror in the hall. I studied my cloudy reflection in the glass. Wide stare, overgrown tumble of waves. Almost as long now, and the exact same color, as Teggie's. A deep, reddish brown.

Chestnut.

Brendan had always explained my pet name by recalling the snack we bought from a city cart at Christmastime.

But Red had been nicknamed for his hair.

Olivia was watching me, her face grown grave. "Nora?" she said, with no abruptness in her tone. "Are you all right?"

I took the lead this time, and Olivia followed me into the sitting room. I picked up one of the photos, not of Greggy, but of his mother. "This is Kat, right? She has such pretty hair."

Olivia continued to look at me, while keeping her distance. We both knew something was coming, like a barometric pressure change building in the air. My head felt thick and hot. And Olivia's strong form looked frail, ready to fall over.

"Everyone admires her hair. Like buttered toast, not a streak of gray in it. Of course, Kat's still pretty young."

"Yes, she must be." I nodded. "How young exactly?"

"Thirty-two," Olivia said, rather wistfully. She was studying another picture of Kat. "She had Greggy when she was only sixteen. That's why she moved so far away, I think. She was ashamed.

Even though I was hardly more than a baby myself when I had her."

There was only one thing left to do.

I took out the first photograph I'd shown to Dick Granger. "Do you know these people? I know the woman's a little cut out of the shot—"

Olivia's fingers were shaking when she took it, but she answered with no hesitation at all. "I've never seen him before. But that's Kat over there on the side."

I wasn't shocked; it was as if I'd known for some time.

"That's Kat's ring right there," Olivia told me. It was a cluster of garnets on the hand resting on Brendan's arm. "I gave her that ring for her thirteenth birthday."

"She had a boyfriend in high school," I said.

"Well, she sure had someone," Olivia replied, sounding a little stronger now, with her own blow still at bay. "Got knocked up, didn't she?"

I winced. "You never knew him?"

"No," Olivia replied, regarding me coolly. "Kat kept to herself some. She's always been mature that way. Began taking college courses while she was still in high school, and moved west to finish. Anyway . . ." She paused to collect her thoughts. "She never brought boyfriends home." She looked at me. "Are you saying that guy in the picture was one of them?"

I dropped my gaze to the photo. "The man in the picture was my husband."

"Oh." Olivia's hand swept across her face. "Oh, Lord."

I finally sat down. This whole conversation had been conducted upright; Olivia still remained standing. "He called your daughter Amber."

Tears filmed Olivia's eyes, not quite yet ready to fall. "Because of her hair."

I nodded. "And he had a brother who died when he was very young. Named Gregory."

Olivia's head snapped straight. "Kat never told me how she came to name Greggy. But she was so insistent. She said she knew she was carrying a boy, and she would only consider one name for him." Olivia hesitated. "She always wanted children."

I recalled the flash of kinship I'd felt with Amber, reading her letters. With Kat.

"The woman you spoke to in Wedeskyull," I began. "Her name was Eileen, wasn't it? Eileen Hamilton." Eileen had to have gotten the photo from somewhere. She'd had some connection, to Olivia, or Greggy, or Kat.

Olivia didn't seem to be focusing, but she answered nonetheless. "That's right. She'd sent checks to Greggy anonymously for years. Starter checks, no name on them. I tracked her down when it occurred to me that she might have some clue as to his whereabouts."

"Eileen knew," I breathed. *Resurrection.* Another boy named Gregory. "How?"

Olivia shook her head. "I've been wondering that myself. Mrs. Hamilton wouldn't tell me. She didn't even let me into the house." For a moment Olivia's mouth compressed. "When things, uh, get back to normal, I'll ask my daughter," she continued. "My best guess is that Kat sent her a baby picture or something. She always swore they couldn't have contact with that side of Greggy's family, and now I understand why. But Kat has a soft spot. Perhaps she took pity on that awful woman."

It occurred to me then, stupidly, late, but it did occur and I forced the thought out. "Brendan, though? He didn't know?"

"No." Olivia shook her head. "No, Nora, if it helps, he didn't. Kat was always very certain of that—that Greggy's father wouldn't have wanted to know he had a baby."

"I wonder," I whispered. How different things might've been if there'd been another boy Brendan could've cared for with the devotion that made him run to rescue his little brother. How different for Brendan, for Greggy, and me.

Olivia went on speaking. "Greggy wanted to search for his dad. It was the one thing he and his mother fought about." A bolt of hope seemed to momentarily strengthen Olivia, and she dropped to the floor before me, leaning forward and gripping my wrists. "Did he find your husband? Or find out he was dead? Is that why Greggy's run off?"

I had already begun shaking my head. I couldn't keep the truth from this woman any longer. Not when I was discovering what a cruel seducer was false hope, and that knowledge could feel light as a balloon in your chest.

"No, Olivia. I mean, I don't know if Greggy found my husband or not. I haven't figured that part out yet. But that isn't why he hasn't come home."

When she spoke, her voice was bloodless. "What part have you figured out?"

I didn't know yet who had killed Greggy. But as soon as one person besides me felt the drive to find out, any role the police played would have to come to light. The more people who have information, and knowledge, and stakes, the fewer secrets can be kept.

I got off the chair, and I knelt in front of Olivia.

The woman crumpled, her hands a protective shield over her face. They hit the floor with a loud, violent smack, and the skin on them flamed as I stroked Olivia's humped back, and told her over and over again how sorry I was, I was so, so sorry.

CHAPTER FIFTY-SEVEN

Back at the inn, I needed to ask one more favor of Dick Granger. I had found two more gifts from Dugger when patting my pockets for tissues for Olivia. An audio recorder and a slim DVD.

"It's not too late, is it?" I asked.

"Not at all, luv." He led the way into the parlor again. "The telly is in here," he said, opening a wooden cabinet.

I thanked him.

The innkeeper stopped at the door, then spoke hesitantly. "Did you talk to Liv, luv? Were you able to give her something to go on?"

I looked up, words not coming to my lips, but the answer probably on my face. This was Olivia's news to deliver now. She had to tell the town. Dick left the room. I could hear his footfalls echoing in the entryway as he headed over to the front desk.

The TV and DVD player came to life and I inserted the disk.

It was nighttime on the tape, and everything was black with a greenish tinge, even the dots of falling snow. The camera had been fitted with a night-vision attachment, turning the scene before me into some sort of Emerald City, malevolent, surreal, filled with challenges too great to overcome. I imagined Dugger sprinting alongside the events he was capturing.

The film jumped around, so it was hard to be sure, but amongst the snow-swept fields, I thought I caught a glimpse of frozen Queek Pond. This was the expensive part of Wedeskyull, full of large, grand homes I had hoped one day to restore.

And then someone burst onto the scene and the video camera caught his flight. He was dressed in jeans and a dark jacket, but that flowing mane of hair was unmistakable. It was Greggy. He ran across the field, stumbling at times, clutching items in both hands so that he couldn't regain balance as fast as he otherwise would.

A cop appeared behind him, his broad, powerful body instantly recognizable. Club. He was moving fast, giving chase, but another gray-clad man was even faster, more agile.

Brendan. Eerily lit, but utterly recognizable. This call must've come in urgently; they'd had to get out of the cruiser without much preparation.

I rocked back on my heels. I hadn't taken a seat, was just watching from the floor. If I hadn't already been down there, I might've fallen.

Here was my husband, alive, in the room with me again.

Shouting.

Words impossible to make out, and then, "Don't run, kid!" A loud crack—a branch breaking maybe—that drowned out whatever Brendan said next. ". . . just want to talk to you! Slow down!"

I began to whimper, hoping the inn-keeper wouldn't hear. If it hadn't been for the man's nearby presence, I might've crawled to the television, tried to summon my husband forth.

Club's distinctive growl. "Go. Don't let him get away. You heard what the Chief said."

Brendan put on a burst of speed, and the cameraman did the same so that for a minute only jarring green ground was filmed, and the lower stalks of trees. Dugger must've been hiding in a perimeter of woods, following along at an equally fast clip.

There was nothing but eerie jade light. Brendan's voice filled the void.

". . . be slowed down on the pond. No way around it—"

"Better run, man," grunted Club, the exertion clearly wearing on him. ". . . faster than me."

Then both men vanished from the shot, because suddenly I was watching a blur, unable to hear anything but a distant rush of wind.

Brendan's lanky, athletic form made

an appearance, Dugger getting close again.

Even when I couldn't see, his voice still carried.

"Stop!" Brendan shouted. ". . . not saying you stole anything, kid! Just let us have a look, and we'll sort this whole thing out!"

A howling swirl of snow from the ground blotted out whatever Brendan must've been glimpsing offscreen, the thing that caused him to raise his voice even louder in alarm.

"Stop right now so we can talk to you!"

"Brendan—get down!" Club huffed with exertion as he gave the command, but only one thing made a cop tell another cop to get down, and my chest pinched with anxiety. Even knowing Brendan's fate, that he'd survived this incident, I was frightened for my husband.

"He's going for something, man! I'm—coming!"

". . . don't want to hurt you!" Brendan himself was hardly out of breath. "Get your hands where we can see them."

There was a third voice, higher and unsure. Greggy's, but he couldn't be seen.

And then he could be, standing beside a green-tinted glimmer of ice, his form small and slight compared to those of the two men. He went down on his knees, stuffing something into one hand, using the free one to scrabble around in his pocket.

Oh, Greggy, don't. I pleaded with events already past, long since set in stone.

"Brendan—get—down! Police! Hands up or we'll shoot!" Club was running hard, but Brendan was closer. And Brendan wasn't doing anything.

Greggy's voice again, repeating the same airy words.

"Goddammit, Brendan, pull your gun!" Club panted. "Shoot him! . . . gonna kill you!"

"Club, wait—" Brendan was at last breathing hard. "He's saying something—"

There was the paper-snapping crack of gunfire, a sound almost lost in the whole of the outdoors.

The camera angle changed. Brendan's boots crunched over snow. He came into focus, crouching down beside Greggy. He felt for a pulse, and his shoulders sank.

Who had opened fire? The recording hadn't caught anyone's finger on a trigger.

As partners, Brendan was the thinker, Club the actor. They worked well together—and were such good friends—because each was so willing to fill a different role.

"He was going for a gun," came Club's voice, unseen in the distance. "You were in danger."

"Are you sure?" Brendan asked thickly. "He was reaching into his front pocket. Strange place for a gun."

"He was saying 'dead.' Kept repeating it."

"Did sound like that," Brendan agreed. "But the front pocket of his jeans? For a weapon? Maybe a pocketknife. Nothing long range . . ." He began to dig around in the dead boy's pocket. "Goddammit . . . did steal the jewelry . . ." He took out several shiny strands, then another item, flat and square. Brendan looked at it, and then he bent over, dropping out of the frame, although noises could still be heard.

The sound of liquid, splattering and sloshing onto the snow.

"Brendan?" Club also stood out of sight of the camera's eye. ". . . the fuck is wrong with you? You sick, man?"

I couldn't follow what was going on; too much information was missing.

"It wasn't . . ." Brendan's words were hard to make out, but that wasn't the fault of the tape. My husband was crying. "Wasn't a fucking gun, Club. He didn't have a weapon."

"What the hell was it then?"

"Goddamn you!" Brendan roared, and both men came into view, their bodies colliding, boots sliding in the puddle Brendan had left, packing down snow with their knees and their fists as they fell. "You murderer!"

"Brendan, man, get off! I was trying to protect you!"

Brendan held something in his hand that the camera couldn't see.

There was a pause, the briefest lull.

Then Club barked a laugh. "A photograph? Kid was going for a fucking photo?"

I inched across the floor on my hands and knees, struggling to see the wavering green images Dugger had fought to preserve. I pressed my face right up against the screen until I could make it out, or thought I could, if only because the shot was so familiar.

The second sliver of Amber picture, this one newly streaked with blood.

My husband's voice came again, broken now beyond repair. "The kid wasn't saying *dead*."

Club stayed silent.

Then came a ragged cry; it sounded like a bird's screaming. "You know what he was saying?"

Club shook his head, a slow, hazy motion in the dark. His features bunched with confusion. Brendan was muttering, putting things together for himself, as he backed away out of sight. "She left. She went to Colorado."

His last words were caught just as he began running. "He was saying *dad*."

* * *

The only thing that remained to be seen on film was the dead boy's body, lying prone in the snow, and the flakes dropping down upon it.

They fell slowly at first so that it was possible to see where each one landed, mark its progress and rate of melt, until before too long they stopped melting altogether and began to accumulate in a thin, white shroud.

READY

Tim sat at the console in the cruiser. They were parked at the barracks, snow falling gently all around. Lately Gil had been driving, and Tim riding shotgun, but tonight that was going to change.

He typed in the coordinates on the GPS. Then he spoke without turning to Gil.

"Tell me what you did to the reporter." It had to be bad. Gil had tied up Club's dog in that smoking wreck of a house without a second's hesitation. And Gil liked animals.

"Nothing that didn't need to be done."

"You took him to the silo."

They had found the place during a raid a year ago—some rich kids from downstate were using it to host pharm parties; Club and Gil had joked about the fact that they took place on an actual farm—and the owners had gone into foreclosure soon after. The whole place still stunk of animal things: breath and fear and waste.

"I did what needed to be done," Gil repeated. "And I doubt he'll be asking any questions from now on."

Tim was to blame. He'd given Ned the lead about Melanie Cooper.

He'd been partnered with Gil the day the call came in from Lenny Paulson's plant about John Cooper. An industrial accident. It wasn't clear from the staticky report what had happened—some part of a container of acid had eroded away, its replacement too long put off probably—and Cooper had been luckless enough to be breathing in the wrong place at the wrong time.

The look in the man's eyes was one Tim hoped he'd never have to see again.

Cooper had managed to get himself

out of the room, even closing the door to protect his fellow workers. Someone had laid him out on a dingy leg of hallway, near an empty water cooler and a coffee station that gave off the smell of something burned. Away from the inner workings of the plant. Wherever all the noise and grinding and bustle of production took place had to have been far off, since where they stood was as quiet and deserted as a crypt.

Cooper was taking shallow, hitching breaths that seemed to cause pain of a sort Tim couldn't imagine. The man's eyes fluttered shut as he went in and out of consciousness, which at least served to blot out the combination of abject horror and mute plea in them.

They got there before the ambulance did. The Chief had always emphasized speed and immediacy of responding. He spoke in a rumble behind Tim and Gil.

"Paulson already radioed, said the call was a mistake. Some worker from downstate must have overreacted. The bus is on its way back to WCH." The

Chief paused. "We'll let Doc take care of this."

Tim felt something crawl up his back. "No way, Chief. Call for it again. This man needs an ambulance. Emergency treatment."

There was silence as the Chief absorbed the protest. Tim's heart clenched like a fist in his chest. But when the Chief spoke, his tone was affable.

"You know, I don't think so," he said. "Those folks at the hospital are only gonna prolong the inevitable. Look at him. You think you'd be doing this fellow a kindness?"

Tim forced himself to take another look at Cooper. His eyes were opening and closing at a rate that suggested things slowing down, ceasing to work, and his mouth hung slackly, exposing the blistered, fiery flesh inside.

"A trip to the hospital will also slow things down here at the plant," the Chief added. "Lenny says it's a bad time for that. Worst possible time." He paused to let his words sink in, although they understood them. "I radioed Doc. He'll meet you on Rural Route 31."

They knew which spot, of course. The leg of road just before the boulder. Gil was already starting to move, hoisting Cooper up in his arms. But Cooper died in the back of the cruiser before Doc could even arrive.

There was nothing to do then. It was an accident, a horrible accident, and it had happened before Tim or Gil had gotten anywhere near. But if Cooper's body was discovered now, things wouldn't look as simple as that.

Gil figured out where to put the man until nightfall. They staggered up the side of the hill to the snow cave, sharing Cooper's weight. They'd hurried because the cruiser had been left on the road. Not many people drove out this way, but someone might.

They had a body to hide and they had to do it before snowmelt. As the Chief had put it, Paulson's loader would come in useful. With spring would come the need to do a better job.

But spring felt very far away.

Tim looked across the seat to Gil. "Get out."

"What?" Gil looked out into the swirling snow outside. "Yeah, right."

Wearily, Tim reached down past the front seat, lifted the piece he'd brought from home—he wouldn't use his service revolver, not for this—and aimed it at Gil.

In a flash so fast Tim had no idea what had happened, the gun was back on the floor, and Gil was on top of him, elbow lodged in Tim's throat.

Tim fought to suck in breath—unable to budge his partner's arm so much as a millimeter—and an image of Cooper dying flashed before his grayed-out vision.

Then suddenly he was free.

Gil loomed above him.

Tim was sputtering and gasping, air like claws in his lungs. Gil didn't even appear to be breathing hard. "What the fuck, man?" he said. "I don't want to hurt you."

Force clearly wouldn't work here.

Gil was strong, and he was trained. But he wasn't all that smart. And he didn't give a shit about anyone but himself. He never had.

"Please," Tim said. "Whatever happened with Cooper or the reporter or anyone else—I know it wasn't your fault. None of this is your fault. But I can't take it anymore. Hamilton couldn't, and I can't, either. I want out."

Every word was true. He just had to hope that the way out Gil imagined him taking wasn't the one he had actually decided on. Or that Gil wouldn't care enough to give the matter any further thought.

"You want out?" Gil repeated.

Tim glanced meaningfully at the gun on the floor. "I need to be alone right now."

Gil studied Tim where he half lay, still angled back against the seat.

Then Gil gave a snort of dismissal. He readjusted his coat from the dismantling it had gotten when he attacked Tim, opened his door, and went out into the night.

CHAPTER FIFTY-EIGHT

When you're in an unfamiliar house, you attune differently to sounds. You don't have to tighten that creaking wood or joist, the balky furnace that comes on won't be yours to adjust, and so these things mostly pass unnoticed. I'd been sitting still for what felt like hours, letting Dugger's video replay in my mind, getting used to the idea that my dead husband had been a father. The sound of the heavy wooden door opening up and someone coming in registered only dimly. But the noise that followed next was too loud and brutal not to note.

The muffled report of a silenced gun.

Someone had found me. But he had found Dick Granger first.

The breath I took stabbed my lungs.

It felt like a long time went by as the headline printed itself across my brain, but it couldn't have been more than a second or two. BED & BREAKFAST OWNER, GUEST KILLED IN SUSPECTED DISPUTE. SEARCH CONTINUES FOR SHOOTER.

There was no link between Wedeskyull and Cold Kettle. Even Ned might not suspect.

I thought again of kindly Dick Granger at the desk, and my body shook with horror.

If whoever had come in went upstairs—assuming me to be in my room—then I might be able to make it to the front hall. So long as I could keep from being heard overhead, I could dash down the entry hall and get out, run to Olivia Peterson's house, to any house at all.

Olivia's was probably staked out. Dear God, I hoped she was all right.

I was formulating this plan when

steady footsteps began to thud. They weren't moving toward the staircase.

I flew to a cold, black window. Raise it and climb out? It was big enough, but these old windows were often painted shut, the double-hung mechanism long past use.

Outside, a gray car rolled up, nearly invisible in the gathering storm, just a shadow amidst flakes. Had all three cops come? In my mind another patrol car, then another, emerged like apparitions from the concealment of snow.

I whirled around, hunting something that could be used as a weapon. What would there be in an inn? I patted my pockets wildly, but the only thing I felt was Dugger's recorder. Hardly even aware of what I was doing, I pressed a button, felt the little machine start to whir inside my coat.

Then Club strode into the parlor, and I ran for the corner of the room.

I had a hunch—based on the way in which Greggy had been shot—that Club wouldn't shoot me immediately upon entering. And in that moment, I also knew who'd killed Aunt Jean.

"Why did you kill her?"

Club was already reaching for his belt, but his hand hesitated then.

"Shut up, Nora," he growled. "Let's do this the easy way, okay?"

Do what? Kill me? Or handcuff me? What was he intending?

"Jean was shot from behind," I answered. "Like you shoot all your victims."

"Victims." Club let out a barking laugh, but the skin around his mouth had gone white. He started to massage the gun in his holster. "You think Aunt Jean was a victim?"

I cast my gaze around. The TV cabinet, several chairs too heavy for me to lift, and an end table whose legs looked deadly but would never make it past a bullet already in the chamber. "What are you talking about?"

Club removed his gun, settling it into a practiced, two-fisted hold.

"She talked shit about my dad," he muttered. "Said he couldn't find anything if it was hidden right under his nose."

I recalled Jean's ransacked kitchen. And something else, too. Jean, taking Brendan's box from me after I had been attacked, and idly stroking its side. At least, I thought then that it had been idle, Jean distracted and distraught over my assault. But that had been the false side she was touching, and now I realized she must've been checking to make sure that nothing had gotten disturbed. When had Jean put the Polaroid inside? When she had gone upstairs to our bedroom after the funeral? Or a long time before that, when the box had still belonged to her brother? The cops had been searching for something for weeks. Burning down houses, stealing, even plundering the box itself, and the crucial bit of evidence had been right there all along. Vern must've known about the picture. He was in it after all.

And there in the parlor, with another body lying dead just one room away, and the kill weapon now trained on me, I tipped a silent glass to Brendan's aunt.

"What the fuck are you smiling about?" Club demanded. "You think the same thing can't happen to you? You think I'm going to be caught? We're never caught, Nora. We can do whatever the fuck we want. And you know what? Someone will thank us for it."

He really seemed to believe it. There was a dark overlay of insanity in his tone.

I shifted my gaze just long enough to snatch another look around.

"So the Chief won't mind if you kill me?" Maybe he wouldn't, I realized. But there was one thing he must've minded. I knew from the Polaroid. "I bet he wasn't too happy about Jean, though. He loved her, you know."

Club had been about to flick the safety on his gun, but I saw his finger jog before gaining control. "The Chief knows things sometimes get out of hand."

Things got out of hand, and the cops did whatever they had to. I refuted Club's claim with all the rage it lit inside me. "Bullshit. I bet he never forgives you for it—"

Club lowered his head like a charging animal, and his stare was ragged, desperate. He must've looked like this right before he shot Jean. There was no stopping him now.

Unless I moved awfully fast. I'd spotted something. It shouldn't have taken me as long as it did. These were the tricks of my trade, and Dick Granger had alerted me to their presence the moment I arrived.

I had a few seconds. Club had to get into position. For all his comfort with weapons, he didn't seem to like shooting anybody straight-on.

I sidled over a few feet.

Club jumped behind me in one ungainly leap.

I whirled on him, even though it meant losing sight of what I'd been going for.

And then I saw something else, and the expression on my face made Club take his eyes off me. I froze, foot already extended in preparation for my next step.

Club swiveled expertly, gun still raised, maintaining every inch of his stance.

Tim Lurcquer stood in the parlor doorway.

I slipped over to the stash of supplies, dropping to my knees. The churchkey fit in my hand like a sixth digit. It would've made a handy weapon in itself, but I might not be able to get close enough to use it. It didn't matter. There was something even better, and just as lethal.

I picked up a can.

CHAPTER FIFTY-NINE

Two things I should've put together. Why did Tim give me the log? And stand stock-still while I drove away from Eileen's when he could easily have given chase?

Because he'd been trying to help.

He faced Club now, a few inches shorter, not quite as powerfully built.

"What the hell are you doing?" For the first time, Club appeared truly baffled, with no idea which way to point his gun.

Tim seemed just as genuine in his appeal to Club. "Too many shortcuts, too many bad outcomes. And it isn't just the dirtbags, who deserve what they get. One of our own couldn't take it anymore. And now he's dead . . ." And Tim turned to me.

I bore down on the can's handle until it branded my palm.

"Shut the fuck up now, Lurcquer," Club growled. "You've gone crazy."

"No, Mitchell," Tim said. "I've gone sane."

Club aimed his gun at me.

"Enough!" roared Tim.

With his voice for cover, I used the churchkey to pry the lid off the can and let it clank to the floor, taking care not to let a bead of its contents touch my hand.

"I said enough!" Tim bellowed again. "Hamilton's already dead. Are you going to keep killing anybody who threatens to say what they know? Who threatens to take one of you down?"

"One of us down?" Club echoed. His next words emerged in a growl. "You're one of us, you bastard."

My arm was still raised, the bucket

not quite motionless, swinging like the world's slowest pendulum.

Club sighted his gun on Tim, who had just begun to withdraw his own weapon. I watched Club's finger depress the trigger; I saw the fear in Tim's small eyes as he realized he wasn't going to be fast enough.

I took one lurching step forward, and hurled the contents of the can.

Catching sight of me peripherally, Club spun to get away, and fired.

On wartime battlefields, in dungeons of torture, or the recovery wards of hospitals where people woke to their pain, there could never have been such a howl of agony.

The gun clattered to the floor. Club's hands ricocheted to his neck, clawing at the liquid that streamed down in rivulets, which only succeeded in searing his palms and fingertips. The paint stripper had mostly hit his clothes and he tore at those as well, trying to rip the fabric off himself, exposing his naked, burning skin.

"Call a paramedic," I told Tim, who

was already shouting into his radio. "Call the police." Then I stopped.

Tim clicked off, keeping the radio low to subdue the ripples of static, and eyeing me. "The State Police," he said. "That's who it'll be up here." He took a look at me. "Let's get you on the floor."

"No, I'm fine," I said, though Tim's expression told me otherwise. "I had to do it, right? He was going to kill you. Us." I frowned. "Why do I feel so funny?" It was as if all air had been sucked out of me by a vacuum.

"Nora," Tim said, in that firm, unyielding voice of his. "Sit down. You're bleeding."

I glanced over at Club, who was writhing on the floor, fingers so burned from trying to wipe the scourge off his skin that they'd become too clumsy and inexpert to unbutton his clothes.

"Tim," I said, and sank. "Oh, God, Tim, what's wrong with—"

He caught me.

I looked down at myself. Blood seeped from a tiny, symmetric hole in my side.

I wondered how long it would take for help to arrive in Cold Kettle.

CHAPTER SIXTY

Club and I rode in the same ambulance. By the time it came, I was weak and shivering, unable to move. I kept looking around blearily, whispering first aid instructions for Club from my position on the floor. Tim had refused to do anything before fetching blankets from the rooms of the inn and wrapping me up. Then he dutifully flushed Club's prone form again and again with tepid water.

Dick Granger's body was left behind so the staties could collect evidence.

All I remembered of our exit was that Weekend had been sitting high on the seat of Club's Jimmy, panting patiently. The paramedics released him into Tim's custody, but first Weekend bounded up to me, all snuffles and barks and licks of reunion.

That may have healed me more than anything the medics did.

I woke in a hospital room. Outside it was light, and I wondered if more than one day had passed. There was an IV in my hand. Except for a hot stitch in my side that somehow refused to trouble me, I felt refreshed, almost reborn.

A man with skin the color of tobacco came into my room. He took my chart from the bottom of the bed, then spoke in a strong accent.

"The good news will be first," he said, and I nodded, which the doctor didn't appear to notice. "The good news is that the bullet did not come anywhere close to your baby. The not as good news is that you will probably require some rehabilitation on your hip."

I struggled to sit up, and a meteor shower of pain sparked inside me, penetrating the cushion of meds I had to be on. It was the drug haze that made me mishear. Or the accent.

"What did you say?"

"Rehabilitation," the doctor repeated. "Your hip was affected by the path of the bullet. We have quite a good unit here at the—"

"No," I interrupted, and the doctor finally looked down at me. "The first part."

He began flipping rapidly through the pages of my chart.

"Mrs. Hamilton," he said. "Did you not know that you are pregnant?"

The weight Teggie thought I was gaining, how the pants Dugger's mother lent me were difficult to close. My aversion to coffee and the hunger that was rampant despite grief. Even the loss of my allergies, which I'd read once was a lesser-known side effect of pregnancy.

A baby.

Though a tinge of panic accompanied that thought—*How the hell am I going to raise a child alone?*—mostly I felt buoyed by a giddy, irrepressible joy. I could hardly even feel the pain in my side anymore and I refused a second dose of meds, even though the hospital staff assured me they were perfectly safe.

"You have a visitor," a nurse announced from the door to my room.

My sister stood behind her.

She took one look at me. "What happened to you? I don't mean this." She flung her hand out, indicating the hospital room. Then she looked again. "Oh my God. You're pregnant."

I burst into tears. They were loud and furious, a tidal wave of feeling.

Teggie waited for me to quiet, then traced one finger along my brow. "You're going to be a wonderful mother."

"You're going to be a wonderful wife."

Teggie stared at me. "Way to steal my thunder. You think taking a bullet and finding out you're preggers all in the same week wasn't enough?"

I fought to smile through my wet face and dripping nose.

Teggie reached for some tissues on a bedside stand. "How'd you know anyway?" she asked.

I gave her a *duh* look, then touched the shiny stone on her left-hand finger.

"Please tell me you'll be moving back to the city now," my sister said.

"Actually," I said, "I think I might try out this town a little farther north."

Night was descending when the door to my room was nudged open and a slice of light fell across the floor. I looked up, expecting a nurse at this hour.

But it wasn't a nurse. It took me a second to place the woman who did enter. She was holding on tight to a shopping bag as she crossed to the side of my bed.

I struggled to sit up, the thin hospital blanket a strangling force. The *call* button dangled and I reached for it.

"Don't," Mrs. Weathers said.

The Chief's wife probably knew the nurse on duty, could slip in past visiting hours.

I swallowed, passing a hand across my belly. Pain flared in my side.

"The Chief is ruined," she said. "If you only knew what you've done. Wedeskyull will never be the same."

I tried to summon a reply. Was Vern here? If he came in, I was going to have to hit that button. No, I was going to scream. Would screaming do any—

"Why did you keep digging in this ground?" Mrs. Weathers demanded. "Brendan didn't ask you to. He didn't even do it himself."

I couldn't come up with a thing to say. Tiny Dorothy Weathers seemed a looming presence, accusing me of sacrificing her husband to protect the memory of my own.

"How could you do this? When all of us kept silent for so long? When I kept—" Something clenched in her face, and she looked suddenly old and ugly. "Do you have any idea what I've had to do?" Mrs. Weathers reached down and grasped my wrist, and then I did let out a scream, or at least a little yelp.

She looked at me on the bed and her expression was one of surprise. "Oh, Nora. Oh, no, you thought—" She broke off, releasing my arm. "I didn't come here to blame you, my dear. No, no. I came—because I wanted to see."

"See?" I finally spoke. "See what?"

Mrs. Weathers peered down at me. "What it looks like to stand up to him."

* * *

Ned showed up the day after that. I was almost ready to be checked out, eating a bowl of the chili macaroni casserole that Mrs. Weathers had brought, when he walked into my room. Ned's arm was bandaged, and his face was mottled with bruises. In and around the glow of color, his eyes stared at me with incredulity, then filled with relief.

"You're okay," he said. "You're okay."

"So are you," I replied.

"I came back the second I could," he said. Then he laid the front page of the *Albany Times Union* on my lap.

Police Chief Vernon J. Weathers resigned today, pending an investigation by federal officials into the department's activities.

Two arrests have been made. Officer Club Mitchell has been charged with one count of murder and one count of manslaughter and will be taken into custody after receiving treatment in a burn unit. Officer Gilbert Landry is being held on charges of kidnapping and assault.

Officer Timothy Lurcquer will serve as acting chief of police until permanent replacement can be found.

Members of the Weathers family have served in the role of chief of police in Wedeskyull for more than eighty years. . . .
See "Hidden Face of Justice" page A-2.

Ned watched as I finished reading. My gaze flitted to the byline at the top.

By Ned Kramer

I shook my head, disbelief and wonder coursing through me.

I had thought I'd never feel safe again. Yet suddenly I did. "I think you might have that book you always wanted to write."

Ned gave me a lopsided smile, wincing slightly. "I don't know. I've got the ending. But there's only bits and pieces from the middle. The beginning took place twenty-five years ago. And that will never be known at all."

"I have a few things that might help," I said softly.

I reached for Brendan's yellow box. Tim had reclaimed it from the inn for me. Its lid sat askew, and would until I could repair it. I took out Dugger's DVD, and his cassette, as well as the bloody picture with Amber in it. DNA could probably still be recovered from that. The camera I'd used in the woods came next. Then the recording device that had captured the final sequence of events at the inn. Ned took all five items with an air of puzzlement.

I handed him Jean's Polaroid. And his whole face changed.

A nurse entered the room. "Mrs. Hamilton? You're all set."

Ned was still studying the photo.

His head only jerked up when I started to rise.

Our eyes met. And we traded a smile that held many things—everything except what a smile should contain. No humor or levity. Sorrow, and satisfaction, and maybe just a hint of salvation.

"We could wait a little while." Ned said, indicating the hospital window, which was dashed with snow. "This looks like it might let up."

"I think we'll be all right," I replied. My hip gave a few piercing twinges as I moved toward the hall, but I knew it would soon be numbed by the temperature outside.

I crossed my arms over my stomach to provide an extra layer of warmth.

Ned led the way out to his car, and we drove off into the snow still falling over Wedeskyull.

ACKNOWLEDGMENTS

I can hardly believe it's come down to this: a cool, rainy day in June, when I am writing the acknowledgments for my debut novel. I began composing these words a decade ago.

My deepest thanks go to three women I call the Dream Team. My editor, Linda Marrow, has a visionary view of fiction that made this novel into the book you are holding—and the one I always meant to write. My agent, Julia Kenny, is passionate, dedicated, and unflagging in her enthusiasm—traits every writer needs to rely on. And Nancy Pickard started out as one of my favorite authors, and became the reason I got published at all.

The people at Ballantine have dazzled me from the minute I was lucky enough to land there. I look forward to meeting many more, but for now want to single out Junessa Viloria, for her constant contact and attention to details; Dana Isaacson, for his sage advice on the tiniest turn of plot; Sharon Propson, Sonya Safro, and Quinne Rogers, for taking one look and knowing just how to introduce it to the world; Kim Houey, for steering and charting courses; Rachel Kind, and the whole team for the magic of overseas sales; the awe-inspiring art department, who took a story and crafted it into a single image; and Jennifer Rodriguez and the entire eagle-eyed crew in production, who went way beyond usage to make suggestions I never would've thought of on my own, and still managed to catch the fact that granola bars don't melt.

To Julie Schoerke, Marissa Curnutte, Sami Lien, Grace Wright, and everyone at JKS Communications, thank you for believing.

There are authors who became literary angels along the way. I hesitate to write this list because it will be incomplete the moment I send it off. A few mentions include John Searles—author of the "literary angel" phrase—and Jacquelyn Mitchard, Louise Penny, Sophie Hannah, Timothy Hallinan, Leighton Gage, Lisa Tucker, Craig Holden, Karen McQuestion, Stefanie Pintoff, Debra Galant, David Harris Ebenbach, and Colleen Thompson, who went out on many different limbs for me. Laura Lippman, Chris Bohjalian, Harlan Coben, Linwood Barclay, and Jodi Picoult offered inspiration, in part by telling me to come find them when my book sold—which I did. And Lee Child, Hank Phillipi Ryan, Julia Spencer-Fleming, and William Kent Krueger all made me proud to enter this world which contains such greats.

If you want to be a writer, join a writers organization. Three of the best I've found are International Thriller Writers—thank you, Carla Buckley, for your book and the invitation—Mystery Writers of America, and New York Writers Workshop.

After you join an organization, become part of a listserv. Without the good hearts and avid mystery lovers of DorothyL and MurderMustAdvertise, I would've had a much harder time not giving up.

I have mixed feelings about writers groups, but three have been essential on my road. To Dorothy from the Little Professor writing group—if you hadn't talked about *The Deep End of the Ocean* almost fifteen years ago, it literally wouldn't have occurred to me to try to get published. Stumps Sprouts lasted an idyllic five days and resulted in friends I'll never forget: Karina, Colin, Sandy, Jessica, Teeta, Bridget, Nina, Becky, and Barbara. If the only thing to come out of the Somerset Hills Writers Salon was meeting Lauren Sweet and her mother, it would've been worth attending a thousand meetings.

Some writers hone their craft at the knees of teachers; I was lucky enough to have literary agents poke and prod me into learning how to put a novel together. If Barney Karpfinger hadn't written a single-spaced rejection letter back in 1999, my work would still be laden with unnecessary interior monologue. Anne Hawkins and Anna Stein believed in me enough to put their very capable skills to work, and I am always excited to see the books they usher into the world.

The community of bookstores is a grand and noble one. There are far too many to name, but Margot Sage-El, Marina Cramer, and the crew at Watchung Booksellers deserve credit for giving life to a certain literary series; and Greg and Mary Bruss of Mysteries and More in Nashville helped kick off Take Your Child to a Bookstore Day back in 2010. Thank you, booksellers across the world, and to paraphrase Neil Young, long may you thrive.

Libraries were my place of respite and salvation from the childhood woes to which writers seem especially prone. My hat is off to librarians worldwide.

The world of bloggers is made up of writers, readers, reviewers, thinkers, essayists, and at least one former book-seller. Thank you, Lelia Taylor, Kaye Barley, Lesa Holstine, and many, many others for the creative work you put out there for people to be inspired by.

I'm not a writer who does a lot of research, but I found it necessary to call upon the husband of a dear friend for one certain detail in the book you've read. Thank you, Greg Fox, for the consult on concrete.

When it takes a long time to get published, it's easy to start believing it will never happen. That's when you need your writing kindred spirits, not to mention a little chocolate. Judy Walters, Karyne Corum, Maryann McFadden, Johanna Garth, Savannah Thorne, Sara Backer, and everyone at the Cozy Café; they deserve great success.

Thanks to friends who've been interested and invested along the way: Lynda Wolf, Tracy Fox, Susan Ezell, Jen Grigsby, Deborah McKinley, Tulasi and Eric Jordan-Freedman, Denise Wendorff, Becky Rubenstein, Tara Munn, Leah Hatley, Kimberly Kirstein, Jana Karam, Annaliese Silivanch, Anne Nedelka, and the members of the Tuesday night book club!

Last because they're not least, thank you to my family.

You already know about my husband: support when things looked bleakest, cook when I got hungry, and a mean editor to boot. To truly thank him would take a novel of its own.

Thanks to my daughter and son, Sophie and Caleb, for carrying a flag—a literal one, in this case, for a parade around the house—imploring Mommy to "gat publisht."

I feel extremely lucky to call not one but two women mother-in-law. My thanks goes to Amy Small, for her unflagging support, and for providing a meal or a party just when we needed one, and for knowing almost everyone. And to Shirley Frank, thank you for coming out to every panel, for reading manuscripts in a way that made me feel like a real writer, and your especial flair with pitches.

Thank you, Eddie, for your creative thinking and generosity. Thanks, Bob, for lending a hand, and for lending your wife. And thanks, Frank, for making a bookstore visit seem like the best way to spend a weekend. (Which it is, of course.)

My father knew when I was ready for *Jane Eyre,* and my mother began many a childhood bedtime story with, "Once upon a time, there was a little boy named Benjy." Thank you.

Thank you to my brother, Ezra, for being my number one fan (an intentionally weird, freaky one who hides behind beds), and to my brother-in-law, James, for sending me news of interest, and for always asking about details.

To my sister, Kari, who comes first in so many ways: Thank you for seeing the dream.

ABOUT THE AUTHOR

JENNY MILCHMAN lives in New Jersey with her family. *Cover of Snow* is her first novel.